A SAPPHIRE SEASON

Also by Lynn Morris

The Baron's Honourable Daughter

Available from FaithWords wherever books are sold.

A SAPPHIRE SEASON

A Novel

LYNN MORRIS

New York • Boston • Nashville

FaithWords
Hachette Book Group
1290 Avenue of the Americas
New York, NY 10104

www.faithwords.com

Printed in the United States of America

RRD-C

First Edition: August 2015
10 9 8 7 6 5 4 3 2 1

Library of Congress data has been applied for.

ISBN 978-1-4555-7561-9 (Trade paperback ed.); ISBN 978-1-4555-7562-6 (Ebook ed.)

To Jackson Gilbert Downs:
You make my heart merry,
and it's as good as medicine.
(After Proverbs 17:22.)
I love you, Grandson.

A
SAPPHIRE SEASON

Chapter One

The scene was perfectly idyllic. A pale lemon drop sun, set in the high blue sky, shone benevolently down on the still pond. On the bank, heavily shaded by old willow trees, a handsome young man and a pretty young girl sat tranquilly, the remains of a picnic between them.

One detail of this pastoral setting was jarring, however. The girl was holding a fishing rod. She didn't appear to be the kind of lady to do such an outlandish thing. Yet the expression on her face was typical of the dedicated angler, one of fierce concentration centered upon her line and the cork float bobbing slightly in the reeds.

She was Lady Mirabella Tirel, daughter of the Marquess and Marchioness of Camarden. Her companion was her oldest and closest friend, Sir Giles Knyvet, Baronet. Sir Giles was fishing, too, but he watched Lady Mirabella's face with secret amusement more than he regarded his own line.

"Neither you nor I has had the slightest nip," Mirabella grumbled. "It does seem that on such a glorious day even the fish would want to surface and take a look." She glanced up at the sky. "I can hardly believe it's All Hallows' Eve. It seems more like June."

"So it does," Giles agreed. "Most unusual for the beginning of November. But I was advised by Old Figge this morning that his bad knees were telling him that the cold rains are on their way, so we'd better enjoy this untimely weather. 'Farewell, thou latter spring; farewell, All-hallown summer!' "

"Mm... *A Midsummer Night's Dream*?" Mirabella guessed.

"No, *Henry IV*."

"You do show out abominably. No one save you reads *Henry IV*, never mind memorizing it."

Giles grinned, and Mirabella reflected again, as she had countless times, how very engaging that grin was. His mouth was well-formed and his teeth perfect and white, but his smile was crooked, boyish. His sky-blue eyes lit up and he had slight grin wrinkles in the corners. His features were fine, not stunningly handsome, but pleasing. He had thick glossy black hair, and with his light-blue eyes he was noticeable. He had a fine figure, too, at five feet, ten inches tall, he had broad shoulders tapering down to a narrow waist and hips, and he always dressed very well. Today he wore a bottle-green claw-hammer coat, blue-and-green-striped waistcoat, buckskin breeches, and Hessian boots polished to a high gloss. His cravat, though simply tied, was impeccable.

If this scene had been a painting, Lady Mirabella would have been the perfect foil for him. She was tiny, dainty, only two inches over five feet tall. Her complexion was as white as an Easter lily's, and she had deep dimples that flashed at the slightest hint of amusement. Her eyes were a deep and dark blue, a startling color that sometimes seemed to have purple depths. Her hair was an unusual shade of ivory blonde with red highlights so subtle that the true color was seen only in bright sunlight. The bloom on her cheeks was extremely delicate, a very light pink, exactly the same color as her favorite rose, *Rosa x centifolia*, more prosaically known as the Old Cabbage Rose. It was by Mirabella's design that her dress was this exact blushing pink, and several centifolia rosebuds trimmed her bonnet. The three flounces of the dress were trimmed with embroidered bluebells and forget-me-nots, and she wore a light fringed shawl of exactly the same shade as the blue embroidery.

Mirabella impatiently jiggled her line. "Oh, I do so want to catch some tench today! I've had such irresistible cravings lately for Monsieur Danton's *tanche à la citronelle*. It's been forever since he's made it, it seems."

"Ah, tench, the noble physician fish!" Giles stood, theatrically placed his hand over his heart, and quoted sonorously,

The pike, fell tyrant of the liquid plain,
With ravenous waste devours his fellow train;
Yet, howsoe'r by raging famine fined,
The tench he spares, a medicinal kind.
For when by wounds distress'd, or sore disease,
He courts the salutary fish for ease;
Close to his scales the kind physician glides,
And sweats a healing balsam from his sides.

"What does that mean?" Mirabella demanded. " 'Sweats a healing balsam from his sides'?"

Giles took his seat again and picked up his rod. "They're oily, you know, tench. Very slimy."

Mirabella gulped. "They are? But—but I thought they had scales, not like eels."

"So they do, but they're still slimy."

"Oh. Oh dear. Anyway, they are good to eat, at least when Monsieur Danton cooks them. And wherever did you hear of that outlandish poem? 'Kind physician' fish indeed."

"I can't recall, precisely. Perhaps I made it up. Just now. At any rate, if you would ever lower yourself to mind your own fish, you'd know all about his healing balsam sides yourself."

"You know perfectly well why I won't do that," Mirabella retorted. "I'll never forget the torture it was for the doctor to get that hook out of my hand."

"You were only six years old, you can't possibly recall it that vividly. In fact, I doubt you would even remember it at all if it weren't for the scar."

"Well, perhaps I don't exactly recall the pain, but still, I'll never forget it, the scar mars my hand. I'm so glad that ladies always wear gloves now."

"Nonsense, you can hardly see it. I'd venture to say that no one has noticed it, or even seen it, save you."

"You have."

"That's because I was there, and I do remember it. I say, Bella, it really was a rum go. I was so surprised you didn't cry. I'm sure I would have."

"I'm sure you would not have," Mirabella scoffed. "You always teased me so unmercifully when tears welled up in my eyes that I'd rather not cry than listen to you."

All through their childhood, she and Giles had fished together as much as they had played together. Taking a small perch off her hook, somehow Mirabella had managed to plunge the hook straight through the tender meat between her left thumb and forefinger. Now she reflected, with some wonder, that she hadn't cried. But then Mirabella had never been weepy, as some women were. She rarely cried. When she did, it was simply a welling up of tears in her eyes, with perhaps one or two tracing down her cheek. In fact, Mirabella could never recall having a stormy cry with great sobs, only slight sniffling and dabbing.

The Camarden family estate, Camarden Court, was only three miles from Knyveton Hall, the home of the Knyvet baronets. The two families had always been close, and when Mirabella had been born in March of 1791, and Giles three months later, it was only natural that the two would spend much of their childhood together. Giles was an only child, and Mirabella was like one, for she had only one brother, sixteen years her senior. Lady Camarden and Lady Knyvet had had them rather late in life, and this bonded the two women even more closely. Mirabella's entire life was filled with memories of Giles. Of course he had been sent to Eton when he was ten years old, and then to Oxford; but still, all his holidays had been spent at home. The only time they had been parted for any length of time had been when she and Giles were eighteen, and he had left to go on the Grand Tour. For almost a year he had been in Rome, Venice, and Florence, and Mirabella had missed him terribly.

But she had been very sorry for the reason he had to return home. His father had died, abruptly, with no warning. The shock had been so great to Lady Knyvet that she fell ill. When Giles returned he found only unhappiness and regrets. His father had been horribly imprudent with his finances, and Giles was left with near-impossible debts. Lady Knyvet never recovered from her husband's death, and died only six months later.

Her broodings concerning Giles's finances weren't at the top of her mind, however. Today was October thirty-first, tomorrow was Sunday, November first, and the second was the first Monday in November, the traditional opening of fox hunting season. The marquess had made this quite an event in the county. He was Master of the Hunt, he had wonderful fox hunting grounds, and he invited anyone who could find a cob to amble along on to Camarden Court for the hunt. Such generous provision for all and sundry, regardless of rank, was a tradition of the Marquesses of Camarden, begun by Mirabella's grandfather in 1756.

Giles had not joined the hunt last year—probably, Mirabella

thought, because he had sold all of his hunters. Naturally she was hesitant about asking Giles if he was to join the hunt this year. She dearly hoped so. But try as she might, she couldn't think of a tactful way to broach the subject with him.

Then her cork bobbed, and she sat up alertly. But no, it was merely a light ripple that had caught it in the thick reeds. They were fishing in the Camarden stewpond, a very old legacy from the Tudor beginnings of the house, and the pond was heavily stocked with carp, tench, pike, and perch.

"This is a waste of time," Mirabella complained. "We may be enjoying an All-hallown summer, but I think that the fish know better, they're not up here in the reeds as if it's spawning season. We should go out in the punt."

In a high falsetto Giles said, "'You thought, Miss! I don't know any business you have to think at all—thought does not become a young woman.'"

Mirabella giggled. The quote was from their favorite play, *The Rivals*, by their favorite character, Mrs. Malaprop. She retorted, "Sir, you offer me a great insult by your implementations as to my becomings." It was their little game; Mrs. Malaprop's particular gift was for using words that sounded like the correct ones but were wildly wrong. By the rules of their game, Mirabella was obliged to reply with a *malapropism*.

"But your becomings are so charming," Giles replied. Then with a sigh he stood up and took off his coat. "It's such a warm lazy day that I'm loath to punt you around the stewpond, but your wish is my command, my lady."

With satisfaction Mirabella said, "*One Thousand and One Nights.*"

Giles folded up his coat to make a cushion for Mirabella, then loaded their fishing gear into the light, shallow-drafted boat. After Mirabella seated herself, he took the long pole and slowly pushed them out away from the bank.

"Look, look over there, Giles, bubbles! Surely those are tench," Mirabella said excitedly. "The poem should have been about how foolish they are to give themselves away by blowing bubbles. No, there, over there." Patiently Giles poled them into the center of the pond and they both sank their lines in the midst of the bubbles.

"They would surely be shocked in London to know that Lady Mirabella Tirel is very knowledgeable of the habits of the tench," Giles teased.

"And I'll make you pay dearly if you tell anyone," Mirabella warned. "Oh, Giles, I must say I'm more excited about this Season than I have been in two years. Finally, finally, Josephine has agreed to accompany me."

"Yes, I know, Lewin told me. I hope this will be agreeable news to you, too. I'm coming to London this year, and Lewin will be coming with me."

Oddly enough, considering their exalted stations, the Camardens and the Knyvets had always been very good friends with their rector, the Reverend Mr. Rosborough, and his family. Mr. and Mrs. Rosborough had five children. Josephine was the same age as Mirabella and Giles, while Lewin was two years older. The four of them had always been close friends.

Mirabella's eyes lit up. "Truly? Oh, how wonderful! You and Lewin will stay with us, won't you?"

"No, we two bachelors have a flat at St. James's that's been loaned to me by a friend who's in Greece. We intend to enjoy all the delights of two dandies on the town, showing out in Hyde Park, doing the strut on Bond Street, strolling about the pit in the theatres, making a nuisance of ourselves calling on beautiful young ladies."

"Nonsense, you're no more a dandy than is Lewin. However, I shall be incensed if you don't call on us often."

"And what other beautiful young lady did you think I was referring to?"

"This is wonderful news indeed," Mirabella said complacently. "Now I know I shall have a brilliant Season. But I'm a little surprised that you managed to talk Lewin into coming to London. He seems much changed since he returned. Of course I know that being a soldier, and in such a terrible war, must sober a man, but he was always so cheerful and high-spirited. Now he seems very grave at times."

Quietly Giles said, "He has good reason." Then he roused and said, "But let's not talk of such dark matters today. And so, after four years you finally managed to persuade Josephine into coming to London. It's a small wonder you're excited."

"Yes, but I must say that her decision not to come out until Constance was married showed great sensitivity and sisterly love." Constance was the eldest of the Rosborough children, and had married only the previous June, when she was twenty-five years old. Mirabella continued, "But I'm a little concerned for Josephine. At first she seemed deliriously happy to have a Season in London, but for the last few days it appears she has doubts. I can't imagine why, she's so pretty, and so charming, I know that she'll be a success."

"You don't know why she's hesitant? That's unlike you, Mirabella. It's her clothes, of course. I thought you always knew all about the earth-shattering importance of the clothes."

Mirabella's eyes widened. "Oh, how could I have been so stupid! Of course, of course, but however did you know?"

"Because after at least eleven years of hearing you nattering on about clothes I finally comprehended that such must be the center of a lady's existence. Also, Lewin told me. I had much the same problem with him, when he learned he had to wear knee breeches and stockings and beribboned pumps."

With determination Mirabella said, "Never mind, I shall take care of that little problem, for Josephine at least. You'll have to worry about Lewin's stockings and pumps."

They fished in silence for a while, and under her breath Mirabella began to hum a tune.

"Sing for me, Bella," Giles said.

Mirabella began to sing a lovely little canzonet by Haydn, "The Mermaid's Song."

Now the dancing sunbeams play
On the green and glassy sea,
Come, and I will lead the way
Where the pearly treasures be.

Come with me, and we will go
Where the rocks of coral grow.
Follow, follow, follow me.

Come, behold what treasures lie
Far beneath the rolling waves,
Riches, hid from human eye,
Dimly shine in ocean's caves.
Ebbing tides bear no delay,
Stormy winds are far away.

Come with me, and we will go
Where the rocks of coral grow.
Follow, follow, follow me.

Mirabella had a lovely voice, not operatic, but clear and sweet and true. Smiling a little, Giles said, "Thank you, Lady Mirabella."

"You're welcome, Sir Giles."

Just then Giles's line jerked, and he began to pull and wrangle the line.

"Oh, how I hope it's a tench!" Mirabella said excitedly.

After much struggle, Giles landed a fat carp that must have weighed seven or eight pounds. "I diligently tried for a tench, but I'll settle for a juicy carp."

Mirabella rolled her eyes. "Monsieur Danton flatly refuses to cook carp. He calls them *poissons stupide sans goût.*"

"'Stupid fish with no taste'? Hm. They may have no taste to Monsieur Danton, but they are certainly not stupid. It's the devil to catch one."

"I cannot understand why you catch more fish than do I," Mirabella complained. "We use the same tackle, the same bait, and fish in the same place."

"Since you won't bait your own hook, or even watch while I do it, then I am obliged to tell you that I never actually do put any bait on your hook."

"You lie, sir," Mirabella said complacently.

"So I do. Anyway, that's the first hint we've had all day that there are even any fish in this pond. I think you must have charmed them with your singing."

Promptly Mirabella sang, "'Come with me, and we will go / Where the rocks of coral grow. / *Monsieur la tanche*, follow, follow me. / Come—'"

A great jerk on her line, and Mirabella pulled, hard. "I have him! I have him, Giles!" She yanked, but the line played back out, the cork went far underwater. Mirabella fought hard, but her strength was small compared to that of the fighting fish. Gritting her teeth, she stood up and strained backward.

Giles was still stringing his carp, but he dropped it, started up, and said, "Bella, no, wait! Let me—"

Mirabella's line snapped. The fishing rod shot up and backward; her feet flew up over her head, and as neatly as if she had practiced it, Mirabella turned a backward somersault into the pond.

Giles leaped in. The water was about two feet over Mirabella's head; she stood on the bottom, motionless. He clasped his arm about her waist and gave a tremendous kick off the bottom. It propelled them toward the bank, into shallower water. With one more hard propelling bound they were in waist deep. Giles immediately picked her up in his arms and carried her out and up the bank. He was deeply frightened for long moments, for she was motionless, her eyes closed. But as he stood looking down into her pale face, her eyes flew open and she started coughing and spluttering.

"Put me down!" she said, choking and pushing against his chest. Giles breathed a sigh of relief and set her gently on her feet.

Mirabella coughed and snorted.

Giles sat down, took off his boots, and upended them so that rivers of water gushed out. "When you were singing, 'Follow, follow, follow me far beneath the rolling waves,' I didn't know you meant it."

Her eyes widened with outrage, but she was unable to speak for a few moments as she spluttered. Finally she almost shouted, "Confound it! How could you let my line break? Why did you not help? It's all your fault!"

"Yes, my lady," Giles patiently said.

"And I didn't even catch the tench!"

"No, my lady."

"Oh! How maddening! And—and—how am I supposed to go home like this?" she said accusingly.

She was a sorry sight indeed. The brim of her straw bonnet sagged limply, the flowers were sodden, and a piece of reed was entangled in her dripping hair. Rivulets of water flowed from the hem of her dress.

"Mm, that is a dilemma," Giles said gravely. "I think I must go to Camarden and fetch you some dry clothing."

"But—oh, you great ninny! That would be simply capital, for you to tell my mother you needed to bring me some clothes!"

"So that won't do? Then perhaps we may go to Knyveton. I'll be only too happy to loan you some of my clothes, Bella."

"Oh, if you can't help, then do be quiet! And don't call me Bella!"

"Yes, Lady Mirabella. Look here, there's nothing for it, you know. We shall have to go home and make the best of it. We can go through the conservatory, it may be that no one will see us. Here, your lips are turning blue. Put on my coat."

Mirabella clasped his coat about her. "That water was freezing. Take me home, Giles, I'm starting to shiver."

They had driven one of the farm carts to the stewpond, and as always, Mirabella had insisted on driving. But now she allowed Giles to help her into the seat and he drove. Miserably she untied her bonnet and wrung it out. Rivulets of water dribbled onto the cart floor.

"I'm fairly certain that one is ruined," Giles remarked.

"And it was one of my favorites, too," Mirabella lamented.

"Mirabella, you must have at least a hundred bonnets."

"What do you know about bonnets? You're only a man."

"True, I apologize for my shortcomings."

They rode in silence for a while. The sun still shone down, warm and kind, and in spite of her continual sniffing, Mirabella began to look a bit less miserable.

Under his breath Giles murmured, as if to himself, "'There is a willow grows aslant a brook, / That shows his hoar leaves in the glassy stream; / There with fantastic garlands did she come / Of crow-flowers, nettles, daisies, and long purples—' "

Mirabella elbowed him sharply in the side, and he mumbled, "Ow."

"I am no Ophelia, thank you. All that girl needed was to show a little backbone."

They reached the back of Camarden Court, but it was impossible to drive up to an entrance. They were obliged to walk through the walled kitchen garden, the herb garden, and the knot garden before they came to the back door of the conservatory.

The marquess had built the conservatory specifically for Mirabella, as she loved gardening, including hothouse gardening. In truth it was more like an expansive, luxuriously landscaped room than a hothouse. Beneath the glassed rotunda, in the center of the conservatory, was a magnificent Venetian wrought iron table surrounded by eight chairs. The family often had breakfast here instead of in the morning room.

But this afternoon there was a different gathering. Sitting at the table, having tea, were the Marchioness of Camarden, Mirabella's mother; Mirabella's aunt, Lady Dorothea Tirel; and Mrs. Honora Rosborough and Mirabella's friend Josephine. The marchioness looked shocked, but then her jaw tightened and she shook her head slightly. Lady Dorothea's face was expressionless, though her dark eyes gleamed. Mrs. Rosborough and Josephine exchanged quick glances of amusement, then both looked down.

Giles took Mirabella's hand and tucked it into his arm, and they came forward slowly, both of them wet to the skin and dripping onto the brick floor. Giles made a bow as courtly as if he were being presented to royalty. "Good afternoon, ladies. As you see, we have suffered a discomfiture, and it is entirely my fault. I imposed upon Lady Mirabella and persuaded her to go out punt-ing with me, and to my deepest regret I overturned the punt. Lady Camarden, may I offer you my most heartfelt apologies."

Lady Camarden frowned. "Giles, you lie most abysmally, it's little wonder that you never gamble. Mirabella, you have been fishing again, haven't you?"

"Mm—er—" She sighed deeply. "Yes, Mamma."

Aunt Tirel, her eyes bright with mischief, asked with polite interest, "Did you catch anything?"

Lady Camarden said, "Dorothea, I forbid you to encourage her. Mirabella, if you must be a little slyboots and sneak off to—oh dear, you're shivering. Go on up to your room, child."

"Yes, Mamma." Mirabella hurried off, still clutching Giles's coat about her.

Signaling to a footman standing to one side of the table, Lady Camarden said, "Matthew, go tell one of the maids to make up a fire in Lady Mirabella's room. And find Colette and send her up."

The footman bowed. "Yes, my lady."

Lady Camarden turned back to regard Giles. He stood with remarkable aplomb considering his dripping coatless state, a blankly pleasant look on his face.

Icily Lady Camarden said, "I would ask you to join us for tea, Sir Giles, but I fear that you might dampen us. I'm sure you, too, would like to repair your sodden state. We'll see that your coat is cleaned and returned to you."

Again he bowed deeply. "Thank you, my lady. Lady Dorothea, Mrs. Rosborough, Miss Rosborough. Bid you good afternoon."

And so, squelching only a bit, Sir Giles Knyvet took his leave.

Chapter Two

Colette's eyes were wide and horrified. "*Ma dame, qu'avez-vous fait?*"

Mirabella rasped, "I've fallen in the stewpond, that's what I've done. Hurry, help me get out of these wet clothes. And oh, what a foul smell."

Murmuring under her breath, Colette soon had Mirabella's clothes in a sodden pile. "Don't even try to clean them, Colette, just throw them out. And I want both my flannel dressing gown and my banyan. I'm frozen."

In heavily accented English Colette replied, "Yes, my lady. But *mais non*, it is too much the waste to throw out your fine clothes. I will take them, *oui*?"

"Yes, as long as you take them out of here. I must have a bath and wash my hair, it smells like fish and pond mud. Tell the maids to hurry, or I'll never be dressed in time for dinner."

Indeed it was a scramble to get Mirabella bathed and dressed in time. During the entire ordeal Colette complained of Mirabella's foolishness in a low whisper, for she was of the firm belief that if she didn't say it in English, and aloud, then Mirabella had no right to reprove her. She was a pretty girl, the same age as Mirabella, with dark curly hair and bright dark eyes, and she was saucy. Her father, Monsieur Danton, was the marquess's *chef de cuisine*, and he was as haughty as any aristocrat, and her mother was their *chef pâtissière*, their own expert pastry chef, and *confiseuse*, a genius confectioner, and she also was temperamental, so Colette came by her impudence honestly. Mirabella enjoyed her lady's maid, for she was bright and fun-loving, and Mirabella's last maid had been an efficient but dour woman of forty-eight. When she had at last retired two years ago, the marchioness had disapproved of Mirabella's choice of Colette as her lady's maid; until then Colette had been a kitchen maid, albeit almost an under-chef to her father and mother. But the marchioness couldn't deny that Colette was accomplished, in that she had a lady's education and air, and she was an excellent seamstress and hairdresser. Mirabella had succeeded in having her way, as she usually did.

"No, not full evening dress tonight, Colette," Mirabella said as Colette was pulling out a fine pink satin gown. "It's just the Rosboroughs and Sir Giles, not formal dinner. Here, I'll have the amber jaconet with the peach sash, and my opals. And Colette, you must hurry down to the conservatory, I have the most glorious snapdragons for my hair, they're precisely the same shade as my sash and slippers."

Colette protested, "But my lady, there is no time, you cannot be late for the dinner!"

"Then find a footman and send him."

"*Ma dame*, the footman, he does not know the snapdragon. *I* do not know the snapdragon."

Mirabella relented. "Oh, very well. I know you'll make do with just the ribbon in my hair."

Colette finished dressing Mirabella in record time, and quickly took the peach satin ribbon and made clever little rosettes with pearl hairpins as the centers. Mirabella's hair was still damp as dinnertime approached, so she couldn't have her usual Grecian knot surrounded by wispy curls. Colette cleverly braided her hair into three strands and arranged an elegant tight knot with the braids pinned in graceful loops beneath.

At last Mirabella hurried downstairs to the drawing room where the party was gathered: Mirabella's mother and father, Giles, Mr. and Mrs. Rosborough, and Lewin and Josephine. The Rosboroughs had spent a pleasant day at Camarden Court. Lord Camarden, Mr. Rosborough, and Lewin had been out shooting, as the pheasant were plentiful. With obvious pride Mr. Rosborough was regaling them with tales of his son's shooting prowess. "He didn't miss a single shot, not one! He used twenty-three rounds, and brought down twenty-three birds!"

Lewin said with affection, "Father, I am in the Ninety-Fifth Rifles, I'm supposed to be a sharpshooter. If I couldn't hit what I'm aiming at I'd be slogging along in the mud with the infantry. Oh, half a moment, I do slog along in the mud with the infantry. At least I'm not a lobsterback." Lewin was tall, over six feet, with brown hair and brown eyes and rather plain features. But the warmth in his countenance, and the light of humor in his eyes, made him very attractive. He was dashing in his uniform, for the Ninety-Fifth had green jackets with black facings and three rows of silver buttons, rather than the usual scarlet and brass buttons. His mother hung on to one arm, and Josephine on to the other, both of them gazing up at him with radiant joy. It was the first time in three years that he had been home.

Clifford Rosborough still beamed. "Nonsense, Son, some of those birds were so far away I could barely— Oh, good evening, Lady Mirabella. Here you are, we were sadly missing you."

"Yes, here I am at last, sir," she said, curtsying to him. "I fear that my *toilette* took entirely too long this evening, I hope you all will pardon me for my tardiness." She looked around and said,

"Where's Aunt Tirel? Am I not the only one who needs forgiveness for being late?"

Lady Camarden answered, "Dorothea said she's fatigued and that she'd prefer a light supper in her room tonight, and she begs all of us to forgive her."

"Oh dear, is she ill?" Mirabella asked.

"I asked the same thing, and she told me quite snappily that she is never ill, thank you," Lady Camarden answered. "But it seems to me that her rheumaticks are bothering her more severely than before. She could hardly get up the stairs without assistance."

With sympathy Mr. Rosborough said, "That is distressing indeed. I have to admit that I, too, feel some twinges in my hands and knees these days." He was a tall, thin, plain man, with undeniably bowed legs. He had gone both prematurely bald and prematurely gray, so he had a very pink pate with a silver fringe that made him look older than his fifty-three years.

His wife Honora, in contrast, was ten years younger than he, and quietly pretty, with still, peaceful, Madonna-like features. Softly she said, "I'll make up some lavender-and-willow-bark compresses, they do seem to help Mrs. Varney. She just turned seventy-nine last week, you know, and suffers cruelly from the rheumaticks."

Lady Camarden said, "Did she have a birthday? I didn't have that on my calendar. We'll take her a couple of baskets, Mirabella."

"Yes, we must. She's really quite amazing. The last time I visited her she was out in the garden on her hands and knees, weeding. I helped her, and it seemed that my knees gave out sooner than did hers."

Mrs. Varney had been a housemaid at Camarden Court for over forty years. Her crippling rhematism had obliged her to retire at age fifty-five. Lord Camarden had given her a pension and a cottage on the estate. It was a good thing that Lord Camarden was so wealthy, as there were about another dozen retired servants he provided for and gave housing.

The butler, Irby, appeared to announce that dinner was served. As they were such an informal party, they all trooped into the dining room as a group, still talking among themselves.

Camarden Court had originally been built in 1530, although all that remained of the original Tudor fortress was a magnificent tower gatehouse. Mirabella's grandfather, the first Marquess of Camarden, and her father also, had extensively renovated and refurbished both the interior and the exterior of the house. But one room that had retained its Elizabethan style was the dining hall. It was a long, massive room, with gigantic fireplaces on all four walls. The floor was of ancient oak, blackened with age but polished to a high dark sheen. The walls were of coffered oak panels and there were several old tapestries hung between the floor-to-ceiling stone-mullioned windows. The ceiling was low and oak-beamed. For many generations hundreds of candles in candelabras had been used to light the hall, but Mirabella's mother had installed four great black wrought iron chandeliers, in keeping with the Gothic atmosphere of the room, that provided superb lighting.

Lord Camarden said, "Mrs. Rosborough, Miss Rosborough, I hate to deprive you of your limpet-like attachment to Captain Rosborough's arms, but I want him to sit by me and tell me great tales of his exploits." Lewin sat on his right, and Mirabella promptly took the seat by him, and Josephine sat by her. Across from them Mr. Rosborough, Mrs. Rosborough, Giles, and the marchioness took their seats. The table seated twelve easily, but they sat in a companionable group at one end.

Even though it was a very informal dinner a footman stood behind each chair, splendidly arrayed in the Camarden livery of maroon and black, with his satin knee breeches, white stockings, silver-buckled shoes, and white wig with a queue. As soon as the footmen had ceremoniously seated everyone, the marquess said, "Mr. Rosborough, will you honor us by asking a blessing upon this meal?"

"Certainly, sir." He stood and prayed a simple, heartfelt grace, asking the Lord to bless the food and the diners, and especially praying for a healing mercy for Lady Dorothea Tirel. The Reverend Rosborough was a simple, humble soul who cared deeply for all his parishioners, from the Marquess of Camarden down to the lowest farm laborer. His sermons were always taken from the Bible, usually sweet, short homilies from the Gospels about the love and mercy of Jesus Christ, and His sacrifice. Mirabella had often thought that Mr. Rosborough was truly pious, with none of the usual disparaging implications of the word.

The footmen began serving the first course, beginning with *potage de Crécy*, one of Monsieur Danton's specialties, a thick creamy carrot-and-potato soup seasoned with leeks, thyme, nutmeg, and other herbs that Monsieur Danton flatly refused to name, as he was very secretive about all his receipts.

After two spoonfuls Mr. Rosborough said, "My lady, how I wish you could persuade Monsieur Danton to share his genius for imparting new and unique flavors to the simplest of dishes. It's a genuine travesty to call this carrot soup."

The marchioness replied, "Sir, I would never dare to attempt such a thing and incur Monsieur Danton's ire. Such a torrent of French imprecations I should have to endure! Although I'm certain I shouldn't understand half of it. I was taught French, of course, but he speaks no French I ever learned. Most of the time Mirabella is obliged to translate for me in our weekly meetings to discuss the menus."

"Mamma, 'tis only that your French is a bit rusty. And Monsieur Danton does speak so quickly that sometimes he's difficult to follow."

Giles said with amusement, "It's amazing that he's never learned to speak the King's English. He's been here since the Great Terror in ninety-four."

"He can, but he chooses not to," Mirabella said, her eyes sparkling. "At least to us. I've heard that he can make himself only too well understood to the kitchen maids."

Josephine said, "Oh, he can speak the King's English perfectly. And loudly. I was in Mr. Causby's butcher shop when the great Monsieur Danton himself came in. He threw a wrapped parcel on the counter and proceeded to tell poor Mr. Causby in no uncertain terms that he had cut the sirloins all wrong. He said that they were as chipped and chopped and shredded as if they were tough old mutton chops, and that they would never grace the Marquess of Camarden's table." Josephine was a lovely girl, with bright dark eyes and thick wavy auburn hair. She had a wide, mobile mouth that turned up naturally at the corners. She was vivacious and sprightly, with her gamine prettiness and lively air.

Giles said, "Oh, so that's how I came by those sirloins at such a pretty price. I had no idea they'd been denigrated by Monsieur Danton." He sighed. "Still, I'm afraid he may have been right. They were of a very odd shape and thickness, and although my Mrs. Gess is a good cook, they were somewhat tough."

"Still, he has no right to go terrorizing the tradesmen," Lady Camarden said.

"And will you reprove him, Audrey?" Lord Camarden asked, his mouth twitching.

"Certainly not."

The serving of the entrées of the first course began, a selection of lamb cutlets, sweetbreads, oyster patties, and rabbit. Lady Camarden said, "Here, here is an example of exactly what I'm attempting to illustrate. Monsieur Danton tells me that we will have *lapin braisé du Provençale*, and I meekly agree. I know that it is braised rabbit, but what is *du Provençale*? I'm frightened to even choose the sauces in my own house."

The marquess said, "I'm sure I don't know, m'dear, but you must admit it is delicious, whatever it is." There was general agreement around the table, even from the nettled marchioness. Lord Camarden frowned slightly and continued, "Speaking of rabbit, I heard some disturbing news from Mr. Fairman today. It seems that poachers broke into the deer park and set some traps. The gamekeepers found a doe with a broken leg and had to put her down. She had a fawn, too, a pretty little doe."

Mirabella dropped her fork and murmured unhappily, "Oh, no!"

Hastily her father said, "Don't worry, my dear. They took her to the stables and Diamond, who foaled seven months ago, adopted her. Apparently she's doing very well, along with Diamond's foal."

Mr. Rosborough was visibly upset. "Oh, my lord, poachers in your deer park? How distressing."

"It's more than distressing, it's criminal," the marquess said grimly. "How dare they encroach on the deer park? I've already allowed them very great liberties in Camarden Wood." For two centuries Camarden had had a fallow deer park, enclosed with a stone wall and an ancient gate that was never locked. The park was lovely, and had a beautiful glade that was a favored picnic spot. It overlooked a meadow, thick with daisies in spring, where one could always see the fallow deer delicately grazing.

The marquess continued, "You know, after the harvest, the gamekeepers began to find traps brazenly set right on the bridle path to Knyveton. Giles's horse almost stepped on one when he was on his way here. When I allow them to trap in the wood! I told the gamekeepers to confiscate the traps, but I didn't punish the poachers. I instructed Mr. Fairman to make certain they understood that if they did such a thing again I'd not only confiscate all of their traps, I'd put them in the lockup."

"Oh dearie me," Mr. Rosborough murmured. "Do you know who the poachers in the deer park were, my lord?"

"I do. Fools, they broke into the deer park to check their traps, and were fairly caught just this afternoon. It's two brothers by the name of Neary. I can't place them, but Mr. Fairman is investigating."

Mr. Rosborough sighed deeply. "I am most heartily sorry, my lord, but I'm afraid they're two of my laborers. They were journeymen, and I hired them last spring. As it happened, I had two cottages recently vacated, and I contracted them as permanent laborers. They and their families were literally in rags, traveling in a broken-down old cart that held only six people. The children were obliged to walk." The benefice that the marquess had bestowed on Mr. Rosborough included a glebe of five hundred acres.

"I see," the marquess said thoughtfully. "They have families, you say?"

"They do. The elder brother, Tom Neary, has twelve children. Will Neary has seven, with another—oh, I do so humbly beg your pardon, Lady Camarden." Such things as pregnancies were never to be mentioned in polite company.

"Nonsense, Mr. Rosborough, all of us here know about the realities of the poor," she said evenly. "What is the situation of the two families? Are they indeed so desperate that their only recourse is to poach in our park?"

Mr. Rosborough answered with clear discomfort, "I can't say that is the case, my lady, for as my lord says, none of the poachers are punished for trapping in the wood, where rabbits are plentiful.

Both families had chickens, but Tom told me that the foxes were so numerous this year that they had killed all of them."

"That is certainly not true," the marquess said firmly. "My gamekeepers have told me that the fox hunt will be hard on the hounds this year, as they think we only have half a dozen foxes on the grounds. And so speak clearly, if you please, Mr. Rosborough. Are these fellows simply so lazy that they're getting the easy pickings in my deer park?"

"I fear that must be so, my lord. It's unfortunate indeed. Both brothers have allowed their cottages to fairly go to rack and ruin, and I'm afraid they're both partial to the drink."

Lord Camarden grimaced. "Then they must certainly be dealt with. The punishment for poaching is three months in the lockup, and a fine of five pounds."

Unhappily Mr. Rosborough said, "Yes, my lord, and I cannot say that is not merciful of you, since by the law of the land you could transport them, or even hang them. It's only that their families will have such a difficult time of it this winter. The eldest boy is not yet fourteen years old, I believe." He brightened slightly. "However, of course the church will help."

"Yes... yes," Lord Camarden muttered blackly. "I will not have families going hungry on my land. It's difficult for me to comprehend that some men simply will not prepare for provisioning their families in the winter. Very well, Mr. Rosborough, later we will discuss what must be done about the Neary brothers."

Mirabella knew that this meant that her father and the rector would go over the various charitable programs the church offered. If ample provision could not be made to the two families, the marquess would invent, and fund, a new charity.

Thoughtfully Mirabella said, "Pappa, I have been thinking. Why couldn't the old mere just north of Camarden Dael be made into a stewpond? We could easily stock it from our pond, it's quite overrun, particularly with carp. If the cottagers could fish all winter, perhaps they wouldn't be obliged to poach so much."

Each person at the table stared at her, bemused.

Mrs. Rosborough said, "But that—that's not possible. Is it?"

Mr. Rosborough said, "I think it's a capital idea, Lady Mirabella. Plentiful fishing would certainly add to the cottagers' cupboards. Of course I have no idea what it might involve."

"Nor do I," the marquess said thoughtfully. "But my gardeners and gamekeepers will. I shall look into it. I do have one question, however. How is it that you know so much about the stewpond, Mirabella?"

Mirabella's cheeks flushed a bright pink and she shot a guilty glance at her mother. Lady Camarden said, "Camarden, I can assure you that you don't want to hear the answer to that question. Now, Captain Rosborough, all of us here would love for you to tell us all about the Ninety-Fifth Rifles, and the war."

Lewin said lightly, "My lady, I'm a poor storyteller. At any rate, most of the story would be of little interest, and very repetitive, for there are long periods of marching, marching, and stifling boredom. The exciting parts are generally short periods of time."

The marchioness was not a particularly insightful woman, but she saw that Lewin was reluctant to talk about the war. Though his tone was casual, his eyes darkened and his face was shadowed. Briskly she said, "I have found that is what most soldiers say when questioned, so I won't hound you. I do wish to offer my sincerest congratulations on your promotion. *Captain* Rosborough sounds much better than *Lieutenant* Rosborough."

"Hear, hear," Lord Camarden said heartily. "A toast to Captain Rosborough!" They toasted him, calling out, "To *Captain* Rosborough!" Lewin blushed like a small boy.

It took a couple of hours for the diners to work through all four courses. Monsieur Danton never served only the three obligatory courses, for Madame Danton had decreed that no one was to partake of her desserts unless their palate had been cleansed by savories. She never made prosaic meat pies, either. The savories were always exotic. On this evening she had prepared angels on horseback, bacon-wrapped oysters seasoned with smoked paprika and then roasted. There were devils on horseback, figs wrapped in Dunlop cheese and bacon and then roasted. There were also two sumptuous tarts, one of tomato, goat's cheese, and basil, the other of Somerset Brie and beetroot. Mirabella ate so many angels on horseback that she couldn't eat any of the selection of desserts.

When everyone had finished, Lady Camarden rose and said, "Ladies, let us retire to the drawing room, for I am seeing the beginnings of a heated discussion between my husband and Mr. Rosborough. Tonight it appears that it will be centered around the scandalous prince regent and the true nature of the divine right of kings. Honora, for years we've had no success in restraining them from discussing politics or religion at table. I have finally surrendered."

"As have I," Honora sighed.

The two ladies led Josephine and Mirabella to the drawing room. Honora said, "In truth, I do find it quite amusing when his lordship and my husband argue. It's the only time I see him forget his station, and neglect to say, 'my lord.'"

"It is one of Camarden's favorite pastimes, baiting your husband," Lady Camarden said. "And poor Mr. Rosborough never seems to recognize what he's doing. Really, as if Camarden actually believed in the divine right of kings! He's as much a liberal Whig as is the rector."

The drawing room was expansive, tastefully furnished with Sheraton sofas, settees, and armchairs. Intricate draperies of sage-green, blue, and yellow stripes decorated the long windows. A grand concert piano stood at one end of the room, surrounded by easy chairs for the frequent musical performances Mirabella gave.

Honora asked, "Lady Mirabella, will you favor us with some music tonight?"

"Actually, ma'am, Josephine and Giles and I have been practicing a piece that I'm anxious to perform for an audience and see if it is acceptable. If there is a request to perform in London, I intend to offer it instead of a solo," Mirabella said eagerly.

"You're always requested to display your musical talent, Mirabella," Lady Camarden said.

"Yes, and I always find it a little uncomfortable when Sir Giles is present," she said with ill humor. "He is so much better at the piano than am I. I find it quite intimidating."

"That's nonsense," Josephine said firmly.

"But he is a much better pianist than am I," Mirabella countered.

"Yes, I know. What I meant was that you are certainly not intimidated by it. Nothing intimidates you," Josephine said with a smile.

"All too true," Lady Camarden said sternly. "Not even the specter of drowning in the stewpond."

"Oh, Mamma, I was never in danger of drowning. You know very well that Giles was with me, he would never let that happen. And so, what did you think of my idea about the village mere? It seems to me to be a workable idea."

Although it was an unorthodox topic for fine ladies, they discussed it with interest, wondering exactly what was involved in turning a simple pond into a stewpond, how one would go about moving the fish from the Camarden stewpond four miles to the new pond. This decidedly unlively topic absorbed them until the gentlemen came into the drawing room.

The marquess and Mr. Rosborough came in, deep in conversation, completely ignoring the ladies. Mr. Rosborough's shiny pate was bright pink.

"No, sir, you entirely mistake my meaning," he was saying passionately. "King Nebuchadnezzar cannot be compared to King George. Nebuchadnezzar's seven years of madness was a punishment of a wicked king by, as Daniel said, the 'great and dreadful' God—the Old Testament God. The sacrifice of Jesus Christ freed us from retribution for our sins. And King George is a devout, charitable Christian man."

The marquess and Mr. Rosborough took, as it were, adversarial stances at the fireplace, leaning upon the mantelpiece. Both Lewin and Giles were grinning as they followed them in. Giles sat by Mirabella on the settee. "Lewin and I had no opportunity to say a single word," he whispered.

"Are you at all surprised?" Mirabella said, watching the two older men, her dimples flashing.

Lord Camarden had a particularly bright, mischievous look on his strong features as he said, "But surely, instead of disagreeing with me, you are in fact agreeing with me, sir. You yourself said that all rulers have a much higher responsibility to conduct themselves nobly and morally, and that the price that must be paid when they neglect to do so is much more onerous than for the common man."

"Sir, you know very well that I was not speaking of King George's madness, I was speaking of the prince regent's continual troubles, both in his public life and in his personal life, which I anticipate will continue if he doesn't change. He is not a moral man, and he does not conduct himself nobly..."

In a normal tone, for the marquess and Mr. Rosborough were talking quite loudly, Giles quoted from *The Rivals*: "'I must confess that you are a truly moderate and polite arguer, for almost every third word you say is on my side of the question.'"

With delight Mirabella responded, "Indeed, my father and the rector are two very collarly gentlemen, and quite matriculate. Well, it seems we'll have no concert tonight. But I have thought of a most amusing exercise for us on the piano." They rose, and signaled Lewin and Josephine to join them. Lady Camarden and Mrs. Rosborough were watching their husbands with clear amusement.

Mirabella said, "Here, Giles, I shall sit on the left-hand side of the bench, and you sit on the right-hand side." She looked up at Josephine and Lewin and said, "I have thought of a way I might at last best Giles on the piano. We shall play 'Rondo alla Turca.' "

"But we've often played that as a duet," Giles said, puzzled.

"Ah, but not this way. I shall play the left-handed fingering with my right hand, and you shall play the right-handed fingering with your left."

Lewin said, "Surely that's not possible. Isn't there some sort of theory that the two sides of your brain control your right and left hands? If your brain has taught your right hand the right-handed fingering, and your left knows the left-handed fingering, can you just turn them arsy-varsy like that?"

Giles said, "I rather doubt it—unless one practices. You wouldn't ambush me in such an infamous manner, would you, my lady?"

Mirabella sniffed. "You would accuse me of falsity, sir? For shame. I highly represent that. Now let's play."

"Rondo alla Turca," the last movement of Mozart's Piano Sonata no. 11, was a complex, quick, lively piece. Giles and Mirabella reached across their bodies, as it were, to play, as Lewin had said, somewhat upside down. Mirabella played the first few bars creditably, but Giles's fingering was clumsy and several times he hit two keys instead of one.

"Neither my brain nor my hands can do this," he complained.

"I'm getting the headache from trying to switch the sides of my brain. And my right hand keeps twitching and creeping up to the keyboard of its own accord to do the fingering."

Lewin, Josephine, and Mirabella all laughed, while Giles, frowning prodigiously, kept trying to play.

Mirabella thought, *Oh, what a wonderful Season this will be! With the four of us all in Town, it is sure to be my best Season yet. I can hardly wait.*

Chapter Three

It was about ten o'clock when the merry party broke up and the guests went home. When Mirabella went upstairs to her bedroom, she was surprised to see under the door that the candles were still lit in her Aunt Tirel's room. She hesitated, but decided that she wanted to get comfortable, and warm. It seemed that she had never quite thawed out since she'd somersaulted into the stewpond. She smiled at the mental image as she went on to her bedroom.

Mirabella had decided long ago that she didn't want to refurbish her room with more contemporary furnishings, as her parents had done to their suites. Her bed was a massive Elizabethan four-poster bed with a full tester, and it was so high that it had a stool with which to climb up into it. In winter the hangings were heavy satin damask, in summer a light airy lawn. The paneling was dark, the walls covered with old tapestries, as in the dining hall. It had a medieval air that Mirabella loved.

Colette assisted her to undress and she put on her old worn banyan. "No, Colette, I don't want you to put my hair up in curling rags tonight. Just brush it out and you can do the braids again tomorrow." When Colette finished, Mirabella dismissed her.

Going to the window seat and throwing open the window,

Mirabella breathed deeply of the night air. It was much colder than the deliciously warm day had portended, and Mirabella was grateful that Colette had thought to bank up her fire. Thin gray clouds scudded across the sky, the stars faintly glimmering in and out as they were shadowed. She thought that perhaps Old Figge's knees had been correct, and hoped that it wouldn't rain on Monday, the first day of the fox hunt.

Mirabella often had insomnia, and she knew that this night would be sleepless, perhaps until the wee hours of the morning. Wondering about her Aunt Tirel, she took a candle and went down the passage to see if the candles still burned in her bedroom. They did, so Mirabella knocked and said, "Aunt Tirel?"

"Come in, child," she called.

Lady Dorothea was sitting up in bed, her hair wrapped in rags and a warm nightcap on. She was wearing her spectacles, and reading a book. As she looked up over her spectacles, they slid down to the end of her nose as she gazed at Mirabella with astonishment. "What on earth is that outlandish costume you're wearing?"

"Oh, it's a man's banyan. My father's, in fact. Three years ago he ordered all new ankle-length dressing gowns, saying that he was getting old and his shanks got cold in a banyan. I purloined it, and I've treasured it ever since." The dressing gown was of heavy quilted satin brocade that was embroidered in red and gold, and it swallowed Mirabella. Although it had been calf-length on the marquess, it was long on her, trailing a demi-train. As in it she often wandered the house at night, and sometimes even went outdoors, it had to be cleaned often and was much faded, and some of the embroidery was threadbare. Still, she couldn't bear the thought of giving it up.

Mischievously she said, "I think that when I'm in London I may sneak off to Pappa's tailor and have a couple of new ones made for me."

"I should think that would be your only re respecting mantua-maker would think of dr in such a thing," Lady Dorothea said. "I'm come to see me to display your execrable dr

"No, I saw that your candles were still lit a about you. Aunt Tirel, I thought you were fatigued? We mis your company very much at dinner."

"A mild reproof, but still undeserved. I was fatigued, and I went to bed and to sleep at eight o'clock. Then I woke up and knew that it would be fruitless to try to go back to sleep. Since I've gotten old I find that my sleep is often disrupted by these episodes. It's really most tiresome." She patted the bed and Mirabella sat down with her knees up, hugging her ankles.

Lady Dorothea was now sixty-four years old, seven years older than her brother, Mirabella's father. She had never been considered a handsome woman, for she definitely had taken after her father, as had Lord Camarden. She was tall and had the same strong features, a square jaw and long imperious nose and wide forehead. She and her brother had inherited their father's thick salt-and-pepper hair. When she was younger she had been sturdily built, but now she was rather bony and gaunt. Still, she didn't look her age, for her face was relatively unlined and she had a certain vigor about her, although she did rely more heavily on the cane she had been obliged to start using the previous year.

Mirabella sighed. "It is tiresome, is it not? I must take after you, Aunt Tirel, for I often have sleepless nights. That's one reason I love this banyan, on cold nights a simple flannel dressing gown doesn't keep me warm. I often wander about at night when I'm restless. The servants think Camarden Court is haunted."

"I'm not at all surprised. But no, Mirabella, I don't think you're at all like me. When I was your age I slept like a stone. Why don't you sleep, Mirabella? Are you that worried, or troubled?"

abella considered this. "No, not really. I think that I'm just ... e perverse opinion that sleep is a waste of time. I'm always so anxious to be up and about, doing things."

"I see. And what things might you wish to be doing tonight?"

"Why, talking to you. Is it too late? Are you about to retire?"

"No, to be honest, it's a relief to have a distraction from this stupid book," she rasped, tossing it down without marking her place and taking off her spectacles. "I thought it would bore me enough to put me to sleep. Instead I just find it irritating."

"What book is it?"

"*Childe Harold's Pilgrimage*. Everyone is so mad for it that I thought I must investigate, but I could barely get through the first canto. I had almost decided to toss it out the window."

Mirabella giggled. "Ah, yes, Lord Byron's masterpiece, it is all the rage now. And perhaps I'm not so unlike you as you think, Aunt Tirel. I was quite unable to get through the first canto at all. Childe Harold is a dreary, drooping, melancholy libertine, isn't he?"

"Excellent observation. I should have realized after reading the introduction, 'To Ianthe,' that it was certain to be syrupy and melodramatic."

"And I should have been well forewarned when I learned that Lord Byron's Ianthe is actually Lady Charlotte Harley, who is is all of eleven years old," Mirabella said scathingly.

"That settles it. It is going out the window."

"That will suit me. My copy went to Giles, for he reads everything, even if he hates it. He's just too intelligent to live. Anyway, Aunt Tirel, I would like to talk to you about something in particular. But first"—she smiled slyly—"I happen to have a secret potion to help me sleep. Madame Danton makes the most delicious orange ratafia for me, with heavenly spices like cinnamon and nutmeg and cloves. Would you care to share a glass with me?"

"I certainly would. And if you won't tell anyone that I'm a secret drinker, then I won't tell anyone that you are."

"I seriously doubt that it's a well-kept secret. You know the servants always know everything. I'll just go along to my room and collect it." She left and came back with a silver tray that held an exquisite crystal decanter and two small glasses. After serving her aunt and pouring herself a glass, she settled back on the bed and sipped lightly. "You see? It has very little brandy in it. When Madame Danton first started making it for me, I kept having to tell her to cut down the amount. Her first concoction made my head spin so badly after only two sips that I thought I was turning somersaults."

"Then I must say that you're not a very accomplished secret drinker."

Mirabella nodded absently. She was deep in thought for long moments. Lady Dorothea waited quietly. Ever since Mirabella was a child, she had confided in her aunt, but sometimes it took a while for her to come to the point. On this night, however, she finally managed it very well.

"Aunt Tirel," she said, frowning a little, "I have lately been thinking a lot about love."

"Have you now? By your countenance I can surmise that it's hardly like the so-rapturous swoonings of our Childe Harold. Is it charitable, familial, godly, filial, parental, maternal, or romantic love we're considering?"

"Hm. Actually, it's some of all of them. Tonight at dinner I was thinking about how I care so deeply for Lewin Rosborough, like a beloved brother. I hate to admit it, but it's very different from my feelings toward Philip. I love him, of course, he's my brother, I think it's just that I hardly know him. And of course I love Josephine as much as if she were my own sister."

"That is quite natural. Your life has been much more intertwined with Lewin's and Josephine's than it has been with Philip's."

Now Mirabella looked amused and the dimples showed ever so slightly. "And also at dinner I was thinking how very dear is Mr. Rosborough. I think if I could find a young man exactly like him I should marry him instantly."

"You would do no such thing. Beautiful, wealthy, intelligent, accomplished, titled ladies of your age never have the good sense to marry a man such as the Reverend Rosborough."

"No, I suppose not," Mirabella agreed complacently. "And I know it wouldn't suit. I'm so busy all the time, I should drive him to distraction. Mrs. Rosborough is such a calm, restful lady, they seem to do very well together."

"They do. I believe they have one of the most successful marriages I've ever known."

"A successful marriage," Mirabella repeated. "How does one ensure that? How does one go about making the decision that this person will make me happy for the rest of my life? How will I know if I can make him happy?"

"I perceive now that we're hardly talking about the romantic kind of love. We're discarding that, are we?"

With a touch of weariness Mirabella said, "I don't know. I don't think I understand at all about romantic love. Once... I thought I did. Now I wonder if such a thing even exists."

Mirabella could tell by the sudden shrewd light of understanding on her aunt's face that Lady Dorothea now knew exactly what Mirabella was trying to ask her.

When Mirabella was seventeen, in her first Season in London, she had met the dashing, handsome Captain James Pryce of the glamorous Tenth Royal Hussars. Mirabella had fallen hard, and quickly, for him. He had been less forthcoming, but after a time he had told her of his deep love for her. Later he had told Mirabella that he simply couldn't believe his good fortune, that he had never thought a lady such as Mirabella could fall in love with him. His family was not particularly distinguished, and he was poor. Mirabella told him that she couldn't care less about either.

By the end of the Season, Mirabella had managed to be alone with him several times, and it seemed that their love was unconquerable and irresistible. Captain Pryce asked Mirabella to elope with him to Gretna Green.

Mirabella had been hesitant. "I dislike deceiving my parents, but I am so afraid that my father and mother would not approve. I must tell you, James, that I don't think they would completely disown me, but it's very possible that they wouldn't give me such a substantial settlement." Mirabella's marriage settlement was thirty thousand pounds.

He had replied, "Mirabella, I wouldn't care if they cut you off without a shilling. That is, I would hate to ask you to live on a captain's pay, for we would be poor indeed. But for my part, I don't care a fig for your settlement." He had kissed her, and Mirabella had breathlessly agreed to elope with him.

But Captain Pryce had not been at all discreet. Either he bragged, or else he was truly so elated that he couldn't keep it to himself. Mirabella often wondered which it had been. He told some of the other men in his regiment, and one of them was a good friend of the Earl of Reynes, Mirabella's brother Philip. When her parents found out, they swept Mirabella back to Camarden Court immediately, and she never saw Captain Pryce again. He returned to the war in France and Spain, and died the next year in the Battle of Corunna. For almost five years Mirabella had struggled, trying to comprehend exactly what the nature of her love for Captain James Pryce had been. And she had ceaselessly wondered about his true feelings for her.

Now Mirabella had only one certainty concerning Captain

Pryce. She had never again known the same breathless delight in another man's company. She had never known the same heady and, yes, passionate depth of feeling again. She had never again even come close to falling so helplessly in love with another man. She was utterly confused. Her father had told her that Captain Pryce was nothing but a shameless fortune hunter. Had she been that deceived by him? Even more troublesome was the question: had she deceived herself? Was it possible that he had been the only man she could ever love? Had it even really been love, or simply a youthful infatuation?

Lady Dorothea watched the changing expressions on Mirabella's face. She asked, "Mirabella, are you wondering why I never married?"

Mirabella managed a small smile. "Yes, I am, Aunt Tirel, although I would never have the courage to be so impertinent as to ask you."

"On the contrary, you do have a great deal of courage, in many ways. But then I know that I'm a fearsome old lady, and if the time had not been right, I would have given you a proper set-to.

"But I think that it is time now. I was engaged once, you see. I was twenty-five years old, and he was ten years my senior. I wanted to marry him more than anything I had ever wished for."

Mirabella's eyes grew wide and startled. "But no one has ever spoken of this. I don't mean gossip, I mean my parents, the family has never told me."

"No, I forbade them to. At first it was so painful for me that I never wished to hear his name again. And then, after a time, it wasn't that it was so painful, it was simply that I had healed enough that I didn't need to dwell on it, and I went on with my life."

"What happened, Aunt Tirel?" Mirabella swallowed hard. "Was it—was it like me?"

Vigorously she said, "Not at all, Mirabella, except for one thing, I suppose. He was a soldier, Colonel John Grandison of the Bengal European Regiment, with the East India Company. He had been orphaned at sixteen, and had joined the army, and had been in India for eleven years. My father, your grandfather, knew him. John had returned to England, he was then thirty-five years old. He loved the army, and he loved India, and he had decided to sever all his ties here and live in India. My father introduced us."

A slight shadow of pain darkened her eyes, and she took the last sip of her ratafia and held out her glass. "I promise not to tell anyone that you took two glasses if you promise not to tell anyone that I did." As Mirabella silently poured the two drinks, she wondered if she really had intruded on a subject too painful for her aunt.

But then Lady Dorothea continued in her normal matter-of-fact tone, "Colonel Grandison and I fell in love, almost from the first time we met. His only hesitation was that he really wanted to live in India, but I was wild for it, and I convinced him that was what I wished, too. We decided to marry. The only request he made of me was that we wait until he could go back to India and make a home for us there. He had a small indigo plantation, and he said that the house was very humble, and that he couldn't bear the thought of me living in a cottage with mud and dust and scorpions." Now her dark eyes lit up with amusement. "I fought him savagely, but he simply wouldn't consider taking me to India until he could provide for me."

"He must have been a very strong man indeed, to win a fight with you," Mirabella said lightly, then she looked dismayed. "That is—if he— Is he—"

"No, you're right. He did die. He had been back in India for two months when he got typhoid. We received word from his commanding officer. I think that perhaps the hardest, most painful thing was that General Mayes said that John had never once been ill all the years he had been in India."

"Oh, Aunt Tirel, I am so, so very sorry. That is so tragic," Mirabella cried.

"It was, and I was devastated, of course. We were so well suited, we were so much alike. I knew that my life with him was going to be such an adventure."

When Lady Dorothea Tirel was young, she'd been something of a rake. She rode to hounds, went shooting, raced her cabriolet, and generally scandalized Polite Society. Mirabella also knew of the greatest scandal, although she had never known the reason for it. When Lady Dorothea was twenty-six years old, she had gone to India with only a maid and a manservant. Lord Camarden had said that once Dorothea made up her mind to do something, no power on earth could stop her.

Aunt Tirel was watching Mirabella with an amused look on her face. "And so I went to India, and to this day I still relish the scandal it caused. It's too ridiculous, I was never an immoral woman. I was just different. I had always chafed from the rigid strictures of society.

"John had left me his property, you see. He was a simple man, and he lived modestly, and had no air of privilege about him. But his plantation, and all of his money, came to over ten thousand pounds."

"Ten thousand pounds? That must have been a substantial fortune that many years ago."

Lady Mirabella rolled her eyes. "Oh, yes it was, back in olden times."

Mirabella looked down into her glass. "And so my grandfather approved of your marriage?"

Lady Dorothea smiled, and it warmed Mirabella. When she smiled her eyes sparkled and her entire countenance looked merry. She may not have been a handsome woman, but she was attractive. "My father indulged me in the same way that your father indulges you. How do you suppose I was allowed to run wild, as I did?"

"Aunt Tirel, I do not run wild. There may be occasional lapses, such as the stewpond incident, but normally I'm perfectly respectable. At any rate, I'm sure one reason my grandfather was so lenient with you was because Grandmother died when you were but seven, and he never remarried a woman to raise you and Pappa."

Mirabella's grandmother had died giving birth to her father. In the course of their marriage, her grandparents had had seven children, but Lady Dorothea and Lord Camarden had been the only ones to survive. Four had died in infancy, and one had died at the age of eleven.

"That may be true, I suppose. How I wish he would have lived to see you, you are so much like my mother," Lady Dorothea said quietly. "Still, his indulgence of me wasn't the sole reason that he approved of John. Your grandfather was a soldier, and an army man through and through, and he greatly respected John. As I said, we weren't even really privy to his financial situation. At my request, my father offered to give John half of my settlement, which was six thousand pounds, before we married, to help with building us a new home. John flatly refused, but it shows how much Father esteemed him."

Mirabella sighed. "So for all of these years you've mourned Colonel Grandison. I understand now why you never married."

"No, you don't understand at all, Mirabella. Of course I mourned him, I grieved for him, I felt terrible loss. I was even angry at God when John died. But as I said, time passed, I healed, and I went on with my life. Later, when I was thirty, and again when I was thirty-two, I considered marriage. But I made a decision that I simply was not meant for marriage. And I realized how much the Lord had blessed me, because I had the means to remain independent, and a wonderful family. I had a loving father and brother, and later I had your mother, and you and Philip. No, Mirabella, I have not been suffering. I've had a good life, a satisfying, rich life. I still do."

Mirabella asked softly, "But Aunt Tirel, haven't you had regrets?"

"Of course I have, everyone does. But remaining unmarried has not been one of them."

"It's so difficult for me to understand."

"Yes, it would be. Because I was right when I said that you're nothing like me, in spite of our mutual disdain for Lord Byron. Don't mistake me, child. I don't expect anyone else to make the same choice I did. I heartily approve of marriage. Well, some marriages, but that is not the salient point. I can see now, my dear, that you are longing for marriage."

"Oh, I am, Aunt Tirel," Mirabella said with relief, now that she could admit it. "I know that I swore when I was seventeen that I would never marry, and—and of course you know the reason for that. And then when I was eighteen I said that I would, perhaps in my third Season. That Season I decided I would wait until the next Season. I have driven my poor Mamma to distraction. But now, just in the last year, I have been longing to have my own home, and family. Especially children."

"I would advise you to select a husband first," Lady Dorothea said. "And have you?"

Mirabella smiled mischievously. "Not yet. I have several candidates, but I shall have to interview them this Season."

"I see. What are your requirements for the position?"

"He must be handsome, of course. He must have a suitable income, and preferably a sizable estate, although there is room for negotiation on that particular point."

"That's very generous of you. Now I should like to revisit our first topic. What about love? The romantic kind?"

Mirabella looked straight into her eyes. "What about it, Aunt? One thing I have understood as we've talked tonight. You never loved another man as you did Colonel Grandison. If you had you would have married him."

She shrugged. "Perhaps, perhaps not. In truth, I just never met another man who would have allowed me my independence, and with the spirit of adventure that John had. I just couldn't contemplate making the compromise."

Mirabella looked crestfallen, and quickly Lady Dorothea continued, "But that was me, Mirabella. You must make allowances for vast differences in temperament, and the desires of the heart."

"But that's just it, Aunt, I don't even know the desires of my heart," Mirabella said passionately. "It seems to me that I may in truth not have any, that I never will."

Quietly Lady Dorothea said, " 'The heart is deceitful above all things, and desperately wicked: who can know it?' I know that Jeremiah was saying that since Adam and Eve, we are all born to sin and are inclined to separate ourselves from God. But think about it. The heart is deceitful, yes. And the only person your heart can deceive is yourself."

Mirabella said, "Oh dear, now you have given me too much to think about. I was convinced that you would solve my problem for me, but here I am with only more questions."

"Surely you didn't think I would decide whom you should marry. I, of all people, despise arranged marriages," Lady Dorothea said tartly.

"Mm. Sometimes I think it might be easier if I allowed Mamma to arrange my marriage. But then again, I've decided to arrange it myself."

"So I understand. But you're not allowed to ask me any

more questions tonight, Mirabella, you've been quite meddlesome enough. I, however, have a question for you."

"I suppose I do owe you at least that."

Lady Dorothea said lightly, "You've spoken of your affection for Josephine, for Lewin, for Honora, and you've confessed your secret longing for Mr. Rosborough. What about Giles?"

"Giles?" Mirabella said, surprised. "Why, I should think that would be obvious to you. He's my dearest, best friend. He's like—like—my old banyan." She plucked at her dressing gown. "I'm so comfortable with him, I trust him, I know I can always rely on him."

"That sounds suspiciously like 'I take him for granted.'"

"Not exactly. It's more that I know I can depend on him, as I know I can depend on Josephine and Lewin and my parents and you. I know that Giles and I will always be close friends."

"Will you?" Lady Dorothea asked intently.

With a touch of impatience Mirabella said, "Of course we will. I can't imagine anything that could cause us to be estranged from one another."

"Can't you? Has it not occurred to you that perhaps this theoretical husband of yours may object to his wife having a man as her closest friend?"

"Nonsense. I would never marry a man who wouldn't allow me to stay close to my oldest friends. I may not wish to have a husband who will let me ride all over, shooting up the country, and dashing off willy-nilly all over the world, as some ladies do, but I won't have a tyrant who would try to control my life. I shall add that to my list of requirements. My theoretical husband will not be the sort of man who would try to control my life."

Lady Dorothea nodded thoughtfully. "And Giles's theoretical wife? I can't imagine that there are many women who wouldn't be insanely jealous of you."

"Oh, fie. Giles would never marry that sort of woman, just as I would never marry that sort of man." Mirabella's eyes lit up. "I have it! Josephine would never be jealous of me. I shall tell Giles to marry Josephine."

"I'm sure he'll be thrilled," Lady Dorothea rasped. She took the last sip of ratafia and handed the glass back to Mirabella. "This sleeping potion is finally taking effect, I find. It really is wonderful, perhaps I can persuade Madame Danton to brew up some for me to take back to Tirel House."

Mirabella picked up the tray and her candle. Slyly she said, "If you would move into the Dower House, as we have all begged you to do, you could have all the orange ratafia you want, whenever you want."

Crossly she said, "I've told you to stop badgering me, child. Go to bed."

"Yes, ma'am." Mirabella stopped and turned back at the door. "One kind of love I do know all about. I love you, Aunt Tirel."

"And I love you, dearest. Good night, and sleep well."

"I think I will, now. Good night." Mirabella smiled sweetly. "And thank you. From my heart."

Chapter Four

"Farewell, thou latter spring; farewell, All-hallown summer,'" Mirabella repeated softly as she opened the window to the cold November morning. Yesterday had been as balmy and pleasant as Saturday, but today the late-autumn weather had arrived. A gust of chill wet wind made her shiver. Quickly she closed the window, threw on her banyan, and jumped back into bed to pull the down comforter up to her chin. A maid had made up the fire about an hour ago, but the room was still frigid.

Colette came in with Mirabella's breakfast tray of tea and toast. "Rrrr, it is too cold," she complained. Muttering in French under her breath, savagely she stoked the fire to a low roar. "Does *ma dame* wish to have fresh hot bricks for the feet?"

"No, this hot tea will warm me," Mirabella answered. "I'm not going to be in bed that long. I've slept late already."

"Bah, for the fine my lady it is not late. It's barely dawn." Long ago Mirabella had given up on trying to correct Colette for answering back.

"But it's late for the first day of fox hunting season. And in a way I'm glad it's turned up cold, for now I can wear my scarlet pelisse."

Colette's eyes grew round. "*O ciel! Ma dame* does not tell me of the scarlet pelisse! Now I must hurry and go ready her!"

Mirabella thought she heard a whisper of "*Malediction!*" as Colette bustled into her dressing room, and she called after her, "Yesterday it was too warm to think of it, Colette, I'm certain it will be fine. And I'll want my black velvet top hat." Clucking and murmuring sounded from the dressing room, with a final sulky, "*Oui, ma dame*" thrown in as a sop.

Last year Mirabella, delighted by the new style of the military look for riding habits and pelisses, had ordered a red velvet pelisse of the same shade as the gentlemen's hunting coats. Trimmed in black velvet, it had wide lapels and braided velvet cords trimming the sleeves and hem. As an added whimsy, instead of the usual frog closures of the military style, she had brass buttons made, such as the men's hunting coats had, embossed with a fox's head. Her top hat was the same shape as a man's, but smaller, with a red velvet band and another of the brass fox buttons anchoring a spray of white swansdown. The pelisse was formfitting, so the dress she wore was of plain white linen, with a jabot of lace at the throat.

Hurriedly Mirabella finished her toast and tea, and went into her dressing room. Originally this had been another bedroom, but when Mirabella came out of the schoolroom her parents had converted it. Entirely covering one long wall were two floor-to-ceiling walk-in oak wardrobes. Between them was an intricately carved rosewood chiffonier with ten shallow drawers holding her underclothes. By the fireplace were two plump settees and a tea table. A hearty fire snapped in here, and the room was warmer than her bedroom.

Colette had put the scarlet pelisse on one of the four mannequins, which were made exactly to Mirabella's measurements. Busily she was brushing it. When Mirabella came in, she said with triumph, "A-la, what do I say? She has two loose buttons."

"I'm sure you'll be able to set them in plenty of time. While you do that I'll take my hair down." Mirabella's hair was thick and healthy, but it refused to curl at all unless it was set overnight in curling rags. She hated them, but as Grecian curly tendrils were all the rage, she submitted to it.

With her customary quick efficiency, Colette thoroughly brushed the pelisse and top hat, repaired the two buttons, splendidly arranged Mirabella's hair, and dressed her. It took barely an hour, and Mirabella was glad, for as she dashed out the door she could already hear the baying of the hounds. It was time for the "lawn meet," when the ladies bid good-bye to the men going on the hunt. Mirabella cared nothing for fox hunting itself; in fact, when she thought much about it she felt sorry for the fox. But she did enjoy the lawn meets, for not only was it a grand event for the huntsmen, her mother had made it a tradition that the ladies have a celebration, too.

The Camarden hound kennels, far from being a series of pens, were a grand structure as fine as the stables, built of the same mellow gold brick as the Court, with three dozen separate stalls. Just by the kennels was another Tudor remnant, the old banqueting house. This was a simple long rectangular room with enormous fixed tables with benches running the length of them. It had been somewhat decayed from disuse, but Lord Camarden had repaired it and installed two massive double doors in the front. When they were opened, it was like a three-sided pavilion. Inside the servants set up tea and coffee and of course the traditional stirrup cup.

The guests had already gathered when Mirabella arrived, and the houndskeepers were letting the dogs out of the kennels. Most of the men were already mounted, but some were in the banqueting house, mingling with the ladies and sipping tea or coffee, or his lordship's fine port, as they chose. As they always were, the dogs were so excited they ran frisking into and out of the banqueting house, and all around the horses, under them and between them, panting and barking importantly. Mirabella loved the hounds; she thought that if only people could enjoy their lives as much as did they, the world would be a happier place.

Mirabella saw Josephine, and ran to her immediately. They kissed, as they always did as a greeting. "Oh, Mirabella, you look simply stunning," Josephine said, her dark eyes dancing. "So you're riding to hounds today, I take it?"

"No, I'm only a poor *poseur.* I know that I look very much like my father as Master of the Hunt, and I admit it was done purposely." She looked Josephine up and down. "You are a picture yourself. The pelisse exceedingly becomes you." Mirabella was glad to see that Josephine was wearing a blue pelisse, trimmed in brown grosgrain ribbon arranged in a fleur-de-lis pattern, that she had given her a month ago. It was going to make her later request of Josephine much easier.

About thirty people milled around, with twenty or so huntsmen and half that many ladies. With the commotion of the dogs, the stamping, neighing, and snorting of the restless hunters, and the loud babble of conversation in the pavilion, it was almost impossible to conduct a conversation at normal speaking levels. Mirabella pulled on Josephine's hand to lead her outside. The sun was shining but a raw north wind blew. Josephine pulled her collar more tightly around her neck. "It's so warm and I adore the color. Thank you again, Mirabella."

"How many times have I asked you to stop thanking me? It's embarrassing, as if I were making some great sacrifice. Once I got this pelisse I'd never wear that one again. So. Let me see who is here, it's such a rout I'm having difficulties sorting everyone out. My father, of course, splendid in his scarlet coat."

Lord Camarden's dress was generally very conservative, even drab, although he was always well tailored. But he loved wearing his scarlet huntsman's coat with the black lapels and four brass buttons.

With amusement Josephine said, "And there is my pappa, splendid in his huntsman's garb and dashing hat." Mr. Rosborough always wore the somber black clergyman's coat and vest, with black stockings and old-fashioned buckled shoes. He also wore the shallow-crowned, wide-brimmed clergyman's hat. As it had a tendency to fly off when he was jumping over stiles and hedges, he anchored it with a long white muffler that bent the brim down over his ears, and was tied under his chin.

Mirabella giggled. "He is such a dear! And there is old Squire Eldridge, huffing and wheezing along on his fat old mare. I do declare, Mr. Eldridge's girth almost matches hers. Oh, wonderful, Pappa loaned one of our hunters to Mr. Fairman. He's such an avid hunter, but his gelding died just a few months ago, and it's my understanding that he hasn't been able to purchase another yet."

"Lord Camarden is kind to lend him a horse," Josephine answered.

"Not really, he has fourteen, and he can hardly ride all of them at once. In fact, I see about another half dozen of ours he's loaned out. Oh dear, I see my brother Philip, I didn't even know they had arrived. Have you seen Clara?"

"Yes, I spoke with Lady Reynes. Apparently they arrived very early this morning."

Mirabella sighed. "I'm sure she noted my tardiness. Come along with me, I'll go find her and make my obeisance."

Mirabella's sister-in-law was a disciplined, humorless, stiff woman. Mirabella had often wondered about her brother's marriage. Philip was, in fact, rather staid and boring, but he wasn't completely bereft of a sense of humor and generally was a low-key, unexcitable man. Clara seemed high-strung and tightly wound. Mirabella had the vague impression she was a product of overbreeding, for on both of her parents' sides were numerous marriages to cousins. Then again, marriage to first cousins was not at all uncommon, and the offspring weren't necessarily brittle icicles.

Lady Reynes was sipping tea and talking to Giles and Lewin. As Mirabella and Josephine neared, they caught the last of an imperious observation she was making. "... patch on your sleeve is very distinctive, Captain Rosborough, I don't believe I've seen that particular insignia. Pray, what does it signify?"

Lewin looked extremely uncomfortable. He answered courteously, but rather evasively, "I received this after the Siege of Badajoz, my lady. It is an insignia that was awarded to many men after that battle."

"Oh, yes? I read of that great victory, in April, was it not? And what do the initials stand for? The *V* and the *S*?"

Rather loudly, rudely interrupting the conversation, Giles said, "Lady Mirabella, Miss Rosborough. Good morning to you ladies." He bowed deeply, as did Lewin.

Mirabella always curtsied to her sister-in-law. She had learned early on that if she extended this sign of deference to Clara it thawed her a bit. Mirabella observed that, as always, the frostiness in Clara's eyes lessened, and her thin pinched nostrils relaxed. Clara was not an unhandsome woman, but her features were somewhat sharp.

Clara said, "Good morning, Mirabella. You look well, I must say. That hue is a bit startling, but it does flatter you."

"Thank you, Clara. As I'm sure you observe, I have shamelessly copied the huntsmen's scarlet coats. I've heard that bolder colors are coming into fashion this year, so perhaps it's not so awfully daring."

"Perhaps not," Clara said with an unmistakable air of disbelief.

"In my opinion it's a risk for young unmarried ladies. But I know you dress as you like, regardless of the dictates of Polite Society."

Mirabella's ire rose, but strictly she stifled it. Somehow Clara always managed to make her feel as if she were slightly indecent. Smiling sweetly, she asked, "Did you bring Alexander with you, Clara? How I long to see him."

"Yes, we did bring him, although I objected, for children shouldn't be exposed to these falling damps. Philip insisted, however, for he says that you and your parents would wish to see him."

"And so we do," Mirabella said. "He's a delightful boy."

The Master of Hounds blew a short blast on the fox horn, and the dogs went wild. All of the gentlemen left the banqueting house and mounted up.

Clara said with distaste, "It's always seemed to me to be somewhat common for the ladies to serve the stirrup cup."

"It's a tradition that dates back to Queen Elizabeth," Mirabella said. "When she was visiting here, the countess herself served the queen and her courtiers, and Queen Elizabeth thought it was such a charming gesture that she appointed her as one of her ladies of the bedchamber. The Tirel ladies have done it ever since then."

"Yes, Philip has told me of that story," Clara said shortly. "It's just a legend, of course."

Mirabella resisted the urge to argue with her sister-in-law. The "legend" was, in fact, documented. Queen Elizabeth herself had written a short proclamation that because of Dorothea Tirel, Lady Reynes's correct and deferential grace in serving her the stirrup cup, it pleased her to appoint the Countess of Reynes as first lady of the bedchamber. The document was one of the most prized in the Camarden Court library, and indeed the third Lady Reynes, Dorothea, had been noted as one of Elizabeth's ladies.

It occurred to Mirabella, not for the first time, that Clara was jealous of the Tirel lineage. The current Lady Reynes was the granddaughter of an earl on her father's side, and the daughter of a baron, but neither family had anything like the long and distinguished history of the Tirel family. Henry V had awarded William Henry Tirel the first barony in 1415, after he distinguished himself at the Battle of Agincourt; Henry VIII had awarded John Philip Tirel, the sixth baron, an earldom after the 1513 Battle of Tournay. The marquessate was a relatively new patent, awarded to Mirabella's grandfather, General Lord Reynes, by George III after he displayed strong leadership in the Seven Years' War, and showed conspicuous gallantry in leading a cavalry charge in the Battle of Minden. When Mirabella thought on these things, she was very conscious of the privilege, and obligations, of her family.

As the ladies went outside, followed by the servants bearing trays with silver cups, Josephine said to Mirabella, "I wouldn't wish to argue with her ladyship, but I find that the ladies serving the stirrup cup is a charitable tradition, in accordance with the charity that your father displays with the entire fox hunt. He invites anyone in the county who can attend, he loans out his hunters and saddle horses to those who need them, and the marchioness herself serves the stirrup cup. There she is, serving your steward, Mr. Fairman. I think that it all shows a greatness of mind, and much generosity."

Gaily Mirabella said, "You always think the best of people, Josephine. I'm not displaying greatness of mind, I'm just having fun." She had noted that Giles and Lewin were riding Camarden hunters. She was glad; it was difficult for Giles to accept favors.

Taking a silver goblet, she went to Giles and handed it up to him. "I wish you good hunting, sir. I send you to the field with a cup of my father's finest port."

He took a sip, his eyes smiling at her over the cup. "It is fine port indeed. It's generous of your father, considering that half of these fellows wouldn't know good port from dark ale. Won't you join me in a toast to the hunt, my lady?"

"You know very well that I don't drink port."

Slyly Giles asked, "Shall I fetch your ratafia?"

"I take it back. I hope you never set eyes on a fox."

Giles shrugged and drained his drink. "That would suit me. I don't relish being in on the kill. I enjoy galloping hurly-burly all over the country, however. As you've told me countless times, I do like to swagger."

"Swagger on, then. I'm going to serve Mr. Rosborough before my mother beats me to it."

Mirabella served the rector, and then a couple of tenant farmers of the Camarden estate. Then the Master of the Hounds sounded a stirring call on his horn, and the dogs immediately formed a pack and dashed out across the park, with the huntsmen galloping hard behind them.

The ladies gathered back in the banqueting house to finish their tea. Lady Camarden said, "Ladies, this year Lady Mirabella has offered to allow all of you to pick your own bouquets from her conservatory." Pleased murmurs sounded from the ladies. "After that I hope you'll join us for luncheon."

Walking by twos and threes, the ladies followed the path through the formal gardens back to the house. Mirabella and Josephine came to Lady Dorothea's side. Her limp was noticeably more pronounced than usual this morning. With concern Mirabella said, "Aunt Tirel, should you like to stay at the banqueting house and let me fetch a carriage for you?"

"I would not. Great heavens, girl, I used to lead the pack on these hunts. I'm not going to start being carted around like an old cripple, for I'm neither old nor crippled."

Mirabella and Josephine exchanged wry glances behind Aunt Tirel's back. "Of course you aren't, Aunt Tirel. Are you coming to the conservatory?"

"Yes, I am, I'm looking forward to visiting with Mary Eldridge again. We're old friends, you know, and I haven't seen her in an age. In fact, why don't you two girls go ask her to walk with me? She won't mind being as slow as a snail. Get along with you, now, I'm perfectly fine."

Mirabella and Josephine asked Mrs. Eldridge to join Lady Dorothea. Mirabella tucked Josephine's arm in hers and said, "There's something I really need to speak to you about in private. Would you come with me up to my dressing room?"

"But surely you can't neglect your guests?" Josephine said hesitantly.

"Fie, they're all practically family, except for Clara," Mirabella retorted. Then her eyes widened and she pressed her hand to her mouth. "I can't believe I said that."

"I can," Josephine said knowingly. "Very well, I'll come with you if Lady Camarden gives us permission to desert our posts."

"I've already asked her, and she said it would be fine if we don't stay too long. I simply must talk to you, I can't wait any longer."

"I'm not at all surprised, you so rarely have to wait to get whatever you want," Josephine teased her.

The two girls slipped through the conservatory, leaving the chattering ladies behind, and went upstairs to Mirabella's dressing room. Mirabella sat on a settee and patted the seat beside her. After Josephine sat down Mirabella took both of her hands, and suddenly looked grave.

"You know, dearest, that I wouldn't offend you for the world," she said hesitantly.

"I doubt that you could offend me, even if you tried."

"I'm happy you feel that way. Because I'm going to ask you a particular favor, and you may find it difficult to grant it."

Josephine looked mystified. "I'm trying to decipher what favor you could possibly ask that I might find difficult to grant, or might find offensive. Do you wish me to launder your smallclothes? Arrange a secret assignation with a lover? Finally tell my father how absurd he looks with his hat and muffler?"

Mirabella smiled with delight. "I do love you, Josephine. No, none of those, although it might perhaps be time to address the hat and muffler. No, I think—I hope—that my request will be easier for you. I want—I want—oh, hang it all, I'm just going to say it. I'm so excited that you're coming to London with me. I want to supply you with a wardrobe for the Season."

Josephine's raven-wing eyebrows shot up. "No, Mirabella, I can't possibly allow you to do such a thing. It would be an incredible expense, and it would be wasted, for I'd have no use for such finery after the Season."

Mirabella sighed. "I knew you'd say that, so I knew that I'd be wasting my breath in offering to buy you all-new gowns. But please, would you consider this? I've been horribly extravagant this year, I've purchased practically an entire new wardrobe because—because this Season is going to be so special to me. That means that I have dozens of gowns that are only a year or so old, and that are not outmoded yet. We're much the same size, you know," she finished in a pleading tone.

Josephine stared at her for long moments, then her dark eyes grew soft and warm. "Mirabella, you thought I'd be offended at this offer? No, no, dearest, not in a thousand years. It's so generous of you, and so kind. Not many women would be so caring as to think of it."

"Actually, Lewin told Giles that you were worried about your clothes, and Giles told me," Mirabella admitted. "But I would have thought of it eventually. So, you will accept?"

"I will, gladly, on one condition. After the Season I'll give the finest gowns back to you. I know that you give all of your clothes to Colette, and I'll have no use for grand ball gowns when I return home."

"Oh, fie on Colette," Mirabella said crossly. "It's not in her service contract for me to give her every gown I don't wear any more, she's just so impudent that she wrangles them out of me. But if that's your condition, then I agree. I have a condition, too. I absolutely forbid you to thank me every time you set eyes on me. It's more blessed to give than to receive, you know."

"Very true, and the corollary of that is that it's harder to receive than to give. But I shall try. I won't burden you with effusive gratitude, I'll take every gown you give me very much for granted."

"Please do, I'll be so relieved."

"So you tell me that my brother told Giles, who told you, that I was worried about being a drab church mouse in London? How extraordinary, that men would give such things a moment's thought."

"I doubt very many men would. But then Lewin and Giles are extraordinary gentlemen, are they not?"

Josephine nodded. Mirabella had released her hands, and she looked down and slowly smoothed her skirt. Quietly she said, "Did you know that Lewin is staying with Giles?"

"He is? He's not at the rectory?"

"He was, but as you know, Constance and John came down for the hunt, and they brought the baby, so it's crowded and rather hectic. I think that it's a good thing for Lewin. He seems to need some quiet and solitude. Giles leaves him to his own devices."

"He would, he's an intuitive, understanding man. And it may

be good for Giles, too. I've so worried about him at Knyveton Hall all alone. You know, my father goes to call on him often, but he hasn't extended an invitation to my mother and me since his mother died. Of course we don't take it as a slight, but we have been concerned."

Josephine nodded. "From what Lewin has told me, Knyveton is in such an odd state that Giles won't think of trying to entertain."

"An odd state? In what way?"

Josephine smiled ruefully. "Apparently Sir Edwin was in the middle of redecorating and refurbishing the Hall when he died. Lewin says the drawing room and the master's and mistress's bedrooms look like a French brothel."

Knyveton Hall, like Camarden Court, had been built in the Tudor period. It was a quadrangle enclosing a courtyard and had a moat, where swans peacefully glided. The ground floor was of gray ashlar and the first floor was half-timbered, with old wavy diamond-shaped paned windows. Unlike Camarden, however, Knyveton had not been renovated; it still retained the medieval atmosphere both inside and out, including Elizabethan furniture and tapestries.

Mirabella sighed. "Yes, my mother and I saw the drawing room and Lady Knyvet's bedroom, spindly gaudy rococo furniture, all white and gilt and flowery upholsteries. We knew the furnishings must have been imported from France, and must have been costly."

"They were. Giles was horrified. He tracked down the old furniture, which was stored in two old barns on the estate. They were carelessly thrown in there, and evidently require some extensive, and expensive, restoration. Giles is sending them to a London craftsman one piece at a time."

"What about the tapestries?" Mirabella asked. "All I saw were those awful sentimental florid paintings, including not one but two prints of *The Swing*."

"Giles was much relieved to find that the tapestries at least were carefully stored, wrapped in linens with marigolds and lavender, up in the attic. He's taken down the silly paintings and replaced the tapestries, although he said that they only make the furniture look even more ridiculous. Did you see the matching armchairs in the drawing room that were in the shape of big swans?"

"I had managed to forget about those eyesores, but yes, now I do recall them. I was shocked when you told me that Lewin said that about the brothel, but if they're still there he's perfectly justified."

"No, Giles showed them to Lewin, he'd tossed them out into the barn. He said that in good conscience he could hardly destroy such expensive chairs, but it also went against his conscience to take money from some half-wit that might want to buy them."

"That sounds like Giles."

Josephine asked, "Did you see the dining hall?"

"No, we hadn't actually dined at Knyveton Hall for some time before Sir Edwin died."

"He replaced the oak floor with encaustic tiles. Not just a border, or a central pattern. The entire floor is covered in encaustic tiles that have a huge red-and-black flower pattern. Giles said that if he ever entertained again he was going to strew the floor with rushes, bring in the dogs to throw them the bones, set up a head table with a throne, and throw away all the forks."

Mirabella said, "At least he's been able to retain his sense of humor over the sad state of affairs his father left him. It's generally known that the Knyveton estate usually makes about ten thousand a year, which seemed always to allow them to live comfortably, both here and with the town house in London. Those last two years of Sir Edwin's life he must have been horribly imprudent, and you know that Lady Knyvet would never have objected to anything he wanted, she was such a meek woman. But to this day Giles has never said one word about it to me, I only know because of some things my father said."

"Mirabella, you know that Giles has such a delicate sense of honor, he'd never complain about his father, or engage in any sort of poor-mouthing. Lord Camarden has been so helpful to Giles since his father died, advising him and counseling him on how to repair the damage, it only makes sense that Giles would confide in him."

Mirabella asked hesitantly, "Josephine, do you know any details of Giles's trouble? I hate to pry into his private affairs, but he is so dear to me that I honestly want to try to understand what he's going through."

"I know you'd never pry just for the pleasure of gossiping, Mirabella. One thing I do know is that Sir Edwin died owing just about every tradesman in the county large sums of money, from the collier to the draper. Apparently there were no small debts owed in London, too. They completely refurbished and remodeled the town house, bought carriages and expensive horses, and ran up debts to the tailors and dressmakers and even some of the jewelers."

With irritation Mirabella said, "My father told us that in the last two years of his life, Sir Edwin suddenly developed high political aspirations. In his years of standing MP for Camarden, he had become good friends with Prime Minister Perceval and seemed to be aiming for leader of the House of Commons. He was working hard to impress the MPs and the Lords. Pappa also said that apparently Sir Edwin developed that infuriating aristocratic attitude that tradesmen need not be paid for months, or even years. I'm sure Giles was absolutely horrified."

Josephine said sadly, "It's even worse than that, in a way. For two years Sir Edwin had refused to contribute to the schools."

The Marquess of Camarden and Sir Edwin Knyvet had established four charity schools in the county, administered by the church. There was one boys' and one girls' school for the children of the villagers, cottagers, and tenant farmers, one academy for young ladies that taught the genteel arts of French, music, dance, and deportment, and another advanced school for young men that taught the classics and mathematics. Many of the young men who had attended this school had gone on to get scholarships to Oxford and Cambridge, and there were several whom the marquess and Sir Edwin had sponsored themselves.

Mirabella moaned, "Oh, no, poor Giles, he must have been so ashamed! Josephine, you should have told me, I would have been happy to make up the shortfall myself." Out of her personal allowance Mirabella contributed generously to the schools.

Josephine said quietly, "Of course Lord Camarden made up the shortfall, Mirabella. I felt so badly for Giles. My father said he was distraught when he found out. Both my father and your father tried to persuade him to simply begin the contribution again in the next year, but Giles was adamant. He said that everyone completely understood that gambling debts were debts of honor and must be paid immediately, and it astounded him that people couldn't see that obligations to charity were a higher debt, of much higher honor. He sold some of his mother's jewelry to pay the funds back to your father."

"Oh, Josephine, this is so distressing, I can hardly bear it. I knew that Sir Edwin had left Giles in a tangle, but I had no idea it was this bad."

Josephine patted her hand. "Please don't be so upset, dear Mirabella. Giles has recovered amazingly, you know. Just think, he's making silly jokes to my brother about swan chairs and Tudor banquets. And he and Lewin are coming to London for the Season, so Giles must be at least a little more comfortable, as far as finances go."

Mirabella brightened. "Yes, you're right, of course. Giles is so clever, I'm sure he's straightened it all out. And speaking of London, and the Season—how did we end up on such a dreary topic? Let's go ransack my wardrobe and look at all of your new gowns!"

Josephine rose, drew Mirabella to her feet, and said sternly, "Your mother may allow you to ignore your guests, but my mother will blame me for your shameful neglect. We have four months for me to steal your clothes. Just now we must go attend to the ladies, or they'll strip your conservatory bare."

"You order me around as badly as does Colette," Mirabella grumbled.

"Lady Mirabella Tirel," Josephine said, smiling, "no one on this earth orders you around."

Chapter Five

On Saturday the cruel November rains swept in. Mirabella despised being forced to stay indoors, and often would brave a gentle rain to take a walk, but the weather was simply too fierce, with dark-gray skies, rain falling in great torrents, and wind blowing hard from the north.

On this bleak day, however, she had two solaces. The first was her conservatory, for it was so lush that it was very like the outdoors. Although Camarden Court had a separate orangery, Mirabella had brought orange, lemon, lime, and citron trees into her conservatory and had placed them and the plants to simulate a real landscape, instead of a flower warehouse. Regardless of how cold it was, the conservatory was always warm in winter. There were two fireplaces at each end, and an ingenious series of flues ran under the brick floor to provide even heat throughout the greenhouse.

Her other delight was that she was playing with her nephew, Alexander. Her sister-in-law Clara had initially demanded that her family return to its estate, Reynes Magna, on Tuesday, the day after the fox hunt. Mirabella and her parents had urged and pleaded with her to stay longer, for they so rarely got to see Alexander. Finally Clara had told them that she was expecting, and wanted to go home. To be fair, Mirabella reflected, Clara had had a very difficult time during her entire confinement with Alexander, and now that she thought about it, and considered it from Clara's point of view, she sympathized with her. She even realized that it was during Clara's pregnancy that she had become so querulous and snappish; she had never been a warm-natured woman, but until then she had not seemed to be morose and glum.

Mirabella's mother had told her that she'd had a long talk with Clara. She was two months along, and so far she'd had none of the debilitating sickness she'd had with Alexander. Lady Camarden had told Clara that often the first pregnancy was the hardest, and subsequent ones might not be so devastating. Clara had seemed doubtful, but still she must have been reassured, for she had agreed that they would stay at Camarden for another week.

Alexander was an audacious three-year-old, bright and energetic, and was already showing signs of a highly creative imagination. One reason he was so engaging was that he was such a beautiful child, with thick tousled black curls, sparkling velvety-brown eyes, a complexion any woman would envy, a mobile mouth and, even at three years old, fine, even teeth. He was in fact very pretty, although he was in no way girlish. Mirabella reflected how strange it was, that Alexander was nothing like either his father or his mother.

How odd it would be, she thought idly, *if I and my handsome theoretical husband had a pudding-faced, dull child. I wouldn't care, I'd adore him or her anyway.*

"Aunt Mirabella, you said we could see the fawn today," Alex urged her.

"Just look outside, Alex. We can't go out in this storm. But you're staying another week, and I'm sure we'll get a chance to go see Dolly. That's what I named her. But surely you don't mind staying here with me? I brought your toy soldiers, and I'd very much like to play with them."

His eyes brightened. "You would? You mean, play with me, not just watch me play with them?"

"Of course I want to play, it wouldn't be nearly so much fun just watching you." She opened the wooden box with the specially designed slots that held the lead soldiers. "Oh, my, there are a lot of them, aren't there? We could have a battle, couldn't we?"

Promptly Alexander said, "I'll be the English, and you be the French. You have to lose. Where can we have the battle?"

"I have an idea for a battlefield," Mirabella said with sudden inspiration. Then she hesitated, looking Alexander up and down. He was wearing what was called a "skeleton suit," a short coat with long sleeves, buttoned onto high-waisted trousers. It was olive green, with a white shirt underneath. She knew that if Alexander got dirty Clara would be extremely vexed. Then recklessly she thought, *However can you raise a high-spirited boy like Alex and never let him get dirty? It's absurd. Perhaps it won't show too much on the olive green.*

"Come along, I'll show you." Mirabella led him to one of the waist-high potting benches. It held a wide shallow wooden box filled with rich soil. Pulling up two high stools, she said, "I think we should make this into a battlefield. We can pile the dirt up to make ramparts, and ditches, and I have some thin wooden stakes we can break up to make fences."

"Oh, yes, do let's!" He waved a stubby hand around. "Can we have trees on the battlefield, too? Like in here?"

"I think I can do that. But first, here, let's roll up your sleeves, since we're going to be digging in dirt."

"Mamma doesn't like it when I get dirty," he said cheerfully. "Does your mamma get upset when you get dirty?"

Mirabella said, "As a matter of fact she does. So I'm going to put on an apron, and I shall roll up my sleeves, too."

They got very busy landscaping their battlefield, with the promised ramparts, trenches, fences, and even trees. Mirabella callously cut several small twig-ends of an orange tree, and stuck them in the ground. They made very credible trees.

Mirabella allowed Alexander to apportion out the soldiers. He did so, carefully considering whether each one was French or English. All forty of them were finely made, carefully detailed, and meticulously painted. Slowly, one by one, the British and French forces took their places on the field. Alex did at least allow Mirabella to arrange her own company of twenty men.

"These are all redcoats," Alex grumbled. "I wish I had some soldiers that have green jackets like Captain Rosbo's." Alex rarely mispronounced words, and when he did, Clara strictly corrected him, insisting that she wasn't going to allow him to "baby-babble." But Mirabella had no such inclination, so she merely smiled.

"Yes, Captain Rosbo's regimentals are handsome. But this is a fine set of toy soldiers, Alex, and you should be grateful to have them."

"I know, Pappa says I have lots of things that other boys don't," he said meekly. "I do like my toy soldiers. When I grow up I want to be a soldier. Like Captain Rosbo, and wear green with silver buttons instead of red. I don't want to be a lord."

As Philip, the heir to the Marquess of Camarden, was entitled to his secondary title, Earl of Reynes, so Alexander, as the heir's heir, was entitled to the third title, Baron Tirel. Although these were courtesy titles, it still meant that Alexander was Lord Tirel.

"I'm afraid you have no choice about being a lord," Mirabella said with amusement. "But lords can be soldiers, too."

"They can? That's jolly. Now let's have the battle. I'm going to attack you!"

Of course the English beat the French resoundingly, and then Alex decided he was going to be the French and Mirabella might be the English. He fought hard, but he still lost, as he insisted. They rearranged their soldiers and their battlefield and fought another two battles, with the inevitable outcome.

Alex looked up and around the conservatory. The sky was still a solid leaden dull gray, and when the fiercest gusts of wind blew, the rain slanted almost horizonally against the glassed north wall. He said, "This time the armies have to fight in the rain. It's storming. Make a storm, Aunt Tirel, please? Please?"

Mirabella couldn't deny Alexander anything, so she proceeded to make a storm.

The back garden door opened to a dismal sight. Giles came in, his top hat streaming water, his greatcoat soaked and dripping. Taking off his hat, he drained the slopping brim. Then he took off his greatcoat and shook it. Huge drops of water sprayed all around him. "Hullo," he said cheerfully. "Wet day, ain't it? Still, I suppose I'm not making any more of a mess than we did last Saturday." He stopped and stared at Mirabella and Alexander. "I say, what's all this about? You've planted toy soldiers, you're watering them, and are now going to grow some new ones?"

He was viewing the extraordinary sight of Alex sitting on a stool, his hands covered in mud up to his elbows, a litter of soldiers and trees and fences wallowing around the mud-filled wooden box. Mirabella was on her knees on her stool, holding a watering can high above and sprinkling down great drops of water.

"Hello, Giles, gracious, you're soaked," Mirabella observed. "No, silly, can't you see? There's a battle going on, and there's a big storm."

"The English are winning. They have to," Alex explained to Giles. "Aunt Mirabella has to do the storm, so I have to be both the French and the English, but the French don't care if they lose."

"I like your war philosophy, my lord," Giles said, coming to stand over the battlefield.

"What's phosphy?"

"That your Frenchmen don't mind losing, and the English always win." He gazed at Alex with amusement, and then looked Mirabella up and down. "You and Alex are a little, um, shall we say, disheveled?"

Mirabella looked down at her apron and Alex's suit, which were both liberally spattered with mud, and their filthy hands. Shrugging, she said, "War is a dirty business."

"Yes, so I see. So much so that you have a streak of mud on your cheek and a blob in your hair, and Alex has mud in and about his left ear."

"Oh dear," Mirabella moaned, climbing down from her stool. "Alex, perhaps we'd better get cleaned up before Nurse comes to get you for luncheon."

"But I want to play soldiers some more," he said plaintively. "Nurse is nice, but she just knits and watches me play. Nobody's ever played with me except you, Aunt Mirabella."

Mirabella and Giles exchanged rueful glances. "Can you resist that?" Mirabella asked.

"Not for the world. Alex, let's say we let your Aunt Mirabella get the mud out of your ear, and wash your hands, and I'll get us a new battlefield that's not quite so stormy. Then we'll split up your soldiers, and you can be the English, and I'll be the Prussians, and together we'll wallop the French."

Alex considered this, then nodded. "Can I be the Ninety-Fif regimen? Like Captain Rosbo? And pretend I have green uniforms?"

"You certainly can, I'm sure Captain Rosbo would approve."

The war lasted another hour, after which Nurse came to fetch Alexander for luncheon and a nap. Nurse Bignell was warm, motherly, and easygoing, and obviously adored Alex. She was precisely the opposite of the type of nurse Mirabella would have thought Clara would engage to take care of her son. Nurse clucked reprovingly when she saw the state of Alex's suit, but she merely said, "Welladay, m'lor, we'll be having to get you all scrubbed up this very minute, won't we? Come along now." Alex protested, but weakly. He was looking a little tired.

Mirabella and Giles went to wash their hands at the washbasin, for now Giles, too, had battle stains. Mirabella took off her apron and rolled down her sleeves. "I'm all mud-spattered, too. But it was well worth it. I'm going to go find a footman and order some tea. Will you join me?"

"I'd like that, thank you. But before you do—will you allow me?" He stepped close and gently pulled on a thick tendril of Mirabella's hair. "You got most of it, but one blob is stubbornly hanging on." After much patient threading of her hair through his dampened fingers, he finally got the last speck of mud out. "Sorry, I fear I've completely annihilated that fetching curl. Shall I call Colette to make repairs?" Giles asked mischievously.

"Certainly not, I'm already dreading what she's going to say when she sees my sleeves. Excuse me for a moment." She left and returned quickly. "Tea is on the way. Let's sit down before we clean up the battlefield, shall we? I'm always amazed at how weary one can get after playing with a three-year-old for only two hours. And Alex goes full bore like that all day, every day. No wonder Nurse doesn't play with him, it's a wonder she can stay conscious."

"He's so bright, you know. With such an active mind, it takes a lot to keep him occupied. I must say your battlefield idea was brilliant. It shows that you're bright, too."

"Hardly, you know very well that it's exactly the same way

we used to play with your toy soldiers, only outside in the dirt," Mirabella scoffed.

"But you thought of the storm, that was creative. If a little messy."

"Speaking of the storm, what are you doing out in it? What a perfectly abysmal day to be out riding."

Giles shrugged. "I prefer being outdoors, even on days like this. At least, for long enough to ride over to see you. Also, your conservatory is as close to the outdoors as an enclosed room can possibly be. I enjoy it, even when you make me help you with your flowers."

"Which you are going to be obliged to do today. Last Saturday I neglected the flowers for the church shamefully, since you lured me into going fishing with you. This week all of the bouquets need to be replenished."

Giles grumbled, "I don't mind grubbing in the dirt, weeding and planting and potting and re-potting and re-re-potting with you. But I refuse to do flower arrangements. Men don't do that."

"I could teach you. You're quite astute, you'd catch on quickly."

"Thank you so much. I'll put it on the list of things I wish to learn before I die. So that should put flower-arranging at about, mm, when I'm eighty-three."

"I look forward to it."

Two footmen came in, each bearing a wide silver tray. Regardless of the time of day, or whether one person or the entire family ordered tea, Madame Danton's teas were always feasts. Aside from the tea tray, the second tray held dishes with four different kinds of scones, filbert, sultana, and lemon biscuits, and puff pastries filled with almond cream, and one dish held assorted dried fruits arranged in the shape of an ornate flower. Mirabella dismissed the footmen and poured while Giles began to help himself to the confections.

Mirabella asked, "So where is Captain Rosbo today? He didn't want to ride out and get thoroughly drenched?"

"He said he'd had quite enough of slogging around in the mud in the last five years, and that I was a pure fool to do it without being under orders to do so. When I left he was in his sock feet, sitting in my favorite armchair before the fire, reading Lord Nelson's memoirs."

"Naval memoirs?" Mirabella said with surprise. "I would have thought he would read books about the army."

"He says that reading about the life of seamen makes him feel better about being a soldier. I agree with that viewpoint wholeheartedly, although I can hardly imagine the life of either. Still, to be in foreign lands for years, fighting a war, seems to me to be preferable to being confined on a ship for years fighting a war. What a nightmare."

"It's a good thing our jolly tars don't feel that way. If I understand it correctly, our navy is the prime reason that England is such a preeminent world power."

Giles nodded approvingly. "You do understand correctly. If we didn't have such a strong navy, we could hardly defend this tiny island from invasion. Also, we wouldn't be able to transport our massive land army to those foreign lands to fight these wars that keep us preeminent. Of course that's another topic altogether, as we've often discussed. Our history of almost continuous warfare. As you said, war is a dirty business."

Mirabella was gratified that Giles was not the kind of man who thought that ladies should have no knowledge, or opinions, about anything besides ladylike pursuits. He always listened to her, and treated her with respect when they discussed serious topics.

"It is, but I don't wrestle too much with fervently hoping that we soundly defeat Napoleon. He's a tyrant and a bully, even to his own people. A toast: Confusion to Bonaparte!" Giles echoed it, and they clinked their teacups together.

Then Mirabella sobered and said, "Giles, I shouldn't like to pry, or ask you to betray a confidence, but I can't help but wonder about Lewin. Can you tell me what's happened to him?"

Giles frowned down into his teacup. At length he said, "It's not about betraying a confidence, Lewin is a soldier and the battles he's been in are well documented. It's simply that the last one, the Siege of Badajoz, was particularly brutal. It affected him deeply."

"I can see that. I did read about Badajoz, and I remember that the casualties were disastrously high. Was that what made it so much worse?"

"Yes. Most battles are ghastly, but Badajoz was really horrific. Especially for men like Lewin. You see, he volunteered for the Forlorn Hope."

"What—what is the Forlorn Hope?" Mirabella asked with a slight frisson of dread.

"When besieging a fixed fortification, the artillery pounds through the walls until there's a breach. The first men to storm the breach are always volunteers, called the Forlorn Hope, because generally it's a suicide mission."

"But why on earth would anyone volunteer for such a thing?" Mirabella cried.

"Any man in the Forlorn Hope that manages to live usually receives a promotion, sometimes cash gifts, certainly the boundless respect of his fellow soldiers. Lewin did manage to come through the breach, although, as always, the casualties among the Forlorn Hope were astronomically high."

Passionately Mirabella said, "But Giles, I still simply cannot understand it. Why would Lewin do such a thing? Surely he must know that with my father's patronage, his career in the army is assured. There's no sense at all in throwing his life away on suicide missions." Lord Camarden had purchased Lewin's commission in the army, and had made known his preference for him.

Gently Giles said, "Bella, you know better than that. Not all men are content to base their lives, and sense of honor, simply from their birthright, or from patronage. Lewin is a soldier, and he did what, in his eyes, was the right and honorable thing to do."

Mirabella looked chastened. "Yes, I suppose I can understand that is why a soldier might do such a thing. I still have difficulty comprehending *how* he can do it. I know I could never, never have such courage."

"You might, under the right circumstances. But I agree with you, I think it's almost impossible for anyone who is not a soldier to completely understand how they can face battle. Lewin has told me some things about Badajoz, but he relates it in a sort of impersonal manner, as if he were reporting it."

"Giles, that patch on his sleeve. He looked so distressed when Clara was asking him about it. Is it some special insignia from Badajoz?"

Giles nodded and looked grim. "It's a very special insignia, a *V* and *S* surrounded by laurel leaves. It stands for Victorious Stormer. Lewin was exaggerating the other day when he said that many men were awarded it. There weren't 'many' survivors of the Forlorn Hope. He said that Wellington wept when he saw the piles of bodies lying at the breach. Lewin didn't even want to wear the Victorious Stormer badge, he said that all those who died didn't get an insignia. I told him that the ones who lived should wear it proudly, to honor them."

"Oh, Giles, this is so hard," Mirabella said. "I do love Lewin so, I hate to see him suffering."

Giles studied her, and then smiled. "Bella, don't be so upset.

Lewin is getting better, day by day. He's healing. Being home, with his family and close friends, has comforted him and eased his mind. Yesterday he even made a joke about going to London for the Season. He's said very little about it, you know, and I was beginning to wonder if it was the right thing, persuading him to come with me, or if I was imposing upon him. But yesterday we were talking about White's, and I was telling him that I hardly ever go there any more, the gambling has gotten so outrageous that I find it a crashing bore. Lewin said that he had no use for the namby-pamby fops in the clubs anyway, he was looking forward to bashing someone at Gentleman Jackson's boxing saloon, preferably one of the abovementioned namby-pamby fops, or perhaps two at the same time."

Mirabella's eyes lit up to a deep dazzling blue. "Oh my, our Lewin, such a bold warrior! I never would have suspected it in him when we were children. He was so much kinder and gentler than you."

"Well, I'm the kindler, gentler one now. I told him that I might match fencing foibles with him at Angelo's, but under no circumstance would I volunteer to be one of the thrashed namby-pambys."

"Coward," Mirabella teased.

"That's what he said," Giles said calmly, "and I don't mind at all. John Jackson's broken nose is hideous. I'm not going to take the chance that Lewin might deface my nose in such an infamous way, simply to allow him to let out his pent-up aggression. He must find some other nose."

"I agree. You do have a good nose, it would be a shame for it to suddenly become repugnant."

"You really think I have a good nose?" Giles asked with interest.

"Yes, I do."

"I'm glad," he said with pleasure. "I like your nose, also."

"Thank you," Mirabella said wryly. "Now, I think we've about exhausted that fascinating topic. Let's do our battlefield cleanup, and then forge on to the flowers for church."

"But we haven't had luncheon yet," Giles protested.

"I haven't invited you for luncheon."

"I invited myself."

"And you ate two scones, two puff pastries, a biscuit, and fully half of that dish of dried fruits. Surely you can survive on that. You can invite yourself for dinner."

"If you insist. I hereby invite myself for dinner. I'm going to invite your mother and father, too. Would you care to join us?"

Affectionately Mirabella said, "Ninny."

"I strenuously object to being branded a ninny. Everyone knows that I'm a namby-pamby fop."

"Then mince on over here and start cleaning up these toy soldiers with your scented hankie. You wash, I'll dry and polish."

"As always, my lady, I am your most humble servant."

Most ladies of high society found winters in the country dull, but Mirabella relished them, and to her this winter at Camarden was particularly agreeable. November had several mild spells, and Lord Camarden had four highly successful fox hunts. To Mirabella's delight they had a perfectly beautiful snow on Christmas Eve and Christmas Day. She always longed for Christmas snow, and secretly even prayed for it, though she knew it was fatuous. Still, she was grateful for this one. On Boxing Day she, Josephine, Lewin, and Giles piled themselves up with furs and took a ride in the open landau. The park and grounds of Camarden Court were stunning with their frothy diamond snow-blanket.

Parliament opened in January, and Lord Camarden went to London to attend the House of Lords. He came home some weekends, and was subjected to extensive interrogation by his daughter concerning Who was in Town and Who was not.

"Mirabella, by now you know that most of the families stay in the country until March," he said wearily. "The only dinner parties I've attended given by ladies were Lady Liverpool's and Countess Lieven's."

Lord Camarden was a powerful man in politics, albeit behind the scenes. He was a close longtime friend of the prime minister, Lord Liverpool, and was one of his most trusted advisors.

Countess Lieven was married to the Russian ambassador to the Court of St. James's, who was also a friend of Lord Camarden's. The countess was something of a political force in her own right. She was extremely clever, haughty, and arrogant, and was perhaps the most ruthless patroness of Almack's, excluding anyone, regardless of birth, lineage, or fortune, if they did not meet her approval.

"Countess Lieven is in Town?" Mirabella cried. "You didn't tell me. At her dinner did you ask her about vouchers for Josephine and Lewin?"

"I most certainly did not. Neither did I ask her about the newest, most fashionable ladies' fripperies, nor about the health of her dogs, nor about Count Lieven's choice of waistcoats, although I did find one of them questionable, it had some sort of bear's head design. At any rate, it's your mother's heavy burden to deal with the hallowed halls of Almack's, not mine."

Mirabella immediately went to her mother to importune her, again. "Mamma, Pappa says Countess Lieven is in Town. Please write to her again about the vouchers for Josephine and Lewin. I know that she would be the only patroness who might possibly deny them."

The Marchioness of Camarden, both because of her own considerable consequence in Polite Society, and because of her husband's political influence, held no little sway with the patronesses. She had been friends with the two older patronesses, Lady Sefton and Lady Castlereagh, for many years, and was on very agreeable friendly terms with the other four ladies. At one time there had been an attempt by Lady Castlereagh, Lady Sefton, and Lady Cowper to name Lady Camarden as a patroness, but she had graciously refused, saying that attending to her own daughter kept her so occupied she could hardly concentrate on anyone else's children.

Lady Camarden said, "Mirabella, I'll do no such thing. I've already heard from Lady Castlereagh that she'll be happy to submit applications for Josephine and Lewin, and has no doubt that they'll be accepted. I hadn't yet mentioned this to you because I thought I might wait to hear from Mrs. Drummond-Burrell, more out of politeness than any other reason. Both of us know that she won't vote against Amelia Castlereagh, who in reality is the most powerful of the patronesses."

"But Countess Lieven is so merciless when it comes to exclusion," Mirabella pleaded. "Surely, if you simply mention them again, it may encourage her to accept them."

"She already responded to my letter, in a conciliating manner, for her. Apparently this victory at Badajoz was so influential in the war that it's been a major topic. The countess was quite knowledgeable about it, and had learned that Lewin is an acknowledged hero in the storming of the breach. Although she didn't specifically say that he and Josephine would be accepted, as her *hauteur* wouldn't allow her to be so kind, I'm satisfied that she'll vote for them."

"Oh, Mamma, this is wonderful news! Thank you, thank you!"

Josephine visited that afternoon, and Mirabella immediately seized her and dragged her up to her dressing room. "Josephine, Mamma told me today that she's all but certain that you and Lewin will receive vouchers for Almack's! Isn't that marvelous?"

"Truly? Oh, it is! And Lewin, too? He'll be so—or perhaps he might not be quite as enthusiastic as we are. All he talks about is having to wear silk stockings, he's really very grumpy about it."

"He'll find it well worth the trouble when he sees all the lovely young ladies to flirt with at balls and at Almack's. And speaking of silk stockings, please listen to me, Josephine. I know that fine smallclothes are costly, and I'd like to—"

Josephine interrupted sternly, "No, Mirabella, I will not allow you to buy lingerie for me. As it happens, I've already bought several things on my own." She smiled sweetly. "You know, Lewin received a cash award for his gallantry at Badajoz. He said that if he was going to throw it away buying silk stockings and pretty little black pumps with ribbons, he might as well give me some money to throw away, too."

"That is so like Lewin. He's such a darling. Very well, then. Shall we go through the half dresses today?" Mirabella asked eagerly. She had been having as much fun in arranging Josephine's wardrobe as in ordering her own.

"What are half dresses again? It's too bewildering. Half dresses, full dresses, morning dresses, day dresses, walking dresses, promenade costumes, carriage costumes, dinner gowns, formal dinner gowns, ball gowns, opera gowns, full formal evening ball and opera gowns—"

"Josephine, surely you remember that half dresses are exactly that, only half as formal as ball gowns. That makes perfect sense, doesn't it? Oh, half a moment! We completely forgot riding habits! I have six—no, eight now, with the two I ordered that only arrived yesterday, and that will be more than enough for us, as you know I prefer taking the phaeton to Hyde Park. That will require carriage costumes, as you well know, in spite of your blustering. Still, we do need to attend to the riding habits, as they'll require some alterations, I'm sure, since they're so formfitting in the bust, and you've had the effrontery to exceed me by an inch or so. Colette will attend to it, she can work pure miracles in alterations, and since I promised her an extra half day off during the Season she's stopped complaining about making alterations to dresses she's already altered..."

Josephine watched and listened to her friend with affectionate indulgence. This was going to be an exciting Season indeed.

Chapter Six

The carriage was now in the jostling, bustling streets of London, which normally was quite an eye-opener for one who had never been in Town. But Josephine had barely glanced out the carriage window, since she and Mirabella were engaged in an extremely serious discussion.

"No, Josephine, I insist!" Mirabella argued. "You see now it's just as I've said, London is so much warmer than the country. We shan't have an opportunity to wear furs much longer, perhaps only another week or two. I doubt if I'll even be able to wear the Hussar jacket with the mink."

"But that is precisely my point," Josephine said stubbornly. "You haven't worn it, because it's brand-new, and I absolutely refuse to start pilfering in your new wardrobe, after I've already stolen an entire Season's worth of clothes from you. I have the blue pelisse and the olive green, which is very fine, and which I like very well. I shall wear it."

"Please, please wear the Hussar?" Mirabella pleaded. "In any case, I don't care if I wear it after you wear it. Tomorrow we're only going to see three of the patronesses." With sudden inspiration she added, "If you'll wear it tomorrow, then I'll wear it on Thursday, when we go shopping. If you won't wear it, I shall refuse to wear it at all."

"Oh, really, Mirabella, you can drive a person batty attempting to reason with you," Lady Camarden said. "Josephine, please wear the Hussar, for my sake. You two have been arguing about furs for the last hour, I declare I almost wish I'd never see one again. Thank heavens we've arrived, I'd rather talk to one of the scullery maids than listen to more of this."

They had arrived in London, at the Camarden town house, which was in fashionable Mayfair, of course. The Camarden town house was not one of the many terrace houses on Grosvenor Square; it was a sizable, elegant freestanding house of six stories, counting the half basement and attic. The large kitchen was detached, and the lot also had a private mews, with stables and the carriage house. Although not as grand and palatial as the mansions lining Park Lane, which bordered Hyde Park, it was still larger than most town houses, and stylishly appointed.

It was the last week of February, and it was cold and damp, so the ladies hurried out of the Camarden town coach and into the house. All the servants were assembled to greet them in the entry hall, a spacious room with black-and-white marble tiles and a grand white marble staircase with an intricate black wrought iron railing.

The marchioness greeted them in her usual brisk manner. "Irby, Mrs. Parmeter, the house looks very well, I'm certain you have everything in hand." The faintest shadow of pleasure crossed the butler's stoic face. In contrast the housekeeper, Mrs. Parmeter, smiled happily as she curtsied. Both of these highest of servants were young to occupy their exalted positions. Irby had just turned thirty, a great hulking man with black hair and eyes and a crude, pockmarked face, but he possessed that economical grace that characterized good butlers. Mrs. Parmeter was twenty-eight, a small sweet-faced woman.

As the ladies took off their traveling cloaks and bonnets, Lady

Camarden said, "You may all resume your duties, there's no call for everyone to be standing about here in this drafty hall. Mrs. Parmeter, we'll have tea in the drawing room."

The entry hall, the dining room, and the marquess's study were on this, the ground floor; upstairs on what was called the first floor were the drawing room and a grand ballroom. The drawing room was a gracious space, with an intricate Adam ceiling and fireplace surround. The marchioness had furnished the entire town house in the light, elegant Neoclassical style of Thomas Chippendale. At one end of the drawing room double French doors led out onto a balcony overlooking the square. The color scheme for the draperies and furnishings was a pleasing Wedgwood blue and deep rose. The ladies settled themselves comfortably near a hearty fire in plush wingback chairs.

As usual, two footmen served one of Madame Danton's sumptuous tea creations. "Mirabella, will you pour, please? My fingertips are still frozen."

"Of course, Mamma." As she poured and served the tea and seedcake she said, "And so tomorrow we shall call on Lady Castlereagh, Countess Lieven, and Lady Jersey, and Wednesday will be Mrs. Drummond-Burrell, Lady Sefton, and Lady Cowper, correct? How I wish we could visit Emily first, I'm so anxious to see her again."

"And Emily is . . . ?" Josephine hinted. "You will please recall that I'm hardly on a first-name basis with the patronesses of Almack's."

"I beg your pardon, Josephine, it's rude to name-drop in such a manner, isn't it?" Mirabella said with good humor. "Emily is Lady Cowper, and a particular friend of mine. She's very warm and amiable, you'll like her, too, I'm sure."

The ladies lingered over tea for an hour, and then the marchioness said, "I find that I'm fatigued after our journey, I think

I'll rest until time to dress for dinner. I'm glad it will just be us and Giles and Lewin this evening. Camarden wanted to have Lord and Lady Liverpool tonight, but I implored him to give me one night to recover before we start tomorrow."

"Josephine, why don't we go up, too? I want to show you your bedchamber, I hope you'll be pleased," Mirabella said.

"I'm sure I will be," Josephine answered. And so she was, for it was a lovely room done in cheerful yellow and green, with an elegant French canopy bed, a slender white secretary, two plump recamiers and a thick carpet with an ivy-and-cornflower design. Like all ten bedrooms at the Camarden town house, it had a separate dressing room.

After Josephine expressed her delight, Mirabella settled on one of the recamiers and said, "Did you wish to rest, too, Josephine?"

"No, I'm far too excited," she answered, settling on the other recamier. "To be honest, I did want to ask you some things, but I didn't like to, in front of the footmen."

Mirabella said wryly, "Yes, that's one of the myriad rules in Town, one always has footmen in attendance in the reception rooms. It would cause quite a scandal to dismiss them."

Josephine looked puzzled. "But in your own home, if you dismissed them, how would anyone ever know?"

"That's another of the rules in Town, everyone knows everything about everyone else. Our servants would tell other servants and soon all of Polite Society would know of my calumny in dismissing the footmen."

"Then you must never commit such a grave sin," Josephine said, her eyes sparkling. "When I have something delicate to discuss with you, we shall make certain to wait until we're hiding out here in our bedrooms."

An oddly pensive look came over Mirabella's face. "It's strange you should say that, for I have a rather delicate matter to discuss with you. But no, you first, dearest. Are you truly apprehensive? Not just about the patronesses, I mean, but about the Season?"

"Oh, no, not at all. I promise you that I'm almost giddily happy to be here," Josephine answered sincerely. "No, what I really meant was that I didn't like to show my own ignorance in front of the servants. I can't help but wonder, since I understand that the Lady Patronesses are the arbiters of Who is in Polite Society and Who will not be allowed to join it, aren't they at the very top of the social ladder? I mean, aren't they considered to have the most exalted position of all ladies in society?"

Mirabella looked knowing. "Yes, they are, and what you're really wondering about is why my mother is calling on them first, instead of waiting for them to call on us."

"Hm, it seems I don't hide my ignorance very well at all. Yes, I was wondering exactly that."

"It's not ignorant, it's a perfectly logical question. The reason is that morning calls are made according to very strict rules, and believe you me, the patronesses are the most rigorous in demanding observance to protocol. The first rule is that a lady of higher rank must make the first call on other ladies of lower rank, and conversely, no lady of lower rank must ever make the first call on one of her social superiors."

"Of course," Josephine said thoughtfully, "I should have known that. With your mother being a marchioness, she outranks everyone else except duchesses. Still, it seems a little odd, since Lady Camarden has been such longtime friends with Lady Castlereagh and Lady Sefton, one would think that friends can call on each other as they wish."

"Oh, later in the Season the rules get more relaxed. For instance, you know that although we call them morning calls, they're really made between two and five o'clock in the afternoon, and ladies who are mere acquaintances and not intimate friends would never actually make calls in the morning. But close friends often do."

Josephine nodded. "This makes more sense to me. Not all of the rules do, you know, for instance, why on earth *do* we call them morning calls when they're made in the afternoon?"

Mirabella looked nonplussed. "I have no idea. You see, you're not the only one who's ignorant."

"Oh, do be quiet, you're not ignorant at all. The daughter of a marquess, you were practically born knowing the rules," Josephine said. "Such as you never have to worry about the depth and supplication of your curtsy, all you have to do is bob politely to everyone but dukes and duchesses and the royal family. I realized when I was practicing mine in front of the mirror that it was ridiculous anyway. I'll be expected to virtually kneel to all and sundry."

"Silly girl, you do a most elegant and charming curtsy," Mirabella said affectionately. "And don't be too impressed with my rank. There are some who aren't. In fact, my grandfather was one of them. He said that a marquess was a Frenchy jumped-up sort of title they gave you when they didn't want to make you a duke."

Josephine giggled. "But he did still take it, I see."

"So he did. Anyway, to continue this stimulating conversation about curtsies, you'll find that I don't do the same polite bob to everyone. There are certain shades of politeness that concern a person's lineage, their age, their status in society. For instance, I curtsy quite subserviently to Mrs. Drummond-Burrell, even though she's not married to a peer, although he will be one day. It's mainly because she is a patroness, and she's so haughty that she fully expects it."

"Yes, you've told me that she's the most straitlaced and icy of the patronesses. What about the others? Tell me all about them."

Mirabella's dimples flashed. "All the juiciest gossip, you mean?"

"Of course. After all, you yourself said it's a rule in Town, yes? Everyone knows everything about everyone else. Now I'm one of the everyones."

"You certainly are. But I'm not going to dissect everyone you're going to meet, we'd be here for a fortnight. I will tell you about the three ladies we're visiting tomorrow.

"As you know, Lady Castlereagh is married to Lord Castlereagh, the foreign minister. She, too, has a reputation for *hauteur*, although she is very elegant and can be charming. She confides in my mamma, as they have been such longtime friends, so she's always been kind to me, and I'm certain she'll show the same cordiality to you."

Mirabella frowned slightly. "Countess Lieven, I fear, may be a little more difficult. She can be extremely arrogant and cold, and can be ruthless in denying vouchers to anyone that she deems unsuitable. However, Mamma seems to be certain that she'll accept you and Lewin; I just hope that she won't seem terribly formidable to you."

"Likely she will," Josephine said calmly, "but I'll say a quick extra prayer before I meet her so that I may not wilt away."

"As if such a thing could happen. You are like your mamma, so serene and graceful, and you always retain your good humor. That's exactly how I know that you'll be such a success this Season, Josephine, those are much-sought-after qualities in a young lady. And you're very pretty, which helps immensely."

"Thank you, it's always so nice to hear such from someone besides your mamma. And so—Lady Jersey? You have told me that she also has a reputation for being overbearing."

"She's really a sort of complex person, in my mind," Mirabella said with uncertainty. "She's mercurial, one might say. She can be unbelievably rude, but she can also be affable and cordial, even to people she doesn't like. For instance, she despises Lady Caroline Lamb, but she always is gracious to her, which, I think, demonstrates a sort of empathy and kindness."

"Lady Caroline Lamb, she's the lady who went so mad for Lord Byron, is she not?"

"*Mad* is a good word for it," Mirabella said. "Ever since they were estranged last year, Caro has been behaving in the most insane manner. She's hardly presentable, even at Almack's. But Lady Jersey has always been courteous to her, even when Countess Lieven and Mrs. Drummond-Burrell have openly shown their contempt for her."

"It is puzzling, for a person to have such apparently opposing qualities in their demeanor, to be on the one hand terribly rude, and on the other extremely considerate."

"Yes, but to me it's always seemed that Lady Jersey is not so much purposely abusive as it is that sometimes—well, perhaps much of the time—she speaks without thinking, and whatever is in the forefront of her mind just comes right out of her mouth. One of her nicknames has come to be Silence, which is perfectly ironic. She has a tendency to continuously talk nonstop. And also, she is an inveterate gossip, and can be extremely indiscreet."

With amusement Josephine said, "That doesn't intimidate me too much, as I doubt we'll supply her with any delectable tidbits."

Mirabella's mouth twitched. "Actually, we will. Or at least I will. That's really the delicate matter I wanted to talk to you about."

Warily Josephine said, "Mirabella, I cannot imagine that you're involved in any sort of scandal."

"No, it's no scandal. It's just something that I've decided I want generally known in Town this Season, and I've calculated that the best way to quickly circulate any information is to tell Lady Jersey."

"Very well, I am mystified. Pray tell me of this evidently good news that we want to be a topic."

Mirabella smiled mischievously. "I have decided that I'm going to get engaged this Season."

The look on Josephine's face was one of absolute astonishment. "What? But—what? Engaged? To whom?"

"I'm not sure yet."

"Mirabella, please explain," Josephine begged.

"Oh, it's simple, really. For the last four Seasons I've managed to alienate several potential suitors because I didn't want to get married. Now I do. But I have no intention of wasting time trying to discern who might be interested in me now. I'm certain that if Lady Jersey lets everyone know right away, it won't be long before—"

"Before the men come flocking around," Josephine interrupted with an uncharacteristic frustration. "But surely you can't mean to choose your husband by simply taking a likely group and eliminating them one by one."

"Why not?" Mirabella said lightly. "That's in essence what the Marriage Market is, although I may say that you expressed it a little more crudely than is generally done. Granted, normally a girl's marriage is arranged by her parents, and I intend to arrange my own, but it's still well within the bounds of the normal convention."

Josephine was silent for long moments, frowning darkly. Then she said, "You know, I hate to admit it, but I do see your logic, and I know that what you've said is often true for women of your rank and position. But still, it seems to me that you of all people could marry for love."

"Oh, really. If you recall, I tried that once and it didn't work out too well," Mirabella said in a hard voice.

"Oh, darling, my dear Mirabella, I'm so sorry," Josephine said softly. "I—didn't mean—I didn't think. Please forgive me."

Immediately Mirabella smiled sweetly. "There is nothing to forgive, dearest, nothing at all. Perhaps I will fall in love, who knows? Or perhaps I'll marry for other, more realistic and tangible, reasons. At any rate it will make for a most interesting Season, will it not? Now let's talk about something of much greater import. The Hussar jacket, with the mink..."

It was indeed much like the jacket that Hussars wore. Waist-length and tight-fitting, it was of midnight-blue velvet trimmed with horizontal rows of fine gold braid. The mink trim was at the shoulder seams and the cuffs, along the facings, and around the bottom, and it had a luscious double row of mink for a collar. Josephine carried a large mink muff. Her straight gown was light blue, a thick, rich grosgrain fabric that was heavy enough for the coldest winter days.

Josephine sighed. "I say again, Mirabella, I would have preferred not to wear any of your new clothes, but seeing how stunning you look, you outshine me enough that it's lessened my aversion somewhat."

In a stuffy tone, with ridiculously pursed lips, Mirabella said, "'What business have you, Miss, with preference and aversion? They don't become a young woman.'"

Josephine giggled. "*The Rivals*. I—I, oh, bother, I can never come up with a Mrs. Malaprop reply, I'm not as quick as you and Giles."

Mirabella's deep blue eyes danced. "'Female punctuation forbids me to say more.' Thank you for the compliment, but I say that neither of us outshines the other, we're just so very different.

I think you look better in that ensemble than I ever will, now that I see it on you, it may be a bit dramatic for a pale blonde. Still, I look very *bewitching* in my *witzchoura*, do I not?"

Lady Camarden said severely, "He that would pun would pick a pocket. And I am at my wits' end, I'm now forbidding you two girls to argue one more instant about your clothing. Both of you look very well indeed."

Mirabella did indeed look stunning in her witzchoura, a long, full mantle made of a deep-puce merino wool that was a perfect blend of brown and purple. It had a triple-tiered cape collar made of silvery gray Iberian lynx, which also lined the bottom of the mantle, and framed her face around her bonnet. She had an enormous muff of lynx. As a touch of whimsy, as Mirabella often did with her ensembles, she had had her velvet slippers lined with the same fur.

They were beginning their morning calls of the Season, and their first call was to be on Lady Castlereagh. The three ladies presented their cards to the butler, who immediately returned to the entryway to invite them into the drawing room, as her ladyship was at home.

Amelia, Viscountess Castlereagh was now forty-one, one of the oldest of the patronesses, the other being Lady Sefton, who was forty-four. She was still a very pretty woman, with a wealth of curly brown hair and delicate features, and she had an undeniable elegance in her posture and deportment. Still, her greetings to her callers had a certain reserve; she was not a warm person.

As she was well known to be the greatest stickler for propriety among the patronesses, she greeted Mirabella and Josephine with courtesy and then addressed most of her remarks to Lady Camarden. Lady Castlereagh was of the opinion that young ladies should speak only when spoken to. They talked of Who was in Town and when other families were expected, and of Lord

Castlereagh's onerous duties as foreign minister, and then she turned to Josephine.

"Miss Rosborough, although it's not generally announced personally, I wish to let you know that because of Lady Camarden's glowing recommendations, your application to Almack's has been approved, and also that of your brother. You should receive your voucher today or tomorrow," she said with her customary coolness.

"I'm honored, Lady Castlereagh, and I thank you for your kind consideration," Josephine said.

She acknowledged this with a queenly nod of her head, then turned back to Lady Camarden. The ladies stayed the requisite fifteen minutes and then took their leave.

Next they called on Countess Lieven, a great beauty with black hair and eyes, and wide full lips. She was much as she always was, haughty and aloof. But she, too, welcomed Josephine to Almack's and asked about Lewin, expressing her hope to meet him soon. "Pray, where is he quartered here in Town? I intend to send him a message to call on me."

Josephine replied with open pleasure, "That's very kind of you, my lady. He and Sir Giles Knyvet have taken a flat at St. James's, number eighteen."

"Sir Giles is here this Season? I am glad, he's so charming, I shall be glad to see him again."

In the carriage, Josephine said, "She was not quite so frightening as I had dreaded. It's most gracious of her to invite Lewin to call."

The marchioness said, "Camarden tells me that Lord Wellington allowed around two hundred veterans of Badajoz to winter here at home, and I believe there are a dozen or so of them here in Town. But Lewin is the only one who obtained a voucher to Almack's."

"And it was certainly all your doing, my lady," Josephine said warmly. "Again, I want to most sincerely thank you."

"I was happy to do it, and as I'm banning all further talk of furs, I'm also banning any further effusive expressions of gratitude. Such exuberance is not proper here in Town. Young ladies may be expressive, but with a certain restrained refinement."

Mirabella winked at Josephine. Instantly Lady Camarden said, "I saw that, young lady, and we'll have no more of your sauce, either. Here we are at Lady Jersey's, and I expect she'll provide more than enough impudence for all of Polite Society."

They presented their cards and were immediately ushered into an enormous, grandly furnished drawing room. Lady Jersey rose to greet them, and the ladies did their curtsies. Now twenty-seven years old, Sarah, Lady Jersey was not considered a beauty, but she had a lovely creamy complexion, and a particular vivacity in her countenance, with sparkling dark eyes and a bright expression.

Eschewing proper introductions, she immediately took both of Josephine's hands and started talking. "Here, let me have a look at you, Miss Rosborough. I see that you're not a great beauty, but you are pretty, even with a somewhat pert nose. Your curtsy was proper and graceful, I'm happy to see, as I can't abide a woman that cannot perform even a passable curtsy, like that awful Mrs. Smythe, she positively grovels, it's really a disgrace. Here, please sit down, so happy to see you, Lady Camarden, Lady Mirabella. Tell me, Miss Rosborough, can you dance as elegantly as you can curtsy? You must, you know, to pass muster with the young men at Almack's. And this year Dorothea is introducing the German waltz, so you must immediately learn it, if you aren't already accomplished in it."

There was a pause for breath, so Josephine said with some puzzlement, "The German waltz? No, Lady Jersey, I'm not at all familiar with it, in fact I can't recall that I've ever heard of it."

Lady Camarden said with surprise, "The waltz? I'm amazed that all of the patronesses gave their approval, particularly Mrs. Drummond-Burrell."

Lady Jersey said carelessly, "Oh, she's always indignant at one thing or another, great heavens, she's the same age as I and she behaves as if she's an ancient dowager, she's so stiff and pious, I declare it only adds to her dowdiness. Mirabella, do you waltz?"

"No, I've heard of it but never observed it. I understand that it's considered to be scandalous, although I could never quite penetrate what about it—"

As Lady Jersey often did, she interrupted. "I think it's total nonsense, it's quite a lovely and graceful dance, they've been doing it on the Continent for years and I haven't seen a precipitous moral decline resulting from it, if anything if those horrid *sans-culottes* of the French Revolution would have spent more time dancing instead of whining and chopping off people's heads they likely wouldn't have had a Revolution in the first instance. I assure you, Audrey, that all of the ladies heartily approve of finally introducing a dance that is so much more modern and fashionable, although at first Clementina was positively horrified, but Dorothea soon convinced her, and of course since Amelia is so widely traveled she's seen the elegance of the waltz all over the Continent..."

Mirabella reflected that her assessment of Lady Jersey had been accurate: she was so impulsive in her speech that she seemed to be rude. She noticed that the expression on Josephine's face was one of lively polite interest, but Josephine could have no idea who the ladies were whom Lady Jersey was going on about. Although Mirabella herself occasionally slipped and used her friends' first names when she was talking to Josephine, she tried very hard to correct herself. No matter what the speaker's rank, it was considered extremely rude, even ill-bred, to speak of people without using their correct titles when someone included in the conversation couldn't know their given names.

Then Mirabella started wondering about the German waltz: what exactly it was, how it was performed, and how she could possibly master it before the opening night of Almack's next week. She was jolted out of her musings when she heard Lady Jersey finally say her name.

"Mirabella, I demand to know, how is it that you haven't married yet? It's so ridiculous, you should have been married three Seasons ago, you're going to end up a spinster if you don't take care. There are any number of suitable matches you could make, but as you get older, both the number and the likelihood of a truly brilliant match lessen considerably. You really must stop frittering about and make a decision, last Season I know there were at least a half dozen eligible young men interested in you, and you callously discarded them all, did you not?"

Finally Mirabella was given the opportunity to speak. "I don't believe I was callous, exactly, as none of the young men were so smitten that I broke any hearts." Taking a deep breath, but speaking quickly before Lady Jersey could go on a diatribe again, she said, "But I will admit I've somewhat changed my attitude in the last year. As you say, I've realized that it's time I started thinking of marriage."

Lady Jersey's eyes brightened alertly. "Oh, really? And are you simply starting to think of it? Or are you actively thinking of it? Is there any gentleman in particular that you're thinking of?"

"I am thinking of it, and no, I have no particular gentleman in mind at this time."

Lady Jersey immediately launched into a long list of young men, enumerating their various good and bad qualities, including their lineages, their present fortunes and prospects, and assessments of their personages, sometimes including her opinions on their horsemanship, their political views, and their cravats. The visit lasted all of thirty-five minutes, with Lady Jersey talking the entire time. They escaped only because Viscount Southam and Lord Trevor Brydges came to call on her. Lady Camarden and Mirabella knew Lord Southam and Lord Trevor, and did manage to introduce Josephine, but immediately Lady Jersey started talking nonstop to the young men and barely took notice as the ladies took their leave.

When they were safe in their carriage, Josephine said, "I'm actually quite breathless. She's very fast-paced, isn't she?"

"She is," Lady Camarden said. "I hope you're satisfied, Mirabella, by tomorrow she will have decided whom you are to marry, and will have told everyone in Town."

Carelessly Mirabella said, "That's fine by me, Mamma, you know very well there is no harm in letting people know that you're interested in marriage. Good heavens, that's practically the sole reason young ladies come to Town anyway."

"It's not the worst thing that can be said of you," Josephine said with amusement. "I expect that she'll mention to everyone that I have a pert nose."

"It's not pert, it's small," Mirabella said decidedly. "But just now the only thing that's worrying me is however are we to learn the waltz before next Wednesday?"

"Oh, yes, that is of the utmost import," Lady Camarden said sarcastically. "I haven't given you permission yet to waltz."

Slyly Mirabella said, "Not *yet*. But you will."

Lady Camarden sighed deeply. "Sauce, young lady. Pure sauce. And yes, I probably will."

Chapter Seven

The following day the ladies called on the other three patronesses of Almack's, Lady Sefton, Mrs. Drummond-Burrell, and Lady Cowper. Against all dictates of fashionable dressing for ladies of high society, Mirabella decided that she loved her witzchoura so well that she would wear it again, and again she persuaded Josephine to wear the Hussar jacket. Josephine protested, but weakly, and soon gave way to Mirabella. The girls were very careful not to discuss it in front of the marchioness.

As soon as Lady Sefton greeted them, she warmly complimented the girls. "Mirabella, you are simply stunning in that color. Not many ladies can wear puce. As a matter of fact I bought a gown once that was exactly that shade, and I declare it made me look as yellow as if I had the jaundice. Miss Rosborough, you look as dramatic and dashing as your brother in his striking regimentals."

Lady Sefton possessed a definite aura of kindness and warmth. She was a small woman, and delicate, with polished elegance.

Mirabella and Josephine thanked her, and eagerly Josephine asked, "So you have met my brother, Lady Sefton?"

"Yes, Sefton and I were riding yesterday in the park, and we met Sir Giles and Captain Rosborough, and Sir Giles introduced us. I remarked that I had found Captain Rosborough to be charming, and Sefton allowed that he did keep a tolerable seat for an infantryman."

With amusement Lady Camarden said, "I wasn't aware that you ever rode with Lord Sefton, I admit I'm surprised he allows you." Lord Sefton's nickname was Lord Dashalong, for the reckless manner in which he drove his coaches all over Town.

Lady Sefton replied, "It's not so much that he doesn't invite me, it's that I'm usually paralyzed with terror. He's relatively calm in the park, however, so I can enjoy myself there at least."

They spent an enjoyable twenty minutes visiting, and then called on Mrs. Drummond-Burrell. She was one of the wealthiest women in England, and she dressed with great style. Her clothes were always sumptuous and obviously outrageously expensive. Her manner in greeting them was overly grand, but in the course of the visit she thawed a bit. She even welcomed Josephine to Almack's. In the carriage Lady Camarden remarked that in private she found Mrs. Drummond-Burrell to be much more affable.

"I, too, have spoken with her at Almack's," Mirabella said thoughtfully, "and found that she can be interesting, and even animated. She's a devout Christian, you know, and she obviously adores Mr. Drummond-Burrell."

"And he adores her," Lady Camarden said. "I find it unusual, in these libertine days. He is a famous dandy, and definitely runs with the fast set. But there's never been a hint of scandal about him, and of course everyone knows that Clementina would never have an affair."

"Unlike some other of the patronesses," Mirabella said mischievously. "Although I must say that personally I find Lord Palmerston so devilishly charming that I can't help flirting with him myself."

Josephine couldn't contain her curiosity. "One of the Lady Patronesses is having an affair with Lord Palmerston?"

Lady Camarden said, "He was rumored to have an affair with Lady Jersey, he definitely had an affair with Countess Lieven, and now he and Lady Cowper are well known to be a couple, although, of course, they're discreet."

Josephine's eyes sparkled. "So, am I to meet this irresistible man?"

"Certainly," Mirabella said. "But I thought you'd be shocked."

"No, dearest, I'd be a simpleton if I didn't know that such things went on, and not only in Polite Society, either. In fact, among the highest circles I'm often more surprised to hear of devoted, loyal couples like the Drummond-Burrells than I am to hear of the famous people who are having affairs."

"That's because the couples who don't indulge in illicit affairs aren't nearly as interesting as those who do," Lady Camarden said tartly. "Who wants to gossip about faithful couples?"

They came to Lady Cowper's home, and were immediately ushered in.

Emily, Lady Cowper was twenty-six years old, and looked even younger. She was a beautiful woman, with a wealth of dark hair exquisitely dressed, dark eyes with perfectly arched brows, a small delicate nose, and full lips. When she smiled, which she often did, she glowed with warmth and grace. She greeted Mirabella with a kiss, and returned Josephine's curtsy with a cordial one of her own.

"Miss Rosborough, I'm so happy to make your acquaintance, Mirabella has written and told me much of you and your family. And I've had the distinct pleasure of meeting your brother. We're all so looking forward to you joining us at Almack's this Season."

"Thank you, Lady Cowper, you're very kind," Josephine said.

"I'm so glad you've met my brother, it seems that he's already making his way around Town quite easily."

"Men can do that, you know," Lady Cowper said. "They're introduced, and then in their dull, unimaginative way, the other men just accept them as one of the fellows. We ladies have a much more laborious task in introducing ourselves. Still, Lady Camarden and Mirabella know everyone, and you'll find that you'll soon be surrounded by amiable acquaintances, and even some friends."

"I do hope so," Josephine said. "I admit I have been a little worried, however, since Lady Jersey said that I have a pert nose. I'd hate to get a reputation for being pert, such ladies are so very annoying. I hope that my nose doesn't come to define me."

Lady Cowper laughed, a soft pleasing silvery sound. "I've only known you for two minutes, and I can already see that you're nothing like those young women that mistake being impudent for wit. I wouldn't be too concerned with whatever observations Lady Jersey makes about your person. She once told me that my bosom is too small, and I should have my dressmaker design a corset to enhance it. What's worse, she said it in front of my husband and Lord Jersey, who never blinked an eye, and even managed not to let his gaze drop to my bosom. But Cowper turned as crimson as blood. Anyway, I've found that life is fairly enjoyable, even with a small bosom."

The ladies were delighted with this anecdote, and Josephine said, "Now I don't feel at all concerned about my nose. At least she didn't say it in front of any gentlemen."

Lady Cowper said, "Not this time, perhaps, but please don't be disconcerted if she says something outrageous in mixed company, you certainly won't be her first victim, or her last. Now, please tell me whom you've met, and how you're finding London."

The ladies spent a pleasurable half hour talking. When they were on their way home Josephine said, "Do you know, Lady Cowper is one of the most gracious ladies I've ever had the pleasure to meet. I find it interesting that the patronesses are so wildly different. Lady Castlereagh, Countess Lieven, and Mrs. Drummond-Burrell were polite, but I definitely detected the sort of condescension one would expect from their exalted stations. But Lady Sefton and Lady Cowper, and even Lady Jersey, in her own may I say unique way, were quite personable and easy."

"It's a nine days' wonder that they ever agree on anything," Lady Camarden said. Then she bestowed one of her rare smiles on Josephine. "But one thing they did all agree on was to accept you and Lewin to Almack's. And so, Josephine, I know that your success in Town is assured."

Lightly Josephine said, "I know I'm going to have such fun, I'm so excited. As for my success, I'll know that I've truly arrived when I have an opportunity to flirt with Lord Palmerston, and see if he will flirt with me."

Mirabella scoffed, "Josephine, you never flirt. You will, however, charm him, I'm sure."

"But I should like to learn to flirt. You could teach me."

"If I catch either of you flirting, I'm instantly sending you back to Camarden," Lady Camarden said dourly.

"Oh, Mamma, we'll be good," Mirabella said.

"I know that, Mirabella. It's not you two girls I'm worried about. It's the young men."

Cheerfully Mirabella said, "Don't worry about the men, Mamma. We can handle them."

Lady Camarden grimaced. "We shall see."

Giles and Lewin came to breakfast the next morning, to Mirabella's and Josephine's delight. It was the first time they'd seen them since arriving in London.

The Camarden town house had no morning room, for it had a fine garden in the back, with a loggia that was used as a breakfast room in fine weather. The dining room was enormous, with a table that sat eighteen. As usual, however, when it was merely "family," they all sat together at one end, close to the sideboard. It was heavily laden with Monsieur Danton's breakfast, which was never simple, and never sparse. Every morning there was a feast. Today there were boiled eggs, fricasseed eggs, and egg-and-cheese pie; ham, chops, veal, beef tongue, and enough bacon to feed a regiment; oatmeal with sweet cream; a steaming mound of jacket potatoes roasted crispy in olive oil and seasoned with thyme; four kinds of bread and three kinds of rolls, and of course butter, honey, marmalade, and seven different kinds of fruit jams.

When the diners' plates were fully laden, they seated themselves with Lord Camarden at the head of the table, absorbed in reading the *Times*. Mirabella said to Giles and Lewin, "I hear that you gentlemen have been so much in demand that I thought we might not see you except at Almack's or some ball or other."

"Yes, we're quite the men about town," Giles said. "We're fairly exhausted from all the strutting we've been doing, especially Lewin, since his new boots are hurting him."

"They pinch something monstrous," Lewin grumbled. "I'm not taking another strutting step until I go back to the bootmaker and tell him that if he doesn't stretch them out he's going to be wearing them on his head."

"Lewin, for shame," Josephine said. "Such violent emotions, and at breakfast, too."

"For my part I can't blame him, this is the first time I've ever known Harrigan not to fit a shoe perfectly," Giles said. "So that's going to be our first call this morning, or Lewin is going to stay in this black mood."

"Quite right," Lewin muttered.

Mirabella asked eagerly, "You're going to Bond Street this morning? We're going shopping, too. Why don't you join us? You see, we're already dressed."

Giles said, "Yes, I had particularly noted that you were dressed."

"You cretin, I meant that we already have our carriage costumes on, and our hair is done," Mirabella rasped.

"I know what you meant, my lady," Giles said mischievously. "I'm a gentleman of such discrimination that I know perfectly well the difference between a morning gown and carriage costume."

"That's more than I know," Lewin said with somewhat more cheer. "What about it, Giles? Shall we join the ladies? If your ladyship is amenable, of course."

"You and Giles are always welcome," Lady Camarden said. "Though you may regret it, if Mirabella goes on one of her marathon shopping tours."

"Not today, Mamma," Mirabella said. "I only want to go to Mrs. Varenne's for a fitting, and to Rundell & Bridge to pick up my opals."

"That will work fine for us," Giles said. "If I'm not mistaken, Mrs. Varenne's establishment is just down from Harrigan's, and, as a matter of fact, I have some business to attend to at Rundell & Bridge."

Mirabella said, "Very good, we shall enjoy your company. But what I'd really like to search out today is to find a good dance master that's in town. Father, could you please look at the advertisements for dance masters?"

"Hmph? What?" Lord Camarden said, appearing from behind

his newspaper. "Dance master? Why should you want a dance master?"

"We must, we simply must find some suitable dance master that can teach us the German waltz before next Wednesday," Mirabella replied.

"Nonsense," Lord Camarden said, and dived back behind the *Times*.

Giles said, "I know the waltz, I can teach you. If you have permission to learn it, of course."

Lord Camarden mumbled something, but Mirabella ignored him. "Of course we have permission, don't we, Mamma? After all, Countess Lieven is introducing it at Almack's, so there can't be anything wrong with it."

Still Giles was looking at Lady Camarden, and though she frowned, she answered, "Yes, the girls may learn the waltz, Giles. If I didn't give my permission there would be no living with Mirabella."

Eagerly Mirabella said, "Giles, when may we have our first lesson? Today?"

"When we return from our errands we can have a session if you'd like," Giles answered. "We two strutting bucks have no engagements this afternoon."

Mirabella smiled brilliantly. "'He is the very pineapple of politeness.'"

Giles's blue eyes sparkled. "I am. After all, 'few gentlemen, now-a-days, know how to value the ineffectual qualities in a woman.' Like getting dressed before breakfast."

Josephine said thoughtfully, "You know, that's one of Mrs. Malaprop's quotes I've never quite been able to fathom. What do you suppose she meant by 'pineapple'?"

"*Paragon?*" Mirabella suggested.

"*Pinnacle?*" Giles offered.

"*Pear,*" Lewin said firmly. "Pear of politeness. In keeping with the fruited theme, you see."

Lady Camarden sighed. "I now know I'll not hear a sensible conversation all this long day."

Indeed, sensible conversation was rather rare. Giles and Lewin rode, while Lady Camarden, Mirabella, and Josephine took the carriage, so Giles's and Mirabella's banter was considerably reduced. Still, Mirabella and Josephine were in such high spirits that they were rather silly. They reached Mrs. Varenne's dressmaker's shop, and Giles and Lewin went down Bond Street to Harrigan's.

Mrs. Varenne was a tall, stately, elegant lady, now sixty, with exquisite clothes, and bright-silver hair that was always dressed fashionably. She greeted the ladies with appropriate deference, but with dignity. She was from a noble family, but her husband had left her an impoverished widow, and she was obliged to make her living as a *modiste*. Her establishment was very exclusive, patronized by elite ladies of the *haut ton*.

Lady Camarden started looking around at the exquisite fabrics and trims on display, and Josephine started to follow her. Mirabella said, "Josephine, please come with me, I want you to see my dress." Josephine followed her into an elegantly appointed alcove dressing room.

The dress was a gown Mirabella had designed herself, and had had made for her birthday ball. Every year Lord and Lady Camarden gave a grand ball in honor of Mirabella's birthday, March twenty-fifth. The gown was on a mannequin form, supplied by Mirabella, that conformed to her exact measurements.

"Oh, Mirabella, it's absolutely lovely," Josephine breathed. "The color, the fabric... such richness."

It was a deep, shimmering royal-blue satin. Mirabella had decided on a very simple design, for she thought that the fabulous glimmer of the satin had little need of embellishment. Above an

Empire waist, the neckline was low, both in the front and in the back, and was off the shoulder. Around the neckline were three deep layers of white Binche lace, as delicate as a spider's web, and the fall of lace formed sleeves, instead of the gown's having cap sleeves. A single band of the lace was at the high waist, and three identical layers adorned the hem, which had a demi-train.

With Mrs. Varenne's assistance, Mirabella put the dress on. "Mm, yes, I see the difficulty now, Mrs. Varenne," she said thoughtfully. "The lace border falls so low on my shoulders that the sleeves have a tendency to slip down. Can it be remedied?"

"Certainly, my lady," Mrs. Varenne said. "All that need be done is to have a very thin strap of satin running just under the top layer of lace. You will need to be sewn into it, of course, but I would be honored to come on the evening of your ball and do the necessary stitching."

"That's kind of you, but it won't be necessary," Mirabella replied. "My maid is extremely skilled, and will be able to accomplish it with no trouble. So please go on and fashion the straps and have it delivered. I'm so happy with it, Mrs. Varenne, you've created a vision, as always."

Mrs. Varenne gave her one of her rare smiles. "It was your creation, my lady, and if I may say, you are the vision."

Their business on Bond Street concluded, the party went into the City of London proper, to Ludgate Hill. In 1789 the distinguished jewelers Rundell and Bridge had been appointed Royal Goldsmiths, Silversmiths, Jewellers, and Medallists. Philip Rundell was rather an irascible man, often brusque, but he was reputed to be the best judge of gemstones in London. In contrast, John Bridge, who was essentially the public face of the firm, was a sophisticated, elegant man, and served his clients with the utmost in understanding and discretion. Walking into their store was like walking into a bejeweled fairyland.

Mr. Bridge immediately came to greet them, and was introduced to Josephine and Lewin, and he welcomed them fully as warmly as he had greeted Lady Camarden, Mirabella, and Giles. "Lady Mirabella, I'm so happy to say that we've restored your necklace without a single sign of a repair. It's such a fine piece that I could not have borne a flaw. Naturally, since it was our own production there will be no charge."

Mirabella's opal necklace, a piece of jewelry that she particularly treasured, had been broken. Now she protested, "Sir, you are too kind. I believe I confessed to you that I broke the necklace myself, trying to remove it without my maid's assistance. I'm only too happy to pay for the repair."

"I'm afraid that will not do, my lady," he said with a smile. "You and your family are much-valued patrons. It's a pleasure to provide you with this small service. If you would be so kind as to wait a moment, I'll go get your ladyship's necklace."

"As if we would mind waiting," Mirabella said. "You know very well, Mr. Bridge, that my mamma and I can barely tear ourselves away."

Mr. Bridge said, "Then I shall certainly give you all the time you need, my lady." He said a quiet word to Giles, and the two of them went into the back, where the offices were.

Mirabella looked around the glittering store, and immediately her gaze was drawn to a display in the center of the room. On a high square glass case was a sky-blue velvet box, beautifully lit by two Argand lamps. She went to it as if she were mesmerized. In the box was a parure of sapphires and diamonds: a necklace, post earrings, and a tiara. The pear-cut sapphires were of the purest deep blue she had ever seen. The stones were not large; indeed, the diamonds surrounding the sapphires were small enough to look more like frost than like hard stones. The pieces were set in silver, but it was silver of such a luster that it seemed to glow of itself.

"Oh, Mamma, look at this. Aren't they exquisite?" Mirabella breathed.

Josephine's eyes widened. "Now I can see why one of the gates of heaven is made of sapphire."

Lady Camarden searched Mirabella's face. Mirabella had never cared for precious gems. She had always said that as small as she was, she'd look foolishly gaudy wearing ostentatious jewelry; and generally she was correct. She preferred her opals and her pearls, and she had some semiprecious pieces of coral, lapis lazuli, and garnets that she often wore.

"They are indeed delicate and ethereal," Lady Camarden agreed. "Do you truly like them, Mirabella?"

"I do, it's the first time I've seen a parure of precious stones that I think wouldn't look ridiculous on me," she said quietly. "Have you ever seen sapphires of such purity, such clarity?"

Mirabella, Josephine, and Lady Camarden lingered over the sapphire parure, admiring it, until Mr. Bridge returned to them. "I see you've found our newest pieces," he said, lifting the necklace and offering it to Mirabella. To Lady Camarden he handed the tiara, and to Josephine he gave the earrings. "Our premier silversmith, Mr. Storr, only finished this parure two days ago."

"Ah, so that's why the prince regent hasn't purloined them yet," Mirabella said. "But Mr. Bridge, please tell me about them. Is this a silver setting? I've never seen such finely detailed silver, it almost looks like gossamer."

"No, it's very difficult to fashion silver in such a small filigree, it does have a tendency to break. This setting is made from a fairly new precious metal called platinum, which is more generally known as Colombian white gold, as Colombia is the only source of it. It's an extremely hard, durable metal, and the means to fashion it into jewelry is a relatively new science."

"White gold," Mirabella repeated. "It's apt. It's such a gleaming silver that it does almost look white. And the sapphires? Surely it's rare to have so many perfectly matched stones."

"You're correct, my lady, they are Ceylon sapphires found in one single rock, and it is almost unheard of to have stones of such quality that match in hue and in clarity, and with no flaws. Mr. Rundell flatly refused to make separate pieces from these particular sapphires."

Mirabella sighed. "I comprehend that what I'm hearing is that this parure is rare and precious, and so the price must be dear indeed."

"Yes, my lady," Mr. Bridge said kindly. "The parure is priced at four thousand pounds."

Three audible sharp intakes of breath sounded from Josephine, Lewin, and Giles, who had gathered around. Neither Lady Camarden nor Mirabella looked shocked, however. Mirabella gave Mr. Bridge a rueful smile. "I'm sorry to tell you this, Mr. Bridge, but if I were buying them you could have charged me more. I was guessing five thousand."

"Of course your ladyship knows that your credit is unlimited here, always," Mr. Bridge said. "And by that I do mean certainly up to *four* thousand pounds."

"You are so obliging, as always, Mr. Bridge, but no, it's impossible," Mirabella said firmly. "They are well worth it, however, and I hope whoever is fortunate enough to acquire them appreciates them."

They stayed a while longer, for the marchioness had decided to order a new set of silver. Mirabella lingered over the sapphires; she had never been as enchanted by any jewelry as she was by this parure.

When they left, Mirabella saw that Giles was carrying a parcel. She thought—hoped—that he had been able to redeem some or all of his mother's jewelry that he'd been obliged to sell to pay her father back for the charity school funds. She knew that Rundell & Bridge generally simply bought and sold jewelry. But often the discreet, courtly Mr. Bridge would make allowances for reputable patrons who were obliged by some financial embarrassment to sell family jewels, and would act more as a pawnbroker, without the vulgarity, of course.

When they were in the carriage, Josephine said, "At first I was surprised that you were so enamored of the sapphires, Mirabella, since you've never seemed to care for precious gems. But that parure was so exquisitely fashioned, it was of such delicacy, that it would suit you perfectly."

"Except for the cost," Mirabella said. "It's entirely beyond my purse, and I fear that Pappa would have an apoplexy if I asked him to buy me a necklace, tiara, and earrings for four thousand pounds. Hm, I wonder who will be sporting them at the opera, or the next grand ball? I have no doubt that Rundell & Bridge won't have them for long. Now, where are Giles and Lewin? I declare that if they dawdle along and don't come for our waltz lessons I'll wring their noses."

They didn't dawdle, so Mirabella wasn't obliged to carry out her threat. They all arrived at the town house at the same time, and promptly the young people went up to the music room. This was a sizable room, specifically designed for the musical *soirées* that Lord and Lady Camarden often gave during the Season. It had a concert piano and a harp, with graceful chairs provided for the audience, and comfortable settees and sofas lining the walls.

Giles said, "Lewin, we must clear out the central space here, as the waltz takes a lot of room."

"I know that," Lewin said indignantly. "I know the German waltz. In point of fact, if I say so myself, I'm fairly adept at it."

"You are?" Josephine said in amazement. "You never said."

"You never asked," Lewin retorted. "Not everything in France and Spain was dirt, drudge, and drear. There were some very nice ladies there, too."

Giles said, "You're a deep old file, Rosborough. Small wonder that you've been getting along so famously with the ladies. Now, Mirabella, come here and I'll give you your first lesson. Let me think, music, music..."

"What kind of music is played for the German waltz?" Mirabella asked.

"Actually, it's the Viennese waltz, and I learned it firsthand in Vienna," Giles answered. "But now I think of it, the music that was played was always Mozart's and Beethoven's *German Dances*. Perhaps that's why here we've come to call it the German waltz. Anyway, I know we've no transcription of them for piano." He thought for a moment, then asked, "Josephine, do you know *Bloomsbury Place*?"

Smartly Josephine answered, "Giles, not everyone has all the music and all the books memorized as do you. Of course I don't know *Bloomsbury Place* by heart."

"The sheet music is there," Mirabella said with amusement.

"Oh. That's all right then," Josephine said, shuffling through the sheet music until she found it. "Very well, I think I can creditably play it, though I know I'll have to patch through some of the more complex passages."

"That will do very well," Giles said. "The important thing is to keep the three beats to the bar. Now, are you ready, Mirabella?"

"I am." She was standing four feet away from him, facing him, as couples do in country dances.

With a crooked half-smile, Giles came to stand close in front of her. She looked up at him, mystified. He said, "Now, hold up your right hand, gracefully, to the side." She did, and Giles took her hand in his left. "Rest your left hand on my shoulder."

"I beg your pardon?" Mirabella said blankly.

Patiently Giles said, "Rest your left hand lightly on my right shoulder. Mind, arrange your fingers gracefully, with your middle fingers together and your pinky and forefinger slightly raised."

"I know how to arrange my fingers gracefully," Mirabella snapped. Tentatively, barely touching him, she rested her left hand on his shoulder.

"And now I do this," Giles said, and slid his left hand around her waist.

Instantly Mirabella lurched backward. "You must be joking!" she exclaimed.

Giles looked amused. "I'm afraid I'm not, my lady. This is how the waltz is danced."

"But—but do you mean people actually embrace each other? In public?"

"Generally a ball is public, yes, although I'm sure that people may dance the waltz in private, also."

"This is not amusing, Giles," Mirabella said between gritted teeth.

He looked repentant. "I apologize, Bella, I don't mean to make light of your discomfort. You don't have to do this, you know."

"I am most certainly going to do this! And I'm not discomfortable!"

Behind her she heard smothered chuckles from Lewin and Josephine, and Giles couldn't help but grin. "Very well, Mrs. Malaprop. Shall we continue?"

As usual, Mirabella's good humor was immediately restored, but she still felt unsure. She turned to ask, "Josephine, do you really think this is quite—proper? If you waltz, what do you think your father would say?"

She answered, "I know exactly what he would say, that in First

Corinthians thirteen it says that true charity thinketh no evil. And I think no evil of it, either."

Mirabella said, "So apparently I'm the only person in London who's discomfortable with the waltz. No, no, I shall be courageous, and allow you to grope me, Giles."

She stepped forward again and assumed the waltz position, her cheeks flaming, but her face set with determination.

"I won't grope you, and neither will anyone else," Giles said firmly. "And this is supposed to be enjoyable, you know. You look as if you were riding in the tumbrel to the guillotine."

"So sorry, I shall attempt to appear as if I'm enjoying it."

"Please do, or else you'll frighten your partner. So, actually, it's a simple dance. It's one-two-three steps, and we turn. We turn to my right first, and whirl around a bit, and then we do a change step and turn the other way. The couples on the floor never pass each other; we dance in a circle, counterclockwise. Josephine, some music, please?"

On the second bar of three beats, Giles stepped forward—and almost knocked Mirabella down. "You mean I must dance backwards? I'm backwards!"

Soothingly Giles said, "Yes, to begin, but remember, we turn and turn, and you'll be dancing forwards half the time. Let's try it again." This time Mirabella haltingly took her three steps backward, and then did a creditable turn. They did well for several steps, and then Giles did the change step and Mirabella trod solidly on his foot. "Ow," he mumbled. "Sorry."

"It is your fault, you know, how am I supposed to know when we turn about? Can't we set a certain number of turns to your right, and then a certain number of turns to your left?"

"But it doesn't work that way, the waltz is very free and flowing, and the dancers turn as they feel. The gentleman is the leader, you see, and he will lead you to know when to turn."

"You said this dance was simple," Mirabella said accusingly.

"And so it is, if you can just relax and enjoy it."

Mirabella nodded, and they began again.

Though she did try hard, she found it terribly difficult to relax; she felt stiff and awkward. Although Giles held her very lightly, and did not press close at all, his arm about her waist still felt overly warm. She was painfully conscious of his nearness. Oddly she felt hot and cold at the same time, unaccustomed as she was to a man's touching her.

And there it is, she thought with no little confusion. *I haven't been so much as touched by a man since Captain Pryce, except for taking their arm and such as that . . . I suppose I must be so flustered because it reminds me of him . . .*

But it didn't, really. Dancing with Giles, his arm secure about her, his hand warm in hers, sensing the solid muscle of his shoulder even with her light touch, was nothing like embracing Captain Pryce. This realization only added to her bewilderment. After a few minutes she stopped and disengaged herself and said, "Do you know, I think it might help me if I could watch this dance being performed. Josephine, I'll play, and you dance with Giles."

Mirabella took her place at the piano, and Josephine easily assumed the waltz position with Giles. They danced very elegantly, from the beginning. Josephine said as they whirled by, "You're probably correct, Mirabella, I'm sure it came easier to me since I saw the steps first."

Mirabella wondered if this was true. After playing for several minutes, she stopped. "I think we all understand the three-beat now. Lewin, would you dance with me? And we can all practice not running over each other."

"It would be my great pleasure, my lady," Lewin said, bowing.

Mirabella danced with Lewin, and was amazed to find that she was much more at ease. *Perhaps it is true, seeing the steps demonstrated makes it easier to learn. Can that be it? Why should I feel so uncomfortable with Giles, and yet I'm perfectly fine now, dancing with Lewin? Could it be that it was just the shock of the first time?*

Lady Mirabella, by her own admission, was a woman who did not know her own heart. And so she dismissed the questions in her mind.

Chapter Eight

Almack's Assembly Rooms was not a particularly imposing edifice on the outside. The grand ballroom, however, was palatial. It was large enough to easily accommodate the hundreds of dancers who gathered there every Wednesday night. Three enormous crystal chandeliers lit the ballroom, and the shimmering light was reflected in the mirrors that lined the walls. At one end was a gilded balcony for the musicians; at the other end was a dais where the patronesses received the invitees in a queenly manner. The long expanse was decorated on each side by gilded columns and pilasters. Between the columns were many comfortable armchairs, settees, and sofas for the patrons to rest on between dances.

On this opening night, even at the relatively early hour of eight o'clock, a large crowd had already gathered. In one alcove stood three young gentlemen, observing the arrivals. Giles and Lewin were joined by a longtime friend of Giles's, Lord Trevor Brydges. He was a tall, athletic-looking man with thick blond hair and flinty masculine features. His expression, however, was generally one of good humor.

"So, here is Lady Mirabella," Lord Trevor said. "A vision, as always. And Rosborough, your sister looks very well indeed. She's charming."

"She is," Lewin agreed. "And even I can see that she's in particularly good looks tonight."

The three watched as Lord and Lady Camarden, Mirabella, and Josephine made their entrance and paid their respects to the Lady Patronesses.

Lord Trevor said, "Lady Mirabella Tirel is a prize, some man is going to be very lucky indeed. Knyvet, I admit I was surprised to hear that she's in the market now. I always thought that you and she had some sort of understanding."

"We do," Giles said shortly. "We're friends. And she's not a *prize* that's in the *market* now. You make it sound like some racehorse at Tattersalls."

With amusement Lord Trevor said, "There, that's exactly what I'm speaking of. You're very protective of her, you always have been. Sorry, old chap, I meant no offense, either to her or to you. So I am correct in assuming that you only regard Lady Mirabella as a friend?"

"Why do you ask?" Giles asked.

"Because I wouldn't want to interfere if your relationship is anything more than that," Lord Trevor answered smoothly.

"Interfere? You mean that you're contemplating throwing your hat into the ring?" Giles demanded.

"Now who's making it sound as if we're betting on a sporting event? But yes, I am. As I said, she's quite a—she would make a perfect wife. She's witty, she's accomplished, she's elegant, and of course she is beautiful."

"And rich," Giles snorted.

"Yes, she is, and that's always an asset. But not everyone would consider that her most attractive quality," Lord Trevor retorted. His father, the Marquess of Levenden, was extremely wealthy.

"No, I suppose not," Giles begrudgingly agreed. "Still, Brydges, are you saying that you've formed an affection for her?"

"No, I've never had the opportunity to get to know her well enough to form any sort of attachment. She's always held men at such a long arm's length, except for you, which is precisely why everyone was under the impression that you were a couple."

How I wish it were true, Giles thought with a pang, though he remained expressionless. He shrugged. "Obviously we are not, since I expect that after two or three weeks Lady Jersey will be announcing Lady Mirabella's engagement to some other poor young fool."

"Besides you, you mean," Lord Trevor said, grinning. "I won't say I hope it'll be me, because despite how shallow you think I am, I would like to at least first get to know the lady somewhat. And I see I'm not the only one, either." Mirabella and Josephine were already being besieged by four gentlemen. "There's Southam, I had a feeling he might be interested. Excuse me." Lord Trevor began to make his way through the crush to the knot of men surrounding the two ladies.

Lewin and Giles watched in silence for a few moments. Then Lewin said, "Begging your pardon for continuing with the sporting allusions, but I'm of the opinion that she won't come up to scratch."

Giles looked at him with narrowed eyes. "What do you mean?"

"I don't think she'll actually go through with it. Do you, honestly? I mean, Mirabella can be rash and impulsive, but it's quite another matter to stand and vow to God to bind yourself to another person for life."

"Mirabella knows that very well," Giles said. "Yes, she can be rash. But in this case I think she's made a rational decision, with a cool head. She's not romantic, you know. She hasn't been since she was seventeen years old."

"Maybe. Still, I think that she's making a mistake. And I think you should dissuade her. You could, you know."

"Perhaps I could, but why should I?" Giles said shortly.

Lewin looked straight into his eyes and said quietly, "You know why."

Giles frowned darkly. *Yes, I know, and Lewin knows, though Bella doesn't. I suppose I've been in love with her all of my life . . . even though I really didn't realize it until I came back after Father died. But I can't possibly take care of her and offer her the kind of life that she's accustomed to, not now. Perhaps in a year, or maybe two, I could . . . if I can recover that quickly. I thought I would have time, but it seems that I've run out of time. Too soon, too soon.*

Giles said with an appearance of carelessness, "You're mistaken, Lewin. She's probably going to be pursued by half a dozen men whose families might represent a fourth of the wealth in England. She deserves to live in the luxury she's always known. Some of those are good men, like Brydges, and Aldington. Mirabella's no fool. If she finds one of them to be agreeable enough, she'll likely make a suitable marriage."

Lewin sighed. "Sounds cold and dreary. Not like Mirabella at all."

Giles thought, *No, it's not like her at all . . . but what can I do? She's a grown woman, she can make her own decisions. And so it seems that I'm the one who is feeling cold and dreary . . .*

Mirabella glowed in her evening gown. It was made of the finest corded silk in a deep peach color. It was simply made, with a high waistline, low square neckline, and short puffed sleeves; it was the unusual embellishments that made the gown distinctive. It was embroidered around the hem in one of the season's newest and most fashionable colors, coquelicot, a bright poppy orange-red. In spite of her sister-in-law's disdain for Mirabella's scarlet pelisse, Mirabella had been correct; this year even young women could wear more daring colors, in trim at least. The embroidery was of the Oriental poppy, with the black center, surrounded by green ivy leaves. The silk bandeau about her waist had an identical design. Colette had fashioned small poppies out of silk that Mirabella wore in her hair, entwined with live ivy tendrils.

Her jewelry was distinctive, too. Rundell & Bridge had made a necklace and earrings that were of Mirabella's own design. The stones in the gold filigree setting were of coral, but instead of the usual round stone or bead, they were square-cut. At her request, Rundell & Bridge had found coral stones that exactly matched the coquelicot trim of her dress.

Josephine looked lovely, too, in a similar gown of creamy mint green, trimmed in white. She wore a single strand of pearls, and white jasmine in her hair.

As soon as they entered the ballroom, they went to the dais to curtsy to the patronesses, who greeted them warmly. Admission to Almack's was considered quite as important to a young lady as being presented in the Queen's Drawing Room, and was choreographed as strictly. If her first appearance at Almack's was considered her "coming out," a patroness was chosen to arrange the young lady's dance partners. Lady Cowper was sponsoring Josephine, and she said, "Miss Rosborough, as soon as everyone has arrived, I shall come fetch you and make known to you all of your dance partners I've chosen. I think you'll be pleased, and will have a fine debut."

Josephine thanked her warmly. Lord Camarden went to join a group of men that included Lord Liverpool, and Lady Camarden went to speak to Lady Liverpool. Mirabella took Josephine's arm and said, "What a rout, but then it always is, on opening night. Let me look around, to whom shall I first introduce you?"

Josephine whispered, "Perhaps to this herd of young gentlemen approaching us? I did warn you, you know."

"Oh, do be quiet, no one likes an I-told-you-so," Mirabella hissed. Then she smiled warmly and curtsied. "Good evening, gentlemen, how good to see you tonight. Please allow me to introduce you to my friend, Miss Rosborough, although I see that not everyone requires an introduction. Lord Southam, we met only briefly at Lady Jersey's, but you do remember Miss Rosborough?"

"Of course, how could I forget such a lovely young lady," he said as he bowed and Josephine curtsied.

Mirabella continued, "Miss Rosborough, I'm happy to present to you Lord Palmerston, Mr. Aldington, and Mr. Smythe. My particular friend, Miss Rosborough."

Bows and curtsies were exchanged. Lord Palmerston said, "I had already heard of the charming Miss Rosborough, I'm honored to finally make your acquaintance. Lady Cowper, I understand, is assigning your dance partners tonight, ma'am, and I have taken the liberty of requesting the first waltz. I hope that is agreeable to you?"

"Perfectly agreeable, my lord, I thank you," Josephine said. Mirabella and Josephine exchanged mischievous glances as he took his leave. He was not a particularly handsome man, but his face was warm and lively, his dark eyes sparkled, and his voice was deep and resonant, like velvet. But it was especially his wholehearted devilish smile that emanated charm, and had earned him the nickname Cupid.

"I, too, have requested a dance, Miss Rosborough," Lord Southam said cordially. "It was, I believe, the fifth one; however, as I'm unsure and I would hate myself if I left you standing, I'll take care to check your card when Lady Cowper gives it to you."

"You're very kind, my lord. Indeed, I should be vexed to be left stranded without a partner, but I promise if such a mishap should occur I won't hate you," Josephine replied. Both Mr. Aldington and Mr. Smythe then began to assure Josephine that they, too, had requested dances.

Lord Southam turned his attention back to Mirabella. In contrast to Lord Palmerston, he was a tall, broad-shouldered, barrel-chested man of quite imposing size. He had dark hair, stylishly arranged in careless curls, deep-set dark eyes, a fine straight nose, and, curious on his manly features, a wide, full mouth. He was older than Mirabella; she thought that he must be thirty-six or thirty-seven. In the exclusive realm of the *haut ton* of London, she had met him several times, and had danced with him twice that she could recall, but he had always been something of an enigma to her.

He said politely, "Your friend seems very amiable, I foresee that it will be a pleasure to make her acquaintance. And so, Lady Mirabella, are all of your dances bespoken yet?"

"Of course not, my lord, we've only just arrived. I've hardly had time to greet anyone yet, and beg for partners," Mirabella said impishly.

"As if you should ever be required to do such a thing. Would you do me the honor of dancing the opening quadrille with me? And I should also like to request the first waltz."

Mirabella smiled. "You are very bold, sir."

"Fortune favors the bold."

"Ah, yes. Virgil's *Aeneid*."

One eyebrow lifted sardonically. "Good heavens, a bluestocking. You don't look like a bluestocking."

"I thank you, since I understand they were reputed to be extremely frumpy."

"Yes, they were, and obviously you have nothing to be concerned about on that score. Tell me, have you actually read the *Aeneid*?" he asked curiously.

"I have."

"In the Latin, or a translation?"

"In the Latin. You appear to be shocked. But let me reassure you, I could hardly cipher much of it without assistance, and I found it to be rather heavy reading. 'Tis a wonder I finished it, I was so wearied of it by the end."

"I am relieved, a lady who thoroughly enjoys reading Virgil is a fearful thing. But we've strayed from the most important topic. Are you, goddess Fortuna, to favor me for my boldness? Am I to have the quadrille and the waltz?"

"You may, sir," she answered, handing him her dance card. He signed it with a flourish.

Lady Cowper appeared to usher Josephine around to make certain she was introduced to her chosen dance partners. Both Mr. Aldington and Mr. Smythe seemed to be about to try to converse with Mirabella, but just then Lord Trevor Brydges came to stand in front of them and bow to Mirabella.

"Good evening to you, Lord Trevor," she said.

"Good evening, Lady Mirabella, may I say that you are a perfect vision tonight?" he said.

"Thank you, sir, you're too kind."

Lord Southam said with a half-smile, "Too late, Brydges, I've already got the quadrille and the first waltz."

Cheerfully Lord Trevor said, "I thought such, but it's of no consequence. There are three more waltzes, are there not? Lady Mirabella, I beg you will do me the honor of the second and third waltz."

"I see that the waltzes are going to be in much demand this evening," she said with amusement. "I'm so glad that I was able to learn it quickly, after what I must admit was a distinctly unpromising beginning. Thank you, Lord Trevor, the second and third waltz will be my pleasure." She handed him her card.

Harry Smythe, a boyish, bright-eyed young man, had barely been able to contain himself while the other, more important men monopolized Mirabella. But now he couldn't resist saying, "Then that just leaves one waltz. Please, Lady Mirabella, may I have the honor? And also for the second dance?" Mirabella accepted these, and then Aldington signed for two dances. Lord Southam excused himself, but Lord Trevor, Mr. Aldington, and Mr. Smythe lingered. Mirabella had known Denys Aldington for years, and found him to be an agreeable young man, with curly brown hair and expressive brown eyes and pleasant features. However, she wanted to visit some of her other friends before the dancing started.

Firmly Mirabella said, "Gentlemen, I must beg you to excuse me. Mr. Smythe, I hope that Miss Smythe is here tonight, I long to see her. Pray, where is she, one can hardly find anyone in this crowd."

Eagerly he said, "She is over there, with my mother. Would you allow me to escort you to her?"

"Thank you, sir," she said, and took his arm. He fairly strutted across the room.

Mr. Henry Smythe was a very wealthy man who owned vast estates in Northumberland, and was also a well-respected MP for his borough. Although his family was not particularly distinguished, he had married a young woman of noble connections, Miss Frances Molyneaux. They had two children, Harry, who was twenty-five, and a girl who was now nineteen, Miss Barbara Smythe. Two years ago, when Barbara had come out, she and Mirabella had become fast friends. Mirabella found her to be charming. She was very pretty, tall and willowy, with thick curly yellow-gold hair, china-blue eyes, a delicate complexion, and a rare sweetness of expression. Miss Smythe was also a little shy, and Mirabella had, in effect, taken her under her wing.

Miss Smythe and her mother were seated on a settee, and Mirabella saw with pleasure that they were talking to Giles and Lewin. When she approached, the two ladies rose and curtsied, as was perfectly proper. Mirabella couldn't help but recall that what Lady Jersey had said about Mrs. Smythe's groveling was unfortunately close to the truth. Her curtsy was much too deep and subservient, and she deeply bowed her head, which one did only with the royal family. Barbara's curtsy was perfectly correct and graceful.

Before Mirabella could greet them, Mrs. Smythe burst out, "Oh, how wonderful you've come as we were speaking of you, Lady Mirabella! I was just saying to Sir Giles that I was desolate when I realized you were in Town, and you and Lady Camarden had not yet found time to call on us. You will do so, at your first opportunity, will you not?"

"Of course, Mrs. Smythe," Mirabella said courteously. "Miss Smythe, I'm so happy to see you again. You look lovely tonight, but then you always do."

"Thank you, Lady Mirabella," she said with some diffidence. "I was unsure about this new shade, Pomona green, but Mamma says it does flatter me."

"So it does," Mirabella agreed. "Good evening, Sir Giles, Captain Rosborough."

They bowed, and Giles started to say something, but Mrs. Smythe gushed, "Sir Giles and Captain Rosborough were kind enough to come request Barbara to dance, of course she's thrilled. Captain Rosborough, I must say that you look quite splendid in your regimentals, I always thought that the green jackets were most dashing, especially in the full dress, with the Hussar jacket on one shoulder, it's so swashbuckling, is it not? And Sir Giles, I must compliment you on the intricacy of your cravat, I do so wish Mr. Smythe's valet had a little more creativity in the matter of arranging fashionable cravats. I was just saying to Mr. Brummel the other day that he alone has made the fashionable cravat *de rigueur*."

"That he has, Mrs. Smythe, a gentleman can hardly show his face in public unless his cravat is exquisite," Giles gravely agreed. He turned to Mirabella. "Lady Mirabella, I observe that your dance card has already been signed several times. By chance do you have a waltz available?"

"I'm afraid not," Mirabella said. "Those were claimed first of all. But you shouldn't mind another dance, I've been waltzing with you all week."

Giles grumbled, "Since I was your teacher, I would have thought you'd be considerate enough to allow me to be your partner at your debut. I suppose I'll settle for a country dance."

Aside to Mrs. and Miss Smythe, Mirabella said, "I hope, Miss Smythe, that Sir Giles's request to you to dance was phrased slightly more elegantly."

Barbara blushed. Mrs. Smythe said strenuously, "No, no, Sir Giles was most courteous and charming in his application to Barbara. That is, of course I didn't mean to imply that he wasn't courteous to you, Lady Mirabella, what I meant was that—er—he's not, of course, on such intimate—that is, I mean friendly terms with my daughter as he appears to be with you. My lady."

Barbara's blush deepened, and Mirabella, as she always did, felt sorry for her, so she replied warmly, "Yes, Sir Giles is a lifelong friend of my family's, and we often treat each other more as siblings than as friends. Sir Giles, you may have the country dance of your choice."

The orchestra had been warming up, and now the conductor announced, "We will now have the quadrille."

As was traditional, the four highest-ranking couples took the floor to begin the dance. Lord Southam came to Mirabella, and immediately Mrs. Smythe trilled, "Lord Southam, how good it is to see you again. Pray, have you spoken with my husband tonight? I believe he wanted to have a word with you concerning some business in the House."

He bowed and said in a cool tone, "Good evening Mrs. Smythe, Miss Smythe. No, madam, I've not seen Mr. Smythe. I'm sure I'll have the opportunity to speak with him soon." He then led Mirabella to the edge of the dance floor to wait for the other dancers to join the quadrille.

"Mrs. Smythe is very solicitous, shall I say," he said.

Mirabella sighed. "Yes, and I feel so sorry for Miss Smythe, for I like her very well, and her mother does embarrass her."

"It's unfortunate, for the girl is pretty and amiable, and she has twenty thousand pounds. But Mrs. Smythe puts men off. Particularly noblemen, as it's clear to see that snagging a title for Miss Smythe is her sole aim in life. Let's not waste more time talking of Mrs. Smythe, I find the topic excessively tedious. Tell me all about Camarden, particularly the famous fox hunt. How was it this year?"

As they danced, Mirabella recalled that Lord Southam was a superb dancer for a man of his bulk. She regaled him with anecdotes of the fox hunt, including Mr. Rosborough's garb and how, unfortunately and inexplicably, Mr. Eldridge's old mare had gotten it into her head that she would back up instead of going forward, and had backed right into a fallen tree, lost her balance, and sat down, causing Mr. Eldridge to slide off backward. Lord Southam showed a flattering interest in her conversation; generally Mirabella had found that men loved more to talk of themselves than to listen to a young lady prattling on. But Lord Southam's repartee, though a little heavy, was clever and engaging. She enjoyed the dance immensely.

There were four more dances before the first waltz, and Mirabella found that she was particularly looking forward to waltzing with Lord Southam. She watched unobtrusively as he did the allemande with Lady Jersey. She talked incessantly, as usual, but he was smiling at her. Her manner was obviously flirtatious.

It was time for the waltz, and there was no little confusion in arranging the couples in a circle, for the dancers were accustomed to dancing only in lines. At length the waltz began. Mirabella noted that Lord Southam held her closer than Giles had done, although of course their bodies didn't actually touch. He was such a big man, and so muscular, that she was very aware of his nearness and warmth.

"Never in this life did I think I'd be waltzing at Almack's," he said with amusement. "Look there, it's as I suspected, Mrs. Drummond-Burrell looks as if she's bitten into a lemon. I can't fathom how they persuaded her to allow it."

"I'm not privy to the patronesses' weekly meetings, but I believe that sometimes Lady Jersey and Countess Lieven simply overpower her. Lady Jersey, in particular, can leave you somewhat breathless, can she not?" Mirabella said brightly.

"In a manner of speaking," he replied carelessly. "May I compliment you on your waltz, Lady Mirabella. You're really quite accomplished and graceful, unlike some others." He nodded to the other side of the circle. An elderly gentleman and an elderly lady were apparently having some trouble with their change step, as every time they switched their direction they fell a little farther behind the couple in front of them. The dancers behind them were getting rather too close together.

"Oh dear, it appears that we may have some sort of jam-up," Mirabella said, the dimples flashing. "Like the carriages on Piccadilly."

He smiled. "Do you know, you are delightful. It's refreshing, for I find many young ladies to be vapid and banal. Here, I think we must compensate, or we're all likely to end up in a lump. We must turn circles in one place until we can manage to space out again."

Again Mirabella found him to be charming. She thought he might ask to take her in to supper, but after the waltz he disappeared.

Precisely at eleven supper was announced. Lewin escorted Mirabella in, and Giles escorted Josephine, and they sat together. In contrast to the ballroom, the supper room was plainly furnished, with straight-backed chairs and long tables covered with white cloths. It was painted an uninspired blue and the sole decorations on the walls were the candle sconces, which were of gold. The food and drink at Almack's was famous, or infamous, for it was so plain as to be insipid. The bread was a day old so that it could be sliced very thinly, the cake was simple and unflavored. No alcoholic beverages were served, only tea and lemonade, and both of those were watery.

Josephine said, "Now I can understand why you insisted we eat before we came, Mirabella. I admit I'm surprised at this lamentable fare. But no, I shan't complain at all, I'm having a marvelous time."

"One can hardly dance for hours on end subsisting on this," Mirabella said, somewhat absently. "Josephine, how did you find your dance with Lord Southam?"

"He's charming, of course. He dances very well for a man of his size. To look at him one would think he'd—well, rather blunder about."

Giles said, "He's a regular at Gentleman Jackson's boxing saloon, and he's a real terror. None but Jackson himself and his assistants will spar with him. It's not simply his size and strength, either, he has, as you say, a surprising grace and lightness of foot." He was watching Mirabella carefully.

With interest she said, "Really? I know very little about him, personally. How well do you know him, Giles?"

"Not very well. He's in Prinny's inner circle, but I don't know him as well as I do some of the others, like Brydges and Aldington."

Mirabella said insistently, "No, no, I mean, what is said about him personally?"

Dryly Giles said, "I see, you mean the best gossip. I haven't heard. I could launch an investigation if you'd like."

"Of course I don't—Giles, stop it. It's not important, I'm just curious. Josephine, I must know. Did Lord Palmerston flirt with you?"

She smiled. "He possesses such overwhelming charm that I believe any time he's speaking to a woman it's mistaken for flirting."

"Come now, tell the truth, you're as terrible as Giles at evasion," Mirabella said.

"Very well. I exerted all of my charm, and finally saw that he was flirting with me."

"Excellent girl!" Mirabella said. Giles and Lewin exchanged glances, rolling their eyes. She continued, "But I'm so vexed, he didn't ask me for a single dance. It's not fair."

Josephine said, "I'm certain that Lady Cowper was the reason for that."

"Emily?" Mirabella said with surprise. "But surely she wouldn't object, I've danced with him before."

"Yes, dearest, I know you have," Josephine said slowly. "But you were never available before."

"Oh, but that can't be..." Mirabella's voice trailed off in confusion. She glanced sidelong at Giles. "I suppose you've heard."

"Everyone's heard, Mirabella," Giles said with exasperation. "Telling Lady Jersey is as effective as taking out an advertisement in the *Times*."

"I've decided I don't wish to speak of this any more," Mirabella said assertively. "Lewin, you're very quiet. Are you enjoying yourself, or are you bored to distraction?"

"I was feeling like a complete ponce, but Mrs. Smythe's effusive observations about my person cheered me considerably," he replied, his eyes alight. "And I did enjoy dancing with Miss Smythe, she's such an amiable girl."

"Who is Miss Smythe?" Josephine asked.

Giles and Lewin began to tell Josephine about the Smythes, and Mirabella's attention wandered. *Giles sounds frustrated with me. I suppose he thinks I was indiscreet, talking to Lady Jersey. But that's ridiculous, what am I supposed to do, keep it a secret? Oh, hang what he thinks.*

I wonder where Lord Southam got to?

Chapter Nine

Mirabella had been right in her prediction of the weather. When the ides of March arrived, London's airs magically transformed from winter's cold grip to spring's mildness, and all of the heavy winter furs went into storage. The morning was glorious, balmy and with the most benevolent golden sunshine that ever was in the coal-smudged city. It was the first time that breakfast was served *alfresco* in the garden loggia.

Mirabella and Josephine came down, both of them looking sleepy-eyed, for they had been out until two o'clock in the morning at Lord and Lady Sefton's ball. Lord and Lady Camarden had retired from the ball much earlier, at eleven o'clock, leaving the girls to Lady Sefton's chaperonage.

Lady Camarden was sitting in the garden at a wrought iron table in the sunshine, by a triple-tiered tinkling fountain. She came to join Mirabella and Josephine at the dining table in the loggia. "You girls do look frowsty and dull," she said, signaling the footman for another cup of tea. "What time did you get in?"

Mirabella yawned. "It was after two o'clock. Then we stayed up chattering for another hour or so. Still I couldn't go to sleep until some time later."

"Mirabella, you are going to ruin your complexion, let alone your health, if you don't start taking a sleeping draught on those nights," Lady Camarden said sternly.

"Nonsense, Mamma, I may not look like it but I'm as healthy as an ox, and I have complete faith in my Floris Milk of Jasmine cream to keep me youthful and dewy. I dislike taking sleeping draughts, they make me feel as if my head is stuffed with wet cotton wool in the morning."

"Sometimes I believe it is, for shame, comparing yourself to an ox, you sound like a dairymaid. Josephine, did you sleep well?"

"Yes, my lady, I'm fortunate that I don't suffer from the insomnia. I always sleep very soundly."

"When Mirabella doesn't keep you up half the night gabbling about young gentlemen, I'm sure."

Mirabella said, "What else is there to talk about? Except our gowns, of course. Has Pappa already left?"

"Yes, and you missed Giles and Lewin. They breakfasted early, I only came down as they were finishing. They were accompanying Camarden to the House, as there is an important vote on funding for the army today. Lord Wellington is going to speak."

"I hope they give him boatloads of it," Josephine said. "Some of the things that Lewin's told us about the privations of the army are blood-curdling."

"I'm of the mind that perhaps they will, this time, after the triumph at Badajoz," Lady Camarden said. "At least that is the conventional wisdom. So, girls, today we must call on Lady Liverpool, Lady Melbourne, and I believe Lady Heathcote, I must consult my calendar again for her at-home days."

Mirabella said brightly, "Oh, Mamma, must we really? We've done so many calls, and have been so taken up with callers on Thursdays, that Josephine and I haven't even had an opportunity to ride in the park yet. After all, those are return calls, I'm sure none of those ladies would mind if you call on them without us."

Lady Camarden was thoughtful for a moment, then replied, "Very well, I must say you've been dutiful these past three weeks. I suppose I should allow you some time to yourselves without dragging you around to all of the dowagers in Town."

"Splendid, thank you, Mamma. And Josephine, I've been thinking, I'd love to take you to Gunter's this afternoon."

"Who is Gunter?" Josephine asked, bewildered.

"No, Gunter's Tea Shop," Mirabella answered. "It's almost as much fun as Almack's, only the food is infinitely better."

Gunter's was a favorite among Polite Society. It was located in the heart of Mayfair, on Berkeley Square, and the Beau Monde loved to gather there before the fashionable Hyde Park riding hours of late afternoon.

As strictly dictated by Mirabella, the girls wore carriage costumes, for they were taking Mirabella's phaeton. Mirabella's was a sarcenet muslin dress of a gentle cerulean blue, with a matching Russian mantle lined with white satin. Josephine wore primrose yellow, with a chocolate-brown spencer trimmed with gold braid. They had spent the morning trimming their bonnets, and both of them looked fetching with satin ribbons and fresh flowers that matched their gowns.

Mirabella's phaeton was one of those jaunty high-perch carriages that was called a "high flyer," with small front wheels and large rear ones. It was painted the Camarden livery maroon color, with black trim and silver fittings. The previous year, for her birthday, Lord and Lady Camarden had given Mirabella a pair of spirited matched grays, with silver-trimmed harness and headdresses with white ostrich plumes. Mirabella was an accomplished whip, and drove with great style.

Two grooms assisted them up into what was indeed a high perch, and Mirabella dismissed them. "We're not even going to be accompanied by grooms?" Josephine asked.

"It's not necessary at Gunter's," Mirabella replied, taking her whip and briskly snapping it far above the horses' backs. With some dancing, the horses started at a collected trot. "In fact, young ladies may even ride alone in a young gentleman's carriage to Gunter's without causing a scandal."

"Truly?" Josephine exclaimed with surprise. "Any young lady might accompany any young gentleman, and no one thinks ill of her?"

Mirabella pondered this, then smiled. "No, that's not quite the way of it, allow me to rephrase. Some ladies could accompany some gentlemen."

Josephine knowingly said, "I see. This is one of those situations where the rules are different for those in highest circles than for those in the lower circles."

"Oh dear, you do make me sound like the worst snob," Mirabella said. "Am I really?"

"No, you are not, Mirabella. After all, they are the rules of your world and your society, and of course you must understand them and abide by them. Actually, when I make disdainful observations about such things, it's really I who sound like a snob. Or I suppose, a reverse snob."

"I think we are both being much too highly introspective on this marvelous day, let us commence being vain and shallow, and think of nothing but whom we shall meet, and, of course, what delicacy we'll order. Gracious, what a throng, but I suppose this is the first day it's been warm enough to enjoy being out in the weather."

The road in front of Gunter's was packed with carriages and men on horseback. Still, somehow in the deep instincts of London Society the sense of hierarchy was strong. It had become traditional for the ladies to line up their carriages across the street from the confectionery shop, in the shade of the gracious maple trees of Berkeley Square. Less grand carriages moved down the street to accommodate the finest town coaches, phaetons, barouches, and landaus. Skillfully Mirabella maneuvered her phaeton under the shade of a spreading tree, finessing the horses until she was parked directly behind a large open landau. The lady sitting in the back was half-turned, speaking to a gentleman on a horse.

Mirabella said with surprise, "It's my friend Lady FitzGeorge. I didn't know she had arrived in Town yet." Two footmen stood at attention at the back of the landau, and Mirabella signaled to them. One quickly came to stand by her and bowed deeply. "Please tell Lady FitzGeorge that Lady Mirabella Tirel sends her greetings, and hopes to speak to her."

The footman delivered the message, and Lady FitzGeorge turned, smiled, and dismissed the gentleman she'd been speaking to. She gestured for Mirabella and Josephine to join her. The footmen assisted them down. They stopped at the side of the landau and Mirabella said happily, "Hello, Rosalind, I'm so very glad to find you in Town. May I have the honor of introducing you to my friend, the daughter of our rector, Miss Rosborough. Miss Rosborough, Lady FitzGeorge."

Josephine curtsied, and Lady FitzGeorge returned with a courteous nod of her head. "I'm so happy to see you, Mirabella. Miss Rosborough, it's my pleasure to make your acquaintance. Both of you, please join me."

Countess FitzGeorge possessed a beauty rarely seen in Englishwomen; her looks were more Slavic than Anglo. Her face was heart-shaped, with an oval forehead and widely spaced dark eyes, slightly uptilted and heavily fringed with thick black lashes, a delicately small nose, and perfect Cupid's-bow lips. Her hair was black, thick, and glossy. Mirabella had always thought that she looked like a kitten.

Mirabella and Josephine seated themselves across from her. Mirabella said, "I didn't know you were in Town, I would have called on you."

"I only just arrived yesterday," Lady FitzGeorge replied in a pleasingly low, warm voice. "I haven't seen anyone yet. But I couldn't resist Gunter's today, I've been haunted by thoughts of their *pâte de guimauve de cerise.* I've continually nagged my cook to make it, but it's hopeless, it's like a great sickening spoonful of cherry marshmallow jam. At any rate, I've already ordered. John," she called to a footman, "go fetch a waiter, my guests haven't yet ordered." The footman set off in pursuit of a man in a black coat and white apron who precariously weaved in and out of the traffic to attend the carriages on this side of the street. The crimson-faced, puffing young man instantly came to the landau. Mirabella ordered coconut macaroons, and Josephine ordered a raspberry sorbet.

"How long have you been in Town?" Lady FitzGeorge asked.

"For three weeks now," Mirabella replied. "Did you come with Lady Chandos and Lady Margaret? I don't believe I've seen them either."

Lady FitzGeorge said carelessly, "They came yesterday, too, but happily they are staying at Lord Chandos's town house instead of with me." She turned to Josephine and said mischievously, "Miss Rosborough, you must forgive me and Lady Mirabella, we are old friends. I have not yet gotten so rude that I exclude my guests from conversation. Baroness Amelia Chandos and Lady Margaret FitzGeorge are my stepdaughters."

Lady FitzGeorge was the same age as Mirabella, twenty-two years old. But Josephine was a woman of elegant discretion, and her expression betrayed no surprise. "I hope I have an opportunity of making their acquaintance, my lady," she said pleasantly.

"I'm certain you shall, for Lady Margaret has just turned eighteen, and is coming out this Season. Oh, Mirabella, how happy I am that Amelia married last year, and can sponsor Meg. I've been buried and smothered in Lincolnshire, it is an absolute desolate wilderness. I thought I would wither away like a dead vine. Miss Rosborough, my husband died a year ago, and I've been in mourning."

"I'm so sorry for your loss, my lady," Josephine said sympathetically. "Please accept my sincerest condolences."

"Thank you. Now I'm here, however, and finally out of the dismal widow's weeds, I assure you I'm in quite good spirits," she said, her dark eyes gleaming. "And now that I don't have parents or a husband to rule my life, and since I'm not saddled with sponsoring a young naïve girl, I intend to have a brilliant time this Season."

The huffing waiter arrived with their confections, Lady FitzGeorge's marshmallow cherry comfits and Mirabella's macaroons on silver trays, and Josephine's ice in a crystal goblet. Lady FitzGeorge said, "I'm going to start on my plan of doing precisely what I want, and be very risqué and remove my gloves. I dislike eating *pâte de guimauve de cerise* with a spoon, but the paste makes your gloves so very sticky. And so here am I, with bare hands, right out in public in broad daylight."

Mirabella said with amusement, "Rosalind, it's plain to see that you have been bored, and also that you've definitely developed a mind of your own. I've never heard you speak quite so—forthrightly."

"Recklessly, I think you mean. But now I'm a widow, I can say and do as I please, within the boundaries of propriety, of course. I hope I'm not utterly shocking you, Miss Rosborough."

Josephine smiled. "Not at all, my lady. I think all women, at some time or other, are chafed by the strictures imposed upon us by society. Saying so aloud to friends shouldn't be cause for offense."

"As long as those friends are females," Lady FitzGeorge agreed. "Mirabella, I did receive your invitation to your birthday ball, and I'm particularly looking forward to it, you always do have the most dashing and eligible young gentlemen in Town in attendance. And here, speak of the devil! Here are Lord Trevor and Mr. Aldington." She nodded to the two horsemen in an encouraging manner.

The two men greeted the ladies courteously, Lady FitzGeorge ascertained that they had been introduced to Josephine, and then she said, "How pleasant to see you two gentlemen. Would you care to join us?"

The men were agreeable, and dismounted and went to stand by the railing of the park, as was customary. Lady FitzGeorge said, "Oh, fie on all of that distant gallantry, come sit by me. If you two gentlemen behave yourselves, I may share my *pâte de guimauve de cerise*."

With evident pleasure the two young men climbed up into the landau. Lord Trevor immediately sat down, grinning. "And so the precondition for sharing your marshmallow cherry confection is that we must behave ourselves? That's an onerous burden, my lady."

"For you, certainly. Mr. Aldington, why do you hesitate? Please sit down."

Denys Aldington said with some distress, "But my lady, I fear I'll muss your dress, the seating is so close."

"Mr. Aldington, I was just remarking that *pâte de guimauve de cerise* is quite sticky, and as you see, I've removed my gloves and my fingers are coated with it. It's quite impossible for me to arrange my skirt. You have my permission to do so," she said, her eyes alight.

He managed a quite elegant bow, given the circumstances. Very gently he took a fold of Lady FitzGeorge's skirt between his thumb and forefinger and moved it aside, then sat down.

Lady FitzGeorge said, "Now I've done it, I see. I was worried about shocking Miss Rosborough, but instead I've quite flummoxed poor Mr. Aldington."

"Not at all, my lady," he said gamely. "Since I had your gracious permission, I was happy to rescue your lovely gown from a muss. I remain your obedient servant, ma'am."

"The perfect courtier," Lady FitzGeorge said. "Please have a confection. We were just speaking of Lady Mirabella's birthday ball. I'm sure you gentlemen are invited, you always are."

"We are, and as always, I'm flattered to be included on such an exclusive guest list, to one of the premier delights of the Season," Lord Trevor said, making a mock bow to Mirabella.

"You all know very well that I don't limit the guest list simply to assume an air of haughty exclusivity," Mirabella said firmly. "It's just that our ballroom only holds one hundred comfortably. I refuse to have one of those routs that are so packed full that one can barely dance."

"They are crashing bores, aren't they?" Lord Trevor agreed. "But I've noted that getting two dances from you, Lady Mirabella, rarely happens at your ball, as I know the gentlemen make their requests as you greet them, the greedy dogs. I'm going to upstage them this year, however, and request here and now the honor of the opening quadrille and the first waltz."

"Sir, how presumptuous you are!" Mirabella said, her eyes dancing. "Requesting dances nine days ahead of a ball!"

Lady FitzGeorge said merrily, "I find it daring, and admire his pluck, Mirabella. Surely you can't refuse such a charming request."

With an appearance of reluctance Mirabella said, "No, I suppose I cannot. Yes, Lord Trevor, you may have the quadrille and the first waltz."

Mr. Aldington said ruefully, "It is genius, Brydges, I wish I'd thought of it first. However, I shall risk being thought a sad mime, and ask all three of you ladies for the honor of two dances at Lady Mirabella's ball."

With amusement the ladies agreed. Mirabella said, "I confess I'm surprised that you don't request the waltz, Mr. Aldington, it's all the rage, and seems to be the first choice of gentlemen. Now that I think of it, I don't believe I've seen you waltz. Is it possible that you haven't yet mastered it?"

Mr. Aldington began to answer, but Lord Trevor, with a devilish air, said, "Oh, he can waltz very well, we all learned it in Vienna. But some people, in particular Lord Byron, have said that it shouldn't be danced in polite English society. He maintains that it's scandalous for couples to embrace in public."

Aldington rasped, "Brydges, at times you go too far. My ladies, Miss Rosborough, I assure you that I think no ill, at all, of anyone who chooses to waltz. He exaggerates, I do not waltz well, I find I'm as awkward as a goat when I attempt it, therefore I save myself from the humiliation."

Mirabella said, "It's really quite all right, Mr. Aldington, we know you would never say the least thing to offend. I myself had conflicting feelings about it when I first learned. In truth, I believe I blurted out the identical phrase that Lord Byron used. I'm amazed that he and I should agree on such a matter."

Mr. Aldington said quietly, "I know that he has a scandalous reputation, but not all of that is his fault, you know. He does possess a great sense of propriety, particularly regarding ladies."

Lady FitzGeorge laughed, a low, throaty sound. "So he does, in public. In private I hear he's not so fastidious."

Mr. Aldington looked slightly distressed but didn't respond. Lord Trevor said lightly, "Oh, Byron's all right, he just has a tendency for dramatics, from one extreme to the other, and he gets entangled, shall we say. I feel some sympathy for him, he's fairly hiding from Lady Caroline Lamb. Her insane antics have reflected, perhaps unfairly, on him."

"Yes, they have," Mr. Aldington readily agreed.

"I suppose he can't be blamed that she fell so rabidly in love with him that their estrangement made her stark barking mad," Lady FitzGeorge said acidly. "That is, except for the part about him making her fall in love with him."

Lord Trevor said, "Our merry party is deteriorating into melancholy, which would suit Byron but does not suit me. Lady Mirabella, by chance are you going to eat all of your macaroons? Since Lady FitzGeorge hasn't seen fit to offer her marshmallow cherry paste, I would be obliged if you would be so generous as to share with me."

"Don't you dare, Mirabella, I did place a precondition on sharing with him," Lady FitzGeorge warned. "And he's been most impertinent."

"So sorry, Rosalind," Mirabella said sweetly, "but I find his request daring, and I admire his pluck. Lord Trevor, you may come sit by me and share my macaroons."

He did so with great enthusiasm, and the ladies exchanged amused glances.

But Mr. Denys Aldington looked wistful, perhaps even doleful. Mirabella thought that she knew the reason why, and felt sorry for him.

But she was wrong.

Chapter Ten

Mirabella and Josephine had another most congenial night at Almack's, and arrived home at three o'clock in the morning. As they were going upstairs Mirabella asked, "Dearest, are you fatigued? Do you wish to retire?"

"No, not at all. Shall I come to your room?"

"Yes, as soon as you're undressed, I'll send Colette to you first, it takes me so much longer because she has to do my hair."

Soon the girls were making themselves comfortable in Mirabella's bedroom. Mirabella said with disdain, "You are so fortunate to have such glorious hair. I despise wearing these curling rags, they look positively ludicrous."

"No one sees you in them except me and Colette and we don't think you look ludicrous."

"Still, I can't bear to look in the mirror when I'm all tied up. In fact, one of them on the back of my head is much too tight, will you help me find the particular demon and loosen it?" This took no little time, for Colette was very conscientious in using dozens of the rags to form the wispy little Grecian curls that Mirabella favored. Finally the offending rag was located and loosened. Mirabella said, "There, I already have the beginnings of a headache. Would you share a glass of ratafia with me?"

"That sounds inviting, after Almack's abysmal lemonade."

"Madame Danton has created a new recipe, it's plum, and it's heavenly. And it seems to me it also soothes me to sleep better than the orange ratafia," Mirabella said as she poured them two small glasses. As Mirabella had only one recamier in her bedroom, it was the custom of the girls to settle on her four-poster bed, sitting up with piles of fluffy pillows behind them.

"And so? What did you think of the evening?" Mirabella asked.

"It was diverting, as always," Josephine answered, her eyes bright. "Do you know, Mirabella, even though I've been accepted into the highest circles of society, I know I'm still an outsider. Please don't think I'm complaining, I would never. As a matter of fact, I find it entertaining to stand aside, as it were, and observe."

"Observe how? Observe what?" Mirabella asked curiously.

"The people. The undercurrents. The nuances."

"Explain, please. With anecdotes."

"For instance, I found it interesting to see the open friction between Lady FitzGeorge and her stepdaughters. Of course that situation must always be awkward, with the stepmother only a year or two older than her stepdaughters. Or is Lady Chandos actually older than Lady FitzGeorge?"

"She is, by a year. Lord FitzGeorge married Rosalind five years ago, when she was seventeen and he was in his late fifties, his second marriage, of course. He'd been widowed for fifteen years. He was always in ill health, and died of the pneumonia."

"I like Lady FitzGeorge, she's vivacious and spirited. It's difficult to imagine her being married to a much older, frail man."

"Mm, I've found her much altered this Season. It was an arranged marriage, of course. Rosalind's family was penniless, but both of her parents were grandchildren of earls, and well connected. Lord FitzGeorge apparently was utterly bewitched by her, and took very good care of her and provided generously for her family. They appeared to do very well together. Rosalind seemed content."

"I see," Josephine said thoughtfully. "I've learned that in your circles arranged marriages are very common, but I find it odd that they can be so successful. This is the first time I've seen Lord and Lady Jersey together, and they appear to be very devoted. It's the same with Lord and Lady Cowper, their mutual affection and warmth is obvious. But surely he knows of her affair with Lord Palmerston."

"Of course he does. I've thought much about such things myself. I've come to the conclusion that an arranged marriage is as likely to be a good marriage as one resulting from supposed helpless, breathless love," Mirabella said with some disdain. "Look at Caroline Lamb. When she married Mr. Lamb in 1805, they were so deeply in love they were almost oblivious to anyone else in the world, and they remained that way until last year, when Byron burst onto the scene, and oh my, again Caro is overcome with romantic love."

"But surely, dearest, Lady Caroline has a tendency toward mental illness," Josephine said.

Mirabella shrugged. "I could give you another dozen examples of both men and women who've made fools of themselves, and utterly wrecked their lives, by falling in and out and in and out of love. I've come to the conclusion that it's usually a fallacy, all this complicated tangle of starry-eyed enchantment."

Hesitantly Josephine said, "Surely you haven't always had this rather cold-blooded view."

Mirabella looked straight at her. "You're speaking of Captain Pryce. It's quite all right, it's of no consequence. 'When I was a child, I spake as a child, I understood as a child, I thought as a child: but when I became a man, I put away childish things.' Now

I understand that it's much simpler if two mature, clear-minded people decide to make a good marriage, commit to it, and get on with their lives together."

"Mirabella, you cannot mean that you don't believe that people meet, fall in love, get married, and maintain that love all of their lives."

"I believe that some few, some very few do. But it's not meant for everyone."

Josephine sighed. "I'm not sure if I agree with you, not completely. But I won't argue with you."

"How glad I am to hear it! In my mind I've gnawed away at stupid romantic love for so long that now I find it quite tiresome. Let's talk of something fun."

"Very well. Of what particular fun shall we speak?"

Mirabella's eyes sparkled. "Of this one. I've come to a decision. No, no, that's not right. I've come to a decision to make a decision."

"Why, yes, this sounds a merry topic indeed," Josephine said sardonically. "The process of decision-making."

"Oh, you may be as droll as you like. What I mean is, there are three gentlemen that particularly interest me, and I want you to help me assess them. I value your opinion extremely."

Josephine rolled her eyes. "You make it sound like choosing a fabric for a gown. No, no, don't fuss, I apologize, I said I wouldn't argue with you any more. Who are these three extremely fortunate gentlemen?"

"Lord Trevor Brydges, Denys Aldington, and Lord Southam."

"Truly? I mean, I have discerned a certain attraction between you and Lord Trevor. But Mr. Aldington and Lord Southam I find somewhat surprising."

Mirabella nodded and said eagerly, "That's because you aren't acquainted with all of the particulars of each gentleman yet, and that's why I want you to help me assess them. You yourself said you enjoy impartial observation."

"One half of my mind says this must be the most preposterous conversation I've ever had, and the other half tells me I shouldn't be at all surprised because it's with you. Please proceed. How may I be of assistance?"

"I'd like to discuss the benefits and drawbacks of each gentleman. In fact, let's be organized with it. Come over and sit at my secretary, and here are three papers. On the first one, entitle it 'Viscount Southam,' and make two columns, *pro et contra*."

Josephine wrote, murmuring, "For and against."

Pacing behind Josephine's chair, Mirabella said, "Now for the advantages of marriage to Lord Southam. He has already inherited his title. I'm fairly certain that his income is twenty thousand pounds or more per annum. He has a magnificent estate in Hertfordshire, and that's close to Camarden. My children will be 'the Honourable Firstname Wetherley,' and when my eldest son inherits, of course he'll be Viscount Southam."

Josephine finished writing, then said, "Darling, I am not arguing, I promise. It's just difficult for me to understand this—this callous calculation."

Coolly Mirabella said, "We spoke of arranged marriages before. Believe me, this is exactly how parents weigh potential suitors for their daughters."

"By making charts?"

"Oh, do be quiet. Now, add to the *pro*: I believe my parents would approve, he cuts a very manly figure and is always exquisitely tailored, and I'm fascinated by his mouth."

"His mouth! Have you kissed him?"

"Certainly not!" Mirabella said indignantly. Then slyly she added, "I have thought of it, however. Oh, don't look so shocked, we both know that physical attraction is an imperative, one can hardly contemplate marrying a troll, no matter how amiable. And I find his person, and his mouth, attractive."

"Mirabella, you are outrageous!"

"Only in private, with friends. Now for the *contra*. I'm unsure whether he is attracted to me. He's somewhat aloof. In point of fact, he's rather a mystery to me, he always has been."

"Yes, that's why I was surprised to hear that you were seriously contemplating him. I hadn't observed him dancing attendance on you as so many of the young gentlemen have been doing."

"No, he hasn't been, and never has. But when he is with me, he makes it seem personal, not just a display of charm and gallantry to a lady. I find it intriguing."

Josephine knowingly said, "I think what you find intriguing is that he isn't pursuing you, and perhaps that may be quite clever of him. He seems to me to be an intelligent man."

"There, you see! That's precisely why I wanted you to help me. So, hm, put in both columns that I find him mysterious. In time I shall discern which it is, for or against. Now, I believe that finishes Lord Southam. Let's proceed to Lord Trevor Brydges."

"Lord Trevor, *pro et contra*. I believe even I might be able to fill in the first *pro*."

"Yes? Go on."

"I think he's possibly the handsomest—no, that's not apt at all. He's certainly not the conventional ideal of a handsome man. He's—rough-hewn, knife-edged, with a sort of blatant masculinity that would affect any woman. At least, that is the *pro* for the factor of physical attraction."

"Oh, no, please don't tell me I'm going to be forced to compete with you for Lord Trevor's attentions."

"Of course not, you great ninny, it would drive me to distraction to be around a man like him all of the time, I'd always be afraid he was going to dash off to fight duels or kill bears or something. I know, however, that you're sure to find him exciting."

"So I do. And diverting, and entertaining, and amusing. Write all of that down. Mm, let me think . . . what else? Although he is the second son, his financial condition seems to be assured, for the Marquess of Levenden is extremely wealthy. I think that he has three or four estates; if I should decide to seriously consider him, I shall have Pappa find out if they are all entailed, or if one of them may come to Lord Trevor. At any rate, put that down as a pro."

Faithfully Josephine recorded Lord Trevor's benefits. "What more? Any certain feature, such as Lord Southam's mouth?"

"No, for Lord Trevor you may write, 'All of his features, from his face to his muscular calves,'" Mirabella replied, and both girls giggled. She continued, "One thing we should add in his favor. Giles thinks very highly of him. They went to Eton and then Oxford together, you know, and so have been friends since childhood."

"Now that is interesting," Josephine said under her breath.

"I beg your pardon?"

"Nothing, I was just muttering as I scribble."

"Oh. So, now for the drawbacks of marrying Lord Trevor. His financial condition, in the future, is also a contra. I have no idea if he has some sort of life benefit, or if he'll be dependent upon his brother, the Earl of Stowe, when Lord Levenden dies and Lord Stowe inherits. Again, that's something Pappa could find out for me, it's generally complicated, with younger sons."

"Younger sons," Josephine repeated, then said, "Oh dear, Mirabella, if you marry him should I have to call you Lady Trevor? I don't think I could ever become accustomed to that, it would make you seem like a stranger."

Mirabella was amused. "Whyever should that be? I'll still be me, and we'll still be fast friends, no matter what I'm called. Actually, the answer is no, I should still be styled Lady Mirabella Brydges."

"But I thought that the wives of younger sons of marquesses and dukes were styled 'Lady Firstname' of the younger son."

"The order of precedence dictates that the daughters of marquesses and dukes are accorded the rank of the eldest son. Since I rank as highly as Philip, I actually outrank Lord Trevor, who is a younger son of a marquess, and I shall retain my courtesy title."

Bewildered, Josephine asked, "But then—doesn't that mean that if you marry Lord Southam, you can still retain your much higher rank in the order of precedence?"

"No, if I marry anyone below the rank of marquess, that is an earl, viscount, or baron, upon my marriage I must take on their rank, and title. It's only if you marry sort of—horizontally, if you will, that I may retain Philip's rank."

"Good heavens, Mirabella, you people have the murkiest and most indecipherable rules, it's a seven days' wonder that anyone, in particular commoners, can ever fathom them."

Mirabella smiled. "My grandfather, and now my father, says that down through the centuries the nobility have designed it precisely that way, in order to keep our society completely separated from the lower classes. I think they're right, and I share their disdain. All of our heads are so stuffed with meaningless trivial minutiae that it's a wonder we ever learn to read and write. Now, for children. Since Lord Trevor is a younger son, they will be commoners."

"So that is a contra."

Mirabella shrugged carelessly. "I suppose. But they will have their lineage, and that will assure them a place in society, so put 'lineage' on the pro side."

Josephine looked up to study her. "This really is not of much consequence to you, is it?"

"No, it's not. When I was younger, my father used to often quote to me: 'Favor is deceitful, and beauty is vain.' I used to hate it when he did, but now that I've gotten older I've come to see the truth of it. Privilege accorded to you simply by your birth is nothing to be proud of. Beauty fades, and the admiration you receive when you're young is meaningless." She smiled slyly, "Of course it's rather nice all the same."

"Mirabella!"

"You know it as well as do I, admit it."

Wryly Josephine said, "All right, I admit that pleasing physical features are nicer than looking like a troll. Are we finished with Lord Trevor?"

"Hm, yes, I believe we are. On to Mr. Aldington. The heading is 'The Honourable Denys Aldington.' He is the heir to Baron Aldington, and so one day will be Lord Aldington. My children will be 'the Honourables,' and my eldest son will one day be Lord Aldington. The Aldington estate, I believe, is around ten or twelve thousand pounds per annum, perfectly adequate. In fact, I've visited Harpendon House, and it's a gracious, sizable manor house. Oh, and also put down as a pro that they have generous succession greenhouses, five I believe, and a lovely conservatory that could easily be expanded."

With amusement Josephine said, "And so we like Mr. Aldington for his conservatory? I'm not at all surprised, about that at least. But Mirabella, I am a little puzzled, for Mr. Aldington doesn't seem to me to be the kind of man who would attract you. His air is, I don't know, somewhat withdrawn and even melancholy."

"I've seen that in the last weeks. I can assure you that he wasn't always so somber. In fact, even last Season he was actually a jolly, easygoing gentleman. But I think that there may be a reason for his change of countenance. You see, his only sibling is a sister, and I think now she must be about twelve years old. She was born mentally defective, and she has severe fits. It's so tragic, they have a terrible time trying to feed her and get her to drink. But the family has never put her in an asylum, they've always taken excellent care of her, Denys included. They had always even brought her to London during the Season, along with her nurses. But I've noticed this year that Lady Aldington didn't come to Town, and it may be that little Charlotte's condition has worsened. I've wondered if that might account for Denys's somberness this Season."

"I see, it's always so heartbreaking to see afflicted children, or adults, for that matter. The Aldingtons have made great sacrifices, and I admire them for it. So you've met the girl? Charlotte?"

A dreamy, pensive sort of look came over Mirabella's face. "Yes, I have, last summer when we were invited to Harpendon House for two weeks. Normally they keep her hidden away, she's quite pitiful. But I noted that Denys would often disappear in the afternoons, and one day as I was walking in their gardens I came upon them. He took her for walks in her wheeled chair, you see. He wasn't at all upset that I saw them, in fact he said that he was glad to introduce her to me. After that I often went with them."

Quietly Josephine said, "I had no idea that you knew him so well. Now I can see exactly what is in your mind. To be sure, such a man would make a fine husband and father."

"Precisely. And also, were you aware that he, along with Lord Trevor Brydges, was with Giles on their Grand Tour? Yes, the three of them were so close that they decided to tour together. When Giles received word of his father's death, Denys insisted on returning home with him. He did return to Florence after Sir Edwin's funeral, but still, it shows a devotion and loyalty to a friend that is rare."

"That is so true, and admirable. I know now that I must add Giles's approval to Mr. Aldington's *pros*, perhaps doubled."

Mirabella smiled. "Certainly. Now for the physical attraction component. Denys is handsome, in that sort of sensitive, expressive manner of some men. His features are, perhaps, unremarkable in themselves, but you must admit that his eyes are so eloquent, not to mention well shaped. And he does have such divine eyelashes, any woman would envy him."

"'Eloquent, well-shaped, divine eyelashes,'" Josephine murmured. "And his physique is admirable, too. He doesn't have the rakish air of a sportsman, but he must exercise in some manner."

"As I said, this rather doleful, distant air isn't like him at all. He is a sportsman, and he boxes and fences. He's also known as a fine horseman, and a good whip hand."

Josephine said ruefully, "So my impartial judgment of Mr. Aldington was utterly incorrect. I thought my instincts were infallible."

"You did no such thing, you're one of the most level-headed, insightful persons I've ever known. Now, I think we've finished our charts, as you so impertinently named them, for this evening at least. I can hardly believe it, but I'm feeling sleepy. We have another week to do further assessments. As I said, I've come to a decision to make a decision, and I intend, at my birthday ball, to decide which of the three I shall consider most seriously."

"I, too, am feeling fatigued, and I must say that the plum ratafia has definite soporific qualities," Josephine said, stifling a yawn. "But please, may I ask you one last question?"

"Of course."

"Do you—how are you envisioning, in your mind, what your marriage to these men would be like?"

Lightly Mirabella replied, "I've been envisioning marriage for at least a year now. I see a comfortable home, extensive gardens, and children, two boys and two girls."

"And you are going to arrange that, also? In what order, pray?"

"Josephine, I think I've had a bad effect on you, you're much more satiric than you used to be. Boy-girl-boy-girl, if you must know. As for my devoted husband, he has never had a face. Soon I hope to supply one."

"You will let me know, will you not? Naturally I'm curious."

Mirabella hugged her. "Of course, darling. We shall convene another assessment meeting. When I'll know who will be the first to be judged."

Chapter Eleven

On the morning of her birthday, Mirabella awoke early and couldn't go back to sleep, she was so excited. Refusing her usual tea and toast in bed, she dressed and went down to have breakfast with her parents in the garden loggia.

"Good morning, Mamma, Pappa," she said cheerily, going to the sideboard to see the delectable breakfast dishes. "A very happy birthday to me, and I wish myself many happy returns of the day. I'm now officially twenty-two years old, and I don't feel any older than I did yesterday."

"You don't behave much older than you did four years ago," Lord Camarden said affectionately. "Before you breakfast, Mirabella, please sit down. Your mother and I have a gift for you."

Mirabella smiled. "I thought you might, but I didn't like to ask."

"Whyever not?" Lady Camarden said. "You don't mind asking at Christmas."

Lord Camarden said, "Matthew, bring Lady Mirabella's gift."

The footman went into the house and returned with Mirabella's gift on a silver platter. As soon as she saw the sky-blue velvet box, Mirabella knew what it was, and she gasped. Matthew set it down in front of her. Slowly Mirabella opened the box. It was the sapphire-and-diamond parure. "Oh, Mamma, Pappa, how could you? It's—I would never think of a gift that is so costly."

"So it was," Lord Camarden said. "Audrey told me you said I'd have an apoplexy, and I very nearly did. But when I saw it, I could see how it suited you, and that it would make you happy. That's exactly what we want."

"I am happy, I'm so fortunate, I'm so grateful," she said in a low voice. A small card was in the box, and Mirabella unfolded it. In her mother's beautiful hand was written the text of Proverbs 31:29. "Many daughters have done virtuously, but thou excellest them all."

Every year her parents gave her a card with this verse, and every year it brought her to tears. She looked up, her eyes luminous and shimmering. "I thank God for you every day," she said softly. "If there is any virtue in me, it's because of the Lord, and because of you and the godly home you've given me. Thank you, with all of my love."

"You're very welcome, Mirabella," her father said, smiling. "Now that's done, you may have breakfast and I shall return to the *Times*."

"No, there's something I must do first," she said as she half-ran back into the house. Soon she returned wearing the necklace, the earrings, and even the tiara. She looked absurdly childlike with her simply braided hair and her plain white morning dress. "I'm going to wear them all day!" she said gleefully.

"Yes, they're so appropriate for day wear," Lady Camarden said caustically. "The servants are going to be scandalized."

"Colette already said that I'm *fou comme un lièvre Mars*," Mirabella said. At the puzzled look on her mother's face, she translated, "As mad as a March hare. She thought I didn't hear her, but I did. I always do. But I don't care in the least, I'm going to wear these all day and all night, for my ball. I may even sleep in them."

"That will assuredly guarantee insomnia," Lady Camarden said.

Soon Lord Camarden took his leave. Josephine came down before Mirabella had finished her breakfast. When she saw Mirabella, she stopped and her eyes widened. "Well, good morning, Your Majesty. I perceive you're already having a happy birthday."

"Indeed I am. Oh, we've so much to do, Josephine, you simply must hurry your breakfast. The flowers will be here any time now, and the floral experts."

Mirabella always insisted on having fresh flower arrangements on the day of her ball. She was so obsessive about the flowers, it had frustrated her no end to try to attend to all of them in one day. Three years previously, when she was visiting the Summer Exhibition at the Royal Academy of Arts, it had occurred to her to question the president and acclaimed artist Benjamin West. She asked who did the floral and fruit arrangements that the artists used for their models. He told her that the Academy always had three or four talented student artists who were skilled in landscaping the backgrounds and creating the model floral arrangements. Since then Mirabella had hired these artists to do the arrangements for her ball.

Lady Camarden said, "Mirabella, don't be selfish. Josephine may not want to spend her entire day harassing those poor young men who try to please you with their arrangements. Josephine, I'm going shopping with Lady Sefton. Would you like to accompany me?"

Josephine glanced at Mirabella, who promptly said, "Of course it's all right, Josephine, I'm perfectly capable of persecuting the florists all by myself. I'd likely forget about you anyway."

Irby came out to the loggia to somberly announce, "My lady, the flowers have arrived. They are bringing them in now. Would your ladyship prefer to supervise how they are to be distributed?"

"Good heavens, no, Lady Mirabella will attend to it," Lady Camarden said. "My intention is to stay out of her way."

"Mamma, may I—" Mirabella said, hurriedly rising from her chair.

"You're excused."

She ran into the house.

Two enormous cartloads of flowers of every description were being taken into the dining room by porters. Mirabella inspected virtually every blossom and leaf, and found them acceptable. The three young men from the Royal Academy arrived, and Mirabella did indeed spend the next several hours supervising them so minutely that the poor beleaguered artists often simply stood by and handed the flowers and greenery to Mirabella to arrange them as she pleased.

Twelve dining tables, each big enough for ten people, had been placed in the dining room. Just as they were finishing the floral arrangements, the footmen came in to place the cloths and set the tables with fine Sèvres china, gleaming polished silver, and crystal wineglasses. The fruit centerpieces for the dining tables still had to be done, but Mirabella realized that she was fatigued. Reluctantly she left the fruits for the artists and went out to the garden to have tea. Seven wrought iron tables, each seating two, surrounded the fountain, and wearily Mirabella sat down at one of them, grateful for the warm afternoon sun. In her excitement she had forgotten to put on an apron, and the front of her dress had gotten damp, as was inevitable when one was arranging flowers in water. She was slightly chilled.

A footman brought her tea, and it was scanty, with only one plate of biscuits. Mirabella wasn't at all surprised. She knew the kitchen must be absolute bedlam. Six cooks had been hired to assist Monsieur and Madame Danton. Mirabella smiled as she thought to herself that her harassment of the florists had likely been mild indeed compared to what those unfortunate cooks must be enduring.

Giles came into the garden, holding a parcel, and sat down with her. He eyed her fine jewels and her damp soiled dress and grinned. "You look just like when you were five years old and played costumes with your mother's jewelry. It's really adorable."

"Thank you so much, sir, every woman loves to hear that she looks like a cute little puppy. Tea? Thomas, bring another teacup."

"I have a gift for you," he said, and handed her the parcel.

Mirabella unwrapped it and said with delight, "*Pride and Prejudice*, thank you, Giles. I'm certain we'll love it, we enjoyed *Sense and Sensibility* so much."

"I haven't read it yet, so I'll ask you to return it to me when you've finished it."

"I most certainly will not. Get your own copy, I have no intention of giving my birthday gift back to you. I never ask you to return books I give you."

"That's because you only give me the ones you despise. And so, it's your birthday. I like your birthday, because it means you're an older woman, and I find older women intriguing."

"Silly man, you know I'm only older than you for three months. And I do not see that you find older women at all intriguing, I've noted that you've been paying particular attentions to Lady Margaret FitzGeorge, and she's barely seventeen, for shame."

"I'm not such a doddering ancient that I can't dance with seventeen-year-old girls. Are you jealous?" he asked slyly.

"What! Certainly not!" she indignantly exclaimed.

"I meant of her youth, since you're now an older woman."

"'Oh! it gives me the hydrostatics to such a degree,'" Mirabella said, her eyes dancing.

"'Since you desire it, we will not anticipate the past,'" Giles quoted. "However, I shall precipitate the future for the ball tonight. I haven't been able to waltz with you yet, so I demand a waltz. I know that you'd rather be publicly embracing other men, but you owe me for my masterful instruction."

"Perhaps I should simply pay you so that I'll be free to embrace other men," Mirabella said icily.

Giles shook his head. "No, that will not do, I won't accept filthy lucre for my dance tutelage."

"Very well, you may blackmail me for a waltz."

Giles's expression grew thoughtful. "The custom is to wish you a happy birthday, and many happy returns of the day. And so, Bella—are you happy?"

Mirabella was surprised. "Am I happy? Of course I'm happy. Why shouldn't I be?"

He searched her face carefully. "I was just asking. I want you to be happy, Bella."

"Well, you may rest assured that I am. Giles, is something amiss?" she asked with a hint of anxiety. "You sound, I don't know, distant."

He rose, smiled down at her, and warmly said, "No, nothing's wrong, at all. I'll see you tonight. Don't forget my waltz."

Lord and Lady Camarden and Mirabella greeted their guests in the entrance hall. At first there was only a trickle of early arrivals, but precisely at nine o'clock the hall grew quite crowded. Still, it didn't stop four young men, including Harry Smythe, from importuning Mirabella for dances; Lord Trevor Brydges and

Denys Aldington had already strictly reminded her that they had precedence. Mirabella was chagrined to realize that all of her waltzes were taken and Lord Southam had not yet arrived. Even as she cordially greeted her guests, she reflected that Lord Southam rarely danced country dances, and she grew slightly anxious that he might not stand up with her tonight.

Lady Caroline Lamb arrived with her husband, the Honourable William Lamb. Mr. Lamb was a fine-looking man, although these days he was always grave. Lady Caroline had once been accounted a great beauty, with lustrous dark eyes and a wealth of curly hair, but in the last year she had deteriorated. She was so thin as to be skeletal, and her eyes were wide and staring, and darted about constantly. Mirabella had barely curtsied to her when Lady Caroline grabbed her shoulders, pulled her close, and in a desperate whisper asked, "Did you invite him?"

Gently Mirabella said, "No, Caro, I'm sorry, but I don't know him at all. I've only spoken to him once in my entire life."

Lady Caroline sighed, a trembling indrawn breath. Without another word she took her husband's arm and they went up the staircase.

Lord Southam was one of the last to arrive. Mirabella thought he looked extremely handsome in his finely tailored black coat and superbly tied white cravat, and of course his muscular legs were always shown to advantage in white stockings. His own dark eyes grew warm with appreciation as he greeted her. "Lady Mirabella, you are glowing with a beauty that even overshadows those exquisite sapphires. Every woman here will be envious."

"You grossly exaggerate, sir," Mirabella said, blushing a little, "but I forgive you, and welcome you."

To her disappointment he merely smiled and went up the staircase.

Mirabella did indeed look dazzling. When she had finished

dressing, she realized that her sapphires were exactly the color of her dress, and in fact, both matched her eyes perfectly. On this night her eyes were almost as brilliant as her jewels.

As soon as all the guests had arrived, Mirabella went upstairs. The ballroom was expansive, spanning the width of the house. It had a marble floor and delicate sage-green-and-white wallpaper, and double French doors at each end opened to balconies overlooking Grosvenor Square in the front and the garden at the back. Two large crystal-and-gold chandeliers lit the room, and along the walls all the sconces were backed by mirrors that added to the brilliance.

Mirabella easily saw Lord Southam, as he was taller than most of the men in the room. He was talking to Lord and Lady Jersey, and Lady Jersey stopped in the middle of a sentence to greet Mirabella. "Darling, I'm absolutely livid with jealousy, you look so smashing tonight, and those jewels! Why, they must be worth a king's ransom, wherever did you get them and more importantly, how much did they cost?"

Mirabella smiled. "They are a birthday gift from my parents, and so I'm afraid you must inquire of them about the cost, as it would be ill-mannered of me to discuss it."

The Earl of the Island of Jersey was an aristocratic-looking man, with fine features. In contrast to his wife, he had a no-nonsense manner and a rapier-sharp wit. He said, "As if Sally would note ill manners, unless it's someone she doesn't like, and she likes you, Lady Mirabella. I'm sure she won't press you, at any rate, for we all know she'll go to—was it Jeffrey's? Rundell & Bridge? She'll be there tomorrow, nagging John Bridge until he tells her down to the ha'pence how much your jewels cost."

"Jersey, I'm standing right here," Lady Jersey said, but with no sign of animosity. "He will speak of me in third person, which drives me to distraction, and he knows it very well. There, now I've repaid him in kind. Mirabella, have you heard the latest of

Caro? Yesterday the mad little fool dressed up as a messenger boy and went to the Albany and tried to get in to see Byron. It caused quite a scene, I understand, and finally they sent to Lamb to come fetch her. I'm surprised to see her here tonight after all that bedlam." Her eyes gleamed with mischief. "I don't suppose you invited Byron, did you?"

"I did not, I'm barely acquainted with the man," Mirabella answered.

Lady Jersey said, "I'm not at all surprised, as Caro so famously said, he is 'mad, bad, and dangerous to know.' I'd wager that she asked you the same question."

"Yes, she did, and she seemed distraught when I told her no."

"Poor Caro, and poor Lamb," Lady Jersey said. "Come, Jersey, let's go see if we can cheer them up, so many people are avoiding her she looks stranded." Resignedly Lord Jersey bowed to Mirabella and followed his wife.

Viscount Southam said, "I believe you owe me an apology, Lady Mirabella, for you accused me of gross exaggeration, a vice that I particularly abhor. You witnessed the first sentence from Lady Jersey's lips, that she was lividly jealous of you."

"Good heavens, it's difficult to give much weight to anything that Sally says, the sheer quantity overwhelms you. Still, sir, I ask your pardon for attributing to you such a detestable trait."

"I will forgive you," he said with mock gravity, "if you will grant me the honor of two waltzes."

"I fear you're a trifle late, my waltzes are already claimed," Mirabella said lightly.

"I'm desolate. Here, let me see your dance card. Ah, that devil Brydges, and Knyvet, and that young pup Smythe claimed two?"

"He did specifically ask for them, and I could hardly refuse in the mere anticipation that you might request them."

He said firmly, "I wish you had done. In order to make it up to me, you must grant me the allemande, and this country dance just before supper, and you must also allow me the honor of escorting you to supper."

"Oh, I must do this and I must do that?" Mirabella said, but she smiled. "I warn you, sir, I'm of such an obstinate nature that I rarely do as I'm ordered."

"I beg you, make an exception for me. After all, your offense was grave."

"Very well, I'll make an exception, but just this one time, mind you."

"Just tonight? Then I intend to capitalize on it," he said, and his eyes gleamed. "You must also allow me the pleasure of dancing *La Boulanger* at the end of the night."

Mirabella's eyes widened. "That's entirely too much capitalization, sir! You know very well that I daren't dance three times with a gentleman unless I'm engaged to him."

Coolly he said, "Yes, there is that."

Mirabella was utterly nonplussed, and involuntarily she drew in a sharp breath. He watched her with amusement, then said carelessly, "I'll settle for the two dances, and supper, but just this one time. Your servant, madam." He bowed and walked away.

In confusion Mirabella thought, *Whatever did he mean by that? That he would only dance waltzes with me from here on out? Surely he couldn't have meant that he would start demanding three dances, that's awful! Isn't it?* Mirabella reflected that Lord Southam was high-handed, but she had to admit to herself that it thrilled her a little. She enjoyed matching wits with him, although, she thought ruefully, it seemed that she never came off as well as he did.

Coming out of her reverie, she grew mindful of her duties as a hostess and circulated around the crowd, speaking to several people. At length she found Josephine and Giles, who were talking with Barbara and Harry Smythe. Josephine looked lovely in an emerald-green satin gown, and as always, Mirabella noted that Lewin did not look at all absurd in his stockings and pumps, as he had an athlete's physique. She said, "Josephine, Barbara, I hope you've found plenty of partners. In truth, it's so difficult to arrange for enough eligible young men, sometimes I despair that so much of the guest list must be taken up by chaperones."

"Perhaps next year you might ask the mothers to form a pool," Barbara said mischievously. "One mamma might sponsor, say, six young ladies."

Mirabella was surprised; normally Barbara said very little, and when she did it was something of an innocuous nature. Then she realized that Mrs. Smythe was nowhere in sight.

Giles said, "I think that's a splendid idea. In fact, why don't we organize it now? Call all of the mammas together, and send five out of six of them home."

"Well, that would certainly assure that my ball would be the most talked-of event of the Season," Mirabella said. "Now here is the quadrille. Where is Lord Trevor? If he leaves me standing for the first dance I'll never forgive him."

"He's right behind you, grinning like a baboon," Giles said.

"I take exception to that, Knyvet, baboons don't grin," Lord Trevor said cheerfully. "Lady Mirabella, surely you know I would never miss a dance with you, they are much too hard to come by. I wish to make you all aware, I was obliged to reserve my two dances nine days in advance. I'm considering making my reservations for next year."

"Such nonsense you do talk," Mirabella said, taking his arm and moving to the dance floor. As they waited, Lord Trevor said, "So I'm often told, but I will say this, and there is nothing nonsensical about it. You are by far the most beautiful lady here. You're always in good looks, Lady Mirabella, but tonight you positively glow as brightly as your jewels."

"I thank you, sir, you are too kind."

The four highest-ranking couples, including Lord and Lady Camarden, performed the first of the set. "Actually, I'm not all that kind, you know. I was merely stating a fact, one with which I'm sure all the men would agree, and the ladies would deny, out of pure envy. Oho, what is this bemused expression on your face, my lady? Someone has anticipated my carefully planned compliment, have they not? It's Southam, I'll wager, blast him, he's as smooth as sweet oil, and just as slippery. Not to worry, I'll think up something more original and spellbinding before the first waltz."

Lord Trevor continued with his outlandish banter during the dance, and Mirabella was vastly amused. She realized, too, that somehow she felt conflicted, because when she considered Lord Trevor and Lord Southam, her impulses of physical attraction seemed virtually indistinguishable. She admired both men's looks, and their unmistakably masculine air. Lord Southam was self-assured, even masterful. Lord Trevor had a certain raw, rough edge that was in no way vulgar. Mirabella found both men exciting.

Mirabella's second dance, a country dance, was with Denys Aldington. It was a lively long dance, with very little opportunity to converse with one's partner. The expression on Aldington's sensitive features was one of polite pleasure, but he had none of the animation that Mirabella recalled from past years. As he took her hand to escort her off the floor, he said, "Lady Mirabella, you are as radiant tonight as starshine. Would you make me the most fortunate man here, and allow me to escort you in to supper?"

"I'm sorry, Mr. Aldington, but Lord Southam has already offered to escort me. There are any number of ladies here who would be glad to accept you, and I hope you will join us at our table."

He sighed. "You are so kind and charming, as always and ever.

I suppose I shall be obliged to settle for a poor second, for no woman can compare to you, ma'am." He bowed and, with a slight squeeze of her hand, left her.

The first waltz was, as solemnly promised, with Lord Trevor, and he was as rakishly charming as ever. "That scoundrel Southam told me that he's taking you in to supper. Blast it all, I should've thought to reserve supper nine days ago," he said with his captivating grin. "All is well, however, for I intend to sit with you and insert myself into your conversation, and if possible monopolize you entirely."

"I'm sure Lord Southam will be vastly intimidated," Mirabella said.

"Oh, yes, certainly, he's so easily daunted. As much as a bull mastiff."

It was difficult to ascertain who was partnered with whom in the long, ever-changing lines of the country dance, but it was easy to see the couples in the waltz. Mirabella had noted that Josephine seemed to be partnered for every dance; with amusement she saw that Lord Palmerston had claimed her first waltz. Giles was waltzing with Barbara Smythe. Later, in the second waltz, which Mirabella had engaged to Harry Smythe, she noted that Giles again danced with Miss Smythe. Barbara was in particularly good looks tonight in her shot silk white gown, Mirabella reflected, and she seemed animated. She also observed that Lord Southam danced the first waltz with Lady Jersey, and the second with Lady Cowper.

He dutifully appeared for the allemande, and as they danced he observed, "Lady Caroline is having the hysterics in the card-room, it's really reprehensible."

"Oh, no," Mirabella moaned. "I was hopeful that she would find the company so congenial that she might enjoy herself. Perhaps Mamma and I should go to her."

"There is no need, Lamb is already preparing to take her home. And I'm sorry, but you are under obligation to me for precisely two dances and supper, and I have no intention of excusing you from either duty."

"It's hardly a burdensome duty, sir," Mirabella said, her eyes brilliant.

They danced again, the last country dance before supper. Mirabella observed that Lord Southam, with his elegant, sophisticated deportment, was ill-suited to the frolicsome long dances.

As he took her arm to escort her down to the dining room, he said, "How relieved I am to be finished with that ordeal. I only endured it for the pleasure of your company."

"You bore it with amazing fortitude, sir. Although you obviously don't enjoy the country dance, you do perform it gracefully."

"Gracefully, I should hope, but I'm always afflicted with the strangest feeling that I'm the only adult dancing with a crowd of children."

Lord and Lady Camarden, followed by Mirabella and Lord Southam, led their guests downstairs to the dining room. As midnight suppers served at balls were so informal, no particular precedence was observed in the procession, and people sat down wherever they liked. The strict protocol restricting conversation solely to one's partner on the left or right did not apply; conversation was general, and couples could converse together without giving offense to their dining partners.

The diners' tables were laden with platters of ham, beef, and veal, sliced paper-thin, with both sweet and savory sauces, salad platters of celery, endive, cucumbers, and pickles, an assortment of cheeses, fresh breads and rolls, and of course a selection of Madame Danton's luscious confections. Mirabella noted that the fruit arrangements looked particularly beautiful, and charitably thought that she could not possibly have done better.

She and Lord Southam seated themselves at a central table. Mirabella was somewhat surprised that he sat down beside her, rather than at the head of the table; she'd had the impression that he was the type of man who would naturally assume the dominant seat. Soon, to her gratification, they were joined by her friends. Harry Smythe escorted Josephine, Giles escorted Barbara Smythe, and at the far end Denys Aldington sat with Lady Margaret FitzGeorge, a rather plain, shy girl. Lord Trevor escorted Rosalind, Lady FitzGeorge. To Mirabella's amusement, he seated Rosalind across from her, and took the seat by her at the head of the table with an impudent wink.

The diners talked among themselves as they filled their plates, but as they began to eat the conversations became more private between the couples. Mirabella saw that Lord Trevor did not come through on his vow to monopolize her; in fact he half-turned away from her and spoke with Rosalind in a low voice. It nettled her, but only slightly, and she gladly turned her full attention to Lord Southam. He asked her about Camarden Court, for he had never visited there. Mirabella described it, and spoke of how happy she was with her long walks, her rides, driving her phaeton all over the countryside, and in particular her conservatory.

"You seem enamored with country life," he said. "It has been my experience that most young ladies regard it as boring and rather stifling."

"I suppose that I have so many varied interests that I'm rarely bored. But surely I must be boring you, with all of my prattling on about Camarden. What about you, sir? I've heard that Wetherley Manor is particularly grand. Do you spend much time there?"

"It is a fine estate, I'm fortunate to have it. But no, I spend very little time there."

With some dismay Mirabella asked, "Then you do not care for country living?"

With a curious half-smile he answered, "I do enjoy country pursuits, such as hunting and shooting and fishing. But I generally spend the fall and winter with friends. I find that entertaining at Wetherley is troublesome, as there is no mistress to provide the ladies with a gracious hostess."

"Yes, I can well understand that giving large house parties would be difficult for a single man. A bachelor's life must be solitary indeed."

"It is. Lately I've been thinking that I should remedy that," he said, staring straight at her. Mirabella could feel her cheeks flush. But as usual, he gave her no opportunity to reflect, or to answer. He went on lightly, "I see that you've finished eating, although you barely ate enough for a bird, as it is with most delicate females. Perhaps I may fetch you an ice?"

"Thank you, I'm longing for a coconut cream ice," Mirabella managed to answer. He rose, bowed, and went to the tables where footmen served the numerous selections of ices, sorbets, cream ices, and cakes.

Lord Trevor rose at the same time and went to the confections table. Rosalind was glowing. "I must say that Lord Trevor is one of the most amusing men I've ever known. He's so handsome, too. But I think your conquest must be equally as enticing. Those broad shoulders!"

"He's not my conquest, Rosalind," Mirabella said. "I hardly know him."

"Obviously he intends to remedy that," she replied with a sly smile. "Do you know, I had a painful crush on him when I was seventeen. Then, when FitzGeorge began to court me, my parents insisted that I'd be a little fool to trade a fabulously wealthy earl for a mere viscount."

Curiously Mirabella asked, "How did you feel about that?"

"Obviously I agreed with them, I married FitzGeorge. But I had very little hope for Southam anyway, he never paid me the slightest bit of mind. I think he prefers ladies with some sophistication about them, and is bored with raw girls just out of the schoolroom. He's quite a catch, Mirabella. You should secure him as quickly as ever you can."

"But I don't—" She broke off when Lord Trevor and Lord Southam returned with the ladies' ices.

As generally happened with late suppers, people began to get up and move around the tables, visiting with friends. Most of the older people retired to the cardroom, and many of the ladies to the drawing room. Mirabella and Lord Southam talked with Rosalind and Lord Trevor for a while. Harry Smythe and Josephine went to speak to Mr. and Mrs. Smythe. Mirabella saw that Giles and Miss Smythe were still deep in conversation and took no note of anyone else. Denys Aldington spoke to Lady Margaret, who kept her eyes downcast and said hardly anything at all. His eyes often rested on Mirabella.

As more and more people began to get up and mill around, Lord Southam said, "Would you do me the honor of taking some air in the garden with me? I find the heat oppressive in here."

"I'd love to get some fresh air," Mirabella gladly replied.

At some houses, couples often met in the secluded gardens for romantic assignations, but such was not so at the Camarden town house. The garden and loggia were well lit by dozens of lanterns, and candles on the dining table and the wrought iron tables. The sideboard held tea, coffee, wine, port, negus, and lemonade, and footmen served the couples enjoying the cool night breeze.

Mirabella and Lord Southam sat down by the fountain, and Mirabella gratefully breathed in the heavily flower-scented air. Occasionally tiny droplets splashed from the fountain and fell on them, and it was refreshing. Lord Southam sat very near to Mirabella, and leaned close. "I'm tempted to keep you here as long as possible, since my time with you tonight is at an end."

"But surely you're not leaving," Mirabella protested.

"No, I'll go to the cardroom, the gaming was excellent until Lady Caroline disrupted everyone with her theatrics."

"You aren't dancing the second set?"

In a low voice he replied, "No, I've danced all I care to this evening, as my favored partner refuses to stand up with me again. I'd very much like to spend more time with you, my lady, instead of here-and-there blurs of waltzes. I know this is very short notice, so it's presumptuous of me, but I have a proposition for you."

Startled, Mirabella blurted, "A what? A proposition?"

He was amused. "Don't be so alarmed, believe me, I have no nefarious intent. No, what I propose is this. On Saturday night there is to be a grand display of fireworks at Vauxhall, and they also have a troop of Chinese acrobats that are said to be so skilled they are almost magical. Would you do me the honor of accompanying me? If you aren't previously engaged, of course."

Mirabella smiled radiantly. "Sir, we are obviously in harmony of mind! We had already planned to attend Vauxhall on Saturday. Perhaps you would join our party?" She faltered at the reluctant look that crossed his features. Uncertainly she said, "But surely you didn't mean—you cannot possibly have intended that I should accompany you alone?"

"Of course not," he said firmly. "Naturally I included Lord and Lady Camarden in my invitation. It's just this notion of a 'party.' I had hoped that we might have an opportunity to be together without hordes of people surrounding us."

"Our party is hardly hordes of people. It's my friends, Sir Giles, Miss Rosborough and Captain Rosborough, and Mr. and Miss Smythe."

"What of Mr. and Mrs. Smythe?" he asked cautiously. "Smythe seems a tolerable sort of man, but I find Mrs. Smythe's company unbearable for more than a few moments."

It occurred to Mirabella that Lord Southam could not be longing for her company very dearly, if he was put off by Mrs. Smythe. Still she answered, "They were included in the invitation, of course. But Mrs. Smythe maintained that my parents, and of course Miss Smythe's brother, would be quite proper chaperones. Mrs. Smythe said that she and Mr. Smythe found the social rounds fatiguing, and would like to spend an evening in quiet at home."

"Is that so? Interesting. So, your party is seven, and with you and me would be nine. May I make a suggestion? My yacht is on the Thames, and it would be a great pleasure if you would allow me to take you all to Vauxhall on Saturday."

"That would be splendid, Lord Southam, I can assure you that all of my party would be so happy to join you."

He picked up her gloved hand and lightly kissed it, a rather bold gesture, but not completely unwelcome to Mirabella. "Then I shall be looking forward to Saturday, madam."

Mirabella didn't see him for the rest of the night.

Giles came to Mirabella for his promised dance, the last waltz. "My lady," he said, bowing over her hand, "at last I can claim you."

"Oh, I'm so glad to see you, Giles," she said happily. "I'm so dreadfully tired, I feel that I'm in that dreamy sort of stupid stage, do you take my meaning? At least with you I can relax, and not feel that I must amuse you with my brilliant wit, or charm you with my ladylike grace."

"You're never obliged to entertain me, but I admit that even when you're dreamy and stupid you're still amusing and charming." He took her in his arms, and they began the elegant, flowing, graceful dance.

Mirabella barely heard him, for she was thinking of what she had just said—*with you I can relax*—and contrasting it with how she'd felt the first time she had waltzed with Giles. Of course it had been her very first waltz, and she had been unaccustomed to men clasping her about the waist, and to dancing close to her while holding hands, and to resting her hand on a man's shoulder. Still, the sensation of touching and being so close to Giles had been wildly uncomfortable, yet she hadn't felt nearly so ill at ease dancing with Lewin only a few minutes later. The raw awareness of, as she had said, "embracing" Giles had lessened with further lessons, but still she was very conscious of his nearness when they waltzed.

What is this, exactly? she mused. *I suppose it's that I've never really been aware of Giles as a man. No, that's silly, of course I know he's a man. I just never have been so conscious of his physical presence, how I can feel the warmth of him, and I've always loved his scent, I wonder what it is, exactly? Something clean and citrusy and spicy, very understated. And his shoulders are muscular, but not bulky, just taut, his chest is broad, his stomach is perfectly flat, and why haven't I ever noticed before how particularly nice his lips are? I noticed Lord Southam's, and surely Giles's lips are just as well-formed, perhaps even more so because they're slightly upturned at the corners, as if he's about to smile . . .*

". . . my mouth?" Giles asked.

"I—I beg your pardon?" Mirabella stammered.

"I asked why you're staring at my mouth. Do I have crumbs, or, heaven save me, a wine mustache?"

"No, no, certainly not, I was just—I was—oh, never mind, as I told you, I'm so fatigued I'm in a staring stupid state. I beg your pardon. What about you? You look as fresh and energetic as when you first arrived, and I've noticed you've danced every dance, too. Aren't you tired?"

"Not really. You have all of the choicest ladies of Town at your ball, every dance is a pleasure."

"'Choicest ladies,'" Mirabella grumbled. "You make it sound like a happy visit to the butcher's."

"How would you know anything about going to the butcher? Your dainty slippers have never graced a butcher's shop in your life."

"Very well, you win. The ladies on my guest list are the choicest in London. I noticed that you must think Barbara Smythe is especially choice, as you danced, in fact waltzed, with her twice. It's really very chivalrous of you."

"Not particularly. She's charming, and a good dancer."

"I know, but most men are so repelled by her mother that they never give her a chance. It's a shame, because she's so sweet, I simply adore her."

"I do, too," Giles said blithely.

"What!" Mirabella made a very slight misstep, and Giles automatically drew her closer to steady her, which for a moment Mirabella enjoyed very much, but it didn't distract her from her shock. "You adore her! What—how can you say that? You barely know her!"

"Actually, I'm getting to know her fairly well. As you say, she's sweet, she's charming, and she can be quite interesting when you have the opportunity—"

"But you can't say you adore her! That's just—just—not right!"

"You said it first."

"But I—but Barbara and I are friends! One might say one adores one's friends without it meaning anything."

"I see. I consider Miss Smythe a friend, too, so therefore I can say I adore her and it actually doesn't mean anything. Also, since I'm your best friend, you must adore me much more than you do Miss Smythe, correct? Even though it really doesn't mean anything, tell me how much you adore me." He was grinning in an infuriating manner.

"Oh! You really are the most tiresome man. If I weren't dancing with you I'd tell you to go away and leave me alone."

"But you are dancing with me. So forget everything and everyone else and just dance with me, Bella." He pulled her even closer, and squeezed her hand, lightly, warmly.

Mirabella found that the last waltz was the best dance of all.

Chapter Twelve

A merry party boarded Lord Southam's yacht, the *Fortuna*, for the crossing to the south side of the Thames to Vauxhall Gardens. The yacht was luxurious, built for comfort and not racing. Since the crossing was so short, no deck chairs had been provided, but the party lined the sides with pleasure, watching the fleet of boats all heading for the Vauxhall water entrance.

Chilled champagne was served in fine crystal flutes. Lord Southam took two glasses and handed one to Mirabella with a small bow. Then he offered her his arm and took her to the prow. The wind was bracing, and warm. As they got farther from the city the air grew cleaner and clearer. Mirabella lifted her face and took a deep breath.

Lord Southam looked down at her with his enigmatic half-smile. "As always, you are lovely this evening, Lady Mirabella. I've heard women complain that such and such shade does not flatter them, but it seems that you can wear any of them and look beautiful."

"I thank you, sir," she said. "I suppose it's because of my coloring. However, I've always said that white does not much flatter me, I look like a ghost. Although it's still so fashionable, this year

I determined I wouldn't wear a white frock, except for my morning robes."

Mirabella's promenade costume was a deep rose color of jaconet muslin, trimmed with a creamy mint green. The high collar was delicate needlework, with three tightly gathered flounces around the hem. The long sleeves were tied with four grosgrain ribbons of green, in the Mameluke style. She wore a mint-green Vittoria cloak, which was short, actually made more like a shawl, trimmed with Spanish fringe. Instead of draping it around her shoulders and arms like a shawl, she wore it gathered and pinned up at her left shoulder by a peridot-and-pearl brooch. The only other jewelry she wore was small peridot drop earrings. Her bonnet was fetching: it was like a full cap, made of the mint-green jaconet, with a small bill. Delicate curls framed her face.

He nodded at the brooch. "I've noticed that you always wear modest jewelry. Your sapphire parure was somewhat of a surprise, but it was small and delicate, which suits you."

"I should look preposterous with extravagant jewels. They would quite overwhelm me, I think."

"I find it amazing that a woman has sensible taste concerning jewelry. Most women's view is that the larger, the more ostentatious, and the more expensive, the better. Do you know, I've been thinking that I have seen some blue diamonds that would become you very well."

"Oh? I don't believe I've ever seen a blue diamond, except the crown jewels, of course. Where did you see them?"

"They were my mother's," he said lightly. "I hadn't seen them for years, as they've been in storage since my mother died eleven years ago. Just last month I sent all her jewelry to be cleaned. I had quite forgotten how exquisite they are. Like you. But see here, I'm neglecting my guests, let's rejoin them."

The crossing was accomplished in a half hour. There was some confusion at the gate, for everyone knew that the admission was three and sixpence. Lord Southam said, "I've already made arrangements for my party, lords, ladies, and gentlemen, so we may go straight through."

They entered into the wide leafy walks, with stately elm, sycamore, and lime trees towering over them. Lord Southam, with Mirabella on his arm, led them straight to the Grove, the large rectangle that held the Temple, a fantastical open-air structure built in the elaborate Moorish style, with much cutwork and topped with spires and pinnacles. The second story held a full orchestra, with a balcony for singers. The orchestra had already started performing, and the gardens were filled with the strains of a Mozart concerto. Already a crowd strolled around, usually couples, most of them finely dressed.

Rows of supper boxes, small open-fronted dining rooms, lined the colonnades and piazzas. Lord Southam had reserved a supper box that directly fronted the Grove. "This is my usual box," he said as the group took their seats at a long table covered with a fine white damask cloth. "I reserve it for the entire evening, so that I and my party may have a comfortable place to rest." Normally the supper boxes were rented by the hour.

As the entire point of having an open-air supper box was to see and be seen, no one wanted to sit with their back to the Grove, so they arranged themselves all along one side of the table. Lord Southam was at the head, Mirabella was by him, then Miss Smythe, Giles, Josephine, Harry Smythe, Lewin, and Lady Camarden, with Lord Camarden at the foot of the table.

"Before we go see the sights, I'd like to invite you to try some of my arrack punch," Lord Southam said. "I mix it myself, with my own recipe, including a secret ingredient that no one has been able to guess. Will you join me?"

They all agreed to partake, and Lord Southam went to a sideboard at the back of the box. An enormous silver bowl held a fragrant clear liquid, and small assorted colored bottles held juices and spices. "This is the true Batavian arrack, fermented from coconuts on the island of Java. One lime and one lemon, very thinly sliced, have been dissolving in it for twelve hours. Now I add sugar syrup, both white and burnt, nutmeg, cinnamon, and my secret ingredient, and stir."

"It sounds delightfully exotic," Mirabella said. "I've never had arrack punch before, I understand it's a heady drink."

"Yes, Batavia arrack is a strong spirit. And the punch is so rich that most people limit their indulgence," Lord Southam said. "Once I had a guest, a lady whose name, of course, I shall never mention, who drank three glasses, and she became somewhat incapacitated. I viewed the entire incident as my personal responsibility, and deeply regretted it. I hope you ladies will understand that I recommend only one small glass."

"Oh? What of the gentlemen?" Mirabella asked. "Do you limit them also?"

"The gentlemen can take care of themselves," Lord Southam said dryly. "But I would not view kindly any man who overindulges in the presence of ladies, as I'm certain every man here feels."

Lewin said, "Then I shall certainly watch my imbibing tonight, my lord. After witnessing your pugilistic skills at Jackson's, I shouldn't want to offend you to the point that you felt bound to challenge me to a boxing duel."

"I've seen you sparring, Captain Rosborough, and I think you would be a worthy opponent," Lord Southam said. "If you like, perhaps I might handicap myself in some manner."

"Unless your lordship tied your hands and feet together, I don't think I'll venture it," Lewin answered.

Giles said, "Perhaps if you were blindfolded also I might take up the challenge. Miss Smythe, do you know of the pugilistic sport?"

"I have heard that it consists of gentleman striking each other, sometimes quite brutally. I fear that I utterly fail to understand the attraction," she said, blushing a little.

Josephine said, "I cannot comprehend it either, Miss Smythe. I think any lady with any sense at all is mystified at the sight."

Barbara's cornflower-blue eyes grew wide and alarmed. "Miss Rosborough, you've actually seen a pugilistic competition?"

"Oh, yes, and so has Lady Mirabella. When we were children, Sir Giles and my brother would mark off a square for a ring and proceed to try to hit each other. It always deteriorated into a pushing and shoving match until one of them fell down."

Lewin said with satisfaction, "I always won. And remember, Josephine, once I did manage to land a good punch and blacked Sir Giles's eye."

Giles said, "That was only because we were both falling down and my face fell on your fist. The hiding my father gave me hurt much more than my black eye."

"Your father punished you for fighting?" Barbara asked.

"No, he punished me for losing," Giles replied. "After that I hadn't much taste for boxing with Lewin."

Harry Smythe said brightly, "For my part, Captain Rosborough, I'd like to try my hand with you. I've been practicing, you know, and I think I could best you."

"I accept the challenge, sir," Lewin said. "Shall we say Monday at Jackson's?"

"Done," Harry said.

Barbara sighed. "Brother, I predict that on Monday you'll be the one falling down."

As Lord Southam stirred his concoction, the party spoke of the gentlemen's varied pugilistic skills, then the talk turned to other sports, hunting, and fishing. Mirabella noted with approval that Lord Southam, who was barely acquainted with Lewin, Josephine, and Harry and Barbara Smythe, took pains to include them in the conversation and make them feel at ease.

At last the arrack was mixed, and Lord Southam poured their glasses and served them, then took his seat by Mirabella. "A toast," he said, lifting his glass. "To the four loveliest ladies at Vauxhall tonight." The men said heartily, "To the ladies."

Mirabella took a very small sip of the punch, but as soon as she had inhaled the strong fragrance, she sneezed not once but twice. "Please pardon me, oh dear," she said, woebegone.

Giles grinned mischievously. "Sorry, Southam, but she's ferreted out your secret ingredient. Cardamom."

Mirabella sighed. "It's true, I'm afraid. Cardamom always makes me sneeze." She darted Giles a wicked glance and said, "But I shouldn't have told your secret, sir, I have more discretion."

"Everyone knows you sneeze at cardamom, the secret was out," Giles replied.

"I beg your pardon, Mr. and Miss Smythe didn't know," Mirabella argued.

Lord Camarden said, "Mirabella, Giles, if you think we all came here to listen to you two squabble, you are much mistaken, we hear enough of that at home. Southam, I compliment you on your arrack, it's fortifying and the taste is pleasing on the tongue."

Lord Southam nodded, then said to Mirabella, "Please forgive me for inflicting respiratory distress upon you, my lady. And now I must find another secret recipe that won't make you sneeze."

"That's very kind of you, sir, kinder than our Monsieur Danton," Mirabella said, sniffing a little. "It enrages him that I have this odd reaction to cardamom, which is one of his favorite spices. He has accused me of imagining it, and keeps making dishes with it, thinking I won't notice."

"And do you?" Lord Southam asked.

Lady Camarden said, "Once we had lamb with a sweet sauce, and Mirabella sneezed so much that I was obliged to dismiss her from the table. It was really quite embarrassing, with Lord and Lady Liverpool there."

"I did try to hold the sneezes back, Mamma, but all I succeeded in doing was a sort of deep hiccupping into my napkin," Mirabella said plaintively. "It fairly made my ears ring."

"Your ears and your nose were very red," Giles commented.

Lady Camarden said severely, "Giles, stop baiting her, she's outrageous enough as it is. Come, Camarden, let's take a stroll before the Chinese acrobats perform."

All of the party decided to promenade. Josephine was arm in arm with Harry Smythe and Lewin; Giles and Miss Smythe slowly walked down the Grand Walk, and Lord Southam offered Mirabella his arm. "Is there any particular attraction you'd care to visit?"

"Whenever I come here I always want to see the statue of Handel," Mirabella answered.

"Curious," Lord Southam said. "But then you are a singular woman. It's this way, I believe." He led her around behind the circle of supper boxes to another wooded grove, with small side paths surrounded by privet hedges. In the center was a life-size statue of the composer.

"Why do you like this statue?" Lord Southam asked intently.

"It's remarkable, because Roubiliac did it in 1738, at a time when life-sized statues were only done of royalty, or of great military leaders. Although he was a great composer, Handel was only a commoner." She smiled up at Southam. "But in truth I like it because it's whimsical. He's in his dressing gown and slippers and nightcap. Handel's music is so stately, so dignified, I like to think of him as having a quaint sense of humor."

"Extraordinary," Lord Southam said in a low voice.

"What is? That Handel should have a sense of humor?"

"No, that you're actually interesting."

"That's very faint praise, sir."

"Not from me."

They went on to make their way toward the theatre, lingering at one of the ornate octagonal pavilions to watch the passersby, and saw and greeted several acquaintances. They strolled in a circle around the golden statue of Aurora, goddess of the dawn, joining Giles and Barbara, and then Josephine and Harry Smythe and Lewin. Together they went to the theatre and found Lord and Lady Camarden. The theatre was grand, with Roman columns and a lofty ceiling, but it had no seats. In the middle of the room was a great circle of torches, casting lurid, dramatic lighting on the acrobats. Ten men performed almost miraculously, tumbling and somersaulting and vaulting each other high through the air in balletic choreography. Not only were they superb athletes, they were as graceful as dancers.

Standing beside Barbara, Mirabella noticed her friend's face. She was obviously captivated, her expression one of sheer child like delight and wonder. Then, in the flickering torchlight, Mirabella noticed Giles watching Miss Smythe. He seemed amused, but he looked warm, as if the sight gave him pleasure. In some odd way it unsettled Mirabella. She couldn't quite put her finger on it for long moments, but as she pondered it she realized that she had often seen that particular expression on Giles's face—but only when he was looking at her. *Great heavens, what's wrong with me? It's not as if Giles never looks at another woman. Barbara is so sweet, it does give pleasure to see her enjoying herself so much.*

Mirabella dismissed the thoughts from her mind and turned her attention back to the acrobats. Their skills earned a very enthusiastic round of applause from the audience.

As it was almost nine o'clock, when supper would be served, the party returned to its box. It was full dusk, and the lanes were growing dark. As they neared the Grove, a loud shrill whistle sounded. Servants were stationed all over the gardens, holding slow matches. As one they lit the thousands of lanterns, and the gardens were suddenly brilliant.

"Oh, how thrilling!" Barbara breathed. "I've never seen a sight to compare!"

Affectionately Mirabella said, "You're such a darling, Barbara. To see your delight has increased mine, I don't think I've ever appreciated Vauxhall so much."

Their table was set, and a waiter immediately served them when they sat down. Lord Southam said, "I took the liberty of ordering everything, for I like to sample it all. I mean no slight to your magnificent Monsieur Danton, Camarden, but sometimes I prefer plain English fare to Frenchified flummery."

"As do I, although Monsieur Danton pays no more attention to my wishes than he does to my wife's," Lord Camarden rasped. "I've always thoroughly enjoyed all of Vauxhall's offerings."

The suppers were simple, but delicious. Cold roast chicken, lobsters, anchovies, and potted pigeon, and of course the famous ham, sliced "muslin thin" so that "one could read a newspaper through it," were the entrees, with sides of salads, pickles, and relishes. Sweets included custards, pastries, and cheesecakes. The diners ate with satisfaction, with congenial conversation at the table, for almost two hours.

After they dined, the party left to wander the gardens again. Lord Southam said, "The fireworks are about to begin. It's been my experience that the full effect is better seen if one gets away from the glare of the Grove, and moves closer to the fire tower. Shall we?"

Mirabella took his arm, and he placed his hand over hers and pressed close to her. They walked up one of the long shaded lanes, where side paths led to small arbors with stone benches. The side paths were called the "Dark Paths," and had a reputation for hosting romantic liaisons, but no thought of caution entered Mirabella's mind as they sat down, and he kept his hold on her hand.

The fireworks began, and they were, as always, spectacular. Mirabella's face was upturned with pleasure, lit at intervals by greenish, then blue, then reddish, then bright yellow-white flashes, accompanied by distant booms. "I love fireworks," Mirabella said dreamily.

"Then you shall have them every day, if you wish," Lord Southam said quietly.

"I beg your pardon?" Mirabella asked, bemused.

He stared at her intently, and always after, Mirabella recalled the scene as somewhat surreal, with the unearthly flashes lighting his face, accompanied by the rhythmic thunder.

He pressed her hand. "I have come to have a great regard for you, Mirabella, and I believe you feel the same for me. We do very well together, and will do. Why shouldn't we make our announcement?"

Mirabella was stunned. "You mean—you can't mean—you're making a proposal of marriage? Now?"

"Of course, why not? We're adults, and both of us know what we want. Isn't that true?" He slid his arm around her waist, pulled her close, and pressed his lips to hers. Mirabella was so astonished that she was paralyzed for long moments. Then she jerked her face to the side, and pushed against his chest. But it was like pushing on a stone wall, and still he held her close. "Sir, what are you doing? Let me go, this instant!"

He seemed frozen, baffled. He muttered, "I never thought you would have such missish vapors, it never occurred to me. I thought this was what you wanted."

Mirabella pushed hard, and this time he released her. She jumped to her feet, stiff with indignation. "You are sadly mistaken! I've given you no signs to take such license with me!"

He frowned. "I hate to contradict a lady, but it's known that you are, at last, ready to marry, Mirabella. You've shown a definite preference for me. Can you deny it?"

"I—I—no, I can't deny that," she admitted with confusion. "But still, I never intended to invite—intimacies."

Evenly he said, "You intend to marry, but not to invite intimacies? I don't think it's possible you're that naïve. I assume that this sudden prudish fastidiousness is your view of how young ladies behave when they become engaged. I assure you that you're wrong. Besides, it was just a kiss, it's not as if I assaulted you."

Mirabella pressed her fingertips to her forehead. "You're confusing me. We barely know each other, it's much too soon! It's an affront to me, sir, that you believe you can take such impudent liberties with me. You can't possibly tell me that my behavior in any way encouraged it."

"But I can," he said, standing up to face her. Now he was gentle, however, and took her hand. "The way you look at me, and the way you smile at me has told me. We're an eminently suitable match, Mirabella. I know that I could never do any better than to marry you. I think, I hope you have thought the same."

His words made her cheeks flush, and she took a deep indrawn breath. *Haven't I been thinking exactly the same thing? But it sounds so—cold, so calculating when he says it.* Of course Mirabella had thought, and said, exactly the same thing in the same manner; but she was in too much turmoil to realize it.

Now she looked up at him and said coolly, "Lord Southam, it seems that each of us has misjudged the other. I have no intention of having a passionate interlude with you, and I never gave you any indication that I desired it. And on my part, I was gravely mistaken because I thought that you were more of a gentleman."

His face hardened and his eyes narrowed. Frigidly he said, "I see. Well, I'm not so much of a cad that I won't apologize to a lady. Please accept my sincerest regrets, Lady Mirabella, for the affront. I can assure you I won't offend you any further with any importunities."

Mirabella was suddenly exhausted. Wearily she said, "I accept your apology with the best will, sir. Perhaps we may return to our party now?"

"Certainly, madam." Stiffly he offered her his arm; he walked a full six inches away from her, staring straight ahead.

As dictated by the rules of Polite Society, they had both regained their composure by the time they returned to the Grove. The fireworks display ended, and the party grouped together again in the supper box for refreshments. Lord Southam was courteous, but he took particular care to engage Lewin, Giles, Harry Smythe, and Lord Camarden in conversation. Mirabella, her mother, Josephine, and Barbara talked about the delights of the acrobats, and the fireworks. Neither Mirabella nor Lord Southam showed the least bit of uneasiness. Mirabella was upset, but she thought she was successful in hiding it, as she smiled and talked with her usual vivacity.

She noticed, however, that Giles's gaze often rested on her face. He was thoughtful.

He knows, she thought with a start.

He always knows.

Chapter Thirteen

Three young bucks strutted down Bond Street, stepping gallantly aside to allow the ladies and their maids to pass. The street was not at all crowded, however, as it was the unearthly early hour of nine o'clock in the morning.

Sir Giles Knyvet was nattily dressed in a well-cut dark blue tailcoat, fawn-colored breeches and top boots. Lewin was, as always, dressed in his manly regimentals. Harry Smythe was as finely tailored as Giles, with an olive-green coat, tight pantaloons, and Hessian boots. Both Lewin and Harry carried small portmanteaux. "Gentleman" John Jackson, whose nickname suited him in all ways, had decreed that any man who boxed in his saloon would wear knee breeches, stockings, and plain soft cotton pumps. "I'll not have fool dandies stamping around the ring in buckskins and boots, like a backstreet brawl," he had said.

Harry said, "I'm feeling vigorous this morning in spite of a late night at the Daffy Club. Would anyone care to make a small wager on our bout?"

Lewin said, "Giles never gambles because he thinks it's a weakness, and I never gamble because I have good sense and no money. Sorry, old fellow."

"No matter," Harry said cheerfully. "I'm going to enjoy my victory all the same."

"Swaggering young pup, ain't he?" Giles observed to Lewin.

Gentleman Jackson's saloon was strictly a sportsman's domain, but it had a spare elegance. One long, low room was designated for training pugilists, a second room was for fencing and the ancient art of stick fighting, which young dandies gleefully did with their walking sticks. Both rooms had highly polished oak floors, kept scrupulously clean. The walls were decorated with prints of famous bouts, portraits of well-known pugilists, and diagrams explaining the science of boxing.

Since his long-ago rough-and-tumble days with Lewin, Giles had never cared for boxing, although he was actually a formidable opponent, for when he did indulge, he hit hard and accurately and was very quick. But over the years he had come to much prefer fencing. However, he did admire Jackson, who had almost single-handedly elevated pugilism not only to an exacting science, but to an art. Giles had frequented the saloon often this Season, partly because Lewin was such an enthusiastic competitor, but also because Giles had come to enjoy exercising with the weights that were standard training equipment for Jackson's students.

They came into the boxing room and were surprised to see a large crowd already gathered and sitting in the chairs that the saloon provided for observers. Normally two or three gentlemen might be sparring with partners, with other gentlemen exercising. Today, however, only two men were boxing on the floor: Lord Southam and Gentleman John Jackson himself. Jackson was not as tall as Lord Southam, but he was fully as muscular. Always, when Jackson sparred, the other men left the floor entirely to him in order to observe his genius.

Giles, Lewin, and Harry took seats in the back row of chairs, as that was all that was available. The crowd of men was quite rowdy; in particular three men in the front row were catcalling and whistling, which was not at all unusual during an exciting sparring match. One young man, his top hat absurdly tipped far back on his head, bellowed out, "Oho, Southam, you're blundering about like a hippopotamus. Too much brandy last night, eh? Eh?"

It was obvious that Southam was not in his usual precise, collected form. His hair was plastered to his head, his face and massive chest streamed with sweat. His face was dark. His footwork was heavy and ponderous.

Harry said quietly to Lewin and Giles, "Southam was with that loud fellow at the Daffy last night, along with those other two. Are you acquainted with them, Sir Giles?"

Giles grimly answered, "I'm sorry to say that I am acquainted with the one with the loud mouth. He's George Whitmer, son of the banker Lord Whitmer. He's not at all a congenial companion. Aside from being crass, he's an idiot. I think the only reason Jackson's allowed him membership is because Lord Whitmer is his banker, and has dealt generously with him. Smythe, did you speak to Southam last night?"

"No, he came in late, and Lord Southam was surrounded by his party and some—er—ladies that accompanied them. I was just leaving, in fact, and I don't think Southam even saw me."

Southam misstepped and almost tripped. Whitmer shouted, "My sister could beat you down today, Southam! Jackson, pulling punches for the old man, are we?"

Lord Southam threw a wild right punch. With lightning speed Jackson blocked it, held his fist, grabbed Southam's left fist, and shouted, "Hold!" Lord Southam immediately dropped his hands and stood still, breathing heavily.

Jackson turned to Whitmer, and his face was grave. As always, his voice was well modulated and mannerly. "Mr. Whitmer, I would hate to think that you've offered me an insult. If that is the case, then I must surely demand satisfaction."

George Whitmer had large, prominent eyes, a long sharp nose, and a weak chin. Stark fear crossed his face, and his eyes bulged. "No, no—no, sir, Mr. Jackson, I meant no offense, no offense at all. I was merely ribbing Lord Southam. Please accept my sincerest apology."

"Accepted," Jackson said evenly. "Mr. Whitmer, calling out to fighters, whistling, shouting encouragement, and even catcalling is acceptable behavior in the excitement of a match. Belittling a man, taunting him, is not gentlemanly, particularly if you're not willing to defend your words."

"Yes, sir," Whitmer said meekly. "I apologize, sir."

"To Lord Southam," Jackson said calmly.

"Sorry, Southam, no harm done, eh?" he said tentatively. "Me mouth takes over me brain sometimes, eh? Eh?"

"It's Lord Southam," he said heavily, "and you will do well to remember it."

Jackson turned back to Lord Southam and said, "My lord, you are much out of form today, the first time I've ever seen you so inept. The art of pugilism demands that you concentrate, that you keep a single-minded focus, and above all, that you *think*. Think, plan, strategize, act, and instantly react. Your physical prowess and skill are exactly the same as they were yesterday, but today you have lost your mental agility. Remember, you are not in hand-to-hand combat with a French cuirassier and his horse. Shall we continue?"

"Yes, sir, and I thank you," Southam said.

The sparring continued, and Lord Southam seemed to recover. Whitmer and his companions were reduced to muttering among themselves and to some of the men sitting behind them. Once the glare of Jackson and Southam's ire was off him, Whitmer looked petulant and cross. Turning to a short, weasel-faced man behind him, he spoke in a mock whisper, just loud enough for the men seated in the chairs, but not the boxers, to hear.

"Old Southam's just out of sorts because he was deep in his cups last night and let it slip that a lady had jilted him," he said maliciously. "I hear that she's quite a fancy bit o' muslin, too. Lady Mirabella Tirel, don't you know, hoity-toity. Admitted he tried to steal a kiss, and she fair roasted him. Heh, heh, Southam's going to be a famous fool now, that kiss cost him thirty thousand!" The men surrounding him laughed coarsely.

Lewin muttered to himself, "*Idiot* is too fine a word for him, he's a chattering imbecile. If Lord Southam—" He broke off at the sight of Giles. His face was white, his eyes sparking blue fire. His jaws were clenched so tightly that his high cheekbones jutted out like a skull's.

Before Lewin could think of something placating to say to Giles, Whitmer prattled on, "This Lady Mirabella, she's the catch of the world, you know, rich and fair easy on the eyes to boot. Seems that she should have been easy pickings for Southam, but it's said she's cold as a fish, eh? She looks down her fine little haughty nose at every man that's ever—"

Giles jumped out of his chair, and it overturned with a crash. He walked to stand in front of Whitmer, reached down, grabbed his cravat in a stranglehold, and yanked him to his feet. Whitmer's hat fell off, and his wooden chair overturned, bashing into the men behind him, which caused such a commotion that the fighters stopped boxing and turned to see what was happening. The room grew completely silent.

"Do you know who I am?" Giles said between gritted teeth.

In a choked voice, Whitmer answered, "Y-yes, sir, you're Sir Giles Knyvet, we've met, sir, haven't we?"

After a bone-crunching shake, Giles let go of Whitmer's cravat, but stepped to stand dangerously close to him. "We have, to my deepest regret. You've insulted the lady, and I resent it."

Whitmer's eyes again protruded with alarm. "But—but, Sir Giles, I didn't know, that is, you aren't akin to Lady—"

"Don't you dare speak her name again. As long as you live, scum," Giles said. "No, I am no blood relation to her. But she and her family—her *honorable* family—are my closest friends. Her brother is not here, or he would surely defend her honor. I'm glad to do so in his stead."

"But—but—but—I meant no offense to the lady, I, along with everyone else in London, am an admirer of hers, I assure you, Sir Giles, I may have spoken foolishly, but no offense, none at all, was intended, and I—perhaps I spoke lightly of the lady, but I didn't mean, I never meant—"

Giles's face was a picture of disdain. "Be silent. It's clear that you have no intention of giving me satisfaction. Very well, I won't attempt to demand it, since obviously you're a coward and have no honor. I will tell you this. If I hear of you again insulting the lady in any company whatsoever, I will find you, and I will make you pay for your insolence. Do you understand?"

"Ye-yes, Sir Giles, I will certainly be discreet and—"

Giles turned on his heel and walked away.

He had every intention of leaving, but just at the entrance he was stopped by Lord Southam calling, "Knyvet, wait. I need to speak to you."

Giles turned and saw that Southam had followed him, still stripped to the waist and streaming with sweat, and unwrapping his gloves. "I'm hardly in the mood for polite conversation just now, Southam. Particularly with you."

"I don't blame you," Lord Southam said, mildly for him. "But I'd like to request that you give me the opportunity to explain, and perhaps mitigate my guilt in your eyes, if only slightly.

Jackson has offered me the use of his office so that we can talk privately."

They went into the office, which was as neat and spare as the saloon, and stood facing each other. The tension in the air was palpable. Southam said, "The only thing I despise more than acting a fool is being obliged to confess I'm a fool. I greatly misjudged Lady Mirabella. But I assure you that I made her an honorable offer, and I was so certain of her acceptance that I kissed her. In no way did I assault her, or importune her. The thought that she was anything less than virtuous never entered my mind, as it never entered my mind that it would offend her to seal a betrothal with a kiss."

Giles crossed his arms and frowned. "As you admit, you misjudged her grievously, and that's because you hardly know her. Didn't it occur to you that no respectable woman is going to allow a relative stranger to kiss her?"

Southam said, "Knyvet, I'm surprised that you're so naïve. I'm thirty-seven years old, I've been observing the machinations of the Marriage Market for years. I can assure you that once a couple has settled on marriage, the lady rarely objects to a simple kiss."

"You were so sure of her, then?"

"I was. All of London knows that she has decided to marry. In the last month she has given me every indication that she considered us to be a suitable match."

Darkly Giles thought, *Suitable match, even I said to Lewin that that's what Mirabella is looking for. I suppose I can hardly blame Southam, in the same circumstances I might have thought the same.*

With some difficulty Giles asked, "And so you were so heartbroken by her rejection that you went out, got drunk, and insanely ran your mouth to a mob of rabble?"

Southam answered evenly, "I was not heartbroken; there was no question of sentimental romantic nonsense between me and

Lady Mirabella. Let us say I was enamored of her, she's lovely, she's bright and clever and amusing, a most congenial companion. All of the young women I've known, it seems, have been mainly concerned with seeking a title and fortune. I knew that Mirabella cared for neither. I had never considered marrying before, and have never made an offer to any woman. It stung me deeply when she rejected me."

"Your pride, you mean," Giles said.

"I suppose. But I admit that I was disappointed, too, and perhaps even a little dejected. It's none of your concern how I happened to fall in with Whitmer and that low crowd, but I was very wrong to be so indiscreet, as I said, I behaved like the worst kind of fool. I regret the pain it's caused you, Knyvet, and that my actions subjected Lady Mirabella to such filthy gossip. I assure you it will never happen again."

After a moment Giles reached out and the two men shook hands. Giles turned to walk out, but Lord Southam said, "One last thing, Knyvet. I can't undo the damage that Whitmer has already done, but I can stop him from continuing to insult me and the lady. I know that you've warned him, but he is a deeply stupid man and I believe that I shall be obliged to take harsher measures to ensure that he keeps his mouth shut."

Giles said, "But it's obvious the man's a coward, he'll never come up to scratch to duel. You're not thinking of some harsher—physical—measures, surely?"

Southam grinned, and Giles thought it looked feral. "He's not worth the trouble. No, Lord Whitmer is my banker, and was long before he was Baron Whitmer, which title, by the way, he owes to my father. I'll threaten to have that wretch's allowance cut off. That will stop his brainless gibbering."

Giles said, rather stiffly, "I'm grateful that you made explanations to me, Southam. You weren't obliged to by any means."

"If you were ready to fight a duel for her, then I think you're rightly owed an explanation. And also, perhaps, for other reasons," Southam said shrewdly.

Giles could think of nothing more to say.

More than a week passed before Mirabella spoke to Josephine about Lord Southam. At the routs and parties and at Almack's, she was wary of meeting Lord Southam, but she didn't see him. Although privately Mirabella was confused and upset, in public she appeared as she always did, vivacious and lively. Wisely, Josephine didn't press Mirabella. Mirabella was close to her friends and trusted them completely, but she confided to them in her own time and manner.

After a very late night at the theatre, Mirabella invited Josephine for a glass of ratafia and a talk. When they were comfortably settled, Mirabella said, "I love music, in particular opera, but I discovered tonight that actually I find *Artaxerxes* to be ponderous and tiresome. Did you enjoy it?"

"I did, very much, but then it's the first time I've seen it. You've told me that it's been featured every Season for time out of mind, so I'm not surprised that you've wearied of it."

Mirabella nodded. She took a sip of ratafia and stared thoughtfully into space. Josephine waited patiently. Finally Mirabella said, "It was something of a surprise to me that Lord Southam visited our box. I haven't seen him since that night at Vauxhall."

"He was very congenial. Sometimes he seems rather aloof, but he can certainly be charming."

"Yes, when he chooses."

Quietly Josephine asked, "Mirabella, did he offend you in some manner?"

Mirabella gave her a rueful smile. "I thought he did, but now I don't know if he did or not."

"Well, that's a bewildering position to be in."

"So it is. You see, he made an offer of marriage to me, and then he kissed me."

"Oh. Um—and so—you're confused about whether you should be offended or not?"

"It just all happened so fast, I got the feeling of being overwhelmed, and then, when he kissed me, I lost my temper completely." She frowned darkly. "I wonder if I overreacted. I've been trying to think, to understand, if perhaps he wasn't actually taking liberties. Do you think that maybe other young ladies wouldn't have gotten quite so hysterical?"

Josephine said gently, "I have no personal knowledge whatsoever of such a situation, dearest. If I think of it in hypothetical terms, however, it seems to me that when a man proposes marriage, and then kisses his betrothed, most young ladies would not have the hysterics. Unless he treated you with disrespect? Did he injure you in some way?"

"Oh, no, it wasn't like that at all, he was—respectful. He's just so—masterful, that I couldn't gather my wits to respond properly."

"And what should have been your proper response?"

Mirabella sighed. "I should have remained calm, and simply told him that it was too soon, and that I'd prefer to take more time to consider his proposal."

Josephine's eyes grew round. "And so you're still thinking of him as a potential suitor?"

"No, not at all. After the way I spoke to him, I'm sure he'll never renew his attentions. But that's not the only reason I've decided that we wouldn't be a suitable match."

Mischievously Josephine said, "His chart looked very promising, what are we to add to the contras?"

Mirabella's eyes danced. "I just don't want to kiss him again. I didn't care for it much."

Josephine grinned. "Oh, really? But I know, in fact I have it in writing, that you consider his mouth to be one of his most attractive features. Whatever could have happened to his mouth that this tragedy has come about?"

"I don't know, I still like the way it looks, but I just don't want to kiss it. I suppose that might present a problem to a husband."

"I would imagine so. By any chance have you contemplated kissing Lord Trevor and/or Denys Aldington? Do you feel a complete aversion to either of their mouths?"

"I'm not going to think of kissing for a while. I'm going to—to—martial my forces, and regroup. Perhaps I've misjudged the correct manner in going about this."

"Surely not. I mean, we've made charts and everything."

Mirabella yawned. "Josephine, I love you dearly, but please leave me alone and go to bed. I think I can sleep tonight."

But she didn't. She lay awake for a long time, staring up at the canopy of her bed with sightless eyes.

In spite of her determination to dismiss him from her mind, Mirabella was thinking of Lord Southam. *Aunt Tirel might have been right, about him at least. I think he's the kind of man that wouldn't look kindly upon his wife's best friend being a man. But . . . that wouldn't necessarily be true of Lord Trevor, or especially of Denys, he's such a good friend to Giles, I'm sure we'd see him often.*

Although the exact logistics of this scenario refused to make themselves clear in her mind, it didn't really bother her. She found that she really had grown drowsy, and fell into a deep sleep. By the morning she had forgotten all about her doubts and worries. As she had almost every day of her life, she awoke excited and anticipating the delights of the new day.

Chapter Fourteen

At times Mirabella still tried to analyze her scene with Lord Southam, and her reaction to his offer. She realized that he had, quite simply, unsettled her to the extent that not only had the situation gone far beyond her control, she had also lost control of herself. Ruefully she recalled the conversation with her mother when she had so blithely said, "Don't worry about the men, Mamma. We can handle them," and her mother had grimly replied, "We shall see."

Mirabella had not been capable of "handling" a man like Lord Southam. Perhaps she was not quite so worldly-wise and sophisticated as she had thought. This revelation made her cautious. For more than three weeks she held herself strictly at arm's length from her admirers. She noted that Denys Aldington was attentive, as he always was, but maintained a respectful distance. Lord Trevor, on the other hand, outrageously flirted with her at every opportunity. Mirabella decided to have one of her *alfresco* breakfasts and invite both of them, along with other friends. It was so much easier to observe people, and see them in a more personal light, without the crush of balls and Almack's and the theatre.

On Wednesday night, of course Mirabella and Josephine were going to Almack's. Mirabella was slightly out of sorts. She was wearing one of her favorite new gowns. The "petticoat," which was actually an underdress, was of an airy silk of icy lavender. The overgown was the same silk, dyed a lavender three shades darker, and trimmed with gold metallic embroidery. It had a squared neckline with a small stand-up white lace collar on the back and sides, and the newest fashion of long sleeves, topped by puff sleeves. Mirabella wore her single strand of pearls, and her hair was adorned with a dozen of the tiniest white rosebuds. She should have felt that she looked very well, but somehow she didn't feel quite as confident as she normally did. It was difficult to pinpoint the cause of her unease; the shade of the dress suited her, it fit her superbly, Colette had dressed her hair magnificently, and each rosebud, with its single small leaf, was perfect.

In the carriage she studied Josephine, who looked lovely in a pale-golden-yellow silk gown heavily trimmed and embroidered with white work, and yellow roses in her hair. The frock had the traditional short puffed sleeves, and Josephine wore long over-the-elbow white gloves. Mirabella reflected that she was unhappy with the short gloves she was obliged to wear with the long-sleeved dress. They didn't seem nearly as elegant as long gloves. Mirabella decided that she would have Colette remove the long sleeves; perhaps she would like the dress better. It didn't help her on this evening, however, as she still felt oddly uneasy. Impatiently she told herself that she was being frail and missish for no reason, and determined that she would have a fun evening regardless of her long sleeves.

On this night it was just Mirabella, Josephine, and Lady Camarden. Lord Camarden had grumpily said that he'd had a most tiresome day in the House, with arguments all day long regarding the Prince of Wales's request for an increase in his funds. Lord Camarden said he had no intention of having a tiresome night at Almack's. They were later than usual, too, as Mirabella had spent an inordinate amount of time fretting over her *toilette*, so the crowd at Almack's was already gathered, and the quadrille had begun.

As soon as they had greeted the Lady Patronesses, Mirabella searched the room and gladly saw that Giles was there, talking to Barbara and Harry Smythe. She grabbed Josephine's arm and hurried through the crowd to them. "Gracious, is tonight more of a crush than usual?" she asked as they exchanged greetings, bows, and curtsies.

"It certainly is," Giles said. "We're honored tonight with a most distinguished and sought-after personage, Lord Wellington. He's over there, completely surrounded by that enormous knot of people, including my friend Captain Rosborough, who callously forsook us as soon as the great man walked into the room."

"I'm sure he's thrilled," Josephine said. "He told me he's seen Lord Wellington twice from afar, apparently very afar. He never imagined he might have an opportunity to meet him."

"For my part, I'm happy to finally see you, Sir Giles," Mirabella said with mock sternness. "Talk of callously forsaking your friends, Josephine and I haven't seen you and Lewin for days. For your penance you must give me the first waltz, and take me in to supper."

Giles bowed slightly. "A thousand pardons, my lady, but I am engaged to Miss Smythe for the first waltz, and have already requested that she allow me to escort her to supper."

Mirabella was taken aback for a moment; she was not at all accustomed to Giles not being, as it were, at her beck and call. But quickly she smiled brilliantly at Barbara Smythe, who looked slightly distressed. "Barbara, you must forgive me, I have a tendency to regard Giles as my own personal dance master and dinner partner, it comes of our comfortable routine at Camarden, I fear. Giles, I'm happy if you would politely request another dance from me. As far as supper, you have two arms and I doubt that Miss Smythe would object to you escorting us both."

Barbara hastily said, "Please do accompany us, Lady Mirabella. We haven't had an opportunity to talk at all this Season, I'd love to visit with you."

"There it is," Giles said wryly. "I'm escorting two lovely ladies to supper, and they're already planning to ignore me."

"You're still a lucky dog, Knyvet," Harry said, "if I do say so myself of my own sister. And Lady Mirabella, it's always such a pleasure to accompany you on any occasion. May I beg the honor of the first waltz?"

"You may, sir," Mirabella said.

He turned to Josephine. "Miss Rosborough, would you do me the honor of the second waltz? And since such detailed supper plans are being made, would you give me the pleasure of escorting you tonight? Perhaps we may engage Knyvet in conversation while my sister and Lady Mirabella neglect him."

"I should be happy, sir," Josephine calmly replied.

Mirabella saw that though Josephine maintained her usual serene demeanor, her eyes were sparkling and she looked pleased. Mirabella again felt an odd, unfamiliar sense of uncertainty. *Am I imagining things? Surely if Josephine were becoming attached to Harry Smythe, she would have confided in me. But no, that's not her way at all, now that I think of it, she's so reserved. But it does seem there is something . . . how is it that I haven't noticed? Have I become so selfish and self-absorbed that I'm not paying attention to my closest friends?*

And Giles . . . and Barbara . . . ?

The quadrille ended and there was a general shuffling about as the couples left the dance floor and rearranged themselves. Denys Aldington came to bow to Mirabella. "My lady, I was searching for you earlier, but one can barely find one's own feet in this rout."

He sighed theatrically. "I assume that, as always, your dance card is already filled?"

"Alas, it is not, sir. I'm afraid that I dawdled so at dressing this evening that I made our party arrive shamefully late. Miss Rosborough and I have scarcely had an opportunity to seek out partners."

"As if you and the lovely Miss Rosborough should ever be obliged to do such a thing," he said gallantly. "May I have the honor of this dance, Lady Mirabella?"

"Gladly, sir."

In the long line of dancers, Mirabella noted that Harry Smythe was dancing with Josephine, Barbara was partnered with a young gentleman whom she slightly knew as Mr. Eberhardt, and Lord Trevor Brydges was dancing with Rosalind, Lady FitzGeorge. Giles was not dancing. Mirabella couldn't help but contrast the delightful enjoyment on Harry Smythe's face with the rather somber smile that Mr. Aldington occasionally gave her. In past years it had seemed that Denys found much more pleasure in the Season than he did now.

The dance ended and Denys took her hand to escort her off the dance floor. Mirabella said, "Oh, my word, there were so many couples dancing I think that dance must have lasted a half hour. By chance, sir, are you engaged for the next dance?"

"No, my lady, I am not. May I have the honor?" he politely asked.

She smiled. "You mistake me, I beg for no partner just now, I'm out of breath as it is. I was just wondering if you would be so kind as to sit with me for a few moments as I recover."

"Nothing would give me greater pleasure." He escorted her to a settee and sat beside her. Mirabella opened her fan and indulged herself in the little breath of cool air it gave her.

"Do you know, Mr. Aldington, tonight I was having grave

reservations about these long sleeves, and now I know why I took a dislike to them. It's very close in here, and they're not helping at all, and it's only April; well, almost May. I've forgotten how stifling London can be. I tell you here and now you'll see no long sleeves on me from here on out."

"I've very sorry you're uncomfortable, my lady. I must say, however, that in that gown you're a vision, and I've noted that the most fashionable ladies in Town are sporting the new long sleeves. You look very stylish in them."

"You notice ladies' fashions, do you, Mr. Aldington?" she asked, plying her fan flirtatiously. "What an unusual trait in a gentleman who doesn't have a bevy of sisters to continually plague him with the topic. But speaking of sisters, I hope I do not intrude on your privacy, but I have lately been thinking much of darling Charlotte. How does she fare?"

He brightened somewhat. "I'm thankful to say that she's better. Our physician recommended that she take the waters at Bath. He and my mother are there with Charlotte, and my mother writes that she seems comfortable and relaxed, and is eating and drinking more."

"That's wonderful news, I'm so happy for Charlotte and your family," Mirabella said sincerely.

"You are too kind, my lady. Such generosity of heart is a rare treasure," he said, then in a low ardent voice continued, "'As fair in form, as warm yet pure in heart, / Love's image upon earth without his wing, / And guileless beyond Hope's imagining!'"

The quote sounded vaguely familiar to Mirabella, but she couldn't quite place it. Lightly she said, "Sir, such effusive compliments are overwhelming, I can hardly imagine an appropriate response, so I will simply say thank you."

Without giving him an opportunity to reply, Mirabella went on talking gaily, reminiscing about the walks in the gardens and down to the lake at Harpendon House with Charlotte. He remained languorous, his eyes heavy-lidded, his expression one of slight melancholy. Mirabella wondered if something else was weighing on him, and she thought she might ask Giles, as he and Denys Aldington were good friends. As they talked, however, it occurred to Mirabella that there was a hint of artifice about Denys's demeanor. She dismissed the thought, for she had always known him to be a man without guile.

As the next country dance commenced, Mirabella saw that Lady FitzGeorge had no partner and was speaking with Lady Cowper. She excused herself and made her way toward them through the throng.

However, Lady Jersey practically popped up in front of her, grabbed her arm, and propelled her into a corner. "Mirabella dear, finally I've found an opportunity to speak to you. Have you been avoiding me? Surely not, we're such good friends, and you know that I would never berate you for jilting Southam, but I simply must know why you would do such a foolish thing. He's one of the prime catches in England, even though he is merely a viscount but still, he's so deliciously rich! Why, practically every woman of any consequence whatsoever has tried to snag him, and he's managed to evade every single one, but here he just dropped right into your lap and you turned him away and broke his heart, hardly anyone has seen him for the last few weeks. The story has become something droll in Town, for it's said that Southam paid thirty thousand pounds for a kiss, and he's not the kind of man that could abide being laughed at, no matter how—"

Normally Mirabella would never consider interrupting anyone, but she was so aghast that she blurted out, "Sally, stop! What are you blathering on about? This—this is awful, it's so insulting both to me and to Lord Southam, how could you possibly repeat such mean, tawdry gossip?"

Lady Jersey was neither insulted nor abashed; her eyes glinted with mischief. "Most gossip is generally based in truth, my dear, as you well know. Are you saying that you didn't turn down Southam? Or that this expensive kiss never happened?"

Mirabella said stiffly, "I'm not saying anything at all, it's no one's concern. Where did you hear this nonsense, Sally? Surely not from Lord Southam."

"Of course not, he's always been a gentleman of the utmost discretion, one can never find out any good tidbits about him, which is why it makes this tale so priceless," she scoffed. "As for exactly where I heard it, I hardly know, you know how it works, one talks to so many people every day, stories just circulate in the ether and one hears them."

"Well, stop repeating this one, I beg you," Mirabella said angrily. "I declare, if I knew who started spreading these rumors I'd challenge him or her to a duel, and gladly shoot them."

"How odd you should say that, there was some vague mention of a duel, but apparently it didn't involve Southam, no one quite knew the circumstances, and it never came to be," Lady Jersey said with frustration.

"That's likely because it's a lie, just as what you've said is so distorted as to be a thousand miles from the truth," Mirabella retorted. "Please, Sally, I'm so distraught, I need to sit down for a moment and calm my nerves."

Lady Jersey took her arm again and led her to an armchair. "Of course, dear Mirabella, I'm sorry I've upset you, I had no such intention, I honestly believe that in a way it's rather a coup for you, to have spurned such a man as Southam, but there! Since you find it so distressing, I promise I shan't utter another word about it. Here's the waltz I've promised to Lord Harmond, the poor old thing does dodder about, but he's so dear I could hardly say no." She patted Mirabella's hand and left her alone.

Mirabella fanned herself vigorously, grateful for the mildest breath of air in the hot crowded ballroom. *Why on earth should I be shocked? This is Town. I've always known the rule that Everyone knows Everything about Everyone Else. It's just that this is the first time I've been the Everyone Else . . . well, since I was seventeen, I suppose, but then I didn't realize how damaging the gossip could be. But now I should have known! Oh, poor Lord Southam, how embarrassed he must be! I must, I must apologize to him . . .*

Mirabella wondered if that might be the correct course; perhaps the best thing to do would be to never mention it to him. With irritation she thought that again, or still, her dealings with Lord Southam confused her. She determined, however, that she would treat him with the utmost courtesy the next time she met him, no matter how cold he was to her. As for the gossip, she mentally shrugged. The damage was apparently already done. She must forget all about it, or if she couldn't forget, at least refuse to dwell on it.

After a few moments she managed to regain her composure, and again went to speak with Lady Cowper and Lady FitzGeorge. Lady Cowper said, "Mirabella, here is a triumph indeed. Rosalind has snagged Byron for her dinner party next week."

"However did you manage that?" Mirabella asked with surprise. "I'd heard that he wasn't accepting any invitations, that he's off brooding all by himself."

"I have my ways," Rosalind said mischievously. "He was reluctant, but I named off the guest list, and when he was certain that I wasn't including Caro Lamb he accepted. And Lady Cowper is one of his favorites, everyone knows."

"I admit I'm a great admirer, as is everyone else in London," Lady Cowper said.

"Almost everyone," Mirabella said lightly. "I'm afraid that I couldn't finish *Childe Harold*. Now I shall have to purchase another copy and brush up on it if I'm to have dinner with the great man himself."

"You didn't care for *Childe Harold*?" Lady Cowper asked. "I thought it was sheer genius, I've never read such vivid and emotive verse."

"Yes, so everyone says," Mirabella said. "It must be that I'm too shallow to enjoy the writhings of a tortured soul. However, I promise I shall try to lower myself into the dismal depths before your party next week, Rosalind."

"Just don't make yourself so woeful that you can't sing," Rosalind said severely. "I've promised everyone that you'll be our musical entertainment."

"Very well, I shall try to keep myself from sinking into such dejection that I'm unable to sing."

Mirabella danced with Lord Trevor, and found him devilishly charming as always; then she danced with Lewin, who had met Lord Wellington and had found him to be an approachable, even personable gentleman, which had astounded Lewin. Then she had her waltz with Harry Smythe. "Your friend Miss Rosborough is a most charming, amiable girl," he said, beaming.

"Yes, she is," Mirabella agreed. "She's very pretty, too."

"I believe she's one of the prettiest girls I've ever seen," he said artlessly, then hurriedly added, "As are you, Lady Mirabella."

"You're very kind, sir," Mirabella said with amusement.

The second waltz was Giles's, and Mirabella was glad to see him come claim her. "You and Lewin have been so scarce these last weeks, I was beginning to think that you might be angry with me. You're not, are you?" she asked.

"I am not. Should I be? Have you done something wicked?" he teased.

"Mm, let me think. I suppose I have, although you couldn't

know of it. I was jealous of Josephine this evening because her frock is prettier than mine."

"Yes, I had noticed that."

"Scoundrel," Mirabella said affectionately. "Now you've promised to attend my breakfast tomorrow, you will be there, won't you?"

"I will be there. I wouldn't miss one of your famous *alfresco* breakfasts for the world."

Mirabella's *alfresco* breakfasts were a favorite with the *haut ton*. One reason was that Mirabella made clear to everyone that the breakfasts were for young single ladies and gentlemen, and she and her parents were of such prominent standing that any young ladies she invited were able to attend under the chaperonage of Lady Camarden.

Another reason for their popularity was Monsieur and Madame Danton. They set up two large, shallow grilling pans on the sideboard in the garden loggia. These "stoves" had been specially designed by Monsieur Danton. They were a variation of the warming pans used for breakfast dishes, but after much trial and error, Monsieur Danton had added several candles to bring the pans to a temperature hot enough to cook eggs. The couple took special orders from each guest for an omelet, and made them fresh and hot right there.

Monsieur Danton was a tall, thin man with flashing dark eyes, a prominent Gallic nose, and sparse dark hair. Madame Danton was short, and was as pretty as Colette, but without Colette's demeanor of sparkling humor. As they adjusted the candles under their pans and tested them by dropping small bits of butter on the cooking surfaces, they spoke together in low tones in

French. Two footmen stood by to attend to serving beverages to the guests.

Mirabella had invited Josephine, Lewin, and Giles, of course. She had also invited Barbara and Harry Smythe, Lady FitzGeorge, Denys Aldington, and Lord Trevor Brydges.

"I apologize that the gentlemen outnumber the ladies," Mirabella said as they all took their seats. "I did invite another young lady, but she had a previous engagement."

Rosalind, sitting between Harry Smythe and Lord Trevor, smiled. "I'm afraid it's all my fault. You invited Lady Margaret, didn't you? My stepdaughter Lady Chandos disapproves of me, you see, and won't allow Meg to come under my disreputable influence."

"Oh? What infamous thing have you done to deserve this censure?" Mirabella asked lightly.

"I'm certain that Lady Chandos could give you any number of examples of my scandalous behavior. But the latest indiscretion is all Lord Trevor's fault. He persuaded me to dance three times with him at Lady Sefton's ball. Lady Chandos demanded to know if we were betrothed. When I told her certainly not, she was obviously appalled."

Timidly Barbara said, "But is that so very scandalous, Lady FitzGeorge? I thought that such strict rules of conduct didn't apply to widows."

"I thought that, too, Miss Smythe," Rosalind said cheerfully. "But apparently Lady Chandos disagrees."

"I forgot to ask Lady Chandos's permission before leading you down the dastardly path of dissolution," Lord Trevor said slyly. "Naturally I take full responsibility, and will mend my ways, my lady."

Rosalind said, "How I hope not."

With amusement Giles said, "I wouldn't worry that Brydges

will reform, ma'am. The ladies are much too enthralled with that rakish charm."

Lord Trevor grinned. "Can't help it, you know, take after my mother, she always cuts a dash. Ain't it amusing, how that works? My brother is just like my father, as dull as ditchwater. He's going to be the prime staid boring earl."

Mirabella asked curiously, "It doesn't bother you, being the second son, Lord Trevor?"

"Bother me? Not at all, the opposite, in fact. I can be the carefree, swaggering younger son without being saddled with all the work and worry. I tell you if I had to sit in that dreary House of Lords day after day, I'd go full-moon lunatic," he said cheerfully.

Rosalind said slyly, "That is all too true, Lord Trevor, you can barely sit still anywhere for any length of time. Lady Camarden, I must commend Monsieur and Madame Danton. Just looking at this table is a feast in itself."

Monsieur Danton turned and bowed; Madame Danton murmured, "*Merci, ma dame.*"

"There you see it," Lady Camarden said. "They do understand English, except when I'm speaking to them."

The table was laden with ingredients for the omelets. There were six kinds of cheeses, four kinds of mushrooms, assorted sautéed vegetables such as tomatoes, celery, leeks, onions, and sweet peppers, crumbled bacon, shredded ham, and one of Monsieur Danton's specialties, tiny cubes of sirloin braised in herbs, pepper, and red wine until they were falling-apart tender. All kinds of bright fresh fruits graced the table, along with elaborate platters of candied fruits and sugared flowers, such as roses, carnations, nasturtiums, and lemon and orange blossoms.

Much discussion ensued about the relative merits of all the kinds of omelets that could be produced from the array of ingredients. Barbara said, "I'm quite bewildered, everything looks so delicious. But all I can think of is how much I'd like to eat the flowers. Do you suppose I could have a flower omelet?"

Monsieur Danton muttered darkly, "*Une fleur omelette! Mais non, hèlas!*"

The guests were amused, and Barbara blushed deeply. Giles said warmly, "I forbid you to be embarrassed, Miss Smythe. Countless times I've witnessed Lady Mirabella strip one of Madame Danton's cakes of all of the flower garnishes without touching a single crumb of the cake."

"That's very true, Miss Smythe," Mirabella said complacently. "I love edible flowers, especially when Madame Danton makes them, they are heavenly. And there is something decadent about eating flowers, which of course makes it all the more pleasurable, does it not?"

Lady Camarden said, "Mirabella, don't tease the child. I see that Monsieur Danton is beginning to look impatient, are we ready to place our orders? Miss Smythe, if you wish to have a flower omelet, I will brave Monsieur Danton's ill temper and order one for you. But I really think you might try the ham, Stilton cheese, and either the black or white truffles as you prefer. And you may eat as many of the flowers as you like without anyone believing that you've fallen into debauchery, regardless of what my cheeky daughter says."

The guests placed their orders, and Monsieur and Madame Danton went to work with their usual quick efficiency. As the diners waited for their omelets they snacked on the fresh bread with butter and fruits. Barbara shyly signaled the footman serving; he placed several flowers on her plate and she ate them with relish.

Giles asked, "And so, Miss Smythe, are you feeling particularly corrupted?"

"Perhaps a little, sir, but I refuse to let it deter me," she answered with a smile. "Here, I shall take three more of these orange blossoms, they are simply marvelous. Harry, don't you dare tell Mamma, she is adamant that I eat entirely too many sweets, and will end up as fat as Lady—" She put her hand over her mouth, her blue eyes wide and alarmed.

Rosalind laughed softly. "Miss Smythe, you really are delightful. Don't worry, all of us here can think of several ladies that would suit your mamma's example."

"So true," Lord Trevor said slyly. "Of course the first to come to mind is Lady—"

"That will do, Lord Trevor," Lady Camarden said. "If you young people don't start behaving yourselves, I'm going to have every dowager in London chaperone the next breakfast."

"That would be a shame, my lady," Lewin said. "For my part, I find it perfectly refreshing to have conversations with young ladies that don't consist of the state of the weather or the latest fashion in frocks. I have finally comprehended that those topics are the only ones approved by most mammas."

Denys Aldington said rather heavily, "That's been your experience, has it, Captain Rosborough? I've found that this Season, much as last Season, the young ladies have a somewhat more literate, informed conversation now."

Lewin said gravely, "Ah, yes, the Lord Byron craze. I stand corrected, many young ladies do discuss *Childe Harold* passionately."

"It has proven to be a most influential work," Denys said. "I found it to be quite a revelation, a new and brutally honest insight into the Peninsular War, indeed, into the brutality and waste of all wars."

Lewin remained silent, his face impassive, as, of course, he was an integral part of the "brutality and waste." Giles said blithely, "Come, Aldington, the ladies won't like to weep into their omelets. You bought a new saddle horse at Tattersalls, did you not? Out of Dangerfield himself, I believe?"

With some animation Denys spoke of his new mount, and the talk turned to horses, and then carriages, and the ladies joined in with their preferences for riding.

Mirabella said, "I do like riding, but I much prefer driving my phaeton, it's such fun for dashing about."

Giles said, "She's quite a whip hand, too, and knows it all too well. She's never let us drive her, has she, Lewin? It's a good thing I'm so secure in my masculinity that I don't mind trailing along with a lady driving me. Miss Smythe, do you ride, or drive your own carriage?"

Barbara looked rueful. "I hate to admit it, but I'm afraid of horses. I have a sweet old mare named Brynn that I ride at home sometimes, but I wouldn't dare ride her in the park, where everyone cuts such a dash. Brynn and I are like two old comfortable married people, just plodding along. And I wouldn't dare attempt to drive a carriage."

Rosalind said, "I can sympathize, Miss Smythe. I wasn't afraid of horses, I just never took the time to learn to ride or drive. But in this past year, during the winter, I was so dismally bored at Ellanthorpe that I learned to do both, and found that I enjoyed riding especially. I attribute my skill to my head groom, who is an excellent teacher, and has a wizard's way with horses."

Giles asked, "So you do ride, my lady? I ask, because I think I've only seen you in the park in your landau, with your coachman driving."

"Oh, yes, I've come to love to ride. I've charged my head groom with finding me a blood mount at Tattersalls," she said eagerly. "I can hardly wait to astound everyone with my equestrienne skills. Mirabella, I'm determined to outshine you."

"I'm certain you will, as the rules for sedate trots are so strict in the park, it's difficult to display my Corinthian expertise," Mirabella said regretfully.

"Yes, I know, we must observe the rules always," Lady FitzGeorge said disdainfully. "In Town, at least. But last year I found myself so enamored with riding, and the exercise, that I bought a hunter and organized a fox hunt at home. Of course, to my stepdaughter, it added two black marks against my good name. Riding to hounds, and the fact that I actually left the house and people saw me while I was in mourning. I did have a most fetching black riding habit, however, which consoled me considerably."

"So you ride to hounds, my lady?" Harry Smythe asked, bright-eyed. "That's right sporting of you."

"Not only that, but I learned to shoot as well, I found it most diverting," she replied, her dark eyes glowing. "I'm so looking forward to grouse season this year, I'm desperately searching for some amiable friends to invite me to their shooting box."

Mirabella said, "Rosalind, I'm amazed, and impressed. You must come to Littlemoor House with us this August. I may even prevail upon you to teach me to shoot."

"That would be interesting," Giles said blithely. "I haven't known Lady Mirabella to fire a gun, but there was one regrettable instance when I got a slingshot for my birthday. She plonked my dog so hard in the head that he was cross-eyed for a week."

Mirabella sniffed. "Shame on you for such a dreadful exaggeration, Giles. He wasn't cross-eyed at all, he completely recovered in a few minutes. Well, perhaps several minutes."

Rosalind said, "Never mind, I don't find that story shocking at all. When I was first learning to shoot, I nearly shot my loader's foot off. And then there was the time that one of my beaters' hats flew off; I maintained that it was because there was a stiff breeze.

The hat was found to have a hole in it, but I said that it was so shabby and worn the hole was likely already there."

"Perhaps it might not be such a grand idea for Lady FitzGeorge to teach you to shoot, Lady Mirabella," Lord Trevor said.

"Nonsense, aside from those two insignificant instances, I haven't come near to shooting anyone since," Rosalind said slyly.

Mirabella studied Rosalind as they dined. She recalled her again as a quiet, rather submissive girl when she married Lord FitzGeorge. She had certainly changed. Now, Mirabella reflected, she was not sweetly kittenish at all. Rather, her smile looked more like a feral cat's.

That's not fair, Rosalind may be more outspoken now, and her behavior may be slightly daring, but she's not cruel or mean. She's so beautiful, and yes, alluring, that men are certain to respond to her, even Giles flirts with her. As does Lord Trevor . . . but he flirts with all the ladies, I've come to see. Denys seems to be immune to her charms . . . he's so much more comforting to be with, he doesn't force me to constantly be on guard, or to continually try to fathom what he wants, and what he means.

She recalled the good-natured, easygoing, cheerful young man she'd known at Wetherley Manor. Denys had playfully teased his sister, and was always able to make her smile. He'd taught Mirabella how to skip stones on the lake. They'd had such fun together in the evenings, playing card games and betting with some object in the room; Mirabella won so often that Denys had joked that she owned the drawing room. Once Denys had, whispering, of course, bet his father, and Mirabella had bet the fire screen. Mirabella had won the hand, but declined to collect her winnings.

Mirabella thought, *I wonder, I wonder . . . ? Surely that amusing young gentleman is not gone forever. Perhaps I can find him again . . .*

Chapter Fifteen

Lady FitzGeorge's selection of guests for her dinner party made for a diverse group. They were eleven, for Lady FitzGeorge always favored the maximum of twelve for her parties. There was the brooding, dissolute Lord Byron; bright and vivacious Mirabella and her parents, the solid, plainspoken Lord Camarden and the acidic Lady Camarden; the clergyman's children Josephine and Lewin; and the gracious and gentle Lady Cowper and her husband, Lord Cowper, who in contrast to his wife had a reputation for dullness, slowness of speech, and little interest in society. Rosalind had also invited Giles, Denys Aldington, and Lord Trevor Brydges.

They gathered in Lady FitzGeorge's sumptuous drawing room, and Josephine and Lewin were introduced to Lord Byron. Mirabella watched Byron curiously. He was a heartbreakingly handsome man, not tall but sturdily built, with dark pools of eyes, thick curly dark hair, and fine, delicate features. The limp from a clubfoot he'd had since birth added to his tragic air. He greeted Josephine in his usual courtly manner, and immediately engaged Lewin in a discussion of the events in Spain in the Peninsular War.

The butler announced that dinner was served, and the guests filed in according to their rank. As they found their place cards at the table and the footmen seated them, Rosalind said, "Last week Lady Mirabella apologized for having an uneven number of ladies and gentlemen at her breakfast, but I make no such apologies. I find it much more enjoyable to have the gentlemen outnumber the ladies. It so rarely happens that ladies may have the pleasure of conversation with one, or even better, two amiable gentlemen."

Lord Byron was seated on Rosalind's right, and he said, "'Tis true, it seems that in Polite Society the ladies far outnumber the gentlemen."

"Particularly in the groups surrounding you, sir," Rosalind said.

Mirabella was seated between Lord Byron on her left and Lord Trevor on her right. The footmen began serving the first course of soups and entrees, and Rosalind immediately began the ritual of conversation by engaging Denys Aldington, who sat on her left, across from Byron.

Mirabella turned to Byron and said, "Sir, we have been introduced but once, very briefly last year at Lady Jersey's. I'd venture that you likely can't remember me, so I'd like to reintroduce myself, as it were."

"On the contrary, my lady, I remember you quite well," he said smoothly. "I'd be remiss indeed to forget such an entrancing young woman."

"Already I see that the rumors of your famous charm have not been exaggerated. Thank you, kind sir, but I beg you, don't fall into a trance, as I was hoping to have lively conversation with my dinner partners."

"I shall endeavor to remain conscious, and am at your service. What is your choice of topic for this lively conversation?"

Mirabella had heard that Byron was generally cordial and gentlemanly to ladies in light discourse, but that he was often impatient when they tried to engage him in discussion of serious topics. He possessed a vast intellect, a sharp and cutting mind, and it was said that he soon grew impatient with insipid conversation. She saw that he was baiting her, and she decided to take a chance. "As ladies so often do, I'll show proper deference to a gentleman, and allow you to choose the topic," Mirabella said in a slightly mocking tone. "Pray proceed, and I will follow."

Byron matched her mocking tone. "Somehow I find that to be unlikely. I've heard that Lady Mirabella Tirel follows no man, and no little woe may befall those who try to command her."

"Surely the genius Lord Byron is not choosing silly idle gossip as a topic for dinner conversation," Mirabella said lightly.

"Generally I find I have no other option when speaking with respectable young ladies. I see, however, that you may be an exception. Very well, as you have been so womanly in allowing me to guide our discourse, I will choose the usual favored topic of gentlemen, and talk about myself. Lady FitzGeorge has told me that you are not one of my most devoted admirers. Now that I've seen you might possibly have a bit of wit about you, I'm curious to hear your opinion. In spite of my lofty opinion of myself, I do value a thoughtful critique." Then he frowned, and contrary to his arrogant air, added uncertainly, "I beg your pardon, madam, for assuming that you've read any of my works. Certainly I know that not everyone on this earth has done so."

"You're forgiven, for you're very nearly correct. I must admit that I only read *Childe Harold* this last week, when I learned that you were one of Lady FitzGeorge's dinner guests," Mirabella said artlessly. "But now I'm glad I did. Once I took the time to read it carefully, I found that I enjoyed much of it, and came to appreciate that you are indeed a gifted poet."

"I think that you're more insightful than to offer such qualified and vague praise," he said intently. "I was sincere before, I would like to hear your thoughts."

Mirabella took a sip of delicious turtle soup. After a few moments she said, "You have a genius for vivid imagery, particularly in the physical scenery. All of the tactile senses are there: sight, sound, touch, smell, even taste. The contrasts you offer between filth and squalor, while still finding exotic beauty in the scene, are poignant and evocative."

"Thank you," he said rather automatically. "But?"

Mirabella smiled, thinking that she had never seen Lord Byron smile. "But my severest critique of your work is not one of quality. It is of the world view. Childe Harold is dissolute, downcast, and hopeless; he is afflicted with 'life-abhorring gloom.' I understand that there are people who feel such hopelessness, but I will never believe that such a desolate judgment of this world is the true perception of it."

"Harold is not insistent that all men, or women, follow his path. In fact, again and again he warns the reader to avoid his follies."

"Yes, but in his heart he believes that his hopelessness is the only reality on this earth," Mirabella retorted, then quoted:

Yet others rapt in pleasure seem,
And taste of all that I forsake:
Oh! may they still of transport dream,
And ne'er, at least like me, awake!

"Obviously he feels that others, who find joy, contentment, and beauty in life, are simply delusional."

A gleam of admiration flashed in his eyes. "You are clever to use my own words to refute me. Still, I think that you unjustly accuse me of a deranged world view. Again and again I've insisted that Childe Harold is in no way autobiographical."

"I beg your pardon, but I find that argument somewhat specious. You are a Christian, sir, and you must know this. No one but Almighty God can create a new, unique human being."

An expression of amazement crossed his face, and then he looked darkly amused, though of course he didn't smile. "And so it must necessarily follow that whatever we create must be a part of us, of our own experience and thought and spirit. Never in life did I think I'd be confounded by a mere girl."

Wryly Mirabella said, "It seems our conversation, which, I remind you, was chosen by you, has somewhat eroded your famous charm and gallantry."

He nodded his head in acknowledgment. "Forgive me, my lady, I grievously misspoke. You are far from a mere girl. You are indeed entrancing, and captivating, and if I may be so bold, I say that you're somewhat formidable. The silly idle gossip is true: woe is upon me for trying to best you."

"Nonsense, I'd never win an intellectual debate with you. I must tell you that I was obliged to look up almost every classical and mythological reference in *Childe Harold*. I'm an avid reader, but my study of classical history has been halfhearted at best. It's a certainty that you could easily confound me with Ovid or Homer."

"I have no wish to confound you, so let us lay aside classical history. I understand that you are quite an accomplished musician, so let's talk of music, another of my passions. Tell me about your music."

Mirabella enthusiastically told him of her love of music, particularly opera. He was knowledgeable, although he admitted he had no musical abilities. They found that they preferred many of the same operas and arias. When he disagreed with Mirabella, he was sharp and concise in his viewpoint, but he was not rude.

After the second course, Lady FitzGeorge "turned the table" and began to speak to Lord Byron. Mirabella turned to Lord

Trevor. "Sir, I beg you, may we have some frothy, meaningless conversation, please? I find that discourse with Lord Byron is somewhat taxing."

"He can be demanding; he continually challenges people to match wits with him. I refuse to play, for I know I could never win his little game, but he tolerates me anyway. And yes, my lady, I'll be glad to speak of inane trivialities, for I have a particular talent for it. Will this suit? Just today I finally got my uniform for the Four Horse Club, and it's such a disaster that I fear I won't be able to show my face next week for our race. The driving coat has fourteen capes instead of fifteen, my waistcoat doesn't fit, and aside from that tragedy the stripes look to me like a sort of putrid orangy thing instead of yellow. Also, my breeches are too short..."

Mirabella listened with amusement as Lord Trevor lamented his tailoring woes. The Four Horse Club, started by the inveterate carriage racer Lord Sefton, or Lord Dashalong as he was aptly nicknamed, consisted of aristocratic young men who were recognized as experts in the art of driving. They had a strict dress code: the club uniform was a long white driving coat with fifteen "capes," or short gathered lengths of fabric, beginning at the shoulders, and two tiers of pockets, a single-breasted blue coat with brass buttons, a Kerseymere waistcoat with inch-wide blue and yellow stripes, white corduroy breeches, short boots with long tops, and a white muslin cravat with black spots. It was quite a sight to see the twenty or so young bucks line up on Park Lane in their resplendent costumes, each of them driving a four-wheeled carriage with four horses, for their twenty-mile race to Salt Hill.

Mirabella again reflected on the contrast between Lord Trevor's physical appearance and his demeanor. His face was roughhewn, with a squared jaw and firm chin and high jutting cheekbones. He had the muscular physique of the athlete that he was, for he was known as a "Corinthian," a man who dressed with exquisite elegance, and was skilled in all the manly sports of boxing, fencing, sword fighting, singlestick, pistols, horsemanship, driving, and of course hunting and shooting. Yet for all his rough masculinity, which Mirabella saw was often paired with a sort of grimness, Lord Trevor was cheerful and witty, and seemed to delight in whatever company or situation he was in. This boyishness appealed to Mirabella. She contrasted it with the somber mien of Denys Aldington. As he conversed with Josephine, she saw that Josephine was smiling, and seemed to be trying to amuse him, but his demeanor remained grave.

Abruptly Lord Trevor paused in his list of tailoring woes and said, "Lady Mirabella, I'm shocked at your behavior. You've transgressed a strict rule of dinner discourse. I saw you watching Aldington while I was trying to impress upon you the gravity of my situation. It ain't fair, I prevailed upon Lady FitzGeorge to seat me next to you, so I did Aldington one in the eye, or so I thought. Now here you are moon-gazing at him."

"I am not moon-gazing, I never moon-gaze. In truth I was also thinking of you, sir. While I was sympathizing with your plight concerning your club uniform, I was also comparing your jovial demeanor with Mr. Aldington's continual somberness these days. He has changed much, it seems."

"Aldington's a good old stick, but he's been infected with the Byron fever. I'd find it dashed boring to mope about so for very long. I expect he'll grow out of it."

"The Byron fever?" Mirabella repeated with surprise. Suddenly she realized that the effusive quotation he'd recited to her at Almack's was a word-for-word passage from *To Ianthe*, the introduction to *Childe Harold*. Frowning, she asked, "Do you mean this sea change in his deportment is due to Lord Byron's influence?"

Lord Trevor shrugged. "He's not the first, nor will he be the last. Surely you've observed that many people of our acquaintance, both ladies and gentlemen, are affecting the tragic hero or heroine. Don't mistake me, Aldington's an old friend and I'm not accusing him of being weak-minded. I think the concept of a helpless, doomed romantic love has a sort of dark appeal to some."

"But not to you, I take it," Mirabella said lightly.

"Not at all, I'd much prefer to have a pleasant, companionable sort of love. I'm much too lazy to exert all of my energy in sighing over some hopeless inconsolable longings. But enough of these heavy musings, I'm already growing weary of them. Do you have any plans to go to the theatre soon? I know there are several productions this Season that are particular favorites of yours."

"And how would you know my favorites, sir?" Mirabella asked archly. "Surely we don't know each other that well."

"We don't, but I'd very much like to remedy that," he said slyly. "So I asked Knyvet, for I know that he's one of your favorites, too. He told me that you prefer Mozart, particularly the comedic operas, and I know that *Così Fan Tutte* is playing at Drury Lane and *Le Nozze di Figaro* is at Covent Garden. I'm sure you're going to see them."

"So I am: we're going to attend *Così Fan Tutte* next Friday, and *Le Nozze di Figaro* on Saturday in a fortnight. Do you plan to attend either of them?"

"Both of them," he replied with a devilish air, "if I can throw myself upon your mercy and beg a seat in your box, my lady."

"Lord Trevor, I know very well that you have family boxes at both royal theatres and so you have no need of begging for good seats. But since I have a generous, pitying nature, I will invite you to join us in our box."

"For both operas?" he demanded.

"Yes, for both operas."

"I shall count the hours to Friday next."

"You should not undertake such an onerous duty," Mirabella said severely. "If you are distracted, you will make a muddle of your tailoring repairs, you likely will not be able to tie your cravat to perfection, your breeches will remain too short, and you will be so engrossed in your numerical calculations that you will lose your Four Horse Club race."

Affecting anguish, Lord Trevor said, "No, no, such tragedies I could not bear. Let us just say that I shall be looking forward with pleasure to *Così Fan Tutte* on Friday."

Smiling, Mirabella said, "And so shall I."

For Mirabella, the other four courses of dinner were enjoyable. Lord Byron's topics were livelier now; he told her of his love of sport, including boxing, and of his friendship with Gentleman John Jackson. He asked her to tell him of her favorite pastimes, and seemed interested when she told him of her prosaic, peaceful life at Camarden Court. He did, however, engage her in some discussion as to whether most people could find joy in such quiet, uneventful surroundings. He used for his argument her love for the Season, and Mirabella was hard put to explain the apparent dichotomy between her love for country life and her love for city life, and to convince him that she could likely be happy if she never came to Town for the Season again. He was so incisive that she came away from the conversation unsure she would be happy never visiting Town again.

Lord Trevor was his usual amusing self, telling her of the latest gossip among the *ton*, including Lady Jersey's newest *faux pas*, telling the venerable old Lady Melbourne that she should avail herself of Floris's newest anti-wrinkle preparation. He also regaled Mirabella with stories of a party at Carlton House, when the prince regent, who had grown very fat, was so amused at some sally of Lord Alvanley's that he almost fell out of his chair, causing hysterical consternation among the gentlemen-in-waiting.

After a dessert course fully as lavish as one of Madame Danton's, Rosalind rose and announced that the ladies would withdraw and leave the men to their port. They went to the drawing room and gathered all together in a companionable group on the sofas and settees.

Rosalind asked Mirabella, "How did you find Lord Byron as a dinner partner, Mirabella?"

"Fierce and intimidating," she replied lightly, "and intriguing and charismatic. I'm truly quite fatigued, mentally at least. Please don't leave me alone with him again, Rosalind."

"Stuff and nonsense, you don't fool me in the least with all your missish airs," Rosalind scoffed. "I know you're one of the few young ladies that could hold his interest for more than four or five seconds."

"I believe he was only interested in engaging me in a serious conversation because of your shameful informing, Rosalind," Mirabella said playfully. "He told me that you had told him that I was no great admirer. However, I'm happy to say that I hurriedly worked through *Childe Harold's Pilgrimage* last week. I believe I was able to string together one or two sentences concerning it that made some sense."

There followed a general discussion of *Childe Harold*, with the ladies offering their views of it. Naturally the topic turned to Lady Caroline Lamb and her sad antics, and other gossip about Lord Byron. He was rumored to be now having an affair with the Countess of Oxford, who was fourteen years older than Byron.

The ladies abruptly cut off their conversation when the men joined them in the drawing room. Rosalind said, "As I promised, Lady Mirabella will grace us with some music."

One end of the long drawing room held a pianoforte and

a harp. Instead of rows of side chairs for an audience, Lady FitzGeorge had arranged comfortable settees and wing chairs around the musical instruments. As the guests seated themselves, Mirabella said, "I and my friends, Miss Rosborough and Sir Giles, have been practicing a trio from *Così Fan Tutte*, and I'm anxious to perform it. Josephine, Giles, please join me?"

Neither Josephine nor Giles had any coy false modesty, so with a will they joined Mirabella. Giles sat at the pianoforte, and Mirabella said wryly, "Sir Giles so excels at the piano that I flatly refuse to accompany myself when he's present, he quite puts me in the shade."

Giles made a half-bow to her and played the opening bars of the poignant "Soave Sia il Vento," "Gentle Is the Wind," only five lines that conveyed heartbreak because a loved one has left. Mirabella sang in her sweet soprano, Josephine in a soft mezzo soprano, and Giles in a clear, strong tenor.

When the aria ended, the applause was enthusiastic. Mirabella made as if to sit down, but Rosalind said sternly, "Mirabella, you did promise me, and one aria will not suffice. Please continue. Miss Rosborough, you have a lovely voice, if you should know any other duets, or trios, Sir Giles, it would give us great pleasure to hear them."

"You're very gracious, Lady FitzGeorge, but 'Soave Sia il Vento' is my sole claim to a repertoire for public performance," Josephine said easily. "I, too, should like to hear Lady Mirabella."

Mirabella made a small curtsy in acknowledgment and said to Giles, "Shall we lighten the mood somewhat? Please play 'Piercing Eyes.' "

With an innocent air Giles said, "I should much prefer another of Haydn's canzonets, I have such fond memories of it. If you please, Lady Mirabella." He played the first few bars of "The Mermaid's Song," winking slyly at her.

She made a very small momentary face at him, then sang the

song that she had sung on that oddly warm and glowing All Hallows' Eve when she had so ignominiously fallen into the stewpond.

Come with me, and we will go
Where the rocks of coral grow.
Follow, follow, follow me.

Come, behold what treasures lie
Far beneath the rolling waves. . . .

She sang the short song through twice, occasionally darting exasperated sidelong glances at Giles. When she finished, the applause was quite as keen as before.

Lord Byron, seated in a wing chair just by where Mirabella stood, said, "If Sir Giles can make requests, then so shall I. I know that 'Voi Che Sapete' is one of your favorite arias, my lady, so I'm certain it must be in your repertoire. Since I've discerned that you are averse to songs and tales of despair and heartbreak, I thought you might have pleasure in performing a lighthearted air."

Mirabella thought she could actually see a slight sparkling of amusement in Lord Byron's eyes, and she smiled. "Then 'Voi Che Sapete,' please, Sir Giles, for my Lord Byron."

Mirabella thought she saw an unhappy shadow cross Giles's face, but it was so quickly replaced by his blandly pleasant expression she told herself she must have been mistaken. She sang the aria from *Le Nozze di Figaro*, the full theatrical version, which was almost five minutes long. Although it was not coloratura, it was still demanding. When Mirabella finished she refused to sing any more. Laughingly she said, "If I sing much longer I shall be croaking a hoarse tuneless alto."

Lord Byron rose and bowed deeply to her. "That would be a tragedy of despair and heartbreak indeed. The sirens were dangerously beautiful creatures who lured sailors to their deaths with their enchanted songs. I can sympathize with them, my lady, for when you sing I would almost wish to follow you 'far beneath the rolling waves.' "

Giles had come to stand by Mirabella, and he said innocently, "I cannot recommend it, sir. If you didn't drown, you would certainly get wet and cold and likely be subject to a tongue-lashing to boot."

Mirabella gaily took Giles's arm and furtively pinched it, hard. Giles's mild expression didn't change, but he blinked furiously several times. Mirabella said, "Sir Giles, it's rude to speak of private jokes to persons who cannot participate in them. Sir, I assure you he hasn't lost his senses, he's merely referring to a silly incident that happened—er—long ago."

Lord Byron cocked one eyebrow. "Long ago? When you were children, growing up together, perhaps?"

Uncomfortably Mirabella replied, "Um—no—that is, it was some time ago."

Giles said, "Some *long* time ago."

"Ah, I see," Byron said, glancing quickly back and forth between Giles and Mirabella. "Well, in spite of the inscrutability of your warning, Sir Giles, I'll make sure that I never follow Lady Mirabella beneath the rolling waves. Aside from a stubborn desire to avoid death, I intensely dislike being wet, cold, and subjected to tongue-lashings."

Rosalind joined them, and slipped her arm through Lord Byron's. "Who would dare to give you a tongue-lashing, sir? I shall put a stop to it immediately."

"I have had a narrow escape, but the danger is now averted," he said gravely. "Now, what is this you tell me of your new faro table? Are we to have some cards?"

"Certainly, we're all repairing to the cardroom now," she said.

The cardroom, like the rest of Lady FitzGeorge's town house, was luxuriously furnished and decorated. The gaming tables were of rich mahogany, the chairs overstuffed and comfortable, the upholstery, wall hangings, and draperies of plush red velvet with gilt embroidery. Along one wall was a massive sideboard, attended by two footmen, that held all manner of refreshment: champagne on ice, several kinds of wine, sherry, port, brandy, tea, coffee, chocolate, lemonade, and fruit ices.

The guests sorted themselves out according to their gaming favorites. Lady FitzGeorge, Lord Trevor, Denys Aldington, and Lord Byron wanted to play faro; Lord and Lady Cowper and Lord and Lady Camarden decided on whist; Josephine, Lewin, Giles, and Mirabella wanted to play one of their favorites that they'd played many times at Camarden, a board game called Pope Joan. The players bet on different compartments on the board: Queen, Matrimony, King, Ace, Game, Nine, Jack, and Intrigue.

The chairs and tables had to be shifted about somewhat to accommodate the various games. While Rosalind and the gentlemen were attending to it, Mirabella got a cup of tea and sat down on a settee. Denys Aldington joined her.

"My lady, hearing you sing is like partaking of ambrosia and nectar, the food and drink of the gods," he said ardently.

Mirabella reflected that Lord Trevor must be correct; such dramatic praise sounded much more like Lord Byron than Denys Aldington. "You are too kind, sir," she said rather automatically.

"I found your rendition of 'Voi Che Sapete' especially moving. I cannot agree with Byron, instead of a lighthearted song I find it especially poignant and full of passion." Mirabella had sung in Italian, but Denys quoted in English:

I have a feeling full of desire,
That now, is both pleasure and suffering.

At first frost, then I feel the soul burning,
And in a moment I'm freezing again.
Seek a blessing outside myself,
I do not know how to hold it, I do not know what it is.
I sigh and moan without meaning to,
Throb and tremble without knowing,
I find no peace both night or day. . . .

Isn't that the very portrait of love's deepest longings?"

Mirabella replied, "Perhaps for some it may be, I suppose. But you've left out the next line, which says to me that the lady is merely indulging herself in sentimental romantic delusions: *But even still, I like to languish.*"

He frowned. "But surely you cannot discount such fervent expressions of love."

Mirabella smiled. "Since they are not part of my experience, I must indeed discount them, for myself at any rate. Come, sir, you are very solemn this evening, and I won't have it. Tell me, do you enjoy the opera?"

With an effort at lightening his expression, he replied, "Indeed I do, and the theatre, also."

"Just this evening I've decided to invite friends in our box next Friday for *Così Fan Tutte*. Would you care to join us?"

"Thank you, I would love to, madam," he said, and for once his expression was happy and his eyes shone with pleasure.

The tables were arranged, and now the group gathered at another sideboard attended by the butler. On it were three great silver bowls and a large leather-bound book with gilt-edged pages. The bowls held gambling fish, the markers used for placing wagers. The fish could be as simple as small pewter rectangles, but Lady FitzGeorge's markers were elaborately carved, realistic-looking fish made of mother-of-pearl. They were of different sizes: the smallest fish was worth one pound, the next size five pounds, the largest ten pounds. Each guest checked out their desired markers and entered them in the book. After play was over, as at the most fashionable gentlemen's club, White's, the guests entered their wins and losses.

Mirabella, Josephine, Lewin, and Giles were the last to check out their counters. Giles said to the solemn butler, "We are making a slight alteration in the denomination of the markers."

"Certainly, sir. How do you wish to value them?"

"They are each valued as a fish. The largest are pike, the next are tench, and the smallest are perch. Each of us will take four of each."

It was, to say the least, an outlandish request, but like all superior butlers for the *haut ton*, he showed absolutely no surprise at the vagaries of the nobility. "Yes, sir, I shall record it as Lady Mirabella Tirel, Sir Giles Knyvet, Miss Rosborough, and Captain Rosborough each withdrawing four pike, four tench, and four perch."

Josephine and Mirabella giggled as they returned to the table where their board game was set up. "He didn't even blink," Mirabella said with delight. "One would think everyone bets fish."

They sat down at the table and Josephine complained, "It's hardly fair, you know. I'm the only one who doesn't fish, I don't know how I shall ever pay my gambling debts."

"Mirabella can teach you to fish," Giles said. "It's quite an adventure, fishing with her."

"Shush!" Mirabella hissed. "You promised you wouldn't tell anyone in London that I fish."

"I'm not telling random persons in London, I'm telling Josephine and Lewin. You see, all of that fun about 'The Mermaid Song,' it so happened—"

"Oh, Giles, do be quiet, I'm never singing that song again as long as I live," Mirabella said crossly.

Lewin grinned. "But I would like to hear the story. It concerns the day that you and Giles came into the conservatory as wet and dripping as drowned wraiths, does it not?"

Mirabella made a face at him, but she didn't object as Giles continued, in a discreet low voice, to tell Lewin and Josephine about Mirabella's dunking. He told it whimsically, theatrically exaggerating the danger and his part in rescuing Mirabella from a horrible death.

As they played, the four went on talking of homey little doings at Camarden, of the stewpond, of the rescued fawn Dolly that now refused to return to the deer park, doggedly following the stablemen around, and who had become a much-beloved and -indulged occupant of the stable. Josephine told them of a letter she'd had from her father, telling of how well the Neary brothers were doing: they had not only worked diligently at stocking and landscaping the village stewpond, they also were working hard in the cattle barns for a wage, and were conscientiously farming their allotment. The four friends discussed other tenants' and cottagers' doings, births and deaths and engagements and marriages. They talked of Mirabella's plans to try to raise some orchids, those most delicate and exotic flowers, in her conservatory. It occurred to Mirabella that she was having as much fun now as she had at any glittering, lavish diversion that she had attended in London.

The gaming lasted for three hours. Although Josephine and Lewin had some small winnings, Mirabella and Giles took the prize pots.

Giles won the large pot from the Matrimony compartment.

Mirabella won the Intrigue.

Chapter Sixteen

As it was a Law of London Ladies' Fashion that they wear their most opulent gowns and jewels to the theatre, Mirabella happily chose her birthday gown, with her magnificent sapphires, for the opening night of *Così Fan Tutte*. Josephine again wore the emerald-green satin gown, and for tonight Mirabella persuaded her to wear one of her tiaras, a small circlet of gold with tiny pearl insets, and Mirabella's pearl necklace.

As they surveyed themselves in Mirabella's full-length cheval mirror, she said complacently, "We look stunning."

Josephine replied, "Don't we? I think we should wear these to church when we get home. Everyone would be 'astonied,' as it says in the Bible."

"I just hope the gentlemen are astonied," Mirabella said.

"Ah, thou wouldst devise an ambushment for the young men," Josephine said, her dark eyes gleaming.

Joining the game, Mirabella intoned, "Shalt not take them with my eyelids, nor let my lips drip as the honeycomb."

"Mm, methinks thou meanest *drop* as the honeycomb," Josephine said.

This set the girls giggling, and they continued their game as they joined Lord and Lady Camarden in the coach.

"Thinkest shalt be sweet music of the sackbut tonight?" Mirabella asked.

Deadpan, Josephine answered, "Aye, and of the psaltery, the dulcimer, the trumpet, the harp, the timbrel, stringed instruments and organs, and the high-sounding cymbals."

Lord Camarden, who was frowning with concentration, now turned to his wife and said, "Ah, I see. They're speaking King James version."

Lady Camarden said, "Yes, the sackbut and high-sounding cymbals rather gave it away."

Mirabella said, "O my father, hast provided wine for our pleasure on this night? For we thirst for a firkin or two of wine."

Dryly Lord Camarden replied, "Of course we'll have refreshments in the box tonight. However, since a firkin is something over eight gallons, I sincerely doubt that Audrey will allow you two girls to have one, much less two."

The exterior of the Theatre Royal, Drury Lane was rather plain, but the interior was palatial. The decor was primarily white and gold. The grand staircase that led up to the boxes was situated under the magnificent rotunda, which was thirty feet in diameter and surrounded by a circular gallery that held statues and busts of famous actors, musicians, and poets. Everywhere, including in each box, were elaborate crystal and gilt chandeliers that held dozens of candles.

The Camarden box was one of the best seats in the house, the second box on the right in the first tier. The box was roomy; it held twelve armless white chairs, with comfortably padded seats and backs of crimson velvet. The box was large enough to accommodate twenty chairs, but Lord and Lady Camarden rarely invited parties of that size. The boxes were tiered by three shallow steps, with the ladies usually sitting on the lowest level, lining the railing. This was convenient for others in the second and third levels, for the ladies' high headdresses did not block their view.

The seating in the theatres was firmly fixed. The ruling class—the aristocracy and the gentry—had boxes. The middle class had seats on the floor, which were called the "stalls," and were simply long benches with no backs. The lower class, servants and the laboring poor, sat in the gallery, the uppermost tier, hot and dirty, crammed against the ceiling. Often the occupants in the gallery were rowdy and noisy, catcalling and sometimes throwing rotten fruit and vegetables at the actors. Mirabella had found, however, that those in the gallery were more well-behaved at the opera, and at first had wondered why. Gradually it had occurred to her that the poor had little opportunity to hear the majestic music of a full orchestra. Obviously the poor could never afford a pianoforte or a harp for their home; at most they might hear superior music if they happened to have a good organ, and an accomplished organist, at church. The realization had made her uncomfortable, as she reflected that she so often took her exalted position, her life of privilege, and her wealth for granted.

None of these humble musings were in her mind, however, as she and Josephine, arm-in-arm and still speaking in seventeenth-century English, ascended the Grand Staircase to the Camarden box. The party was early, as they were expecting guests, but Giles had already arrived. He was standing, conversing with the Camardens' butler Irby. Mirabella had not been indulging in a fantasy when she had asked her father if he had provided firkins of wine. Although the Drury Lane theatre had a luxurious Grand Saloon where gentlemen could go to enjoy refreshments, and could also order bottles of wine, sherry, various cordials, and other beverages to be delivered to their boxes, Lord Camarden had found that often the Grand Saloon was crowded and busy, particularly during intermission, and so he had done away with that nuisance by having a small sideboard installed in the box, and stocking it with his own crystal glasses and refreshments. When he had first devised this, Lord Camarden had intended for one of the under-footmen to attend the guests in the box, but Irby had, with an abnormal awkwardness, requested that he be allowed to attend them at the theatre. Lord Camarden had remarked to his wife and daughter that he thought it was an odd request, for the butler, the highest-ranking servant, never actually served meals or refreshments; generally he would have been horrified to be so "demoted." Mirabella had thought it odd, too, until she had noticed the rapt, intent expression on Irby's face during plays or operas. Still she wondered at his apparent enjoyment. Usually the theatre presented two or even more productions, so Irby was obliged to stand for sometimes five or six hours at a time, for no servant would ever, *ever* sit in the presence of his employers. Every time Mirabella had stolen a glance at him, however, he had seemed wholly immersed in the performance.

Giles turned to greet them, and said, "Irby has just been telling me of the delicious new concoctions Madame Danton has made for us. I'm having great difficulty in choosing between the raspberry-cherry shrub, or the pineapple-coconut punch."

"Pineapple-coconut punch?" Mirabella repeated, bright-eyed. "That sounds wonderful, Irby. Giles, where is Lewin?"

He bowed deeply. "Captain Rosborough asked me to beg your indulgence this evening, and excuse him from the pleasure of attending you. Two soldiers from his regiment are here in Town, and they are attending the opera this evening. As they are to return to Spain soon, he hoped that you would understand his desire to sit with them, and forgive him for his absence."

"Good heavens, there's no need for such pomp and ceremony from Lewin," Mirabella scoffed. "Where are they sitting?"

Giles walked to the front railing, followed by Josephine and Mirabella. He said, "There, in the ninth row."

Mirabella saw Lewin, his face upturned, gazing at the box, and two young men in a much humbler version of the uniform of the Ninety-Fifth Rifles, for they were common soldiers and not officers. Lewin spoke to his two friends, who were gazing around, wide-eyed, their mouths gaping open. They looked up at the box. Mirabella nodded in a queenly manner to them. All three stood up and bowed deeply.

Mirabella said, "Giles, go to them and ask them to join us. We have plenty of room, I've only invited Lady FitzGeorge, Lord Trevor, and Mr. Aldington."

With an indulgent half-smile on his face, Giles replied, "That's kind of you, but it really won't do, you know."

"What do you mean? Surely you aren't turning into a snob, are you?"

"I hope not, for it seems to me that such persons, regardless of their station, seem to be in a perpetual state of indignation about one thing or another, and therefore can't possibly be very happy. What I meant was, it simply won't do for Mr. Olliff and Mr. Prichett, the two gentlemen accompanying Lewin. Mr. Olliff is the son of a butcher, and Mr. Prichett is the son of a carter. I'm fairly certain that neither of them has ever set eyes on a member of the nobility, much less ever been introduced to an aristocrat."

"But I'd be nice to them, you know I would," Mirabella insisted.

"Yes, you would, but the point is that they wouldn't know how to be nice to you," Giles patiently explained. "They're fine fellows, but their manners are unpolished. Imagine, the little education they've had somehow did not include how to address a marquess and marchioness, and how to behave around such exalted beings. They'd be deeply embarrassed to be presented to you and your parents."

"But Giles, you know that my parents aren't snobs either, we would take pains to make them at ease," Mirabella said stubbornly.

Josephine said, "We know that, Mirabella, for we've seen how you and your parents treat everyone with such courtesy at Camarden, but the congenial atmosphere you've created there is the exception, rather than the rule. And the social interaction is still limited, isn't it? I mean, can't you think of how horrified old Mrs. Varney would be if you invited her to a dinner party?"

This threw Mirabella into a brown study. Josephine and Giles were right, of course. It wasn't fair, and it wasn't the way God had intended His people to live together in communities, but it was the truth. To demand that such people as Mrs. Varney and the soldiers interact with her on her level would place an impossible burden on them, much as if an illiterate man were required to read the Scriptures in church.

Then another realization dawned on Mirabella. For the same reasons, she would not, could not, be welcome at dinner at, say, Mr. Causby the butcher's home. This gave Mirabella the strangest, most uneasy feeling. She was so accustomed to being liked, to being sought out, to being welcomed in company. It had never occurred to her that there was any place or circumstance in which this would not be so. She was at a loss to know what to do about it, and decided that she would talk to Giles.

There was a stir in the box, and Lady FitzGeorge, Lord Trevor, and Denys Aldington all arrived together. After all the greetings, the party sorted itself out to get seated, for it was nearing performance time. Josephine, Mirabella, and Rosalind sat in the front row. Although there were two empty seats at the ends of the first row, Giles, Denys, and Lord Trevor sat behind them in the second row. Lord and Lady Camarden sat in the third row, in the corner, effectively withdrawing themselves from the young people while still providing the required chaperonage.

As usual, the ladies spoke on the most important topic first: their gowns. Rosalind was wearing a dramatic gown of glossy satin that was a deep copper color, neither red nor brown, but glimmering with those colors as she moved. Her headdress was the newest fashion, a turban made of the same satin, wound about her head but allowing tendrils of curls to escape around her face and neck. The turban was anchored on the side by a large square-cut emerald set in gold filigree, and holding three pheasant feathers that were not upright, but were rakishly set to brush against her shoulders and back.

Mirabella sighed, "I'm so envious, Rosalind, for I know very well that I ought not wear that daring color, even though we're much the same age."

"You must get married and then widowed, darling," Rosalind said. "Then you'll be allowed all sorts of freedoms."

The gentlemen were eavesdropping, and behind them Lord Trevor intoned, "Rather hard on the husband, wouldn't you say, Lady Mirabella? To sacrifice himself so that his wife might dress up as a Turkish sultana?"

"Do be quiet, Trevor, you can't possibly understand the suffocating rules we ladies must endure," Rosalind scolded. "Besides, you might have meant it as a compliment, but now you've conjured up a mental image in which I look like a raisin."

This caused general merriment in the group, and Lord Trevor, instead of apologizing, merely grinned. The orchestra began playing the overture, and they all turned their attention to the stage.

Mirabella loved the opera in many different ways, and for many reasons. She wholly admired the operatic voice, both male and female. She marveled at the strength required to project such a strong, emphatic, ringing voice. The grandeur of opera generally meant that the costumes and sets were more elaborate and enchanting than those of plays. Only in opera was there a blend of the spoken word and music that was mysterious and visceral, for it affected her on a deeper level than a symphony, which gave her an enjoyment mostly based on her intellect and her affinity for music in general, as she was a musician. Often she experienced a deeper involvement with the music of some majestic hymns: one of her favorites was Martin Luther's "A Mighty Fortress Is Our God," and she never failed to feel a thrill when she sang it. The sensations, or more likely moments of revelation, awoke in her reverence and awe.

The opera was different. It seemed that Mirabella felt true passion, the human, natural emotion of passion in all its intensity, and only when she was in such thrall could she catch at least glimmers of the true fires of passionate love that could exist between a man and a woman. As she immersed herself in the music, one part of her mind, a secondary and very quiet, unobtrusive voice, was wondering if this was the only way she would ever feel such passion—only vicariously. If so, was that a good thing or—

Both her absorption in the music and her deep inner musings were interrupted. Mirabella realized with dismay that directly behind her, Denys Aldington was speaking to Giles. He was not whispering; he was speaking in a low voice that was discreet, so much so that Mirabella couldn't actually hear the words over the music. Still, it was an almost intolerable distraction to Mirabella. She glanced at Rosalind and Josephine, and neither of them appeared to be affected at all.

Reluctantly she had to admit to herself that Denys had committed no social breach, for the protocols at the theatre were rather vague. It was not considered ill-bred or rude to talk during a performance. Indeed, in many of the boxes, comings and goings to other boxes and to the Grand Saloon took place constantly.

Still, Mirabella had always had the distinct impression that some people preferred to enjoy the music or play in silence, and by all rules of social gatherings, the host and hostess set the tone and timbre of interaction. Casting about in her mind, Mirabella thought that usually parties in the Camarden box didn't converse, or get up and mill about. She thought that Denys, being a well-bred gentleman, should be more sensitive and perceptive. The realization that this was an unreasonable and illogical demand—not to mention uncharitable—didn't lessen Mirabella's irritation. She just wished Denys would be quiet.

She noticed that Giles was either responding with voiceless expressions such as nods and smiles, or else was speaking in such a low whisper as to be inaudible. Eventually Denys's low rumbles came to an end, and again Mirabella was able to lose herself in the music.

The time seemed much shorter to Mirabella, but intermission came in a little over an hour and a half. Everyone stood up and walked around a bit, both to stretch their legs and to order a refreshment from Irby. Mirabella got a second glass of Madame Danton's delectable pineapple-and-coconut-cream punch and went to stand at the railing, looking around and acknowledging nods and bows from her acquaintances in the other boxes, for the premier reason for most of the Beau Monde to attend the theatre (except for people like Mirabella) was to see and be seen. Mirabella scanned the floor and saw that, as always, hundreds of faces were upturned to ogle the Quality. She caught Lewin's eye again and smiled. Again he rose and bowed, smiling back up at her. Then she saw, with dismay, that the Smythes were seated in the humble stalls, about the tenth row back, and on the other side of the theatre.

She went to join her friends, who were standing in a loose circle behind the chairs in the third row. Her parents were still sitting in the corner, talking together in low voices. "Giles, I've seen the

Smythes sitting down in the stalls, on those dismal benches. Please go down and invite them to join us."

He gave a small bow. "As always, I'm at your service, my lady."

As he left, Rosalind rolled her eyes and said to Lady Camarden, "Madam, please do me a great service and take the empty seat by me. I declare I cannot endure Mrs. Smythe's flutterings and grovelings for four hours."

"I regret I cannot rescue you, Rosalind," Lady Camarden replied tartly. "My husband *will* fall asleep at the opera, and I'm in constant fear that he'll fall out of this spindly armless chair, it requires constant vigilance on my part."

"I only wish you'd let me bring my old wing chair and footstool here, it's the only sensible solution," Lord Camarden said grumpily.

"It most certainly is not, for when you nap in such comfort you snore," Lady Camarden snapped. "At least here all that happens is that your mouth gapes open, and when you start dribbling I know it's a signal to awaken you."

Lord Trevor said, "Lady FitzGeorge, if you will allow me the honor and pleasure, I'd be happy to save you from Mrs. Smythe's clammy clutches, and take the seat next to you."

"Thank you, sir, you are Sir Galahad personified," Rosalind said fervently.

"Please, madam, just because I called you a raisin, you'll demote me to a knight?"

More verbal sparring ensued between Rosalind and Lord Trevor, and Josephine and Denys began talking about the opera. Mirabella stood silent for a few moments, watching Denys. She had noted that he had displayed very little amusement at the witticisms in their conversations; only a slight gleam in his eyes had shown that he even understood the humor. He did affect the Byronic tragic hero well.

Mirabella was irritated with Denys's silly phase, for she had begun considering Denys Aldington as a possible suitor, and future husband. After the confusing and vexing speed that had overwhelmed her with Lord Southam, Mirabella had been much more cautious and analytical when considering marriage to Denys. She still thought much as she had when she and Josephine had made their "charts"—that he would make a fine, honorable, dutiful husband and in particular would be a wonderful father. But as for a lifetime companionship, Mirabella felt very hesitant, considering this somewhat heavy-spirited man who bore so little resemblance to the good-natured, animated gentleman she had known before.

Mirabella recalled that she had meant to ask Giles about Denys, and she thought that just a few moments ago she had so blithely decided to talk to him about the wide gulf in social status between them and Lewin's friends. She realized, regretfully, that she'd had no opportunity in the last two months to speak to Giles alone. She saw him almost every day at Camarden; but then life was so different in Town. She resolved to buttonhole him and demand some private time together.

Gradually everyone drifted back to their seats. Denys and Lord Trevor slightly rearranged the front row of chairs so the ladies could converse with those behind them without craning their necks. Lord Trevor then, as promised, took the empty seat by Rosalind. Mirabella said to Josephine, "I know you won't mind, dearest, if Barbara sits between us? I've barely had a chance to speak to her this Season."

"Of course I don't mind," Josephine said. "I like her, too, and would like the opportunity to get to know her better." Then she added in a whisper, "But I do promise not to talk to her during the performance. Methinks you grew exceeding wroth at the vain babblings behind us."

Mirabella whispered back, "Aye, verily, but I am constrained to turn from such iniquity, and not regard it forever."

Giles arrived with the Smythes, and the proper greetings, curtsies, and bows took place. Although Mirabella and Rosalind had deftly planned the seating arrangements, the Smythes were not aware of their assignments, and took seats that proved most satisfactory to Rosalind, and most unsatisfactory to Mirabella. Mrs. Smythe, at Lady Camarden's invitation, took the seat next to her with apparent bliss, and Mr. Smythe sat by his wife. To Mirabella's consternation, Giles held out the seat by him, and Barbara sat down, smiling up at him. Now she sat in the second row between Giles and Denys.

Harry then came to Josephine in the front row, and requested the honor of sitting next to her.

Josephine turned to Mirabella and asked, "Do you mind?"

Mirabella was still staring at Giles and Barbara and answered absently, "What? But I—oh. Oh, no, of course I don't mind, dearest."

For a moment Mirabella considered asking if she might sit between Giles and Barbara. She had, after all, wanted to have some time with Barbara.

Then the wild absurdity of such a request—not to mention the rudeness—hit Mirabella. Also, a small timid voice somewhere in the back of her mind mumbled, *But wouldn't it be less intrusive, maybe even fitting, to sit between Denys and Barbara? After all, you are considering him as a suitor, and he knows it and seems to welcome it, and that way you could also sit by your friend, as you intended.*

But that was not at all what Mirabella wanted, and angrily she silenced this bizarre Other Person talking in her head.

So what *did* she want?

No, no, no, just stop it this instant. This entire . . . thing . . . idea . . .

train of thought is ludicrous! What difference does it make where everyone is sitting? That's right, it makes no difference at all!

But as she watched Giles and Barbara, their heads close together, speaking in low tones, she realized that she was in truth nettled at the sight. She told herself that on her right, Josephine and Harry were talking, and on her left, Rosalind and Lord Trevor were talking privately, and that it was perfectly permissible and proper for them to do so. It so happened that in such a small group the ladies and gentlemen engaged in conversations as couples—

Couples? Giles and Barbara Smythe—a couple?

This upset Mirabella, and then she was puzzled as to why she was so upset, and then she grew vexed at herself for being upset, and then her thoughts were thrown into so much turmoil that she wished she could just get up and leave, and get some fresh air, and be alone for a while to sort it all out.

But that was impossible, of course. With a tremendous effort she wrenched her mind back to her surroundings. She realized that Denys must have said something to her, for he was staring at her with that quizzical expression of one who has spoken to a companion who is paying no attention at all. Then she became aware that not only Denys, but everyone in the loose circle was looking at her. Apparently the conversation had changed from couples (Mirabella still mentally stuttered over the word) to general group discourse.

Smiling brightly, she said, "Oh, I do beg your pardon, I was woolgathering. You are all looking at me so expectantly, I surmise that someone has spoken to me, so I'll summon my wits and try to behave like a civilized human being."

Gallantly Denys said, "Please, madam, you could never be other than the most elegant and gracious of ladies. We were discussing opera, and I said that though I enjoy *Così Fan Tutte* and

Le Nozze di Figaro, I prefer *opera seria* to *opera buffa*, which I find a light and frothy diversion. In contrast, *opera seria*, such as Gluck's *Orfeo ed Euridice*, Purcell's *Dido and Aeneas*, and Handel's *Tamerlano* present noble, eternal, tragic themes that enrich both the understanding and the soul. Knyvet said you would disagree with me, and I was interested in your thoughts."

Mirabella felt suddenly impatient with Denys's airs, and she answered somewhat brusquely, "Certainly *opera seria* consists of eternal and tragic themes, since generally they all ultimately end with death. But *opera buffa* is no less thought-provoking, for it, too, illustrates timeless themes. *Così Fan Tutte* deals with fidelity and loyalty, and *Le Nozze di Figaro* explores such human concerns as the complexity of love, and betrayal and forgiveness. Simply because *opera buffa* incorporates the element of merriment and appeals to one's sense of amusement, such as do satire and parody, it does not necessarily mean that it is any less profound."

Denys looked bemused, and Giles said, "I did try to warn you, Aldington. Leave it, you can't win."

Barbara sighed deeply. "I have no pretensions to such clever insights. In fact, I have difficulty understanding most opera on any count, for although I can speak French tolerably well, my Italian is lamentable. I'm not even certain exactly what *Così Fan Tutte* means."

Airily Giles said, "The literal translation is 'Thus Do They All,' but it's understood to mean 'Thus Do All Women,' or 'Women Are Like That.' "

Spiritedly Mirabella retorted, "Oh, yes, understood by *men*, by misogynists. I must point out that it was Ferrando and Guglielmo that placed a wager on their fiancées' faithfulness, and then proceeded to try to seduce each other's fiancée. If that's not betrayal, I cannot imagine how you would define it."

Giles said, "I must agree with you, for the subtitle is *Ossia la*

Scuola Degli Amanti, 'The School for Lovers,' not 'The School for Ladies,' and so it's obvious that Mozart never intended to besmirch the ladies only. However, I must take exception to you naming me a misogamist. I don't hate marriage, at all."

In a high and unnatural voice Mirabella said, "Marriage! Who was talking about marriage? I certainly wasn't!"

Gently Josephine said, "Mirabella, it was a malapropism, you see. *Misogamist*, not misogynist."

Mirabella stared at her. "Oh. Oh, yes, of course. Misogamy." She looked around at the group. Harry and Barbara looked bewildered, Denys looked confused, Lord Trevor looked amused, while Rosalind had the tolerant half-smile on her face that people tended to assume when they had no idea of the point of the joke. Giles grinned and winked at Mirabella, which for some reason irritated Mirabella even more.

The intermission ended. Mirabella found that now she had a difficult time concentrating on the performance. Her thoughts were still in a whirl, mostly of speculation about Giles and Barbara Smythe. Again and again she tried to focus on the splendid music, but she kept finding that her attention wandered. She told herself that it was because she was distracted; behind her Denys kept whispering to Barbara. Mirabella assumed that he was whispering translation to her, so as not to embarrass her. Again, she couldn't hear the words over the music, but she did keep hearing the sibilant *s*'s that are so keenly audible to the human ear. By the time the performance had ended Mirabella's nerves were so taut that she felt she could cheerfully strangle Denys Aldington. The vehemence of her emotions was an unpleasant surprise to Mirabella, as the offense was so trivial and innocuous. Generally she was not so highly strung. Severely she told herself to calm down and stop acting like an insane person.

The second intermission arrived, for as usual in the theatre, there was a second production. It was to be Thomas Dibdin's pantomime, *Harlequin and Mother Goose; or, The Golden Egg*. Giles, Lord Trevor, and Denys begged leave to go and visit acquaintances in the other boxes, a common pleasant intermission diversion for the gentlemen and one strictly forbidden to the ladies. Mr. and Mrs. Smythe, with effusive thanks, took their leave, asserting that they rarely stayed for second productions due to the lateness of the hour. They secured Lady Camarden's assurance that she would not mind chaperoning Miss Smythe, and said they would send back the carriage for Harry and Barbara.

Lady FitzGeorge, deprived of the male company she seemed to prefer, talked to Lord and Lady Camarden—mostly Lord Camarden, Mirabella noted wryly. Her father was immune to flirting, he seemed utterly tone-deaf to it, and her mother knew it. Lady Camarden's expression was one of narrow, dry amusement.

Josephine and Harry were talking together quietly, and Mirabella took the opportunity to sit down by Barbara. After some small talk, Mirabella said brightly, "It seems that you and Sir Giles have become friends. He's a lot of fun, isn't he?"

"Oh, yes, he's witty and clever and a most congenial gentleman," Barbara agreed, blushing a little. "He's very kind to me."

"He is a kind man, I suppose," Mirabella said. "Although he does tease me unmercifully."

"But that's not unkindness, he enjoys matching wits with you, for you're fully as sharp-witted as he. I'm not nearly so intelligent, so he treats me differently."

"Barbara, you are not unintelligent, it's merely that there's a wide variance between peoples' interests, education, background, and tastes. Mm—how, precisely, would you say that he treats you?"

Her smooth brow wrinkled. "He's one of the few gentlemen that actually take an interest in what I have to say, in my opinions, in my viewpoint. At least, he appears to; as I said, he may simply be kind."

"No, Giles is not artificial in that way," Mirabella said thoughtfully. "It seems you've had opportunity for much conversation with him. Isn't that—well, rather unusual? What I mean is, it's so difficult for a single young lady to have any meaningful conversation with a gentleman, our discourse with them is so restricted, as we're always so closely chaperoned, and critically observed, too, in social situations."

"That is generally true, but I've found that Mamma has eased her fanatical hawk-eyed oversight of me this Season. I think that she's come to trust me more, and also she's seen that Harry takes very good care of me. As for my friendship with Sir Giles, it's really because of Harry. He and Sir Giles and Captain Rosborough have been spending much time together, and so naturally I see Sir Giles, and Captain Rosborough, more than I see other gentlemen."

"What do you mean? How does that come about?" Mirabella said in a tone much sharper than she had intended.

Barbara seemed not to notice, however. "Sir Giles and Captain Rosborough call almost every day to see Harry, for they've gotten into the habit of going to the Great Piazza Coffee House for breakfast. Also the three of them much enjoy Gentleman Jackson's saloon, and Angelo's Fencing Academy, and Sir Giles and Captain Rosborough are always dropping in to see if Harry wants to accompany them. One day they all took me and Mamma to Gunter's, and Sir Giles and I sat together and talked for the longest time about the different confections we liked, and the ones we hated. And now Mamma allows me to ride in the park with only my groom and Harry as chaperones, although I'm only allowed to ride the Ladies' Mile, and not Rotten Row. Often Sir Giles and Captain Rosborough ride with us."

This so nonplussed Mirabella that for long moments she said nothing. Her mind furiously darted around, thinking that here was the reason she'd seen so little of Giles, this was why he and Lewin weren't coming to breakfast or calling at the town house, this was why she hadn't seen them in Hyde Park, for Mirabella drove only on Rotten Row.

Finally she managed to say, "You're a fortunate young lady, then, to have two eligible bachelors so accessible. Most of us have to go through contortions to get a sentence or two alone with them. Tell me, darling, do you, perhaps, enjoy a pantomime more than you enjoy opera? It seems most people do."

Barbara's childlike blue eyes sparkled. "I must admit that I do, at least pantomimes are in English. Don't you find Mr. Grimaldi's performances to be absolute genius? He's so skillful, so acrobatic, so athletic, he's truly a marvel at physical comedy..."

While Barbara continued with her raptures, Mirabella was thinking that she and her parents and Giles must be the only people in London who found pantomimes and farce boring. To Mirabella the slapstick humor, sophomoric antics, stock characters, and unvarying plots could be truly entertaining only to children, like Punch and Judy shows.

Mirabella determined to forget, or at least put aside for the moment, the worrying questions she had about Giles's relationship with Barbara. She listened to her friend with affectionate indulgence, for Barbara was so sweetly innocent, so full of childlike delight, that Mirabella couldn't help but enjoy her company.

Finally the gentlemen returned. As Mirabella was sitting by Barbara, Giles again sat down on Barbara's left, and Denys Aldington sat by Mirabella. Mirabella felt a momentary pang, thinking that in the past, in such shufflings in the box, Giles had always taken the opportunity to sit by *her*.

Harlequin and Mother Goose began, and Mirabella resigned herself to be bored, but determined not to show it, which would have been rude and condescending. Surreptitiously she looked around at the other boxes, and saw that almost every patron seemed convulsed with merriment, including such clever people as Lady Cowper and Count and Countess Lieven and even Mr. and Mrs. Drummond-Burrell. Her own companions laughed loud and long, except for her parents and Giles, who kept a permanent indulgent smile on his face.

Mirabella, now that she sat next to Denys, could observe him closely. She saw that he had lost his morose demeanor, and guffawed heartily, sometimes slapping his knee. It came time for the harlequinade, when the setting, characters, and stage scenery magically transformed from the fairy tale world to the rambunctious world of Clown and Harlequin. Now Clown shouted his famous stock phrase, "Here we are again!" and Denys roared it along with most of the audience. Again, when Clown asked his second famous phrase, "Shall I?" Denys gleefully shouted "Yes!" laughing uproariously.

Mirabella's smile became a rictus, for she was gritting her teeth. *How could I have possibly thought I could marry such a man? Even if he does finally throw off this silly Byronic persona, I could never countenance such a childish taste in humor, it's insufferably tedious and eventually I'd go balmy . . .*

It didn't occur to Mirabella that her reasons for *not* marrying were much less coherent and logical than her reasons for marrying. In fact, her aversion to being kissed by Lord Southam and her disdain for Denys Aldington's sense of humor were so strong that they were passionate. Mirabella would have vehemently denied that she felt any sort of passion, had her mind gone to this particular place. But it did not.

She began again to think of Giles and Barbara Smythe.

Chapter Seventeen

Returning home from the theatre at three o'clock in the morning, Mirabella knew only too well that she would have another sleepless night. She had no desire to talk to Josephine, so she made an elaborate show of fatigue and went straight up to her room. As Colette readied Mirabella for bed, she eagerly asked all about the women *ma dame* had seen, their gowns, their jewels, their hair, their headdresses. Normally it amused Mirabella to recount all this to her maid, but tonight she said shortly, "Colette, I'm deathly tired, don't press me now."

For once Colette was obedient, and said nothing more until she was ready to leave. She asked if Mirabella required anything else, and Mirabella merely shook her head.

She was wholly absorbed in thinking of Giles and Barbara Smythe. She thought over the last three months, and how she had noted that Giles always danced with Barbara twice at Almack's and at balls. At first Mirabella had told herself that this was nothing unusual. Giles was well known to be so kind that he often sought out un-partnered girls and danced with them. Barbara had a stigma attached to her because of her mother, and Giles was just being his usual thoughtful self in paying attention to her.

That must be it, even though he denies it, with his usual gentlemanly courtesy. He pities her, much as I do, and takes pains to show friendliness to her, Mirabella thought with relief.

Instantly a sort of clangor set up in her head: *Pities her? Escorting her in to supper every single time? Calling on her? Rides in the park? Taking her to Gunter's? How many times? How often? What do they talk about?*

The noisy questions, which were very much like the annoying shrill clangs of a bell, made Mirabella squint her eyes painfully and press her hands to her ears.

On the nights when Mirabella was upset (which was rare) or simply bursting with energy (which was not rare) she often wandered around the grounds and gardens of Camarden. Being out of doors, breathing fresh country air, whether the gentle warm airs of spring and summer or the bracing gusts of fall and winter, always seemed to refresh and cleanse her in both mind and body so that she could go to sleep.

It was more complicated here in London, for one of Irby's strictest duties was to lock up the house at night. Mirabella was so desperate to get out of the room and *breathe* that she considered waking Irby and demanding the garden door key. Most of the nobility would never have given this a second thought, but Mirabella, as she had been taught, had regard and consideration for the servants and rejected the idea. She could, however, at least go out onto the balcony overlooking the garden. The French doors were only bolted on the inside.

Taking a fat pillow, a single candle, and a glass of ratafia, Mirabella stole silently down to the ballroom and out onto the balcony. Settling comfortably on the pillow, her legs crossed Buddha-style, she sipped her ratafia and concentrated simply on taking deep breaths. She missed the ever-changing panorama of the night sky at Camarden, and the mysterious bloodless light of the moon, for in London the night sky was always a flat matte black. She closed her eyes.

From ages ago, she heard an echo of her old nurse when she was cross: *Wot's all this then!*

Mirabella smiled, wondering to herself why on earth she had gotten so panicky. What was wrong with Giles being friends with Barbara Smythe? Giles was friends with many people in Town, men and women both. He was a particular favorite of many ladies of the *haut ton* for the reasons that Mirabella had already reflected on: he was congenial, amusing, kind, and always willing to round out a table, gallantly pairing with any young lady, no matter how plain, shy, or boring.

But this is different, Mirabella thought, and again began to feel uneasy. Why?

Echoes of her old nurse had made her smile, but the sudden unbidden recollection of her conversation with her Aunt Tirel made her frown darkly.

"Has it not occurred to you that perhaps this theoretical husband of yours may object to his wife having a man as her closest friend?

"And Giles's theoretical wife? I can't imagine that there are many women who wouldn't be insanely jealous of you."

She was so perturbed that she spoke aloud, her voice sounding harsh and jarring in the silent night. "Jealousy? Me? Jealous—of Barbara? That's absurd, I'm not jealous of Barbara!"

It would be utterly ridiculous to be jealous of Barbara, she scolded herself. She wasn't at all jealous of Giles's attentions to Josephine, or Lady Jersey, who constantly flirted with him, or Lady Cowper, who particularly liked Giles and invited him to almost every party she gave.

Again she thought, *But what if Barbara's different? What if Giles has formed an affection for her?*

And then the thought was like a shout in her head: *What if Giles is in love with her?*

Suddenly Mirabella felt the most miserable sensations she had ever known, first a sort of hot rush throughout her body that made her catch her breath, and then just as suddenly a cold bleak chill that made her feel slightly nauseated.

Giles . . . marrying Barbara. Giles marrying . . . ANYONE.

Giles marrying . . . anyone but me.

She set down her glass of ratafia and buried her face in her hands.

I am jealous of Barbara, because I want to marry Giles! Am I in love with him? What does that mean? When did this happen? How did this happen?

From here her mind spiraled downward into a series of what seemed like nonsensical, unconnected images: She and Giles as children, when she'd fallen and skinned her knee and he had tenderly dressed it with a piece of cloth he'd torn from the tail of his shirt. Giles at about seventeen years old, at dinner at Camarden, teasing her about her helpless revulsion toward oysters on the half shell. Giles at Knyveton Hall, pale and drawn and sorrowful, when his mother was dying. She and Giles playing the piano, singing, laughing. That golden day when she'd fallen into the stewpond.

Gradually she realized that these images were not at all unconnected or random; they were the fabric of a life, her life, that had been so closely interwoven with his.

How could I have been so dismally blind? How on earth could I have not realized this long ago?

The answer to the first question came to her instantly. She realized how selfish, how self-absorbed and self-serving she'd been. Aunt Tirel had been right. She had simply taken Giles for granted, as callously as she took for granted that she could walk and talk and was pretty and that men liked her and that she would arrange her life and that Giles would just be at her side, like a faithful dog.

All of that was true, but then a sort of mitigating factor occurred to her, although it gave her no comfort; in fact, it depressed her even more deeply, if that was possible. Giles had given every appearance of contentment with their friendly relationship. He had never given her any indication that he wished otherwise.

Never once has he acted as if he thought of marrying me. He's not in love with me. And I'm in love with him.

The full enormity of it hit her with the force of a hard gale in a snowstorm. In love, real love, genuine longing and passion and desire. But it wasn't just a physical longing, she wanted to live each day with him, she wanted to go to sleep with him at her side and wake up to him. She wanted to have his children. She wanted to be his companion and comfort and friend every day until they were old, and for the rest of her life until she died.

Abruptly Mirabella felt utterly drained, and couldn't bear to *think* any more. She was so exhausted that she wondered how she would ever gather the strength to get back to her bed. She sat for a long time, staring blankly at the unfriendly night sky, until she realized that her crossed legs were numb. As if she were an old woman, slowly and painfully she rose and gathered her things.

Back in her bed she thought that she would never be able to sleep. But she did: quickly she sank into an oblivion that was dark and heavy. Her last thought was, oddly, a vivid image of the sweet picnic glade in the deer park, with the daisies in riotous bloom, and Giles, smiling at her.

Giles and Lewin were having breakfast at the Great Piazza Coffee House, as had become their habit. Their flat had a small kitchen, and Giles's valet, Minard, who was also serving as butler, footman, maid, and cook, would have been happy to prepare simple meals for them. But Giles and Lewin enjoyed the coffeehouse, even though it was sadly out of fashion for gentlemen. The coffeehouses had been the premier gathering place for the aristocracy and gentry in the previous century, but once membership in the exclusive gentlemen's clubs such as White's, Boodle's, and Watier's had become *de rigueur* for any man with social status, the coffeehouses had become the haunt of laborers, storekeepers, clerks, pensioners, soldiers, and crusty old men who had no liking for the rarified, dandified atmosphere of gentlemen's clubs. Though the accents heard were usually wildly different from those in the prestigious clubs, the atmosphere was not so unlike. Men ate breakfast, read their papers, and talked quietly with friends about the war or politics or the Exchange while smoking cigars and drinking great quantities of ale, beer, tea, or coffee.

Giles and Lewin had their usual breakfast, a loaf of hot fresh bread and hunks of piquant Cheshire cheese. Giles always drank coffee, while Lewin, to Giles's continued amusement, drank cup after cup of chocolate. At first Giles had teased him about drinking "nursery pap," but it was nothing like the warm milky sweet stuff that children drank. It was sweet, yes, but steaming hot, thick, and seasoned with cinnamon and a very small dash of pepper. Lewin had told Giles, "In the last three years I had exactly one cup of chocolate. While I'm here I'm going to drink gallons of it."

On this early morning, however, Giles didn't seem to be amused at Lewin's choice of beverage or anything else. He had said almost nothing as they walked to the coffeehouse, and now he sat staring glumly into his mug of coffee.

Lewin said, "Friend, I don't mean to be ill-mannered—well, perhaps I do mean to be, because I'm going to be. You're very poor company this morning."

Giles replied, "I know, and I suppose that makes me ruder than you. I beg your pardon. It's just that I'm thinking about Southam, and the morass he got entangled in, and how embarrassed he was, although I suppose most of that was of his own doing. And now it's Aldington, and it's worse. I'm afraid he's going to get hurt, and hurt badly."

Quietly Lewin said, "I don't require or expect you to display your heart on your sleeve for me, but do be honest with yourself, Giles."

Giles's jaw clenched, and he said heavily, "You're right. I'm not worried about Southam, he's fully capable of taking care of himself. I am worried about Aldington, but that's not what's really bothering me. You know very well that I'm thinking of Mirabella, and what I'm feeling has nothing to do with charity for my fellow man. I'm jealous, and I'm cursing myself because of it."

Lewin nodded. "I know it's been hard on you. Even though we haven't talked about it, I've seen it. No, don't look so horrified, no one else would ever guess, especially Mirabella. In company you've been the same charming, affable chap you've always been. It's only because I've seen you in private, as it were. But now, since we're talking about it, let's talk about it. And let's play Mirabella's game, and forget all about love. Why, why, why don't you declare yourself to Mirabella? From what I've seen in the past months, the two of you would suit much better than these other fellows, and I know you could convince her."

"Again, let me reiterate: I can't support Mirabella in a proper manner, I won't be able to do so for another year at least, perhaps two, and it almost sickens me to think of sponging off my wife.

"But putting that aside for now, as for me persuading her to marry me, I think that would be impossible now even if I wished to. I think Mirabella's set her course and made her plans. I knew that after we'd been here for about a week, and I saw the men she'd decided to choose from."

Lewin looked mystified. "You knew what the first week? About Southam and Aldington?"

"Yes, and Brydges, who's next in line, if she doesn't stick with Aldington, and after last night I think he's in the wastebin. You mean you didn't see all this from the beginning?"

"No, I haven't seen anything but Mirabella being herself. She's always lively and charming and amusing."

"She flirts with them," Giles said bluntly. "I don't mean that she's a wanton heartless tease, but she plainly communicates to them that she's interested in them, and they understand that she means she's interested in marrying them. So that's another point. She doesn't flirt with me."

"But your relationship with Mirabella is so much more than a simple flirtation."

"So it is, and yet she's never once communicated to me that she's interested in marrying me. Anyway, I'll come back around to my first objection to asking Mirabella to marry me. If I did, I'd look like the worst kind of fortune hunter. You've seen people in this town, you know what the gossip would be. In fact, Mirabella may even see me in that light. You'll note that she's particularly chosen titled, wealthy men."

Now Lewin had doubts himself. Although he'd known Mirabella just as long as had Giles, her relationship with Giles was completely different. For one thing, Giles had a particular insight into Mirabella that he lacked; Giles was acutely intuitive about her. And though Lewin and Mirabella were close friends, she had never really spoken to him of intimate things such as her longing to have children, which she had often talked about with Giles.

Perhaps Giles really did see the truth of the situation, and Lewin was the one who had no understanding of it.

But Lewin was a simple man, and he simply felt that Giles and Mirabella belonged together. He sighed deeply. "All I can say is that I think Jessica was right, love is blind."

"Who the devil is Jessica?" Giles asked grumpily.

Lewin grinned. "Well, I suppose she didn't actually say it, Shakespeare did. I can't believe I bested you with a quote."

"What? Oh. *The Merchant of Venice*. 'But love is blind, and lovers cannot see / The pretty follies that themselves commit.' Not really apt, for reasons that escape me right now but with which I'm sure I'll crush you later."

"Likely you will, and I'll take my thrashing like a man. I'm going to go see Josephine and take her for a walk, I haven't talked to her alone for forever, it seems. Do you want to come?"

"As you might imagine, I'm in no mood to entertain Mirabella just now. I think I'll go to Jackson's and see if I can find someone to pick a fight with."

"I'm sorry for him," Lewin said lightly, "but if it'll lighten your mood, I hope you beat him to a bloody pulp."

Lewin called at the Camarden town house and found his sister and Lord Camarden having an amiable breakfast. That is, they were sitting together amiably, but as always Lord Camarden was wholly absorbed in his newspapers, and Josephine ate in companionable silence. Lord Camarden was just as easy with the Rosboroughs as he was with his own family.

Lord Camarden grunted a welcome to Lewin, and Josephine gladly bade him sit down and have breakfast, but he declined. "I've already had breakfast, thank you. Just a cup of tea will do.

I must say, Sister, I'm surprised to find you awake this early. I thought you had become a grand lady of leisure, not to grace us with your presence until at least midmorning."

"Sometimes I am very grand and leisurely, and lie abed until ten o'clock or so. When I'm feeling especially dissolute I sleep until noon. But country habits die hard, Brother, and sometimes I awaken at dawn and can't go back to sleep upon my life."

"Good, I was hoping that you'd join me in being provincial and unfashionable and go for a walk in the park."

Josephine's eyes sparkled. "I'd love to, it's ages since we've had a chance to visit, just us two. Will you wait until I dress? I promise to hurry."

"I'll wait, unless you take all morning as Lady Mirabella does."

"I'll never be that grand. Just half a moment, I'll be right back." She dashed into the house.

Lord Camarden carefully laid down his newspaper. "The news from Spain is encouraging. It seems Wellington has them on the run at last."

Lewin nodded. "Yes, my lord. I expect to receive my orders any day now."

"Expect to—and hope to?"

"I know that it's difficult for the ladies to understand, but I am anxious to return to my regiment."

Lord Camarden said, "It's not just the ladies, Lewin. Any man who doesn't have the calling of a soldier, and I do believe that it's a calling, can never quite comprehend it. I got some glimpses of it from my father; even though he was a general, they had to virtually lash him to a chair before every battle to keep him off the front lines. At any rate, it's probably best that the ladies don't know until you actually receive your orders."

They talked more of the army's progress in Spain, and of Lord Wellington's political finesse in commanding what was now the

Sixth Coalition, allying the English with the forces of Austria, Prussia, Russia, Portugal, Sweden, Spain, and some miscellaneous German states.

Soon Josephine returned, slightly breathless and hurriedly tucking some curls up into her bonnet. Casting a harried look over her shoulder, she said, "At least Colette didn't follow me all the way down here. She was really quite shrill when I jammed on my bonnet before she'd finished my hair. It's the first time in my life that I've regretted speaking French. Let's hurry before she catches me."

Grosvenor Square was only two blocks from Hyde Park. At this early hour it was almost deserted, except for a few elderly gentlemen taking a quiet, restful carriage ride. The sun was a watery blob in a smoky blue sky. Delicate little tendrils of mist rose from the Serpentine River.

Josephine sighed. "I miss home."

"Do you? Are you ready to go home?"

"Not quite yet, I suppose." She sounded unsure.

"No? Are you staying because you've come to love the glittering world of the Beau Monde, or are you determined to keep on being Mirabella's nanny?"

"As for the first, I still enjoy observing the *haut ton* in their natural habitat, although I've found that they're fairly predictable. As to the second, I wouldn't tackle that job for all the guineas in London."

Lewin grinned boyishly. "Ah, so it's Harry Smythe after all."

"I forbid you to tease me about Mr. Smythe, it's none of your concern, and I don't wish to talk about it."

"I wish he had the same delicate sensibilities, for he continually talks about you." He grew sober and said, "He is in love with you, you know."

"I don't think I knew for sure . . . maybe until just now."

"And you, Sister? What are your feelings toward him?"

Josephine was silent for long moments. Lewin knew that though their demeanors were completely different, Josephine was fully as reserved and private as their mother. Even now she parried the question. "The Smythes live almost three hundred miles away, in Northumberland. Mr. Smythe will inherit the estate."

Lightly Lewin said, "'For this cause shall a man leave father and mother, and shall cleave to his wife.'"

"Yes, that all sounds well and good, but—Lewin, I told you I don't want to talk about this, so just stop this instant."

"Very well. Shall we talk about some other ill-starred lovers, like Mirabella and Giles? Could someone please explain to me what Mirabella thinks she's doing?"

"She thinks she's deciding on the man she'll marry." Lewin frowned darkly, and Josephine held up her hand. "I know, I thought the same as you did at first, that she's being foolish and shallow. But from the things I've seen, things I've heard, things I've discerned here, I've finally come to understand that it's exactly the way most marriages are decided on with these people. Sometimes the parents arrange it, if the girl is very young; even when couples decide themselves, they hardly ever base it on being in love."

Lewin said with exasperation, "'These people.' It's another world. Being here, it's like—like living in Vauxhall Gardens. It's lively and all sorts of fun, but it has nothing to do with the real world."

"But it is the real world for most of these people. Giles, and Lord and Lady Camarden, and Mirabella, and even Lord and Lady Reynes are exceptions, because they seem to have lives away from London and Fashionable Society that they enjoy very much, and that's our world. So how is Giles?"

"You know, men don't tear their hearts out and endlessly dissect them like women do. All I know is that he's in love with Mirabella, he has been for a long time, and he has no intention of telling her."

"Yes, I thought so. Could you tell me why he won't declare himself to Mirabella, without breaking his confidence?"

Lewin mulled this over, then answered, "I don't think it would be betraying his confidence, because I think that if you and he had a long private conversation he'd confide in you himself." He then went on to relate to her what Giles had said.

Thoughtfully Josephine said, "You know, I do understand his reasoning. I've had the same reservations, particularly about the 'fortune hunter' part. Mrs. Smythe would always think that of me."

"If you love Harry Smythe, don't let anyone or anything stop you from marrying him."

Serenely Josephine said, "If I come to be sure in my heart that I love him, and that he is the man the Lord intends me to marry, then nothing at all would make me hesitate for a moment."

"Good for you, Sister! But again, without breaking anyone's confidence, do you think Mirabella really does love Giles, but she just doesn't realize it?"

"I don't know, I truly don't. I realized that maybe you and I always thought Mirabella and Giles should marry just because it seemed sort of inevitable. But now I think there's a possibility that Mirabella feels about Giles the way I do. I adore him, I love his company and never tire of it, I know that in his way he loves me and would do anything for me, and I feel the same about him. But *in* love with him? Wishing to marry him? The thought's never entered my mind."

Lewin argued, "But still, even if Mirabella's not 'in love' with Giles, doesn't it seem to you that she'd be happier with him than with all these other fellows that she's not in love with?"

"That would seem logical, except for two things." Josephine hesitated, then went on, "I know you won't misunderstand this, because you know Mirabella and love her as I do. She's mindful of rank, and fortune; not so much in a greedy way, but as a sort of safeguard to rule out fortune hunters, after what she went through with Captain Pryce, you know."

Lewin murmured, "I see. It's hard, because in a way it does justify Giles's thinking. No one who knows him, including Mirabella, could ever think he was a fortune hunter. But I can see how a man in Giles's situation could wonder such a thing, if maybe even a little tiny thought of 'He's marrying me for my money' might come into his wife's mind. So what's the other pea under the princess's mattress?"

"Oh, Lewin, don't joke, it's not funny. At least, it's not laugh-funny, but I admit it is rather odd-funny. You see, Mirabella takes it for granted that she and Giles will always be close, will always be best friends, that he'll always be there for her and she'll always be there for him. She has this idyllic vision in her mind of her titled, wealthy, nameless, faceless, silent husband, a fine estate with a conservatory of course, four children, and Giles next door, and they all live happily ever after."

"So she is blind after all. That will never happen."

"No, it won't," Josephine agreed unhappily.

"Giles can hardly bear to be around her now, if she marries I think he might just run off back to Italy and never return to England. Come now, seeing Giles every day like she does at Camarden? She won't even be at Camarden, she'll be at Estate with Conservatory. Mirabella's not stupid, how can she not see this?"

Josephine shook her head helplessly. "I've sort of pointed this out in some of our talks, but she just merrily glides right over it. I just don't know."

Lewin said sturdily, "Well, I do know. I know that Giles loves

Mirabella, and I know that she cares deeply for him. I may not understand about her little fancies and airs, but I know that Giles would make her the best husband, and would make her happier than anyone else ever could."

Josephine said admiringly, "Good heavens, that is so simple, but profound. I always thought of you as my silly older brother, not a man of such insight and intelligence. I always thought I was much more clever than you."

Lewin grumbled, "Marvelous, I'm intelligent, you're clever, a great lot of good it does. The other thing I know is that we'd better pray that Mirabella and Giles come to their senses before it's too late, and they both live unhappily ever after."

Chapter Eighteen

It took all of Mirabella's resolve to drag herself out of bed at eight o'clock for breakfast and church. Over the years she had grown accustomed to nights with very little sleep, but on this morning she felt sluggish and dull. She didn't have a full-blown headache, but there was a dull throb in the back of her neck. Her mirror revealed a pale face and lackluster eyes.

After soaking her eyes and forehead with a cool wet cloth, and with some expert application of rice powder and rouge by Colette, she looked and felt better. She knew that when she was ill, she always felt worse at night. When she was upset, she always felt bleaker at night, and when morning came her spirits revived.

Now she reflected that the situation might not be as hopeless as she had thought. It was true that she had finally comprehended that she was deeply in love with Giles, and that presented a myriad of questions and problems. But she might have been imagining, or at least exaggerating, his regard for Barbara Smythe. Last night she had hysterically mired herself in a dither, when the solution—or at least the first step—was to simply talk to Giles. Before she decided what to do, she must at least understand the nature of his relationship to Barbara.

At breakfast her mother had news that cheered Mirabella even more. "It came by special messenger at dawn," Lady Camarden said happily. "Clara was delivered of a boy last night, and it seems that she had an easy time of it. Philip writes that the baby is very well, and they've named him Tiberius after your grandfather, and William Henry after your father."

"How wonderful!" Mirabella cried. "Can we go see him?"

"Not quite yet, for Clara's parents and sister and her husband are attending her," Lady Camarden answered. "But Philip assures me that in a couple of weeks he and Clara will welcome us."

"Oh, how I hope so," Mirabella said fervently.

Josephine offered her congratulations to the family, and said that Tiberius William Henry Tirel was a noble name indeed. Lady Camarden remarked acidly that if Mirabella shortened it to "Tibby" as she had shortened Clara's preferred "Alexander" to "Alex," her daughter-in-law would likely have the vapors.

Mirabella only half-heard the rest of the breakfast conversation, for now it was occurring to her that her simple first step might not be so simple after all. What was she to say to Giles? How could she casually lead him into a conversation about his true feelings for Barbara? She couldn't think of a way to question him about it without being intrusive. Though she and Giles were so close, they were careful not to intrude on each other's most private feelings without an invitation, as it were. After all, Giles had not questioned her about her plans for marriage. Apparently Giles hadn't really cared enough to discuss it with her. He certainly hadn't shown any jealousy.

But Mirabella was by nature high-spirited and not subject to fits of despondency, so she matter-of-factly made up her mind to stop obsessing over Giles. They were best friends, why shouldn't she talk to him? She toyed with the idea of sending for him, but decided that it would seem artificial. She would see him at Lady Cowper's ball tomorrow night, and devise a way to tell him she'd like to speak to him alone. Surely, as had been the case all her life, things would be better after she talked to Giles. Somehow everything would come out right.

But as had been happening often lately, Mirabella was wrong.

Mirabella dressed very carefully for Lady Cowper's ball. Her gown, which was new and a particular favorite of hers, was of Indian mull, the lightest and most gossamer muslin made. The shade was a deep warm ivory, and it was "shot" with gold threads and heavily embroidered in gold around the hem, waistline, and sleeves. Her long gloves were dyed the same shade of ivory, and had gold embroidery along the tops. Mirabella had specially ordered satin slippers with gold thread and bows. The only jewelry she wore was a small, delicate crucifix with blood-red garnets and tiny drop garnet earrings. In her hair Colette skillfully threaded a gold ribbon studded with garnets.

As usual Josephine finished dressing first, and came to talk to her as Colette finished Mirabella's *toilette.*

"You look lovely in that deep-rose gown," Mirabella complimented her. "I think that every shade you wear is your best, and I've come to see that you look very well in any color."

"Thank you. You look lovely, as always. I've been somewhat concerned, for I thought that you were looking a little pale. But tonight you seem your usual glowing self."

"Yes, I suppose I have been a little distracted the last couple of days," Mirabella said vaguely. She had decided that she wouldn't tell anyone that she'd finally realized that she was in love with Giles. For one thing, she felt singularly foolish. For another, in spite of her best efforts at being optimistic, the dreaded thought that Giles might actually be in love with Barbara—or even worse in a way, that he simply wasn't interested in marrying Mirabella—made her determine that no one must ever know of her feelings for him.

"Was it because of Mr. Aldington?" Josephine asked sympathetically.

"I beg your pardon?" Mirabella said blankly.

"Mr. Aldington. Have you been worrying about how you might gently disentangle yourself from him? Even though we haven't talked about it, I could see at the theatre that you've lost interest in him as a potential suitor."

Mirabella felt a slight shock. She hadn't had a single thought about Denys Aldington since that night at the theatre. Had it really been only three nights ago? It seemed much longer. "Oh, yes, Mr. Aldington. No, I hadn't been particularly worried about him. After all, we weren't exactly *tangled*, so I can't see any difficulty in disentangling."

With some distress Josephine said, "But Mirabella dearest, don't you think it's possible that he might get hurt? He seems to be so interested in you, romantically, I mean."

"He's interested in Romance, not me," Mirabella said tartly. "In fact, I may be doing him a great favor. I think he'd like nothing more than to have a tragic, lost, hopeless love. Oh, don't look so upset, Josephine. I've known Mr. Aldington for years now, and he's never shown the slightest interest in me as far as a romantic attachment. Believe me, in a day or two he'll be falling helplessly in love with someone else."

In spite of this rather callous dismissal of Denys Aldington's feelings, Mirabella felt uneasy in trying to work out how to handle him. Normally she knew instinctively how to distance herself from men, without thinking too deeply about it. But she was distracted this evening, and was a little impatient with the idea of employing delicate finesse in communicating to Denys Aldington that she was no longer interested in him. She must simply try to avoid him as much as possible, discreetly of course, and to be friendly but impersonal when she saw him.

Lady Cowper's ball was very grand, so a master of ceremonies announced the guests. "The Most Honourable the Marquess of Camarden; the Most Honourable the Marchioness of Camarden; the Lady Mirabella Tirel; Miss Rosborough." Looking out over the three-hundred-plus crowd, at the far end of the room Mirabella saw Denys Aldington turn alertly to the ballroom doors, and start to make his way toward her. She couldn't see Giles or Lewin anywhere. Close by, however, she did see Lord Trevor Brydges, with Lady Jersey and Lady FitzGeorge. Grabbing Josephine's arm, she hurried toward them.

After the formal greetings, Lady Jersey said, "Darling, here you are, we were just gossiping about you. The word is that Aldington's out, poor dear, although I never thought he was quite suitable for you, he's only going to be a baron, and not a particularly rich one at that, and Lord Aldington is so hale and hearty you might have been a gray grizzled grandmother before Denys ever inherited, and it was all due to some bizarre thing at the theatre, wasn't it, Rosalind? So do tell, Mirabella, who is next on your list?"

"Sally, you are incorrigible," Mirabella said, her cheeks flaming. "I have no intention of discussing my personal life here and now. If you're going to gossip about me, I beg you will do it behind my back and not to my face."

Far from being repentant, Lady Jersey laughed and said, "Very well, I'll hold my tongue until you've left."

"I seriously doubt that, you'd likely explode into bits if you couldn't talk, Sally," Lady FitzGeorge said.

"Likely I would," Lady Jersey carelessly agreed. "Oh, look, Aldington is making his way over here, with that pitiful hangdog expression he's been wearing this Season. I'll head him off, Mirabella, don't say I never did you any favors." She went to him, threaded her arm through his, and promptly turned and marched him off in another direction.

"Oh dear, I hope she doesn't harangue him about me," Mirabella said.

Lord Trevor said, "Stop troubling yourself about Aldington, he'll spend the next few days lamenting his ill-fated love and quoting from *Childe Harold* and *Hours of Idleness* and in a week or so he'll be starry-eyed over some other young lady. Enough about Aldington, I say. Lady Mirabella, I'm going to be honest with you and tell you that I am going to gossip behind your back, but I'd much prefer talking to you in front of your face. Will you grant me the honor of dancing the first two waltzes with me, and allowing me to escort you to supper?"

Mirabella, who was still avidly, though discreetly, searching for Giles, replied absently, "Certainly, sir, it would be my pleasure."

Lady FitzGeorge said slyly, "I may not be privy to your list, Mirabella, but I can plainly see who is hoping to be next on it. Come, Miss Rosborough, let us give Lord Trevor an opportunity to speak privately to Lady Mirabella's face. The Smythes came in earlier, and I know you'll be wishing to see Mr. Smythe, and your brother of course. He and Sir Giles came in with them, if we can only find them in this crush." Rosalind took Josephine's arm and began to thread through the throng.

Mirabella said with exasperation, "It seems that all of my friends are determined to embarrass me this evening. I hope you're not offended, sir."

"Offended? Why should I be? You're a beautiful, clever, elegant lady whom any man would eagerly pursue. The only thing that's offended me is that you considered Southam and Aldington first. All along it should have been me," he said with his devil-may-care grin.

"Sir, please, you, too, are embarrassing me," Mirabella said, flustered. "I—I must protest that I've been—that my demeanor—or my actions—have been misunderstood, or misconstrued."

"Please accept my most heartfelt apologies, my lady, I wouldn't embarrass you for the world. I promise to cease and desist this instant. Come, it's already as hot as blazes in here, shall we go have some refreshments? Oh, deuce take it, I knew I wouldn't get a moment alone with you."

Lord Southam bowed deeply to Mirabella. "Lady Mirabella, Brydges. Madam, if you aren't already engaged, would you do me the honor of dancing the quadrille with me?"

"Why, I—that is—no, sir, I am not engaged, I shall be happy to." She took his arm.

Lord Trevor said, "I'll be waiting right here, my lady, for I intend to guard you until my waltz."

"Not to worry, Brydges, I won't spirit her away," Southam said sardonically. They stood at the edge of the dance floor, watching the opening couples in the first movement.

Now Mirabella was even more perturbed. She had seen Lord Southam several times in the last two months at balls and parties and while riding in the park, but she hadn't spoken with him. Mirabella didn't have any delusions that she had broken his heart, but she knew that since gossip had been rampant about their estrangement (if it could be called that), he must have been embarrassed, and had been avoiding her. Now, tonight, just when she needed all her wits about her to manage the morass that she had carefully constructed and then deliberately waded into, all she could think of was Giles. With a supreme effort she marshaled her thoughts and determined not to appear to be an utter half-wit to Southam.

"You dance so rarely, sir, all of us ladies feel very fortunate when you request the honor," she said brightly. "I thank you."

"The pleasure is all mine, I assure you." The second movement began, and they joined a "square" with three other couples. As they danced, Mirabella kept unobtrusively searching the dancing couples and the crowd for Giles, but she didn't see him at all, nor did she see the Smythes or Lewin or Josephine. She did notice that people were staring at them, and some ladies watching the dance appeared to be whispering behind their gloved hands or fans. Lord Southam gave no sign that he was aware; as always, he danced with grace and dignity, his eyes squarely meeting hers.

Mirabella felt that she was completely incapable of clever repartee on this night, but she also knew that she owed it to Lord Southam to make some sort of explanation, and reparation, if she could, for her behavior to him. He was regarding her gravely, but with no rancor. Finally she said, "Sir, I owe you an apology. My behavior to you, and some of the things that I said, were inexcusable, and very wrong. Will you forgive me?"

Lord Southam rarely smiled, and when he did it was a rather cold expression that barely reached his dark eyes. But still his smile, and his words, warmed Mirabella. "I will gladly forgive you, my lady, and hope that you can find it in your heart to forgive me, for I, too, must apologize. Shall we call it pax, then? Without the kiss of peace, of course," he added ironically.

Mirabella's cheeks colored, but her smile was glowing. "Pax it is. I hope we can still be friends?"

"It would be my honor and pleasure, my lady, to remain so," he said with his customary formal gallantry. He said nothing more for the remainder of the dance. Taking her hand, he returned her to Lord Trevor. Before he released her hand, he bowed deeply over it and smiled at her once again, and then he began to make his way through the crowd. As she watched his tall figure, head and shoulders above everyone else, Mirabella felt an immense relief.

Lord Trevor had been joined by two young gentlemen, Mr. Eberhardt and Mr. Strack. Mirabella had been introduced to them, but knew them only slightly. Lord Trevor said with mock annoyance, "I was determined to monopolize you this evening, Lady Mirabella, but I should have known better. These two young pups are hoping for a dance. I don't suppose I could dissuade you, and steal you away for that glass of punch?"

"Nonsense, it's a ball, we're required to dance," Mirabella said. "You know very well that you love to display your manly skill in dancing, Lord Trevor, not to mention your best opportunities for outrageous flirting. Mr. Eberhardt, Mr. Strack, I should be happy."

And so the evening went as usual, with Mirabella never lacking for a partner. Her two waltzes with Lord Trevor were amusing and lively, for he flirted with her as he always did, but he made no more comments about her all-too-well-known betrothal plans. In the second waltz she finally saw Giles, dancing with Barbara Smythe. They smiled and nodded to her from across the dance floor. When the dance ended, Mirabella was determined to follow them and talk to them, but Lord Cowper requested the next dance, and she felt that it would be rude to deny her host.

The Cowper town house was sizable, but the ballroom was not large enough to accommodate over three hundred. Of course many people went to sit in the other principal rooms: the drawing room, the music room, the cardroom, the billiard room. Still, the crowds surrounding the dance floor were packed tightly, and Mirabella lost sight of Giles again after her dance with Lord Cowper.

Lord Trevor claimed her for supper, and the crowd began to file into the dining room. The dining room was only slightly larger than the ballroom, and thirty tables, seating ten each, made for very crowded seating. As everyone sorted themselves out, Mirabella saw that Barbara and Giles, along with Josephine and Harry, were seated together, and she and Lord Trevor joined them. Soon they were joined by Lord and Lady Jersey, Lady FitzGeorge, and Lord Southam. Mirabella didn't see Denys Aldington in the crush. She sat by Josephine, and across from her were Giles and Barbara, while Lord Trevor sat at the head of the table.

The gentlemen helped the ladies fill their plates from the delectable dishes of veal, lamb, pheasant, and assorted salads and relishes. Mirabella nodded to a nearby table and said to Josephine, "Lewin has reached the pinnacle of London society, I see, dining with such august company." Lewin was seated with Lord and Lady Castlereagh, Lord and Lady Cowper, Mirabella's parents, and Count and Countess Lieven.

Josephine frowned slightly. "Yes, I know. From what I understand, there is much news from Spain, and of course Lord Castlereagh and Count Lieven have all the latest dispatches."

To Giles Mirabella said brightly, "So is Lewin privy to more news than we humble reading public get from the newspapers, Giles?"

"If he's been receiving dispatches from Lord Wellington, he's said nothing to me about it," Giles joked. "He's a close old file, you know."

The group talked for a while about the war, but as the supper progressed, as usual, they broke up into couples privately conversing. Mirabella noticed that Lord Southam, Lady FitzGeorge, and Lord and Lady Jersey all talked with animation at the end of the table. Josephine and Harry, and Barbara and Giles, began talking in low voices to each other. Lord Trevor said to her, "You know, the races at Ascot are in a couple of weeks. Do you and your family have plans to attend?"

"We're not really very dedicated gamblers," Mirabella answered. "We've only been once since I came out. I enjoyed the spectacle, but I was completely downcast that I lost four pounds on a mare that was named Donna Bella. I was certain I was fated to win."

"Then you must come this year, and recoup your losses. I assure you I can advise you on a winner. My family has an estate in Berkshire that's only a couple of miles from Ascot, and this year we're inviting a party to come stay for the entire week. May I invite you and your parents to join us?"

"Well—I—I don't know, I hadn't thought of attending Ascot," Mirabella replied vaguely. She was having trouble concentrating on Lord Trevor, for Barbara and Giles, heads close together, seemed to be having a soft-spoken, intimate conversation. It also came to Mirabella's attention that Mr. and Mrs. Smythe, along with four other couples, were seated at the table next to them, which was situated very close. Mrs. Smythe's voice, always strident, was steadily growing shriller. Several people turned to see who was speaking so loudly. Mirabella saw that Mrs. Smythe was addressing Sir Thomas and Lady Heron, an elderly couple who were both very hard of hearing.

Sir Thomas said crossly, "I cannot fathom what young people are about now, in my day it was considered rude to mumble and murmur in conversation. Are you talking to us, Mrs. Smythe, or whispering to yourself?"

"I beg your pardon, Sir Thomas," Mrs. Smythe bawled in his ear. "I was just saying that Sir Giles Knyvet has been very attentive to my daughter for some time now, we have every reason to expect a happy announcement soon. And of course our Harry is much caressed in Town, we're certain that he'll make a most fortunate match when the time comes, for he's still young and can choose among the young ladies at his leisure."

Mrs. Smythe's words were such a shock to Mirabella that her ears began to ring and for a few moments she could hardly hear anything except an odd distant rumbling. Her eyes, wide and startled, were fixed on the couple across from her. Barbara's face was lowered, and her cheeks were flaming. Giles's amiable expression didn't change. He leaned closer to whisper to her. Then he gently took her hand and threaded it through his arm, and they stood up. Giles nodded courteously to Mrs. Smythe, and they left.

Slowly Mirabella became aware of Josephine, who was half-turned away from her. She could see Harry's face, and his expression was one of deep distress. He was talking in a low urgent tone, and Mirabella heard Josephine say, "It's quite all right, Mr. Smythe. Do you know, I believe I'd like to get a glass of punch and go out onto the balcony for a few moments of fresh air. Could I interest you in accompanying me?" As they left, Mirabella saw Lord Jersey, and even Lord Southam, give them sympathetic nods. Rosalind and Lady Jersey looked vastly amused.

Lord Trevor said, "Poor old Knyvet, what a coil. But for any man that even looks Miss Smythe's way it's to be expected from that old harridan."

Mirabella swallowed hard. "Is—is Mrs. Smythe simply imagining things, then, do you think? I know you're friends with Giles, has he indicated to you any sort of—plans as far as Miss Smythe is concerned?"

Lord Trevor looked surprised. "You're much closer to him than I. Knyvet's not the sort of man to talk much about his personal life, at least to me. You two haven't discussed it, I take it?"

"No, we haven't," Mirabella said dully. "We haven't had much opportunity for private conversation lately."

He searched her face and his eyes narrowed. "You seem upset, my lady. May I impose upon you and ask why?"

Mirabella took a deep breath and assumed a careless tone. "As you said, I am one of Sir Giles's closest friends, and I like Barbara, too, very much. Whether it's true or not, I hate to see them so humiliated."

"I agree completely. And your friend Miss Rosborough, too, and Harry's a good fellow, it's a shame we can't choose our parents, but then I suppose we'd all choose royal princes and princesses or at the very least dukes and duchesses, and there's hardly enough of them to go around," Lord Trevor said with a return to his usual high spirits. "So what about Ascot? You were about to accept my invitation, I hope?"

"First I must talk to my parents, I really have no notion of whether they'd care to attend or not." Mirabella knew that her parents would accept or decline the invitation according to what she wanted. Just now Mirabella had no idea what she wanted. "I have no idea what invitations my mother may have already accepted for that week."

"You know that London practically empties out for those four days. I don't wish to impose upon you with arguments—but then again, perhaps I will. I'd really like for you to come. Please."

Wearily Mirabella thought, *London empties out for the races... but Giles certainly won't go to Ascot. Maybe it would be better if I got away... oh, how I wish I could just go home!* She reminded herself again that Josephine and Harry Smythe did seem to be growing close, and it would be horribly selfish of her to go home early and take her away from him. Finally she answered, "It's so kind of you, Lord Trevor, and I shall certainly consider your invitation. I'll speak to my parents tomorrow."

Mirabella endured the rest of the evening with a sort of numbness. Resolutely she refused to look for Giles any longer; in fact, it was her desperate wish that she wouldn't see him again. She caught a glimpse of him only once, talking to a group that included Lewin and Lord and Lady Cowper, and quickly she turned away. Lord Trevor importuned her to meet him in the park tomorrow. Mirabella said that as she and Josephine generally rode every day she would surely see him. He seemed frustrated at her impersonal answer, but said good night to her with his usual flirtatious grin.

She was subdued in the carriage on the way home, and Josephine and her parents noticed it. Lady Camarden said, "Mirabella, aren't you feeling well? I haven't been obliged to scold you once this entire evening, so surely something is wrong."

Mirabella managed a smile. "Nothing at all is wrong, Mamma, may I not simply behave for one evening?"

"You may, but you rarely do."

When they reached home, Mirabella said tentatively, "Josephine, would you care for a little talk tonight? Or are you too fatigued?"

"Of course not. A glass or two of your ratafia sounds very good after that rich supper," she replied.

With her usual efficiency Colette soon had the two girls undressed and in their nightclothes. When Josephine went to Mirabella's room, she was standing at the open window, looking out on the featureless night.

"I miss seeing the stars, don't you?" Josephine said as she poured out her glass of ratafia and settled on the bed. "Sometimes here one can't even find the moon, the pall over London is so thick."

"It certainly is," Mirabella agreed in a distant voice. She stood motionless for long moments with her back to Josephine. Then she arranged a smile on her face and turned. "I see you've helped yourself, you might at least have offered me a glass." She poured out a generous portion of ratafia.

"I would have done, but the way you were staring outside so longingly, I thought you might have been about to go on one of your night wanders."

"Not with you here to keep me company." Then she added somewhat awkwardly, "Josephine, I know I don't express it often—or perhaps ever—but you mean so much to me. You're a good and true friend, and I thank you for it."

"You're very welcome, dearest, and I feel exactly the same for you. And so, why are we so solemn this evening? I thought it was a fine ball, although I must say that Lady Cowper does have a tendency to stuff us all in like sheep in a fold."

"Yes, she's so kind she dislikes limiting her guest list, she invites anyone and everyone, so her balls tend to be routs. But you did enjoy the evening?"

"Yes, I did. Didn't you?"

Mirabella said with distress, "Oh, Josephine, how can you possibly be so composed after that horrid scene at supper with Mrs. Smythe? I know that you're reticent about displaying your feelings, and I wouldn't wish to intrude on you, but it's obvious that Harry Smythe is in love with you, and unless I'm a complete dolt I think that you are attracted to him. You must be upset at those things his mother said."

"I am attracted to him, yes," Josephine said quietly. "But I barely know him. You may say it's obvious that he's in love with me, but he's never made any overtures to me, so Mrs. Smythe only showed her own ignorance with that foolish speech tonight, which was obviously intended as a slight to me. You heard her, the entire tirade was utterly wrong, and I hate to use this word, but it was stupid."

Mirabella became still and alert. "You don't think that Giles is interested in Barbara, then?"

"Of course not. I mean, he likes her, I know, and enjoys her company, but he has no intention of marrying her."

"How do you know?" Mirabella demanded. "Have you talked to him about her?"

"Well—well, no, I haven't. But I just know that he's not thinking of marrying her."

"Has Lewin said anything to you about them?"

Josephine replied insistently, "Not exactly, but I'm absolutely certain that he's not thinking of marrying Barbara Smythe." She cocked her head and gazed hard at Mirabella. "Mirabella, you're the one who sounds upset. Are you worried about Giles and Barbara?"

Mirabella averted her eyes and took a long sip of ratafia. When she looked back up, her face was settled into lines of amusement; the dimples even flashed. "Oh, I'm just being selfish, as always. Giles is my particular friend, and he hasn't asked my permission to marry anyone, the scoundrel. Although I know that he'd be exactly like you, he'd be cautious, and want to get to know a lady thoroughly before he decided if he wanted to marry her or not. Anyway, regardless of what you think, dearest, it seems to me that he's spending a lot of time with Barbara. You've been with the two of them more than I, at balls and parties. They do very well together, don't they? They always seem to have much to talk about."

Josephine answered carefully, "Yes, they have become friends, I suppose. As it turns out, Barbara has always longed to travel, and of course Giles loves to talk about his time in Portugal and Italy. She dislikes living in the north, it sounds rather depressing and hardscrabble, even though her family is wealthy. She longs to live in the south, in the country, and Giles can't tell her enough about Knyveton and even farming in general. But Mirabella, I *promise* you that Giles is simply being kind to her, partly because he's such good friends with Harry, and partly because he feels sorry for her because of her mother. Mrs. Smythe's vulgar machinations have almost guaranteed that any young man interested in Barbara, unless he's titled, will never get within two feet of her. And naturally the ones with titles don't wish to come within two feet of her. Or I should say her mother."

"Except for Giles," Mirabella said lightly, "but then he always was courageous enough to face a woman like Mrs. Smythe. I don't wish to talk about them any more. Let's talk of something a little less thorny, such as you and Mr. Smythe. As I said, you're my particular friend, too, and so I warn you that as soon as he speaks to your father, I fully expect him to come beg my permission to pay his addresses to you. You must tell him that."

"I'll do no such thing, and as you've already interrogated me about Mr. Smythe and Giles and Miss Smythe, it's my turn to choose the topic. What about Lord Trevor Brydges? He was most attentive to you this evening. Am I correct in thinking that we've moved on to the last, although I still maintain the handsomest, man on your list?"

Mirabella sighed deeply, and for a moment her eyes were dark and shadowed. "Do you know, to tell the truth I've suddenly realized how fatigued I am. I think I can sleep now, and I know that you can, you're so sweet to indulge me in these late-night talks when you could be asleep and dreaming of Mr. Smythe."

Josephine rose and set her empty glass down. "I'll be leaving you now. I fully expect that in the morning, after a good night's sleep, you'll stop talking such silly nonsense. If you don't I'm going to refuse to speak to you at all. Good night, dearest."

Of course Mirabella did not get a good night's sleep. She felt odd. It was as if somehow, deep in the recesses of her mind, she had been dreading a sort of impending doom, and she supposed that she really had, deep down, known that Giles was falling in love with Barbara Smythe ever since the night at the theatre. Josephine had been vehement that it wasn't so; but Josephine didn't know Giles nearly as well as did Mirabella. To her, the affection that Giles held for Barbara, now that she was facing it dead-on, was perfectly clear.

Now that the fatal knowledge had become real, Mirabella felt only a sort of weary surrender. She would never marry Giles, and the thought was intolerable; but then the thought of the long years stretching ahead of her without marriage and family was equally intolerable. The dilemma went around and around in her head until she fell asleep from sheer mental exhaustion. On this night she had only one tiresome, monotonous dream over and over. She stood at the window, staring out into the black night, waiting for the dawn. In her dream it never came.

Chapter Nineteen

For the next few days Mirabella was in such a turmoil of emotions that sometimes she felt almost ill. She went through several stages. For one day and endless night she was depressed and it was an effort just to get out of bed and go about her day. Then she grew angry. She was angry at herself for being so stupid, angry at Giles for betraying her, angry at Barbara for entrapping him, angry at God for giving her such an overwhelming love for a man she could not have. Then she started praying in earnest, begging God to somehow work it out that Giles and Barbara would be estranged, and that he would come to her and realize that she was the right woman for him after all.

But Mirabella had been a Christian all her life, and she didn't deceive herself for long. She had been demanding that the Lord "give" her Giles, and that was just as grave a sin as demanding that God give her riches or beauty or a son with blond hair and blue eyes and a genius for architecture. One did not order God; that was the first sin, the original sin, of pride. She humbled herself finally, and as she prayed in truth for comfort and strength, she found that she was comforted, and she did have strength. It was a strength that surprised her. Mirabella, with resignation and a certain small relief, knew that in her heart she wished Giles only well. She wanted him to be happy. If marrying Barbara Smythe would make him happy, then so be it.

All of this emotional wrenching about went on under the surface. Mirabella had been strictly brought up in all manner of deportment, as had every well-bred young lady. At all times a lady was expected to be graceful, with exquisite manners and etiquette, elegant, and poised. No highs or lows of emotion must ever be displayed in public: neither inappropriately high spirits, with too much laughter or smiling or especially, heaven forbid, giggling, nor melancholy or gloom. Josephine and her parents knew that something was bothering Mirabella. Her mother, and even her father, who normally was consumed with politics and the House of Lords and the war, often stared at her pensively. Gently Josephine tried to get Mirabella to confide in her, but skillfully Mirabella avoided any further mention of Giles, except carelessly in passing, and she determined that even at home, in private, she would work harder to hide her grief.

And so, to Society, Mirabella was as vivacious and bright as she always was. That included Lord Trevor Brydges, who at every opportunity stayed close to Mirabella. She saw him at Almack's on Wednesday night, and he danced with her twice (the waltz, of course), took her in to supper, and talked to her as often as possible between dances.

After one waltz, as he was escorting her off the dance floor, he said, "There's old Knyvet, with Miss Smythe, as usual. They're all the topic, you know, and not just from Mrs. Smythe, although I must say that she's quite the loudest. I tried to get Knyvet to tell me all, but he's as closemouthed as a clam."

"Good heavens, sir, if you demand that Giles explain his feelings for Miss Smythe you're as bad as Mrs. Smythe," Mirabella scolded. "How should you like it if your friends interrogated you about your private life?"

"Now that you mention it, I do have one friend to whom I'd very much like to explain my private life. That friend would be you, my lady. And although I'm extremely glad that you're coming to Levenden Lodge for Ascot, and that will afford us some time together in relative privacy, why should we wait for two weeks to start to really get to know one another?"

Lightly Mirabella said, "I hardly think that Almack's is the place for close confidences among friends, unless you wish for them all to be known by every lady and gentleman in the place by the end of the evening."

"Yes, that is my exact point. May I beg the honor of a more private venue? No, no, nothing improper," he added hastily at the look on her face. "What I was thinking was that I could call on you tomorrow and take you to Gunter's. I'll even humble myself to allow you to drive me in your phaeton, although an acknowledged whip such as I must suffer cruel jibes from all of Society. For you I'll gladly bear it."

Of course Mirabella knew what was in Lord Trevor's mind; although she had gone through a sea change in her outlook about marriage, as far as anyone else knew she still had every intention of arranging her marriage this Season. Mirabella spent another fruitless moment—and there had already been many—berating herself for her foolhardiness. Now her future was as impenetrable as a thick London fog; but all the same, she knew that someday she must marry. She wasn't thinking specifically of Lord Trevor Brydges, but she did like him as well as any man she'd ever met (other than Lewin and Giles, of course) and he was extremely entertaining. She never completely forgot about Giles, but when she was with Lord Trevor, he was diverting enough that she forgot her sorrow. She agreed to go with him to Gunter's.

They went to talk to Giles and Barbara, and Mirabella found that she could behave with perfect equanimity. She and Barbara began talking about their gowns, while Giles and Trevor talked of some successful maneuver in Spain by Lord Wellington.

Denys Aldington came up to them and bowed. Mirabella felt slightly guilty, for this was the first time she'd actually seen Denys face-to-face since that fateful night at the theatre. Cordially he said, "Here are two of the loveliest ladies in the ballroom, and neither of you dancing. Lady Mirabella, Miss Smythe, may I have the honor?"

"Would you like to partner with both of us next dance?" Mirabella asked mischievously.

Denys didn't smile but his eyes gleamed slightly. "Actually, I'd like that above all things, for it would certainly make me the hero of the Season, but I'm afraid that the Lady Patronesses may take exception to it. So rather than all three of us getting blackballed, may I beg the next dance, my lady, and Miss Smythe, the one after that?"

The next dance was a lively long dance, and as usual, the partners had very little opportunity to speak to each other. When Denys took her hand and led her back toward Giles, Barbara, and Lord Trevor, he said in a low voice, "My lady, it was an honor and a pleasure . . . all of it. I always knew that you were a star far beyond my reach, but I shall never regret the few moments I had in that starlight."

He bowed and slipped away. Mirabella thought that the speech had been somewhat rehearsed and artificial; and with her newfound, exquisite sensibilities about the nature of love, she detected no true sorrow in him. She still felt regret, as she had with Lord Southam, at placing him in a position that had proven embarrassing. *I've been so thoughtless, so selfish, so careless . . . Lord, forgive me, may I never use anyone so callously again.*

Giles asked for the next dance, and she smiled and he smiled and they danced well together, as always. Afterward he said, "You look lovely in that green frock, but I must tell you I've noticed an error in your consummate skill in dressing for the evening. Both you and Josephine are wearing green, and I know that you two make careful plans never to wear the same shade. In fact, Josephine says you're a tyrant in telling her what and what not to wear. What were you thinking to so infamously neglect your calling?"

You'll never know, Mirabella said defiantly to herself. Smiling, she replied with one of their old favorite quotes from *The Rivals*: "Oh mercy! I'm quite analyzed, for my part!"

Uncharacteristically, Giles didn't play the game and reply with another malapropism. "Bella, the man or woman that analyzes you must be a genius indeed."

It was the first time in a long time that he'd called her by his affectionate nickname for her. It smote her heart.

The stress on Mirabella had one curious but welcome effect on her. To always appear to be lively and lighthearted was very wearisome, and she was so tired at night that for the first time since she was a small child she easily fell into a deep sleep.

That night she went to bed, trying to plan what she would say to Lord Trevor the next day, again thinking what a supreme irony it had been that she'd so rashly said that she could "handle" the men. She decided that she would quite simply tell him the truth. Exactly, precisely what that truth was escaped her for the moment, but still she was comforted. Her last reflection was that if one had to make detailed plans to tell the truth, something must be wrong...

The next morning she awoke, and as on every morning recently, the weight of her unhappiness immediately pressed upon her; but with determination she reset her mind and said her morning prayers. Although she felt no special anticipation for her outing with Trevor, still she dressed carefully in one of her favorite carriage costumes, an icy pink muslin trimmed with white with a matching shawl. She had special-ordered a pink Oriental silk parasol, elaborately decorated with pagodas and pretty ladies, with an intricate white satin fringe. As Colette dressed her and chattered on in her half-French, half-English dialect, Mirabella reflected whimsically that in spite of all this tragic woe she had several things to be thankful for. For one, regardless of the circumstances, she always felt better when she took care to look her best; for another, she had decided to allow Trevor to drive her, and so she could use her pink parasol, which of course she could not when she was driving the phaeton. She thought of poor Lady Caroline Lamb, and thanked God that she wasn't of such a high-strung disposition that the loss of her love was driving her half insane. Also she found herself looking forward to Gunter's coconut macaroons.

Lord Trevor came at precisely two o'clock to collect her. As he helped her up into the high seat, he said, "Am I dreaming that I'm receiving a special favor, or is this a first? I don't believe anyone has ever witnessed a gentleman driving Lady Mirabella Tirel's phaeton."

"I'm afraid that the only special favor I'm feeling today is for my parasol. As I dressed I realized that I've never been able to carry it because I'm always driving, but today the sun is so fierce that I must shelter from it, or else I risk breaking out in freckles. Obviously if that catastrophe happened I shouldn't be able to show my face for the remainder of the Season."

"All of Society would be devastated if that happened, especially me. And although you tell me that, alas, you aren't bestowing a personal privilege on me in allowing me to drive, I'm still grateful to your parasol."

Their light banter lasted for the two blocks to Gunter's. Mirabella noted with admiration that Trevor was indeed an excellent whip. She herself had to maintain a certain focus and concentration when she was driving the tricky carriage and the spirited team, but he effortlessly negotiated the crowded streets and maneuvered it into a cool shady spot underneath the maple trees.

After they had received their orders—Mirabella's macaroons, and Trevor's cooling lemon ice—he turned to her and instead of having the usual rakish gleam in his eyes and expression, he looked grave. "I know that generally I act the devil-take-it fool, but I can be serious when I really wish to be. Such occasions are very rare, but I wish to be now. May I?"

"You may," Mirabella said calmly.

He frowned, and it was true that such gravity was alien to him. "Thank you, madam," he said formally. "I also think that we are both mature enough that I might speak frankly. I've admired you ever since you conquered Society five years ago, but I knew—all of your friends and acquaintances knew—that you were out of any man's reach, until this year. I like you very much, and enjoy your company as much or more than any lady's I've ever known. I hope these feelings are mutual?"

"They are, with one qualification. Although we've been acquainted for a number of years, you really don't know me at all, nor I you."

"That's true. And therein lies the problem. The rules of Polite Society regarding a gentleman and a lady getting to know one another are a blasted conundrum. Young ladies must never be alone with a gentleman, except in rare circumstances such as this short outing, unless they are betrothed. And so it seems that a couple must become betrothed without ever really having much opportunity for private conversation, to truly get personally acquainted."

Unless the couple are blessed enough to have been lifelong friends, but no, it's surely been no blessing for me, flashed through Mirabella's mind. It was beside the point anyway. "You're correct, sir. In such cases, when it does represent a problem to the couple, I believe the convention is for long engagements."

"Exactly. And now surely you must know of my direction. I think that we would do very well together, Lady Mirabella. I have no intention of repeating South—" He drew himself up and quickly went on, "Of making the error of importuning you too quickly, for I know that you're a lady that determines your own way and will. In fact, that's one of the many things that I admire about you. So I'm not making any demands on you now. All I'm asking is if you would grant me the great honor of allowing me to pay my addresses. Under any circumstances, for any amount of time, that you'd like."

Mirabella stared at him with bemusement. This conversation had been completely different from what she'd anticipated. It was obvious to her that he was sincere, that his generous offer was heartfelt, and so he truly must have a great regard for her. How could she simply say, *No, I'll never consider marrying you because right now I'm suffering from being in love with another man that I'll never have?* It dawned upon Mirabella that that really wasn't the truth, and she had vowed to herself that she would tell Trevor only the truth. Again she felt the insistent refusal to contemplate spending her life alone, the defiant clinging to the hope of marrying someone, after time and her Heavenly Father had healed her grief. It seemed improbable now that that could ever happen, but thanks to her Aunt Tirel's wisdom, Mirabella knew in her heart that one day her love for Giles would no longer be a sorrowful, depressing burden.

And in truth Mirabella agreed with Trevor. She liked him very well, she found him amusing and even exciting. One day they might make a happy, though perhaps not sublimely joyous, couple.

She knew that she had been staring at him, wordlessly, for long moments. He waited patiently. Finally she said, "Sir, I'm honored by your regard for me, and your generous offer. But I must tell you that in spite of—that is, I've come to realize that this Season my—my—actions, and—oh dear, I'm making a muddle of this. As you've been so honest and open with me, I will do you the same courtesy. I've had a change of heart, you may say, and I'm not considering marriage just now. I think it will be some time before I begin to think of it again."

He remained somber for a few moments, then grinned his usual heartbreaking grin. "I see. But I think if you correctly parse what I said, my lady, and I mean no offense, I'm not making you an offer of marriage. My original point was that we should take some time to get to know each other, as long as you like, and that in that time I wish I may be allowed to 'pay you my addresses,' which to me seems a sort of vague and watery thing, but there it is. That's hardly declaring to you that I'm going to your father to demand your hand in marriage, and that we shall be married in two months, and that as the little woman, you'll of course comply with my wishes."

With a smile Mirabella said, "You could try that, but I think that my father might laugh so hard that he'd be unable to wish you all good luck with your intentions. Still, I'm confused as to exactly what you are asking, sir. Do you intend that we should have some sort of—status? As in—promising to think of promising to possibly become engaged at some future unnamed date?"

"That would do me very well for now, if it's suitable to you," he said cheerfully. "I did mean what I said, that I should like to have as much opportunity to be with you as is possible for us. Couples, or I beg your pardon, couples-perhaps-to-be-at-some-time-in-the-future do manage to sort of gravitate together at balls and parties, you know, and though I've seen that your dance cards are generally filled up until Season after next, is it truly necessary that you dance every dance that occurs in London? And then we'll have some time at Ascot. And what about shooting in August? I heard you invite Lady FitzGeorge to Littlemoor. Knyvet tells me that the shooting there is without compare, even to Scotland. Couldn't I cadge an invitation, with my newfound happy status of maybe-possibly-comparably like a suitor-to-be?"

Even with the sharp pang it caused her to hear Giles's name, Mirabella still was amused. It seemed to her that what Trevor was saying indicated little threat that she would cause him any upset if she decided that she couldn't marry him; and she admitted that she found him so diverting that getting to know him might help her not to obsess quite so much over Giles. "Very well, Lord Trevor. Perhaps I may forego a dance or two for the pleasure of your company, I will converse personally with you at Ascot, and I'm inviting you to Littlemoor in August. That's as much of a commitment as I'm prepared to make today."

"I'll take it, and be glad," he said. "I have only one more request to make of you, madam. Are you going to share your macaroons with me, or not?"

The slight buoyancy that Mirabella had felt in Lord Trevor's company dissipated as soon as she left him. He brought her home, and as it was Thursday, it was their at-home day, when Lady Camarden, Mirabella, and Josephine received callers from three o'clock to five o'clock. A succession of ladies called, and Harry Smythe called, as he had done the last four Thursdays. Although the ladies were well aware that he was calling on Josephine, of course they never left her alone with him; Josephine would have been horrified.

Mirabella endured the calls, making an effort to be cordial and bright. At five o'clock she felt utterly exhausted. She had found that along with falling asleep immediately at night, she longed to take naps during the day. In fact, she thought that if she could, she would sleep for days and nights on end; it was a blessed release for her. Tiredly she took a short nap before dressing for Lady Liverpool's dinner party.

The guests, and the conversation, at the dinner were mostly political, with only Lord and Lady Camarden, Mirabella, Josephine, Lord and Lady Castlereagh, and Count and Countess Lieven attending. Mirabella found it a great relief that none of her "set" were there, including and especially Giles. That night she slept long and dreamlessly, and didn't awaken until almost noon.

She went down, yawning, and found her mother and Josephine, who were already dressed, and were sitting in the drawing room writing letters. Lady Camarden said, "Good morning, or should I say good afternoon? I suppose you were up all night, prowling about."

"No, actually I slept quite well. You two are already dressed very prettily, in promenade costumes, I see. Are we promenading today?"

"I thought we might do some shopping," Lady Camarden replied. "We'll be back in time for you girls to ride in the park this afternoon. But Mirabella, Camarden left me a message that Lewin and Giles stopped by this morning and invited themselves to dinner tonight. I'm glad we had no previous engagement, for Camarden says that they particularly wished to speak to us this evening, and asked if we might have an early dinner. I've arranged it for six o'clock, so your time in the park must be cut short today."

Mirabella asked, "This is rather odd, isn't it? Did Pappa give no indication of what they wished to speak to us about?"

"Not at all, but surely it's important for Giles to make such a request," Lady Camarden said.

Mirabella asked Josephine, "Do you have any idea?"

Thoughtfully she replied, "I'm not sure. I suppose we ladies must just wait, as usual, to see what the men are all about."

Mirabella thought she knew what it was all about. As her parents were practically Giles's surrogate parents, he must be planning to speak to them about his intention to marry Barbara. Immediately Mirabella wished that she could run back up to her room, crawl into bed, pull the covers over her head, and hide for the rest of the day, perhaps for several days. Of course it was absurd, and Mirabella told herself that she must get dressed, go shopping, and go to the park, all with a good will and a smile. How she would endure the evening she couldn't fathom. Listlessly she thought that even though it would surely be the worst evening of her life, she would live through it.

All day Mirabella performed credibly, although she was uncharacteristically quiet. Underneath her smiles, however, she was in a state of dreadful anticipation. As she began dressing for dinner, she said to Colette, "I wish to wear my blue silk gown this evening." It was a delicate sky blue, and Giles's favorite color for her to wear, Mirabella thought with poignant sadness; she wondered if he would even notice, or remember.

Giles and Lewin arrived at a quarter of six, but as this was an informal "family" dinner, there was no standing about curtsying and bowing in the drawing room. Mirabella thought that Giles looked particularly handsome, with his well-tailored blue coat, discreet blue-and-gray waistcoat, and black close-fitting trousers. How could she not have seen and admired, always, how well built he was, slim but muscular, how fine his features were, how his blue-black hair was always so attractively arranged, the striking contrast of his coloring with his blue eyes, with what manly grace he moved and talked?

This plaintive and, Mirabella scolded herself, rather pathetic admiration of Giles's person was interrupted when he greeted her with, "I see you've repented of your shameful neglect of your fashion duties. You're wearing my favorite blue silk, and Josephine is wearing that pretty shade that I believe the ladies are calling Pomona green."

Mirabella replied, "Yes, I've come to realize lately that I've been neglecting several things, and have been obliged to repent often."

Giles stared at her quizzically, but just then Lady Camarden said, "We're not standing on ceremony tonight, of course, dinner is ready, let's go in."

They all sat at one end of the dining table, with Lord Camarden at the head, Lady Camarden, Josephine, and Lewin on one side, and Mirabella and Giles on the other. As the footmen began serving the soup, Lord Camarden said, "As Audrey said, we're not standing on ceremony tonight. You may as well go ahead and tell them, Lewin."

When her father started to speak, Mirabella had taken a deep indrawn breath, and clenched her jaw. When she heard the last word, she was so startled that she forgot to breathe.

Lewin took his sister's hand and said simply, "I've received my orders. I'm to return to duty in Spain by July first. There is a transport ship leaving from Portsmouth for San Sebastian on the fifteenth of June."

A heavy silence followed. Josephine sighed, and Lewin patted her shoulder.

Lady Camarden said, "Lewin, naturally we're so sorry to hear this news, but it seems to me that you're hardly devastated."

"No, my lady," he said calmly. "I'm a soldier, and I belong with my men, in Spain. I'm sorry, Josephine."

She said, "No, Lewin, don't apologize, for you're courageous, and you know exactly what God has intended you to be, and you honor Him by fighting for your country. I only hope I'll be brave, and say good-bye without burdening you unduly with grief."

Giles said warmly, "Spoken like the chivalrous lady that you are, Josephine. You've inherited your mother's beauty and grace, and your father's faithful heart."

"Thank you, Giles," Josephine said softly. "Those are the highest compliments I could ever hope to receive."

Mirabella had recovered from her astonishment, and said, "But Lewin, did you say you must leave on the fifteenth? That's barely two weeks from now."

"Yes, and that's the rest of my announcement. I'm going home, of course. I'm leaving early in the morning."

"I want to go home with you," Josephine said instantly. "I'm sorry, Mirabella, but I know you understand."

"Certainly I do," Mirabella said. "It's all rather sudden, but I'm sure we can get enough of your gowns packed up tonight, and send the rest after. Lewin, you weren't planning on taking the stage-coach, were you? Pappa, we must send them in the town coach."

"Although we've all grown accustomed to you ordering our lives, Mirabella, I've already taken the liberty of arranging just that with Lewin," Lord Camarden said.

The rest of the dinner was spent in talking of the details of transporting Lewin and Josephine home, and Lewin spoke, with spirit and undeniable eagerness, of the progress Wellington was making in Spain. "Old Boney had never made a strategic error, and very few tactical ones, until he was foolish enough to invade Russia. He's still putting up quite a fight, but now it's mostly defensive, instead of a crushing offensive."

As the talk went on, mostly among the men, Mirabella was able to gather her thoughts. Surreptitiously she studied Giles. He spoke with intelligence and knowledge about the war and the politics of war. Mirabella wondered with self-deprecating humor what she thought she would see in studying him so closely. *I suppose I'm still thinking he's going to stand up, burst into song, and tell us of his rapturous love for Barbara . . . how silly I've been—again! I* know *that Giles will be prudent and circumspect about such an important decision as marriage!*

When they finished dinner, instead of observing the convention of the ladies' leaving the gentlemen to their port and brandy, they all went to the drawing room. The men were still deep in conversation, and the ladies naturally sat together to talk of how to get Josephine ready to leave in the morning. Mirabella said, "After Lewin and Giles leave, I'll go up with you, and I'm sure with Colette's help we can get you packed quickly."

"Thank you, dearest," Josephine said gratefully. "Although I had anticipated this, I wasn't quite prepared for how quickly Lewin would have to leave. Lady Camarden, I suppose this puts a social burden on you, to make my apologies for the engagements we've accepted? When I get home I'll be glad to write personally to the ladies, but . . ." Her voice trailed off uncertainly.

Mirabella blurted, "Oh dear, Josephine, you won't be able to say good-bye to Mr. Smythe! He'll be crushed!"

Calmly Josephine said, "Mirabella, you presume too much. He and Giles and Lewin have become close friends, I'm sure that Giles will explain to him."

Unaccountably Mirabella had been thinking that because Giles had mainly come to London for the Season for Lewin's sake, he would return to Knyveton when Lewin left. But of course now he had another vitally important reason to stay in Town. Suddenly Mirabella felt the overwhelming and debilitating fatigue that had plagued her so much in the past days, and she grew silent.

Lady Camarden told Irby to get her engagement diary, and together she and Josephine went through the invitations they'd accepted in June, and Josephine took down all the addresses of the ladies to whom she would send her apologies. "We have no engagements with the Smythes," Lady Camarden said in her businesslike manner, "but we're sure to see them somewhere or other, and I'll explain to Mrs. Smythe the grave necessity of you leaving Town."

Josephine said, "I'm sure she'll receive the news with great joy."

"Yes, until I recount to her, in great detail, what an amiable and personable gentleman is her son, and how much you enjoyed his company this Season," Lady Camarden said with satisfaction. "I presume I may have your permission to speak so freely, Josephine."

"You may, my lady, and thank you," she said with amusement.

Giles left Lewin and Lord Camarden and came to sit by Mirabella. "I know you're upset about Lewin, but it seems you're a little pale and out of sorts. Are you?"

"As for being pale, I hadn't really noticed, but I'll surely tell Colette that we must think about some rouge," Mirabella replied lightly. "As for out of sorts, I suppose I am, but it's as you said, because of Lewin. It seems I'm the only one who didn't see this coming, even Mamma didn't seem surprised. I suppose I've been so much distracted of late that I was hardly paying attention to anyone but myself."

"Yes, you have had a busy Season, haven't you?" Giles agreed carelessly. "But seriously, you're lacking your usual glow, you really must take your self-prescribed dosage of ratafia. I know you, you've likely been up haunting the halls and frightening the servants all hours of the night."

You don't know me nearly as well as you think, Mirabella thought sadly, but she merely said, "Yes, sir, of course I'll follow your orders to the letter as always."

Giles grumbled, "As if that's ever happened in the history of the world."

"Of course not, what could I have been thinking? Perhaps my head has been muddled by sleep deprivation. Anyway, Giles, I was wondering, I—I don't suppose you will return to Knyveton, now that Lewin's leaving?"

He looked puzzled. "No, of course not. I've monopolized him enough, he really wants to be with his family these last two weeks. And though I'm sure my social calendar is nowhere nearly as full as yours, I have accepted some engagements for the rest of the Season. By the by, I heard you're going to Ascot to stay at Lord Levenden's house. Brydges said there's going to be quite a party, you should really enjoy yourself."

With a supreme effort Mirabella made herself smile. "It seems to me that wherever Lord Trevor goes, there is generally a party. Surely he invited you?"

"He did, but he knows very well that I don't gamble, and that's about ninety percent of the fun, or so I'm told, though I'll never understand it. Anyway, even though Town will be almost deserted that week, I'm sure I'll find something to do to amuse myself."

"I'm sure you will," Mirabella said with a sinking heart. "I've noticed that you, too, have been much in demand this Season."

It came to their attention that Lewin was saying his good-byes. "I must report to the War Office at dawn tomorrow, and I still must pack, though I know it won't be nearly such an onerous task as gathering up all of your fripperies and gewgaws, Sister. Giles, are you coming now, or are you staying?"

He stood up. "I'm ready, I think we must leave the ladies to their toils. Good night, Mirabella. I'll see you soon." He bowed and he and Lewin took their leave.

Mirabella had found her entire conversation with Giles curiously impersonal, even strained. But she was so drained, mentally and physically, that she couldn't work out whether the strain was all on her side, or Giles's, or both. It took all the strength she could summon to help Josephine with her packing. After about an hour, Josephine said to her, "I know very well that something is wrong with you, you're pale and as listless as I've ever seen you. Are you getting ill, dearest?"

"No, of course not, I'm never ill. I wish everyone would stop telling me I'm pale, I declare I'm going to have Colette paint me up with so much rouge that I'll look like one of the *demimonde*," Mirabella retorted crossly.

"Why yes, what a capital idea," Josephine said sarcastically. "Just listen to yourself, I don't think you even know what you're saying. Colette, I'm ordering you to take Mirabella to her room, dose her liberally with ratafia, and put her to bed. If she wants to stay up and wander around, sit on her. I'm perfectly capable of packing a trunk by myself."

With unusual meekness Mirabella obeyed. Happily, it wasn't necessary for Colette to sit on her; she was almost passed out before she had put on her nightclothes. Eagerly she embraced sleep; for now, and she suspected for a long time to come, it was the only peace she knew.

Chapter Twenty

Lewin's and Josephine's leave-taking made Mirabella feel disconsolate indeed. The weather did not help: the dawn was dark, with a heavy sullen rain that turned to steam as soon as it hit the streets. London had been unseasonably hot for May, and it seemed that June would be as close and unbearable as July and August always were in Town.

That night Mirabella and her parents went to the theatre, as guests in Lord and Lady Jersey's box, which included a large party of sixteen people. The play was *A Midsummer Night's Dream*, which was one of Mirabella's favorites. But on this night she felt so dispirited that she could hardly carry on a conversation, or even pay attention to the play. Against her will she found herself searching for Giles. But she didn't see him, or the Smythes.

Lord Trevor visited during intermission, and Lady Jersey immediately asked him to join them. He sat with Mirabella, and though she smiled at his banter and did manage to respond to him in a sensible manner, she knew that he was aware of her distraction. Private conversation was not possible, of course, but as they left the theatre he whispered in her ear, "May I call on you tomorrow?"

As if she were an automaton, she replied, "Yes, of course."

That night, although she was fully as exhausted as ever, she didn't fall asleep immediately. All she could think, over and over, was *I'm so tired. How I miss Josephine. I'm so very very tired of London, of all of it, of the parties and balls and working so hard to be bright and happy when all I want is to get away, to go home, to have some peace... I'm so very tired...*

Instead of feeling her familiar dreary despondency as soon as she awoke, she sat up abruptly, alert, and stared into space. *How very odd... is that You, Lord? Somehow You spoke to me while I was sleeping? It must be, for as silly as I am, it would never occur to me.*

She rushed through dressing and hurried downstairs to her mother, who was always an early riser. Without morning greetings she sat at the table and blurted out, "Mamma, I want to go home."

Lady Camarden was not the kind of woman to be easily shocked, especially where Mirabella was concerned. She finished chewing, delicately patted her mouth with her napkin, and said, "Would you? Am I to order the carriage now, or may I at least finish my breakfast?"

"Oh, I think I can wait until you finish. I'm sorry, Mamma, of course I wish to explain. I—I'm just so tired, you see. For for some reason I—I—this Season—oh, it's so complicated. I miss Josephine, I didn't realize how much her company meant to me. I miss Camarden. And I—I'm tired."

"Yes, so you said, and so I've noticed these past weeks. When would you like to go?"

Mirabella sighed. "I wish I could go now, but tomorrow would be soon enough, I suppose."

Cautiously Lady Camarden said, "You do know that we've accepted several invitations for the next month, including a week at Lord Levenden's for Ascot."

"Yes, I know, and last night as I was thinking of how much I wanted to go home, all I could think of was of my social obligations, and how irresponsible it would be for me to neglect them." She brightened a little and went on, "But the most peculiar thing happened to me this morning. When I awoke, the only thought that was in my mind was 'It's no sin to go home.' I think—I think that it was the Lord, you see. I know that it's rude to cancel invitations already accepted, but it is certainly not a grave sin. Is it? Or do you think that I've suddenly lost my senses? My social sense, at any rate."

"No, I do not," Lady Camarden answered briskly. "The Bible tells us that the Lord will direct our steps, so I find it completely reasonable that under the circumstances He's telling you to go home and heal. Do not give me that cheeky look, Mirabella, I know that you're not ill, but I also know that something is troubling you." Her gaze grew softer, and though her voice was not tentative in tone, it was gentler. "We have never been the closest of *confidantes*, but you are my daughter, and I love you dearly, and I want above all things for you to be happy. Would you like for me to come with you, or were you thinking of being alone for a time?"

Mirabella swallowed hard. "I'd like for you to come home with me, Mamma. I know that you'll be embarrassed to take such an abrupt and ungracious leave from all of our friends in Town, and I apologize."

"Nonsense, girl," Lady Camarden said, returning to her normal crispness. "Ever since you came out I've endured London mostly for your sake, and because your father is so much happier when we're here. But he'll understand, as will all of our friends, our real friends, that is, for all I intend to say is the truth, for both me and you, and the gossips may natter on as they please. We've found the exertions of the Season fatiguing, and wish to retire to the country early. I only have one question, Mirabella, and I hope you will not think me too intrusive, but I am not a blind fool, and you know that. What do you intend to do about Lord Trevor Brydges?"

"He's calling on me today. I know it's unorthodox, Mamma, but I beg you will leave us alone for a few minutes. As I said, it's complicated, but I feel I owe him a more personal explanation."

Her interview with Lord Trevor was uncomfortable. Mirabella simply told him the truth, much as she'd told her mother that morning, although in a much more organized, matter-of-fact manner.

He looked incredulous, then stood up to pace a few steps. "Are you saying that you're leaving Town tomorrow morning? Just like that?" He snapped his fingers, a hard brittle sound.

Mirabella was more surprised than offended at his brusqueness. "You sound angry. I don't understand. I thought that our agreement, I suppose you could call it, was not of such a nature that either of us would feel any sort of obligation to the other."

For a moment his eyes narrowed grimly, but then he relaxed and sat back down. "I beg your pardon, my lady. You're right about our 'agreement,' but you're wrong about my reaction. I'm not angry, I'm just surprised and disappointed. I suppose this means that you won't come to Levenden Lodge for Ascot?"

"I'm afraid not. Again, I hope you'll forgive me, sir."

"And what about Littlemoor, in August?"

"Naturally your invitation still stands, and I hope you'll plan to join us."

With a hint of frustration he asked, "And for the next two months? In no way do I mean to impose upon you, but I've always meant what I've said, that I do think that we should take as much opportunity as we can to at least get to know each other better. I understand—I think—your wish to go home to rest, so I won't beg for an invitation to Camarden. But would you at least consider corresponding with me?"

Mirabella smiled. "Do you know, Lord Trevor, that in spite of your careless flirtatious ways, I find you to be refreshingly direct when you wish to be? You know that it's not seemly for us to correspond, because—"

"Yes, I know, the old Polite Society conundrum, a lady and gentleman may not correspond unless they are betrothed. I don't suppose you'd wish to *pretend* that we are engaged for two months? No? I suppose it's just as well, I'm a lamentably poor letter-writer anyway." He stood up and bowed. "Then this is good-bye for a time, Lady Mirabella. I thank you for your consideration in speaking to me personally, and please extend my sincerest gratitude to Lady Camarden for allowing me such a privilege." Although his words were courteous, his manner was coldly formal.

After he'd left, Mirabella thought that aside from her physical and mental and emotional weariness, she was thoroughly, completely tired of trying to figure out how to deal with men.

In some ways Camarden did heal Mirabella. She passed her days doing all the old, sweet, comforting things that she loved. Every day she did some gardening, whether in her conservatory or in one of the several splendid gardens of Camarden, for it seemed to her that this particular June they were more bright and brilliant than they had ever been before. She and Josephine and Lewin, along with their younger sister and brother, toured and inspected the new village stewpond. Josephine had a brilliant idea: as she had said, she had no use for Mirabella's year-old very fine satin and silk gowns, but she suggested that they donate them to the girls' school, to remake into usable frocks or trims or embellishments. The young girls were as excited as if they had each received all-new wardrobes themselves, and Josephine and Mirabella spent five enjoyable days working with the girls on their sewing skills.

They had been home for two weeks, and Lewin was leaving the next day. The three friends decided to picnic at the Camarden stewpond, and Lewin wanted to fish. Josephine and Mirabella said they'd be content watching him do all the work, but they'd be happy to eat any fine catches he might make. The first fish he landed was a fat ten-pound tench. Mirabella vividly recalled last All Hallows' Eve, of "The Mermaid Song," her dunking, Monsieur Danton's delicious *tanche à la citronelle*, and of course . . . Giles.

And this was how coming home to Camarden Court had presented new difficulties to Mirabella. Every scene she saw, every green vista, every expansive night sky, everything she did, all the pleasures she had, reminded her of Giles. The pain she felt was not nearly so keen as it had been at first. Now it was like a dull ache, a tenderness, like a healing bruise. But it would have been immeasurably worse if Giles and Barbara had been at Knyveton Hall.

With resignation Mirabella accepted this, and found herself, in effect, saying good-bye to Camarden, or at least anticipating the fact that she must someday. Beyond that she could make no plans at all; there was only the insistence in her mind that she could not, would not live her life alone. Occasionally she thought of Lord Trevor Brydges, but as the days went by she learned to mentally stop herself from trying so desperately to arrange her life, for it had certainly worn her down to exhaustion in London.

Their good-byes to Lewin were poignant, but not really sad because they had all learned to accept that he was called to be a soldier, and he was anxious to rejoin his men. Mirabella learned a lesson from this. Not every parting was tragic; some were just meant to be.

In addition, Mirabella was actually excited and looking forward to the next two weeks, because Clara and Philip had invited them to Reynes Magna for a visit to meet their new son. Mirabella was also very glad to learn that her Aunt Tirel would be there.

When Baron Tirel had been awarded the earldom in the sixteenth century, the fourteen thousand acres included three estates. The houses had actually been fortified castles of varying sizes, already old by Tudor times. Over the last two centuries various earls had refurbished, renovated, and rebuilt the fortresses. Reynes Magna (Large Reynes) had become the home seat of the earls; a mile away, Reynes Parva (Small Reynes) had been variously occupied or empty, according to the needs of the earl's eldest son. Mirabella's grandfather had given Lady Dorothea a life tenancy at the smallest manor house, which had been renamed Tirel House.

Reynes Magna was now a spacious, gracious Palladian mansion, and Mirabella's grandfather had engaged Lancelot "Capability" Brown to landscape the grounds. Wide vistas of rolling grass, little green hillocks, stands of trees, and still small plain lakes were not at all to Mirabella's liking; she loved formal gardens and the buoyant, vigorous English cottage gardens. Still, she saw that Reynes Magna, situated on a hill above a silvery serene lake, had a simple grandeur.

Her brother Philip, a younger, taller image of their father, greeted them with his usual stolid friendliness, and chucked Mirabella under the chin as he had done since she was a small child.

With exasperation she said, "Philip, I'm twenty-two years old now, you simply must stop treating me as if I just learned to toddle and will be allowed a sweetie if I'm good."

Clara greeted them with more warmth than usual, looking happier than she ever had before. She dutifully kissed Mirabella, then said, "I suppose as soon as you've taken off your cloak and bonnet you'll be dashing up to the nursery to see Tiberius. Very well, come along, I'll take you up. And Mirabella, I warn you, he is *not* to be nicknamed Tibby, that makes him sound like a barn cat." But she gave Mirabella a small tight smile as she spoke.

Tiberius had just finished his midday meal, and the nurse was rocking him to sleep. Mirabella begged to be allowed to rock him, and Clara readily assented. But already his nurse was possessive and looked askance at Mirabella, as if she suspected her capable of foul play with her baby. But Clara said, "Newens, stop fussing and fidgeting about and give the baby to his aunt, she's perfectly capable of rocking him to sleep. Go down to the kitchen and have some tea, Mirabella will send for you when she's ready to come downstairs."

Clara bustled out, and with only one backward suspicious glance, Nurse Newens left, but Mirabella barely noticed. Already she was enchanted with her nephew. He gazed up at her with no sign of alarm at this new person attending him, only, it seemed to her, a mild curiosity as to who this new adorer might be.

"Hello, Tibby," she whispered. "I'm your Aunt Mirabella, and we're going to be great friends." He clasped her finger as if in assent, and for the first time in many days Mirabella felt a pure, unblemished joy. She started singing "The Mermaid Song" softly, and by the time she had finished, he was sound asleep. A vision of Mirabella rocking her own son rose in her mind, and she prayed, *Please, Lord, soon . . . soon . . .*

For the next few days Mirabella spent much more time in the nursery, and outside playing with Alexander, than she did with the rest of her family. But on the fourth night, she decided that she would go talk to her Aunt Tirel. On the one hand she'd been longing to confide in her, but she had also been hesitant, because she felt ashamed of her childishness, embarrassed at her foolishness, and guilty for her selfishness. But she knew that her aunt had never judged her, had never censured or condemned her, and always comforted her. Taking a candle, she went down the hall and saw the candlelight glowing underneath her aunt's door, just as it had on that night seven months ago.

"Come in, Mirabella," she called. Mirabella went in, and the scene was almost exactly as it had been then, too: Lady Dorothea was sitting up in bed, her hair tucked away in a nightcap, her spectacles balanced on the end of her nose, reading a book. "I wondered when you'd be ready to confess all, you've been looking suspiciously sheepish these last days."

Settling comfortably beside her, Mirabella said, "*Sheepish* may actually be giving me too much credit, sometimes I think I'm much more foolish than the stupidest sheep that ever lived."

"You are not stupid, you're intelligent and clever, and you very well know it. As for being foolish, I agree with Puck: 'Lord, what fools these mortals be!' That includes you and me and every other human who's ever walked this earth."

"How odd you should quote that, we went to *A Midsummer Night's Dream* on our last weekend in London. That line was one of the few that I recall actually hearing."

"I'd love to claim a special prescience, but I practice no such mysterious art. I'm reading *A Midsummer Night's Dream*, you see. And so proceed, child. Tell me why you quit your glittering Season so early."

Haltingly at first, and then in a flood, Mirabella told her everything. "And so here I am, a forlorn, silly, foolish girl. I was so certain that there was no such thing as romantic love, and I was so wrong and how I wish I had been right. Still I've seen, thankfully, that my temperament doesn't seem to be of the sort that experiences ecstatic flights of bliss, nor cataclysmic throes of despair. I've prayed much about Giles, and I've found that I've rather—evened out, you might say."

Curiously Aunt Tirel asked, "And so what is the exact nature of your feelings toward Giles?"

"It seems so trite, but there is no other way to say it. I'm deeply in love with him. But after all my struggles and resentment and anger and jealousy, I've come to a point where I only want him to be happy, even if that means for him to marry Barbara."

Aunt Tirel said approvingly, "Then I would say that now you do understand the true meaning of real love. The thirteenth chapter of First Corinthians gives us a perfect picture of it. Real, long-lasting, godly love is completely unselfish, and wishes only well for the beloved. In some ways your instincts were right, Mirabella. Romantic love does exist, but it has nothing to do with the kind of love that represents a lifelong commitment between a man and a woman. It's simply an emotion, a sentiment, a passion. In my long years I've seen that it almost always passes away, and if there is no foundation of godly love between a husband and wife, it also almost always means a troubled and unhappy marriage."

Mirabella sighed. "Yes, I've come to understand that. But the emotions, sentiment, and passion are still real, and even though, as I've said, I'm not running melancholy mad, it's still difficult for me to overcome the grief. I thought I would find sanctuary and peace at home, for I was certain it would be so much easier if I didn't have to see him with Barbara. But I was wrong, at Camarden I think of Giles even more, and miss him more painfully. I just cannot think what I shall do, Aunt Tirel."

"Mirabella, ever since you grew old enough to have a mind of your own you've always forged straight ahead to what you're going to do, before you look around and see exactly what it is that needs to be done, if anything. Before you force me into drawing up your charts and tables and lists as you did poor Josephine, allow me to clarify some points. Have Giles and Miss Smythe actually made an announcement of their betrothal?"

"No, but as I told you, their mutual attraction is obvious, they were spending much time together, and I know Giles well enough that he wouldn't—wouldn't—dally around with a young lady unless his intentions were serious. And of course there is the fact that even though they've made no public declaration, Mrs. Smythe has confidently let it be known that they are a couple."

Lady Dorothea almost snorted. "Oh, yes, of course Fanny Smythe knows all the intimate details of Sir Giles Knyvet's affections and intentions. I'm surprised at you, Mirabella, you know very well how silly that woman is. Even I know she's a prating, title-hunting busybody, and I haven't seen her for more than fifteen years. And as for Giles, he's an amiable, popular young man, and he's perfectly capable of making friends with a young lady and enjoying her company without being dumbfounded in love with her."

With a hint of impatience Mirabella said, "But I'm telling you, Aunt, that with Barbara he's different. I can see it, and sense it."

"How is that? Exactly what are you seeing, and sensing?"

Mirabella reflected ruefully that in her mind she might have glossed over the memories of her Aunt Tirel's difficult questions. Lamely she answered, "I see that they seem to have a measure of mutual warmth and affection when they're together. And—and—I suppose I sense that Giles has been treating me differently lately. He's been more distant, more aloof, and I must assume that it's as you tried so hard to tell me, he knows that any woman might object to me being her husband's close friend."

"I'm not so certain that you're *seeing* or *sensing* things at all clearly just now. That last little speech of yours included 'it seems thus' and 'I suppose this' and 'I assume such and the other.' But never mind, one thing I do see clearly is that we could argue about this all night, and it's a waste of breath. The first thing you must *do*, child, is ask Giles about this girl. I cannot fathom why you haven't thought of that one simple thing."

"But I have thought of it," Mirabella said in a small voice. "I can't, I simply can't. I so resented my friends asking me, or teasing me, about Lord Southam and Mr. Aldington, and I even suffered a jibe or two from Lady Jersey about Lord Trevor, although we had only been—whatever we are—for a few days. I would never embarrass Giles so. Mrs. Smythe's syrupy public declarations are bad enough for him to endure."

"There is something in that," Lady Dorothea agreed. "But still, Mirabella, if the opportunity presents itself, I think you could talk to him about Miss Smythe without making him uncomfortable."

"Perhaps, but *I* should be horridly uncomfortable. I don't think I could keep my countenance if I had to listen to Giles talk about being in love with another woman." She looked down and shook her head slightly. "No, I think I shall try to avoid any private conversation with him at all, assuming that the occasion ever again arises."

"It will, and I think it's entirely possible the circumstances may be very different from what you anticipate," Lady Dorothea said, somewhat obscurely to Mirabella. But immediately she went on, "Now, what's all this about young Aldington?"

"Aldington? Do you mean Lord Trevor Brydges?"

"Yes, yes, whoever," she said testily. "I found your explanation of what you two are doing so vague as to be meaningless. What exactly do you want from him, Mirabella?"

"Why, I don't want anything at all from him, at least not now, and I think I made that perfectly clear to him, and I think that he's content."

"Then why are we talking about him at all?"

"Because—because—I know I'm not like you, Aunt Tirel, I want more than anything to marry and have children and a home of my own. And Lord Trevor is—well, he's handsome and diverting and exciting, and—and—"

"He'd do as well as anyone? When you decide that you're ready to return to your list of fiancé-marriage-home-children?" Mirabella looked so downcast that Lady Dorothea immediately softened. "I apologize, I'm a crusty impatient old woman, and you don't deserve to be spoken to so harshly. I love you so much, Mirabella, and it pains me to see you making mistakes that I know will hurt you in the end, so let me try to explain. You said that you had been praying much about Giles, and the Lord has given you comfort and strength?"

"Yes, ma'am," Mirabella said softly.

"Of course He has. We should always ask Him for grace and mercy in our times of need. But Mirabella, there is so much more to being a faithful Christian than merely attending church and being charitable and seeking God when we're troubled. The only way that we can know true peace, and find the right and righteous path for our lives, is when we obey Him. To obey Him, you must know His perfect will for you. Have you sought the Lord about whom you should marry, or even if you should marry at all?"

Long moments passed before Mirabella answered. "No, ma'am, I haven't. I'm afraid to. I'm so afraid that He'll say I should not marry. It only makes sense, doesn't it? I mean, I'm in love with Giles, so how could it possibly be even fair, much less virtuous, to marry a man when I'm in love with another? I know all this, I've thought of this, though I've tried hard to ignore it. But I suppose I can't, not really."

"Not any more," Aunt Tirel said gently. "But you must come

to this surrender yourself, in your own spirit, Mirabella, so I'll say no more about it. I will tell you this, from long experience, that most of the time when we think we are giving up something for the Lord, we actually gain much, so much more than we lose. Christ Jesus said, 'My yoke is easy, and my burden is light.' I think you'll find that whatever the Lord has planned for you will be so much easier and full of light and more joyful than you can imagine."

After breakfast the next day Mirabella followed Philip to his study. "What are you on about this morning, Macaroon?" he asked. He had always called her "Coconut" or "Macaroon" because they'd been her favorite sweet since she was two years old.

"I'd like the keys to Reynes Parva, please. I'm of the mind that I'll go see it, I haven't been there for so long I can barely remember it."

He unlocked a drawer in his desk and handed her a bunch of very old keys. "Touring the manorial holdings, eh? Do you want me to send my steward with you to show you around the grounds and outbuildings?"

"Thank you, no, I just want to poke around in the house a bit."

She rode a calm old gelding, and she allowed him to dawdle along, as she was in no hurry. In fact, she was half-dreading going into the house, for she had a specific reason for doing so, and it was going to be hard for her. As she made her slow way, Mirabella felt exasperated amusement at herself. *As Aunt Tirel said, I'm a "doer," I simply must make a plan and then step by step follow through it until I reach my goal. I'm hardly the adventurous, spontaneous type, am I?*

Reynes Parva was aptly named, as it was much smaller than Reynes Magna. The last of the renovations had been done in 1710, the finished product a graceful two-story manor house with a symmetrical façade of mellow golden brick. At dinner on the previous night there had been much discussion in the family about Reynes Parva. The house, along with eight thousand acres, had come out of entailment when Philip had turned twenty-eight. At that time one of Clara's cousins, General Yerby, had just retired from the army. He had a house in Portsmouth, but he wished to live in the country, so Philip had granted him a life tenancy in Reynes Parva. He had lived there quietly and simply for the last ten years, and had died in February. The talk at dinner had been about exactly what to do with the house. No landowner ever wanted to sell any part of his holdings, so there was no question of that, but Philip and Lord Camarden had discussed whether to shut up the house and leave it empty, or try to find a new tenant and lease it.

Acidly Clara had said, "It's almost impossible to find desirable tenants. Our sort of people are rarely interested in leasing, they either have their own estates or would only wish to purchase one. We should put it back in entailment and close it up until someone in the family needs it."

It was not a matter for Clara to decide, of course; in fact, it wasn't even up to Philip, it was solely a decision to be made by the Marquess of Camarden. Lord Camarden, however, had no strong feelings about it one way or the other, so they had agreed to Clara's suggestion.

Mirabella reached the house, and thought it looked forlorn, with all the shutters closed and the front lawn looking straggly and unkempt. Inside it was dark and musty-smelling. Mirabella opened some shutters and windows, and for a moment stood entranced, watching dust motes dancing in the lustrous sunshine pouring in. She wandered around the drawing room, musing that it seemed much smaller than she recalled.

Furnishings and accessories were sparse, for the general had lived in a Spartan manner, and everything was swathed in ghostly white dust sheets. Mirabella uncovered a tall shape in a corner, and was surprised to find a bust of Socrates, finely modeled, on a graceful Corinthian column stand. *I like this . . . I could use this.*

She hesitated. Her impulse was to explore the entire house and look at all the furnishings, but she resisted, knowing that she was only searching for excuses to delay her difficult task. Resolutely she walked through the drawing room and down a side hall that led to a covered walkway on the east side of the house.

The oldest and most beautiful part of Reynes Parva was the lady chapel. It was tiny, with only four benches in the nave, and a small chancel and plain altar. But above the altar was a magnificent stained glass window with the Holy Virgin holding the infant Jesus, surrounded by intricately shaped panes of glass of every color. Mirabella knelt at the altar and gazed up at the beautiful window.

Her mind refused to coalesce into a coherent prayer, so she said the litany that her wise Aunt Tirel had brought to mind the night before.

Charity suffereth long, and is kind;
Charity envieth not;
Charity vaunteth not itself, is not puffed up,
Doth not behave itself unseemly,
Seeketh not her own,
Is not easily provoked,
Thinketh no evil;
Rejoiceth not in iniquity, but rejoiceth in the truth;
Beareth all things,

Believeth all things,
Hopeth all things,
Endureth all things.

Mirabella's mind was clear, and for a moment she knew that rarest of blessings, complete inner silence. Then she began to speak, and was somewhat surprised to find that, in contrast to the formal recitations of her usual prayers, she talked to the Lord in an effortless, even a conversational tone.

"Dearest Heavenly Father, You know why I'm here. I'm sorry I've been fighting this so hard, and for so long. Now I will say it, even though I'm still feeling a little stubborn about it, but of course You know that. If You don't wish me to marry, then I won't."

She stopped and found herself listening, and realized how ludicrous that was.

She went on, "I know that with Your grace and blessing, I could live here, or somewhere, by myself, and You would be my home. Thank You so much for all of the many countless blessings You've given me, but most of all thank you for sacrificing Yourself so that my sins are forgiven, and I'm clean and whole. I ask now that You will show me Your perfect will for my life, and I'll do my best to obey. Amen."

She stood and gazed up at the window for a long time, still with a vague expectancy that she would immediately know God's decision concerning her marriage.

She didn't hear a voice in her head, much less an audible voice, but perfectly formed and clear the thought came: *After all, we don't have to decide about marriage today.*

She was one of the Lord's blessed sheep, and the sheep knew His voice. Mirabella smiled.

Chapter Twenty-one

Mirabella didn't instantly inhabit heavenly realms of complete serenity. Whenever she thought of Giles, which was often, she still keenly felt pain and loss. But she conditioned herself, at these times, to literally *change her mind*. It was much like mentally turning a sharp corner; she simply made herself ignore the pain and think of something else. The something else was usually either a quick prayer, or a passage of Scripture. Many times a day she thought, *Love suffers long, and is kind . . .*

As the days passed, she found that the best way to describe her state was as one of calm. Sometimes she was sad, when she was happy the vividness of it was diminished, but always she was tranquil.

Only one thing troubled her: she couldn't decide what to do about Lord Trevor Brydges. It was true that their relationship was hazy and ill defined, but Mirabella had a strong sense of social responsibility, and she felt that she should sharply delineate to Lord Trevor that now she was not thinking about marriage at all, and had no plans to contemplate it in the near future. Still, there was the old conundrum, that it was strictly forbidden for a young lady to write to a gentleman unless they were betrothed. It was such a strict rule that to break it was considered almost as scandalous as a lady's visiting a gentleman's home. She could explain to him when they went to Littlemoor in August, but she felt that was inadequate. In spite of the nebulous nature of their agreement, in London the talk had already begun of the two of them as a couple. Mirabella sincerely didn't want to cause Lord Trevor such embarrassment as she had caused Lord Southam and Denys Aldington.

When they returned to Camarden, Mirabella found that this particular problem had been solved, in a peculiar twist of irony, by Lady Jersey. A fat, closely written letter awaited her. Mirabella and Sally corresponded sporadically. Usually Lady Jersey wrote only when she had particularly juicy tittle-tattle to share.

Mirabella took the long letter up to her bedroom and read it all the way through, and then slowly read it again. Sally wrote much as she talked, with many flourishes and parenthetical phrases and paragraph-long sentences. When she finished, the letter fell through Mirabella's fingers and fluttered to the floor, unnoticed. She stared unseeing into space.

Three days previously, at Lady Heathcote's ball, Lord Byron and Lady Caroline Lamb had met face-to-face for the first time of the Season. Words were exchanged, although even Lady Jersey had not been able to ferret out the exact conversation. Lady Caroline had run headlong upstairs to a lady's withdrawing room, had broken a crystal wineglass, and had cut herself several times. Lady Melbourne was the only witness to the actual event, but Lady Caroline's hysterical cries had echoed throughout the house, and a group of people had rushed upstairs, Lady Jersey included. She had seen Lady Caroline covered in blood and fainting. In the hurly-burly Lady Heathcote directed that she be carried down the hall to a guest room, and everyone crowded around Lord Heathcote and followed as he carried her to the bedroom.

When the door was flung open, they found Lord Trevor Brydges and Rosalind, Lady FitzGeorge. Apparently they were not in such extremity as in the euphemism *in flagrante delicto*, "in blazing offense," but this was the longest passage in Sally's letter, and she described the scene in such vivid terms that Mirabella well understood the couple had been caught in a scandalously compromising position.

Sally wrote that they all had thought that Lord Trevor and she were virtually betrothed, but now they all knew that they had been sadly mistaken, and she berated Mirabella for being "entirely too much a woman of mystery, for shame, you didn't confide in your oldest friend that you had added Brydges to the list of men whose hearts you have broken." All of that was nonsense. Lady Jersey was an amusing, lively acquaintance, but was not really her friend; and Mirabella had broken no one's heart. All she felt at the news was a sense of relief that she need not worry about her obligation to Lord Trevor Brydges any longer.

The majority of the letter was about the juicy scandal of Lady Caroline and Byron, but one other tidbit of gossip, added almost as an afterthought, affected Mirabella deeply. Sally wrote that the vague but all-encompassing "they" were expecting an announcement at any time now about Barbara Smythe and Mirabella's "best friend," Sir Giles. Apparently Mrs. Smythe, understanding how much Sir Giles loved shooting, had prevailed upon Mr. Smythe to purchase an estate in Scotland, and was planning a shooting party in August, and Giles was going. Sally wrote, "That awful Mrs. Smythe has invited practically everyone, but of course most of us already had plans, or quickly invented them when her invitation was offered. There are always various sad hangers-on, and here I'm not speaking of Giles, you know I'm crazy for him, who are happy to accept any invitation they can beg, so I understand that they've managed to scrape up quite a large party."

Although Mirabella no longer entertained any hope for her and Giles, still, this was another blow. It took her all day, and much of the night, to struggle against the depression it caused her. But finally she did manage to overcome it, and the next day she again felt the uncanny serenity she'd known since she had prayed in the lady chapel at Reynes Parva.

The next day she had intended to work in the conservatory, for she had found that when she was gone for as much as two weeks, it always seemed to look rather straggly and unkempt regardless of the care of the hothouse gardeners. But it was a lovely summer day, and Mirabella longed to go outdoors. She decided to walk to the deer park and picnic. She dressed carelessly in a worn frock, a yellow muslin sprigged with peach-colored roses entwined with green ivy, and wore a poke bonnet with a deep brim to protect her face from the sun. In a leather gardener's satchel she packed an old faded blue shawl to sit on, some apples and grapes, cheese, and sliced bread, and the book Giles had given her for her birthday, but that she hadn't yet had time to read, *Pride and Prejudice*. Startled, she realized she'd forgotten Giles's birthday, which had been thirteen days ago, on June twenty-fifth. She hadn't forgotten his birthday since they'd been children. With bittersweet amusement she thought that at least now she wasn't an "older woman."

To add to the delightful prospect of the picnic, Mirabella decided to take the fawn Dolly, who was now a year old and was no longer considered a fawn but was not yet a fully mature doe. She had become as tame as a dog, and a particular favorite of practically everyone on the estate. She followed the stablemen around and contentedly grazed close to the stables when she was let out of her stall. When the gardeners tended the deer park, they would always take Dolly with them. So far she had shown no interest in rejoining the herd. Like a horse who knows when he is on the way home, she always eagerly followed the gardeners back to the stables.

Mirabella had visited Dolly every day since she had come home, and now she greeted her gladly. "Hello, my lovely," she said as the doe gently nosed the handful of grapes that Mirabella had brought her. "I've missed you. And just look at you, you're getting plump. I must not be the only one slipping you treats." Fallow deer were smaller than other breeds of deer, and Dolly now was about three feet tall at the shoulder, with a delicate frame, slender neck, and daintily thin legs. Her summer coat was a rich light tan with white spots, and a snowy white belly. Her brown eyes, like those of all deer, were large and lustrous and angelic. Mirabella was sure, however, that Dolly's expression was much more alert and intelligent than those of other deer. "Would you like to come picnic with me and visit your cousins? I have some apples I'll share with you, and if you're very good, perhaps some more grapes."

Dolly apparently agreed, for she readily followed Mirabella out of the stables and walked alongside her for the half mile to the deer park. The gate, seven feet high and made of solid oak, was old and weathered, but the gardeners kept it well hung and oiled, so it swung open easily. Below her the meadow spread out in a small valley, and the deer herd was there, dotted around as picturesquely as if posing for a painting. Far to her right was a thick wood of oak, maple, alder, and elm. On her left was a low hill, crowned by a carefully maintained stand of silver birches. As Mirabella began the climb she watched Dolly. The doe took a few tentative steps out into the meadow and stopped, her ears pricked forward alertly. Some of the deer looked up at her, and then began again unconcernedly grazing. After a few moments Dolly turned and followed Mirabella. "That's all right, darling," Mirabella said affectionately. "Just wait three or four more months, you'll be much more interested in the young gentlemen deer. Like all of us foolish women, you'll likely fall in love with one of them."

At the top of the hill, just inside the sylvan glade, Mirabella spread out her shawl and sat down, contented for a while to simply watch the deer. It was a fairy-tale golden day, with the verdant green meadow spread out below, the virginal white of the daisies shining in the bright cheerful sun. The sky was deep blue, with fat white clouds lazing along. It was almost hot, but not quite, and occasionally light dancing airs of a breeze, wonderfully scented of rich earth and green grass, touched her face and teased the light strawberry-blonde curls that framed her face. She took off her bonnet. Lifting her face to the sun, she closed her eyes. All she was thinking was *Thank you, Lord Jesus . . . thank you . . . for all of it, for everything . . .*

Mirabella had a very sensitive nose, and she became aware of a faint aroma, carried on the breeze. The fragrance was unfamiliar and oddly complex: one moment it seemed to be heavily spiced, but she could also detect a tantalizingly sweet scent, and in the next moment the smells were intermingled so completely that she had difficulty sorting them out. Mirabella was intrigued. After standing up and turning this way and that, and pointing her nose into the air and sniffing (Dolly watched these antics curiously), she discerned that the scent was coming from behind her. In the wild, birches grew very close together, but in the deer park the gardeners kept them thinned out enough that they didn't grow as close as a thicket, and they cleared all underbrush so that underfoot was only grass. Behind her, in the deep of the glade, the trees did grow closer together than in the picnic spot, and far above her the canopy of leaves was so thick that beneath them was almost unbroken shade.

Mirabella gathered her things and, followed by Dolly, made her way deeper into the sculptured wood. The silvery white of the slender tree trunks, marked with the solemn black "eyes," the soft carpet of grass underneath her feet, the sunlight playing in the leaves above, turning the light into a magical gold-green, all enchanted Mirabella. As she went farther and farther back, the elusive scents became stronger and more defined. Then she noticed that ahead, instead of the solid grass carpet, she saw gleams of white intermingling with a lighter green.

Suddenly she stood in a sea of white flowers and lacy lime-green leaves. The aromas now filled her senses, and she knew them. Falling to her knees, she caressed a stalk that had symmetrical rows of tiny bell-shaped blooms. It was lily of the valley, and she wondered now that she hadn't at first recognized the familiar heavenly sweet scent. Taking one of the nearby fern-like leaves in her hand, she crushed it and held it to her nose. The spicy smell, piquant and strong, was that of wild thyme. Mirabella marveled that either plant was thriving in such deep shade; normally they required lots of sunlight. She noted that both types were smaller than normal, but they didn't look stunted or sparse. Looking about her, she saw that she was in a clearing, but the green canopy was still thick overhead, and the light occasionally glinted sun-diamonds down through the softly rustling leaves. It was a bright, secret, quiet place. Suddenly and unaccountably, tears filled Mirabella's eyes.

It occurred to her that even though she had known such sorrow over Giles, she had never cried; but she was not weeping because of him. What she felt was an almost unbearably poignant love, of this place, of the wonderful day, of her home and family, of her entire life. It was mingled with a gentle bittersweet regret for the things that would never be, but Mirabella felt no remorse, no sorrow, only an understanding that pain must be suffered as a part of life in this wicked old world, but that when she went home with her Lord and Savior Jesus Christ, she would eternally know only joy. At last Mirabella was at peace.

The tears ran down her cheeks, and Mirabella felt that they were somehow cleansing. Dolly nosed her bent knee, and then buried her face in a thick clump of heavily flowered lily of the valley. Abruptly Mirabella came out of her deep reverie, and said sharply, "No, no, Dolly, those are poison!" Before she could pull the doe's face away, however, Dolly lost interest in the flowers and began to pointedly nudge the satchel lying by Mirabella's side. Mirabella marveled, thinking that Almighty God, who watched over the humble sparrows, had also lovingly given Dolly such wisdom that she refused to eat even sweetly scented poison. For some reason this made the tears flow even more freely, and Mirabella had the unusual sensation, for perhaps the first time in many years, of crying so hard her nose was running and was undoubtedly red. Lifting her skirt, she wiped her nose on the hem.

"D'ye know, these little bell flower thingamagums always make me cry, too."

Giles walked out of the thick of the wood and came to stand beside her, his arms crossed and looking down at her. Mirabella's heart stopped beating for a moment, but she took a deep breath and managed to smile. "They're lily of the valley, as I think you well know, and that's not why I'm crying. That is, I'm not really crying. Oh, never mind. Hello, I'm surprised to see you, Giles."

He helped her to stand, and then took her crumpled shawl and spread it out for them to sit on. "Hello, Dolly, hello, Mirabella, and I'm surprised to finally see you, too, for I've been looking for you everywhere. Likely I never would have found you, except I heard you talking to Dolly. I can see why you're hiding here, though, this is surely an enchanted glade, it looks as if fairies and naiads and dryads and sprites might dance by at any moment. The scents are bewitching, too."

They sat down on Mirabella's shawl. With easy grace Giles cocked one leg up and rested his arm on his knee; Mirabella sat with her legs tucked neatly to one side. Surreptitiously she wiped her nose one final time.

Giles watched her, and his gaze grew steady and grave, his eyes deepening to a royal blue. Quietly he said, "I suppose you've heard about Brydges."

"Hm? Oh, yes, I have. A letter from Lady Jersey was waiting for me when we arrived yesterday, describing the lurid scenes in endless detail," she said carelessly.

Giles looked slightly puzzled, and asked slowly, "Are you—upset?"

"About Lord Trevor and Rosalind? No, certainly not. In fact I'm relieved, for I know there was a lot of nonsensical talk about me and Lord Trevor in Town, and this will surely put paid to it."

He frowned. Reaching aside, he plucked up a stalk of greenery and crushed it, rolling it back and forth between his fingers. "Hm, thyme, isn't it," he said absently. "Yes, there was talk of you and Brydges, some of it from him. He said that you were leading him a merry chase, but he didn't really mind, he thought that you were well worth waiting for."

Sarcastically Mirabella said, "Apparently my definition of 'waiting for' someone is wildly different from Lord Trevor's. It doesn't signify anyway, Giles, and I don't really want to talk about him. I had understood that you were going to Scotland this month, I didn't expect to see you here."

"Half a moment, Mirabella. I thought—everyone thought that you had finally decided on Brydges. Obviously now you would never consider marrying him, but under the circumstances it seems that you'd be much more distressed."

"As I said, I'm not distressed, I'm relieved. As for this talk of me and Lord Trevor, I suppose it's my own fault, for I've been criminally stupid, but at least I've realized it and come to my senses," Mirabella said uncomfortably. "Do we really have to talk about this any more?"

"Yes," he said bluntly. "So—so you're saying that since this has happened with Brydges, you haven't quite decided on who else you might consider?"

"No, I've decided that I began this Season as an idiot with an imbecilic plan, but thankfully I ended the Season, as they say, wiser but sadder." He still looked at her with utter bafflement, so she decided to speak plainly. "I thought that I wanted to get married, but I don't."

"You—you don't?"

"No. That is—no."

"Oh. I see," he said blankly, and blinked several times.

Brightly Mirabella said, "I'm glad that you do, for I honestly, really, truly do not wish to talk about it any more. Again, I thought you were going to Scotland?"

"Scotland?"

"Yes, Scotland. That cold, mountainous land to the north, where the indigenous inhabitants speak with a rolling burr-r-r-r," she trilled, "and not only the females, but also the males wear skirts."

"Why on earth would I go to Scotland?"

Uncertainly now Mirabella said, "I understood that you were going with the Smythes for grouse. To their new shooting box. In Scotland."

"Smythes? Shooting box?" He shook his head as if to clear away a cloud of troublesome gnats. "That's absurd, I have no intention of running off to Scotland with the Smythes or anyone else."

"You don't?"

"No, I don't."

"Oh. I see," Mirabella said, although it was obvious that she didn't.

"I'm glad," Giles said sardonically, "and I have this eerie feeling that we've already had this conversation, don't you? Anyway, that rumor must have gotten started from Mrs. Smythe, but it's all claptrap as usual, or at least it mostly is. I invited Harry Smythe to come home to Knyveton with me, and I suppose Mrs. Smythe talked herself into believing that I was coming back to their shooting box with him in August, although I never once agreed to do so. I didn't even know it was in Scotland."

Very slowly Mirabella said, "And so Harry Smythe is here, at Knyveton, now? Did you invite Barbara?"

"Barbara? Miss Smythe? Good heavens, no. Why would I invite Miss Smythe to Knyveton? If I did, I'd have to have the whole family, and although Mr. Smythe is an agreeable-enough fellow, I wouldn't be able to endure Mrs. Smythe for more than an hour at most. It's an outlandish notion anyway, for Miss Smythe has no interest in coming here."

"She doesn't? But I thought—that is, everyone thought—thinks—"

Severely Giles said, "Mirabella, please don't tell me that you've paid any mind to all of the balderdash about me and Miss Smythe. The entire thing is fabricated from Mrs. Smythe's fertile and wishful imagination, and she's so transparent that I thought surely you would know how ridiculous the gossip about us was. It had no foundation whatsoever, for though Miss Smythe and I find each other's company to be agreeable, there was never any question of a romantic attachment."

Mirabella was so astonished that she was dumbstruck. She stared at him, her eyes wide, and even her mouth was slightly open, as her jaw had literally dropped.

With amusement he said, "Mirabella, close your mouth, well-bred young ladies do not conduct polite conversation with their mouths gaping open. That is, I hope that we'll have more polite conversation. I find it hard to believe that you're speechless, I've never seen you so. I don't much care for it."

"But—but—but I thought—do you mean that you're not in love with Barbara?"

"I can't think of any plainer way to say it. No, I am not now, have never been, and do not intend ever to be, in love with Barbara Smythe."

Again the tears started flowing, completely unnoticed by Mirabella. After long silent moments, Giles pulled a handkerchief from his coat pocket and handed it to her. "Your nose is running again," he observed clinically, "because you're crying again. Why are you crying now? I thought I knew and understood you through and through, but today I'm thoroughly confounded."

"I don't know why I'm crying," Mirabella said plaintively, and blew her nose. "I'm terribly confused, because I'm not sad, and that's why women usually weep, isn't it? Anyway, I'm not sad, I'm happy. I mean, I think I'm happy. Yes, that is true, I'm happy."

"Then let us solve this conundrum together. If you're—" He stopped abruptly, for now Mirabella was laughing.

"No, no, I'll have no more conundrums, ever. I'm happy, Giles. Can we just leave it there?"

"No, we cannot. I know that something isn't right with you, and I can't fathom what it is. You used to talk to me, Bella, can't you talk to me now? I know I can help you, as I always have."

"Yes, you always have," she repeated softly, and wiped the last tear from her cheek. "I do want to tell you, Giles, but I'm afraid."

"Afraid of what?"

"I'm afraid that you'll be embarrassed, or uncomfortable at least. I'm afraid that it will affect our friendship, that we may not be able to be such close friends any more."

Her eyes were averted. He reached over and took her hand in his, and she admired the grace of his hands, his long supple fingers. In a low, intent voice he said, "Bella, never in this life do you need to fear anything from me. I can't conceive of anything you could possibly do or say that would cause me any discomfort whatsoever. And I promise you, I vow to you, that I will always be your closest, most faithful friend."

Mirabella looked back up at him. "Thank you, Giles. What I want to tell you is that I love you. Well, of course I've loved you for my entire life, but what I mean is that now I've fallen in love with you. Not just now, this instant, that would be silly, but I have finally, slowly realized that I'm *in* love with you. Please know that I'm perfectly happy that you're not in love with me, for I believe you, I know that in your way you'll always love me, and I treasure that and am content."

Giles frowned, a more fierce and forbidding expression than she had ever seen on his affable features. In a guttural voice he said, "I think I misunderstood you. Would you please repeat that? And simplify, please."

Helplessly Mirabella said, "I love you, Giles."

He stayed very still for a long time. "I had no idea . . . you were so determined to marry, you were so certain that you'd never know real love. Are you sure?"

"It's one of the few things in this world that I am sure of. You aren't upset, are you? We can still be friends, can't we? We need never mention it again, and I promise that I'll be a good friend to any lady who is fortunate enough to marry you."

Now, finally, Giles's sky-blue eyes crinkled, and he grinned his familiar old crooked grin. "Actually, I should very much like for that lady to be you. I love you, Bella. I've been in love with you for a long time."

"You—you have?" Mirabella spluttered. "But I never knew, in my wildest dreams! You never showed it, at all!"

"Neither did you. Haven't we done a clever job of fooling each other?"

They stared at each other, Giles still half-grinning. Slowly a smile, filled with delight, lit up Mirabella's face. She leaned forward and gently put her lips on his. At first he seemed frozen, but then he put his arms around her and kissed her, a long sweet lingering kiss. When their lips parted, he clasped her tightly to him, and she put her arms around him and rested her head on his shoulder.

"I can't believe it," Mirabella whispered. "Thank you, Lord... thank you."

Giles said, "Amen. Lady Mirabella, would you do me the greatest honor, and marry me?"

"Oh, yes, yes!" Excitedly she sat up and took his face in her hands and gave him an exuberant kiss. "We can get a special license from the bishop, so we could be married as soon as next month! August weddings are a little unusual, I suppose, but what does it matter, and I wouldn't want to have a big ostentatious production at St. George's anyway, of course we'll want to be married here, at St. John's, by Mr. Rosborough—"

Giles put up one hand. "One moment, please. It's impossible that we marry so soon. The primary reason—or at least one reason—that I never declared myself to you was because I'm simply not in a position to marry you right now. You know that I'm having some financial difficulties, and I don't expect them to be fully resolved for at least another year. I couldn't support you in the manner to which you've become accustomed, and which you deserve. And the one thing that would embarrass me deeply is to live off my wife. It's a matter of honor."

Mirabella's expression slowly changed from incandescent joy to outrage as he spoke. She jumped up, stamped her foot, and shouted, "Hang your honor! That's the stupidest thing I've ever heard in my life! You won't marry me because I have money?"

As Giles got to his feet, he said dryly, "I did get my wish that you would talk to me, I might be obliged to think that over." He put his hands on her shoulders. "Of course I want to marry you, more than anything in life. But it isn't too much to ask that we wait for a year, is it? Many couples have at least a year's betrothal."

"We're not many couples, Giles. After what I've been through, I can't bear the thought of waiting for you for so long. Please, please, Giles, forget all of this worry about money. It's not really your honor anyway, it's simply pride, and that's the deadliest of the seven sins. As your betrothed, I must point that out to you and tell you to repent," she cajoled him.

"It's not that simple," he said sternly. "What I can't bear is the thought of marrying you with barely a ha'pence to my name that's not owed to creditors."

Mirabella's eyes flashed deep sapphire blue. "Very well, then. What I shall do is tell Pappa to deposit my settlement into your bank account, and refuse to take it back. Then you'll have thirty thousand pounds, and I'll be penniless. Would that satisfy your honor?"

"Of course not, that would be absurd," Giles rasped. "I wouldn't accept it."

"That's what would be absurd, if it was sitting there and you refused to spend it. What about this, then? I will loan you all the money you need, and we will draw up all the necessary documents, and you will repay me each month, with appropriate interest, of course. Oh, wait a moment. Again, that would be ridiculous, for you to transfer your money to me, when actually by law all of my money will be yours. Let me think, let me think, oh, now I have it. I wish to purchase your little black mare, she's quite a spirited, lovely thing and honestly, Giles, she's too small for you. I'll give you thirty thousand pounds for her."

"You're not going to allow me to get away with this, are you?"

"No, I am not. I demand that you marry me next month, or I swear, Giles, I really will put my money into your account."

"This must be the most bizarre conversation I've ever had," Giles said. "But I shouldn't be surprised, you always get your way, Bella. Would you do me the honor of marrying me—next month?"

"I will."

Their second long savory kiss was interrupted by a loud crunching sound at their feet. They had completely forgotten about Dolly. She had managed to get Mirabella's satchel opened. She was contentedly eating an apple, staring up at them with deep contemplation.

Giles laughed. "I'm surrounded by females that always get what they want when they want. I'm going to be the most pathetic, browbeaten husband on earth."

"And you will love it. Come, Giles, you must go speak to Pappa now. Help me get my things, and hurry, please."

"My lady, your wish is my command."

Chapter Twenty-two

Arm in arm, Mirabella and Giles argued, affectionately of course, all the way back to the house. Mirabella stopped mid-sentence when she burst into the drawing room, where Lady Camarden was writing letters and Lord Camarden was reading. "Pappa, Giles wants to speak to you," she said excitedly. "Oh, never mind, that's silly, of course, Mamma, you can hear. Tell them, Giles."

With one long-suffering glance at Mirabella, he said, "Sir, and—er, madam, I would like to beg that you will grant me the greatest honor, and give me your daughter's hand in marriage."

Lord Camarden looked them up and down. "You two have finally come to your senses, have you? About time. As for giving you her hand, I gladly do so, although I know you're only indulging me, I couldn't give Mirabella's hand or anything else of hers to anyone unless it's what she wanted. You're very kind to an old man, Mirabella, thank you for the gesture."

Lady Camarden said, "Thank the gracious Lord, at last. It's the most sensible thing you've done in years, Mirabella. Now I suppose I must rewrite all of my letters. Have you set a date yet?"

Mirabella said, "I want to get married next month—"

At the same time Giles said, "I was hoping for the end of September—"

That started the argument again, for Giles had been begging Mirabella for at least a little time to ready Knyveton Hall, while she insisted that she didn't trust him to do the things that needed to be done to her future home, and she would see to any repairs and refurbishments herself. Although the discussion was slightly heated, they were holding hands, and absently Mirabella led him back out into the entrance hall and out the front door, to go to assess Knyveton Hall.

Lord Camarden said, "I'm glad they'll be so close. One happy result of it is that they can quarrel there instead of here."

"Look here, I've written seven perfectly good letters today," Lady Camarden lamented. "And now we won't be going to Littlemoor, so I'll have to write everyone, except that villain Brydges and that sly skunk Rosalind FitzGeorge, and cancel. I suppose I'll wait to do my rewrites until I find out if the wedding is to be in August or September."

"I would wager on August," Lord Camarden said, and returned to his book.

On the way to Knyveton Hall, Mirabella and Giles were still engaged in their spirited discussion, but at odd intervals they would stop and look at each other, amazed again that their entire lives had changed in the last two hours, and there was more kissing. Finally they reached Knyveton, and paused for a few moments on the bridge leading to the entryway, watching the swans gliding majestically. "They are so heartbreakingly lovely," Mirabella murmured. "Oh, I have just had the most capital idea! At Aldington House they have an entire flock of black swans—are they called a flock?"

"I believe it's called a bevy of swans," Giles said warily.

"A bevy of black swans that Lord Aldington acquired from

New South Wales. Surely he would let us have a couple, wouldn't that be splendid? I shall put it on my list. Unless—you don't think that Mr. Aldington is too upset with me, do you?"

"Actually, I think that you might have granted his fondest wish, for right now at any rate, considering the bizarre Byronic mood he's been in. You gave him a star-crossed love affair to lament. Last month Aldington joined me and Harry and Miss Smythe quite often, riding in the park and at balls and parties. I had a difficult time of it for a while, for I was obliged to console both Smythe and Aldington for the loss of their lady loves. Soon, however, Aldington began to take comfort in Miss Smythe's company, and before we left Town I noticed that she was cheering him up considerably. I expect that soon—if she isn't shouting it from the rooftops already—Mrs. Smythe will be telling everyone how Miss Smythe broke a baronet's heart, but her one true love is the heir to a barony. So that will be satisfactorily settled, I think. I only hope that Harry can have a happy ending, too."

"Oh dear, I'd forgotten all about him. You did say that he's here?"

"Yes, although I feared I was going to have to engage a mule team to drag him here. He's hopeless as far as Josephine is concerned, you know. He's convinced that she cares nothing for him, and I've almost talked myself into an apoplexy telling him otherwise."

"Are you so certain she loves him, then?" Mirabella asked cautiously. "I've tried hard to discern her feelings, but she's such a private person that it's been difficult for me to be sure."

"Lewin and I talked it over, and we both think that she does care deeply for him, although she may not be starry-eyed, somersaulting in love with him as he is with her. We believe that she has reservations, and with good reason. In the first place, Northumberland is so far away from her home, and by all accounts is a cold and dreary county. In the second place—and perhaps I should have named this first and foremost—Mrs. Smythe has already been a right Tartar to Harry about her, and I can fully empathize with a reluctance to face a life with Mrs. Smythe as a mother-in-law."

"Ugh, how dreadful, poor Josephine. And poor Mr. Smythe. Is he aware of this?"

"Of course. Harry dutifully loves his mother, but he's flatly refused to countenance her nagging about Josephine, and for once his father has even stood up to Mrs. Smythe. And also, Harry hates Northumberland, too, he's told me that unless his father entails it, he's going to sell the whole estate when he inherits and move to one of the south counties. I think that if he and Josephine get engaged, he'll find some nice estate close and either buy it or lease it, and say a cheery good day to Northumberland, and his mother, too, if she continues to behave so badly."

"Oh, that would be wonderful, to have our close friends nearby!" Mirabella said excitedly.

"Mirabella, you may box my ears for this, but I absolutely forbid you to go barging around arranging Josephine and Harry's marriage. Your past record on that is not exactly exemplary."

"I shall astound you and agree with you, for you're entirely correct. Anyway, I'm going to be far too busy arranging my own marriage."

"Yes, about that. What list?"

Giles soon found out all about Mirabella's list, for it was begun that very afternoon, and was lengthened considerably in the following days. The black swans were first on the list, and in considering them, Mirabella discovered that the moat needed dredging and cleaning, and the stone bridge needed repairs. She toured every single room in Knyveton Hall (much to Mr. Smythe's astonishment) and openly expressed her horror at the furnishings.

"Lewin said the bedrooms looked like a French brothel, and he was right," she fumed. "I'm not sleeping in that rococo monstrosity, not for even one night. Where are the old beds?"

"In the barn, along with about eighteen other pieces," Giles replied. "Lewin said my house looked like a French brothel?"

For the next week, Mirabella came to Knyveton, usually so early in the morning that Giles and Harry were still at breakfast. Finally Giles's elderly butler Pitkin ceased sniffing his disapproval at Mirabella wandering about Knyveton by herself, and his steward, Mr. Leith, grew accustomed to answering to Lady Mirabella as much as he answered to Sir Giles. Within a week Mirabella's list included obtaining the swans, repairing the bridge, maintaining the moat, repairing and renewing all the old furniture including replacing the upholsteries, constructing a conservatory at the north end of the quadrangle, redecorating one of the guest bedrooms and making it into a nursery, removing the vulgar encaustic tiles in the dining room, and restoring the old oak flooring. These were only the major undertakings of the list, for it also included, as Giles said, approximately ten thousand other minor tasks and details.

Ultimately this was the reason, to everyone's amazement, that Giles got his wish that the marriage be delayed until Knyveton Hall was more presentable for its new mistress. Mirabella agreed that she didn't wish to spend the blissful first month of her marriage in a house with four or five crews of laborers. But then she had the bright idea that they could go on a bridal tour to Italy.

"Your dearest wish has always been to return to Florence," she said to Giles. "This way we could make all the arrangements with the workmen, get married next month, and while we're away Mr. Leith can attend to everything."

"No, my dearest wish is to marry you, Bella. And if you think that I want to spend the first month with my new wife on an arduous, boring, cramped, dirty sea voyage with a hundred strangers, you need to think again."

"There is something to that," Mirabella agreed reluctantly. "But someday I promise you, we'll go to Italy."

"We shall see," Giles said. "Listen, Bella, would you please add one item to your interminable list? It's very important."

"Of course."

He came close to her and looked down into her eyes. "Would you please wear that satin blue dress and your sapphires for our wedding? In my life I've never seen anything so beautiful. When I thought you were lost to me, I'd think of you in that dress and your sapphires, and tell myself that maybe such an exquisite creature wasn't meant to belong to a mortal man at all."

She put her arms around his neck. "You were wrong. I was meant to belong to you."

On October first they were married, and the small parish church, St. John's, was filled to overflowing. Practically every person from Camarden attended, of course, and many of Mirabella's and Giles's friends from London came, too. Denys Aldington attended, with Mr. and Mrs. Smythe and Miss Smythe; Mrs. Smythe alternated between beaming at Denys and glowering at Harry and Josephine. She had another reason, although not an excuse, for her ire, for in the previous month Harry had leased Reynes Parva from Lord Camarden for a life tenancy, and had moved in two days after the arrangements had been made.

It was a very good thing that Giles had talked Mirabella out of traveling to Italy. In January Mirabella knew with certainty that she was expecting, and it would have been dangerous indeed for her to travel home by sea. The new year was happily greeted for another reason, too, for Harry and Josephine became engaged, and were married in June.

Mirabella had an easy and ecstatically happy pregnancy, insisting from the first that she knew it was a boy, and his name would be Giles William Edmund. She was correct. On August first she gave birth to a boy with black hair and blue eyes.

Mirabella and Giles knew that something was wrong in the first moments after his birth. Josephine's brother-in-law, Dr. Tarver, attended Mirabella. As soon as baby Giles was born, Dr. Tarver's face grew grave. After cutting the umbilical cord, he took the baby by the heels, suspended him upside down, and lightly spanked his bottom. Only then did the baby make a sound, and the cry was so weak it could barely be heard. After cleaning him up and swaddling him, Dr. Tarver gave the baby to Mirabella. "He's very small," she said quietly. "And his skin is tinged yellow."

"Yes, my lady," the kind, bespectacled doctor said. "He is jaundiced. But that's not too uncommon with newborns. It's possible that once he has mother's milk in him to cleanse his blood, the jaundice will disappear."

But baby Giles would not eat. Mirabella and Giles tried a wet nurse, cow's milk, goat's milk, even heavy cream with molasses added to it, but to no avail.

Three days after his birth, Dr. Tarver said sadly, "I've seen this condition before, and we have no explanation for it, we've never discovered any disease or defect that causes it. Sometimes babies are born, and it seems that the Lord in His infinite wisdom decides to take them home soon."

"How soon?" Mirabella whispered brokenly.

"It's very difficult to know, but I think perhaps a week at the most."

That very night Mr. Rosborough came and baptized baby Giles in Mirabella and Giles's bedroom. Josephine and Harry stood as godparents. Tears streamed down Mr. Rosborough's face during the entire ceremony, and Josephine and Harry had a very difficult time with the responses, for they kept choking up.

Mirabella and Giles, both as pale as parchment, held hands and kept their eyes locked on baby Giles.

Mirabella and Giles moved the rocking chair into their bedroom, and virtually lived there. They took turns holding Giles and rocking him, all day and all night. He slept; he rarely opened his eyes, and then for only a few moments. He never cried, and he hardly moved. At dawn on the ninth of August, in his sleep, little Giles simply stopped breathing.

The next days were dismal blurs to them. Mirabella's mother was at Knyveton, of course, and to Mirabella's vague surprise, Clara came and stayed. She never bothered Mirabella and Giles, she spoke to them only when they spoke to her, she made sure that they had meals served to them wherever they were, and she ran the entire house with her ruthless efficiency.

Giles and Mirabella buried their son, and exhausted, they went to their bedroom, fell onto the bed in their mourning clothes, and held each other. After a time Giles began to weep, and then to sob. Mirabella held him as if he were a small child. "Oh, Bella, Bella, how shall we ever bear it?" he groaned.

"I will tell you how, my beloved husband," she said quietly. "We will grieve, yes, but we will rejoice, too. For a long time I thought that children were the greatest blessings God could bestow, but I was wrong. The best, most loving, most precious gift that the Lord has given us is marriage. I am bone of your bone, and flesh of your flesh. We are one person, and there is no force on earth that is as strong as the bond between a man and a woman that God has joined together. Our love is so powerful that together we will bear all things, believe all things, hope all things, and endure all things, and we will rejoice that we have each other until we die and join Him in heaven."

The summer ended, then a crisp bright fall turned into a cold wet winter. Giles and Mirabella struggled, every day, with their loss; but each day the pain lessened, just a little, and each day they gained a little more strength.

In December, Mirabella seemed to brighten up considerably. Although she and Giles still consoled each other in a hundred different ways every day, she said nothing to him about her sudden buoyancy of spirit.

On the fifteenth Josephine and Harry came to Knyveton, for they visited there often, but this time Mirabella especially wanted to plan a special Christmas party for friends and family. She had often teased Giles about converting the dining hall into a Tudor great hall, and on this Christmas she thought it would be a marvelous idea to have a Tudor Christmas party, complete with head table, two thrones (for her parents, of course), a gigantic wassail bowl, big turkeys as the only roasts of the evening, the Yule log, and fragrant evergreen rushes on the floor.

Josephine was smiling, but her gaze was sharp. "You're certain, then, dearest, that you feel like giving a party for thirty or so people?"

"I'm certain," Mirabella replied. "You see, I think—I'm fairly sure that I have some very good news. It's early days yet, but..." Her voice trailed off, and her sapphire-blue eyes sparkled, for the first time in four months.

Josephine said excitedly, "You mean—can you mean that you think you're pregnant?"

"Yes!"

"That's marvelous, dearest! And now—now I feel I can tell you—so am I!"

Giles and Mirabella had some anxious moments in the months that followed. But together they decided that they would not now, or ever, let fear ruin their lives. "Perfect love casts out fear,"

Giles said to her. "God's love for us is perfect, and may His perfect will be done. And my love for you, Bella, may not be perfect, but I love you as much as mortal man will ever love a woman, now and forever."

Exactly a year to the day after their son died, Mirabella gave birth to a healthy, hearty baby boy with the same straight thick black hair and sky-blue eyes as his older brother and his father. "We'll name him Giles, for that's my favorite name in the whole world. He won't mind, you know," she said. "When he went to his real home, the Lord gave him his real name. It will help me to remember him with joy."

Two days later Josephine gave birth to a baby girl. Scarcely a week later, both women were feeling well enough to visit, and Mirabella and Giles took baby Giles to Reynes Parva.

"Josephine, Harry, she is absolutely gorgeous, just like a little dolly," Mirabella said. "What is her name?"

Josephine and Harry exchanged glances. "We wanted to name her Mirabella, but both of us felt that was a little too *haut ton* for us commoners," Harry said, grinning boyishly. "And so we've named her Bella."

With delight Mirabella looked at the two babies in their cribs. "Giles and Bella, how perfect," she said. "Surely they will be great friends."

"Hm," Giles said thoughtfully. " 'History, with all her volumes vast, hath but one page.' "

Harry said with bewilderment, "What does that mean? I *never* know what old Giles means with his deep and dark quotes."

Tentatively Josephine said, "It's Lord Byron, isn't it? *Childe Harold?*"

"Pay no mind to Giles," Mirabella told Harry. "He's just showing out, as usual. It's that old cliché—history repeats itself—

but Giles is too intellectually superior to all of us to say it simply."

Giles was staring at the two babies, side-by-side in their cribs. He slid his arm around Mirabella's waist and said, "We shall see, my love. In a few years, we shall see..."

Epilogue

Sixteen years later, in the merry month of May, the Smythe family and the Knyvet family gathered together for the May Day holiday. It was their long custom for the two families to spend holidays together. In the early years of their marriages, Harry and Josephine had traveled the eleven miles from Reynes Parva to stay at Knyveton Hall, but as the families grew, Knyveton Hall proved to be entirely too small, so Lord and Lady Camarden, still hale and hearty in their seventies, happily invited everyone, from the ever-growing Rosborough clan to Clara and Philip, to holiday at Camarden.

As they had done so many times, Mirabella and Giles and Josephine and Harry were having afternoon tea in the conservatory, which may not have looked quite as polished and organized as when it had been Mirabella's realm, but was still a lovely, congenial arbor. The four of them had changed very little. Harry, still bright-eyed and eager, looked ten years younger than he was. In the last years Josephine had grown slightly plump with childbearing. She and Mirabella often talked of how their youthful figures had been wasted wearing frocks with Empire waists. Now that the natural waist, with an hourglass figure, was stylish, they mourned the never-seen twenty-inch waists of their teens and twenties. Still, Mirabella had remained tiny and dainty. She had some silver streaks, but they showed very little in her strawberry-blonde hair. The smile creases at the corners of Giles's blue eyes had deepened, and he had a dashing sprinkle of white hair at the temples, but otherwise he too showed little sign of aging.

On this day the conservatory was crowded. Harry and Josephine had seven children, four boys and three girls, from sixteen-year-old Bella, who resembled her mother but had her father's exuberant temperament, to their youngest, Clifford, a lively two-year-old. Mirabella and Giles had had three more children after Giles: next was Audrey Josephine, twelve years old, Tirel was nine years old, and Edmund, their youngest child, was a six-year-old boy who was so like Mirabella, in a masculine way, that it was almost uncanny.

Not all eleven of the Knyvet and Smythe children were in the conservatory, for Bella and Giles, who had always been great friends, had disappeared. However, there were actually eleven children racketing about. Alexander, Lord Tirel, was twenty-two now, had just finished with a first at Oxford, and was taking a short holiday before he joined the army. Tiberius, a serious, intelligent young man who planned to become a clergyman, had just celebrated his eighteenth birthday and was on holiday from Cambridge. The younger children were delighted at the two older boys' presence, for Alexander and Tiberius had made up several battlefields out of potting crates, as their Aunt Mirabella had taught them, and landscaped them, and were now gathering up watering cans to inflict terrible storms on the battlefields. Alexander had brought his old set of forty tin soldiers, and the fact that they could not be split up evenly among the nine children had caused much strife, including shameful amounts of shouting, arguing, pushing and pulling, and tears. Tiberius had finally settled it mathematically, giving each child four soldiers and forming a rotation of troops so that everyone would have the opportunity to have five soldiers. The battles commenced, and they were in some ways like real battles, for they were short, confusing, and very very loud.

"I can barely hear in this din," Harry grumbled. "Why are our children so loud, Josephine? I'm not loud. You're not loud. It must be some sort of inherited trait I've passed on to them from my mother."

"For shame, Harry, she's been a perfect angel ever since Bella was born, and I'll hear nothing against her," Josephine said severely.

"She's been angelic because ever since Bella drew her first breath she's been planning to marry her off to some unfortunate nobleman, preferably at least a viscount, since she succeeded in entrapping a baron for Barbara." Miss Smythe and the Honourable Denys Aldington had been married fifteen years ago, and now they were Lord and Lady Aldington. They had never had children, so Mrs. Smythe had directed all of her energies to her schemes to marry off Harry's children, all seven of them.

"Never mind, Harry, my three children are making fully as much noise as your six, and besides, it sounds to me as if Alexander is the loudest of them all, with his wild war whoops and shouting orders at the top of his lungs," Mirabella said.

Just then General Lord Tirel shouted, "No, no, Cliffie, that's not a battlefield—" They heard a loud crash, and then two-year-old Clifford Smythe came running around from behind a tall mass of plants and flowers and trees, holding a blood-red geranium that still had its roots attached, and another broken bloom trailing limply. "Flower thank you Mamma," he said proudly to Josephine.

She took the muddy mess gracefully. "No, you say, 'This flower is for you, Mamma,' and I say, 'Thank you.'"

"Weckome." He ran back on short fat legs to rejoin the battle.

Mirabella watched him with great affection. "I think that two-year-olds are the most adorable of all, but then I think that same thing at every age my children reach. Each and every year of each and every child is a blessing."

"So they are," Josephine agreed. "But you know, it's also wonderful to see couples like Barbara and Denys, who don't have children but seem to have a rich, full life and happy marriage all the same."

"And like Lewin and Anne," Giles said. "The more I get to know her, the more I like her. Now there is a woman that's full of surprises."

"To say the least," Mirabella agreed. "Do you all recall the first time we met her? We thought that she was very sweet, but on first acquaintance she seemed so very shy."

"We were right, but we were wrong," Harry said. "She is sweet, but she's not at all shy, she's as bold as a tigress. Can you believe that she actually rode a camel?"

Lewin had remained the ultimate career soldier, serving with distinction and finally achieving the rank of colonel. After duty in India, he had returned to England five years previously and accepted a position as adjutant to the secretary of state for war and the colonies. He bought a small cottage in Clerkenwell, just east of the City of London. There he met Anne Meynell, the daughter of a watchmaker. She was thirty years old, and of course was considered an elderly spinster. Two years later, after her father died, Anne sold the business and married Lewin, and the two proceeded to go all over the world, as Lewin's position often gave him the opportunity to travel with various envoys, diplomats, secretaries, and undersecretaries. In the last three years they had been to India, Egypt, Cape Colony in South Africa, and various islands in the British West Indies.

"Where are they off to this time?" Mirabella asked. "I forget."

"To Mauritius," Josephine answered. "Apparently there's some dustup there between the sugar planters, and one of them is a distant connection of Lord Grey's, so he must be attended to immediately."

Mirabella sighed. "It's been too many years since I've studied globes. I've heard of Mauritius, of course, but I have no earthly idea where it is."

Giles said, "It's one of the Mascarene Islands."

"What?" Mirabella said blankly.

"Mascarene Islands. Mauritius, Réunion, and Rodrigues."

"There he is again," Mirabella said to Harry and Josephine. "Showing out. As if we care that you know everything about the entire world, Giles."

"That may be a slight exaggeration."

"Oh, you are still so infuriating, even after all of these years I've tried to train you."

Giles grinned, his old crooked, mischievous grin. "But you're still madly in love with me just the same."

"Yes, I am," Mirabella said serenely.

Another thunderous crash sounded from the other side of the conservatory, accompanied by loud groans, shouts, and outraged cries. Alexander's cheerful face popped out between a lemon tree and a citron tree. "No worries," he shouted. "It's quite all right, really, a minor setback in the prosecution of the war."

"No bones broken, no one bleeding?" Harry called.

"No, sir."

"Very well, carry on."

Josephine rolled her eyes. "Of course, as long as there are no major injuries. So, Mirabella, Giles, how are your plans coming for your trip to Italy next month? Are all of the arrangements finalized?"

Because of the children, Giles and Mirabella hadn't been able to go to Italy as they had always planned. Now that the fast, relatively comfortable, and safer steamships were crossing the Atlantic, and because Edmund was now six years old, they had decided to take their bridal tour, now commonly called a honeymoon. Josephine and Harry had generously offered to take care of the children for the three months that Giles and Mirabella planned to spend in Rome, Venice, and Florence.

Mirabella's eyes sparkled, the same deep royal blue of her youth. "We had made all the arrangements, yes. But I'm afraid your brother-in-law flatly refused to give his permission for us to go."

Josephine said, "John? Why on earth would he object to you touring Italy?"

"I'm surprised you're asking that question, Josephine, I would have thought you'd grasp it instantly. It's not the tour of Italy he's forbidden, it's the sea travel. It's not at all the thing for ladies in my delicate condition."

Josephine said excitedly, "Oh, Mirabella, how splendid! After all these years, thank the Lord!"

"Congratulations, old boy," Harry said to Giles.

"I may catch up to you yet, Smythe," Giles said.

Harry was such a close friend that he'd heard all of Mirabella's and Giles's stories. He asked Mirabella slyly, "So, is it to be a boy or a girl this time?"

"I have decided that it will be twin girls to make up for Edmund having the cheek to be a boy," Mirabella replied with a thoughtful air, "and then I could start all over again with the next one which, of course, will be another boy. After that I plan to get back to my original schedule and have girl-boy-girl."

"That's only ten," Giles complained. "If I'm to best Smythe we must have at least a dozen."

"Well, as the Lord so memorably said to me once, 'After all, we don't have to decide today,'" Mirabella said.

The rear door of the conservatory opened, and Giles and Bella came in. Arm in arm, they hesitated in the doorway, and two puddles quickly formed around their feet, for they were both dismally sopping wet. Giles swallowed hard, then propelled Bella forward until they were standing by the table. "Mr. Smythe, Mrs. Smythe, please accept my most humble apologies. We were at the stewpond, and I begged Bella to let me take her out in the punt. Unfortunately I'm not a skillful punter, and I upset the boat. It was all entirely my fault, and I'm terribly sorry."

Giles and Bella had that look of dread on their faces that all children assume when they know they have done something that is going to get them into deep trouble.

They couldn't believe it when it happened, and they never knew why it happened. Their parents glanced at each other, and then burst into laughter.

Reading Group Guide

1. Mirabella finds fulfillment in outside interests: her gardening and her love of music, particularly opera. Do you have a hobby or special interest that enriches your life? If not, have you asked the Lord to show you how you might *renew your mind* (see Ephesians 4:23) through the wide and varied gifts he's given each and every one of us?
2. Lady Mirabella Tirel lives a life of wealth and privilege that few of us will ever know. Still, she's conscious of her blessings, and is grateful to God for them. Do you take special care to acknowledge the blessings that God has given you? Do you faithfully thank Him every day?
3. When writing historical fiction, writers often help the readers immerse themselves in the period by including current events in the plot. In 1813 to 1814, the period in which *A Sapphire Season* is placed, the Napoleonic War was a constant, overriding topic in England. Did you find that my touching on the war (by making Lewin a soldier, giving brief summaries of the Siege of Badajoz, making references to Lewin's duties) helped you to more fully involve yourself in the book? Or did you find such peripherals a distraction?
4. Mirabella's closest confidant is her Aunt Tirel. Mirabella is able to tell her most secret, heartfelt longings to her aunt. Do you have a friend who "sticketh closer than a brother" (Proverbs 18:24)? Have you asked the Lord to bless you with such a friend? More importantly—and of much more

difficulty—have you asked the Lord to *make you* that kind of friend for someone in need?

5. One of the hardest tasks a writer has is to describe a setting, whether it's an outdoor scene or a house or a single room. In *A Sapphire Season*, sometimes I described a room in detail, while at other times I tried to give a more general, but visceral, impression of a place. As a reader, which do you prefer? Details or impression? (Note: Through the years I've found that there is no question such as this pertaining to ladies' clothes—the answer is always "Details!")
6. In this book, the ultimate Christian theme is "Thy will be done." Through a wrenching and difficult process, Mirabella must come to this surrender in one of the most important decisions we make in our lives, that of marriage. But what of the lesser decisions, even the day-to-day choices we make or petitions we make to the Lord? Most of us haven't reached the point in our walk where we make every choice according to the Lord's perfect will, or always qualify the things we ask for by adding, "Thy will be done." Please join me in prayer today, and every day, that we will know the joy of this final surrender.

> *Thy kingdom come. Thy will be done in earth, as it is in heaven.*
>
> —*Matthew 6:10*

ALSO LOOK FOR THIS REGENCY ROMANCE BY LYNN MORRIS

The Baron's Honourable Daughter

When her stepfather suddenly dies, Valeria Segrave must take charge of her grieving mother and the vast estate that now belongs to her six-year-old half brother, the new Earl of Maledon. Each day brings a new struggle as she tries to establish her authority with servants, stewards, and solicitors—all men. As a young woman with no blood relation to the earl, she is all too easy to dismiss.

Valeria must rely on the assistance of her stepfather's distant kinsman, Alastair, Lord Hylton. He is handsome and noble, and Valeria senses that she never measures up to his expectations for a refined lady, making the burden of gratitude to him hardly bearable. Even when Valeria leaves the country estate for the glittering London Season, where she gets into a series of escapades, Lord Hylton is always there to witness, criticize, and correct her behavior. But if Alastair insists on engaging in a battle of wits and wills with the lively Valeria, she'll stop at nothing to prove that he's met his match.

Available now in print and electronic formats from FaithWords wherever books are sold.